"Compelling and dramati[
Audrey, Amazon US

CW01498008

"Filled with suspense, pe[
softened by tragedy, it is ... . novels I
have ever read... You will not hear this from me very
often: this is a must-read! Readers of all genres, unite!"
Anca, Reviews with a Twist Blog

"An extremely well written, capturing novel."
Richelle, Goodreads

"First Time Author Darren Sugrue hits the mark with a 5
star novel... This book is awesome."
L. Frier, Amazon US

"I loved this book! It was emotionally intense, suspenseful,
and so very touching and beautiful at the end. I cannot
remember the last time a book brought me to tears..."
Judy Schechter, Amazon US

"I finished it in one sitting - amazing. This book deserves
to be read!"
Mika, Goodreads

"Once you get hooked, you won't want to put the book
down"
Allison James, Goodreads

"The ending twist was just genius... I feel this is one of the
few books anyone would enjoy no matter whether you are
a romantic, thriller, horror or sci-fi reader."
Gadget Girl Reviews

"Hard to believe this is the first novel by this author..."
James Phillips, Amazon US

"The story is well written, moves at a good pace, with well-developed characters and a twist I really didn't see coming."
James Walsh, Amazon Australia

"There is something brilliant and enticing about a novel where one of the central conflicts is that you very much want for two mutually exclusive things to happen."
Anne Doucette, Reflections & Echoes Blog

"Fast, easy draws you in, surprise ending."
Nina, Goodreads

"Heart pounding suspense, lost love, regret, lost, murder, betrayal, it's all there. Mind blowing plot twists that you have to pause to process... Drop everything, send the kids outside. This is an incredible read."
Doseofbella, LibraryThing

"You really could not ask for more in a book."
Angie, Readaholic Zone

"...one of those books that after you are finished, it will leave you thinking about it for days...I could definitely see this book being made into a feature film... among one of the best books I have read all year..."
Jael, Amazon US

"Wow! Loved this book!"
Heather, Goodreads

"Mr. Sugrue is a gifted writer, & I think this book could be a best-seller if given the opportunity."
Susan, Goodreads

The Prediction

DARREN SUGRUE

ISBN: 978-1-78280-305-8

www.darrensugrue.com

To Charlotte & Kieran

Prologue

The street performer who was dressed as a statue of James Joyce was beginning to wonder if his costume was *too* realistic. A pigeon had already landed on his shoulder that morning, and few passers-by barely glanced in his direction. *It seemed unfair,* he thought, *that a mime dressed as Darth Vader attracted more interest.*

His thoughts were distracted by the screeching brakes of an approaching car. He turned his head and saw a Nissan Almera speeding out of a side street. It ignored all the signs and mounted the pedestrian zone in the middle of O'Connell Street. The mime's eyes widened as he realised the direction the car was heading; straight for him. It was one thing a pigeon mistaking him for a real statue, but he wasn't taking any chances with this joyrider. He jumped from his pedestal as the Nissan crashed through it, sending the few coins he had collected that morning all over the pavement. The James Joyce mime threw his walking stick hopelessly after the car, as it came off the pavement and rejoined the traffic on the other side of the street.

The driver of the Nissan glanced in her rear-view mirror, angry at the near miss, but relieved that she hadn't harmed anyone.

'Fucking mimes! I nearly ran into him.' Zoe screamed from the driver's seat.

Daniel was sprawled out on the back seat trying to keep pressure on the wound in his stomach. The bump coming off the pavement sent pain through his body. He raised one hand before him and saw lots of blood. It had seeped through the cloth he was holding against the wound: a futile attempt to reduce the blood loss. It was now all over the place, beneath every fingernail and even between the links of Daniel's wristwatch. Closing his eyes, he begged

1

the pain to go.

'Stay with me!' Zoe screamed at him from the front. The GPS navigation system emitted a warning beep that she was driving too fast.

Daniel opened his eyes. He glanced out the window and watched the city speed by. From his angle, all he could see were tops of lamp posts, buildings, trees and road signs. His sense of direction had vanished. He had no clue where in the city he was. Even worse, he couldn't recollect how he ended up in the back seat of his own car with such an injury.

What the hell happened?

His hands moved to the wound in his abdomen. He felt the blade first - at least part of it - and then the handle of the knife. It took another moment before he remembered; before he remembered everything.

Stop the car.

His injury hurt like hell. The car flew over a speed bump almost knocking him from the backseat. Daniel let out a scream of agony.

'Stop the car,' he moaned.

He could see his wife crying. She was in no state to drive, especially at this speed.

'Zoe, please.'

She continued to keep her eyes on the road and her foot on the accelerator.

Daniel's head dropped to the side. He spotted something green sticking out of the pocket of the seat in front of him. All he could think of was Sean, his son. Daniel's bloodstained hand reached over and grabbed it. It was a green napkin with two holes cut out, a makeshift mask of a comic book superhero. Daniel had a quick flashback to the time his son had made it. Sean had cut out holes that were too close together, meaning he had looked more like a crossed-eyed villain than a masked crusader. It had made himself and Zoe laugh, but neither of them had the heart to tell him.

Daniel grasped it tight and pulled it close to his chest. A tear escaped down the side of his face. Deep down, Daniel knew. Could he stop it?

'*After 300 metres, turn left,*' the GPS device announced with a remarkably calm voice that didn't match the emergency situation it was part of.

Zoe continued and then slammed on the brake as she took a sharp corner. She placed her foot on the accelerator again and continued to speed through the city.

'Please stop the car,' Daniel mumbled from the back. He took a deep breath and, with his last ounce of energy, roared, 'Now!'

She glanced behind. 'You're going to bleed to death if I don't get you to a hosp...'

A cold shiver covered Daniel as he caught a glimpse of a red traffic light fly by. This was followed almost immediately by screeching brakes. A car coming from the left clipped them from the back, spinning them out of control across the street. Another sound of burning rubber filled the air before an oncoming van hit the Nissan. Pain exploded through Daniel as the car flipped and slid on its roof to the other side of the street, almost back to where they were first hit. Daniel let out a cry as gravity flung him onto the roof. The weight of his body pushed the knife further into his abdomen. Blood now seeped onto the lining fabric of the interior roof, as the car came to a standstill. The green superhero mask landed an arms-length away.

Sean

Daniel felt faint.

I'm sorry Sean. You'll be okay. I promise.

He heard his wife crying.

'Daniel?'

'I'm here Zoe. Don't be afraid. I'm here.'

Zoe still sat in the driver's seat, but her head was pushed against the roof.

'I'm scared, Daniel.'

Daniel let out a cry. The pain was becoming too much. He tried to be strong. He pushed himself onto his side to ease the pressure from the knife. He was unsure if it would do any good. He picked up the green superhero mask and, with the same hand, reached out and held his wife's hand.

'Don't be… scared,' he said almost in a whisper. He continued talking to her, trying his best to comfort her.

Suddenly he felt dazed. His grasp loosened. Zoe tightened her grip. The green napkin mask remained in place, between the two parents. Daniel's pain seemed to subside. Was that a good sign? He closed his eyes. It felt good to close them. He could hear his wife in the background. She was becoming fainter. Was she being rescued from the car? He felt comfortable now. He wanted to stay where he was.

A strong stench suddenly attacked Daniel's senses. Instead of becoming more alert, a floodgate of memories opened from his student days when he worked part-time in a petrol station. He loved the smell in a strange kind of way.

Suddenly he heard a voice. It was a male voice. One he recognised strangely enough. Were they being rescued?

'Turn around when possible.'

His hopes were dashed. It was the GPS device offering one last piece of navigating advice.

The scent of petrol grew stronger. Then everything went dark.

Part I

The clock of life is wound but once
And no man has the power
To tell just where the hands will stop,
At late or early hour.

Robert H Smith

01

6 Months Earlier

The tower crane swayed slightly as a gust of wind blew. A whistling sound filled the grey sky as it blew across the criss-cross framework of the jib; a giant flute for Mother Nature.

Daniel Geller's initial reaction was to tighten his grip on the levers in front of him. As if that would do any good if the crane actually toppled. His reaction was similar to the purpose of the yellow hard hat that lay on the dashboard in front of him. Officially, he was expected to wear it throughout the entire day. Unofficially, he wore it only on the journey up in the morning and back down at the end of the day. What was the point of wearing it while sitting in the crane? If something were to fall on the building site, he was in the safest place. He often wondered if the policy was made before Newton sat beneath the apple tree.

And as for the crane itself? Well, if that were to fall, he would need more than a hard yellow hat to live that one out.

The gust of wind passed, and Daniel released his grip. He exhaled heavier than he meant to, like a fighter pilot who had just survived a flight through enemy territory. He turned his head and looked at the streets below. After all these years, he still got the jitters when he looked down from such a height. At the same time, he loved observing Dublin life from above. Dog walkers, joggers, students, shoppers, business people, inner city children up to no good, cyclists in their luminous yellow vests weaving their way through chaotic traffic, motorists, double-decker buses, homeless people, pensioners, every walk of life. They all had different destinations, each with their own stories.

Daniel kept a pair of old binoculars in his cabin. Although he used them mostly for work - checking the progress of his colleagues before and after manoeuvres - he would often zoom in on people below and enjoy his very own silent movie. It was a way to break up the days, some of which were slow with less than five or six manoeuvres in an entire day. Although he always had a book to break the monotony, and a Rubik's cube that he completed every time he picked it up, he was grateful for the 360 degrees view he had of Dublin. It felt like his city.

The current project he worked on was that of an apartment block that still miraculously had finances behind it. Maybe it was the location that kept the construction going. The building site - and future apartment block - was on the North Circular Road, near the entrance to Phoenix Park; one of the largest city parks in Europe. This meant Daniel had an excellent view of the park itself, the Zoo, the Old Jameson Chimney in Smithfield, the River Liffey and of course the Spire (not that the Spire was anything to look at).

On a clear day he could make out the Wicklow Mountains to the south and the Mourne Mountains all the way up in County Down. He wondered if other people in Dublin had that kind of view. The city wasn't renowned for its tall buildings or breathtaking skyline, but there was plenty of beauty if you knew where to look.

The tinfoil from his sandwiches lay open on the floor. He didn't have to worry about mice. He was sixty metres high. To be honest, he wouldn't mind if a mouse *did* find its way to his cabin. A bit of company from time to time would break the long day.

The crane cabin, or his "office" as he would often call it, was not the most modern one he had worked in. On his previous project - an apartment block in Ballsbridge - Daniel found himself in a brand new cabin. The seat still had plastic on it and it had that inevitable new smell. But that was during the height of the Celtic Tiger. Now he found himself in a cabin at least twenty years old. Although it was clean, he could tell that it had been filthy in the past. A scent of stale smoke seemed to linger in it, offering a glimpse to its past. It was like buying a used-car from a chain smoker. No matter what the owner of such a car would attempt before handing over the keys, the scent would always offer the new owner a truthful glance into its past.

Daniel pulled some levers and transported a huge steel structure to the scaffolding to the west of the apartment construction. As soon as two of the builders on the scaffolding caught hold of it and prevented it from swinging, he lowered it until the wire rope became slack and the steel structure was resting where it should be. The journey was over.

'Okay, it's released. You can pull away, Daniel,' came a voice over Daniel's radio.

He pulled the lever and the hook rose from the scaffolding. He rotated the crane back into its original position, facing into the wind. The position made him feel safer, especially on windy days like today.

He never forgot his first week on a building site, more than ten years ago, and the horrific sight of a crane falling over. The operator was killed instantly. The accident report said that it was down to shoddy parts that held the crane together, parts that should have been replaced years previously. The report even went as far as to include that the operator was not wearing his hard yellow hat (at the time), but admitted that this was unlikely to have caused his death.

Daniel often wondered what went through the crane operator's mind when he knew the crane had lost its balance. That split second when it began to fall. What it must have felt like to be trapped inside such a confined space, so high up. No escape. It must have been awful, realising the inevitable…

His radio came to life again.

'Daniel, someone here to see you.' It was Keith, the construction site foreman, on the radio.

Daniel looked at his radio on the dashboard with a puzzled look. He picked up the radio and spoke into it. 'There's someone to see *me*?'

He waited for a response.

'Yes.'

He couldn't understand the conventional way the foreman spoke as if he was a secretary outside his office announcing his next appointment.

'Do you want to send him up?' he asked casually.

'Very funny,' came the response back in the radio. It went silent for a moment before the foreman continued. 'You're finishing up anyway, aren't you? Just thought I'd let you know that there's someone asking for you.'

'Okay, thanks.'

Daniel looked at his watch. It was indeed the end of the working day. He scrunched up the tinfoil from his sandwiches into a ball and threw it into a white plastic bag. This was followed by the book he was reading, *How Not to Be Wrong: The Power of Mathematical Thinking* by Jordan Ellenberg, and a Lucozade bottle of pee. This was wrapped in an extra plastic bag as a precaution. He usually peed into it once a day to save a trip down. It was the least glamorous part of his job.

As he opened the door of the cabin, he felt the wind immediately. He climbed onto the platform and closed the door behind him. There was no need to lock it after him. If a thief was willing to risk his life climbing all the way up to steal a Rubik's cube, Daniel didn't want to disappoint him.

Slowly, rung by rung, he made his journey downwards. His journey home started here. As others throughout the city were shutting down computers, rinsing coffee mugs, changing out of uniforms, Daniel was climbing down a huge metal structure.

He had near misses in the past. Particularly on wet

days. The mast however wasn't made up of just one ladder from top to bottom. Instead, each segment of the mast had a diagonal ladder, each separated by a small platform. This meant that, if he did miss a step, the most he would fall would be twelve steps or so - at least in theory.

Adrenaline still pumped through his body on his homeward bound journey, especially when he was near the top. As he got closer and closer to the ground, the adrenaline subsided. In a different life he could be Jack and the crane his beanstalk. He took his time coming down, though. A giant was never chasing him.

Daniel jumped the last few rungs and landed with both feet on the ground. He walked towards the prefab buildings to meet the mystery guest. Before he had taken two steps he heard someone call out his name.

'Daniel Geller?'

He turned to the side and saw his visitor standing next to a cement mixer. The man was tall, late forties, with a good head of dark hair. He wore a shirt, a loosened tie and long overcoat. He could have passed for a business man if it wasn't for the shoddy brown leather bag he held. It screamed academia. The bag had two side buckles, of which only one worked. It had more scratches and cuts on it than an ice skating rink. The shape probably didn't even allow the transport of a laptop. And as for a tablet? It was probably designed when the term "tablet" was more commonly associated with the stone type.

Daniel nodded as he stopped and turned towards the stranger. Hand outstretched, the man introduced himself, 'John Redmond.'

Daniel was about to shake his hand when he stopped and stared at the man. 'I remember you.'

John kept his hand out for several awkward moments before retracting it. 'Of course you do.'

'I remember all the support you gave me in developing my ideas before turning your back.'

'It wasn't as simple as that, Daniel.'

'My arse it wasn't. You believed in what I was trying to do. You supported me all the way and then just abandoned me on the final hurdle.'

John shook his head. 'Daniel, it wasn't just my decision. It was a decision that the entire mathematical faculty at Trinity had to make. I was new at the time. I was at the bottom of the food chain, so to speak. My influence was minimum.'

Daniel looked towards the half-built construction that he had, moments earlier, lowered the steel beam onto. He took a deep breath and turned back to John.

'Why are you here? I mean after all these years?'

John looked at the huge steel crane and then back to Daniel. 'Your thesis.'

Daniel said nothing for a moment, unable to believe that his thesis from all those years ago could be the reason. 'My thesis?'

'I think everybody deserves a second chance.'

'What do you mean a second chance?'

'I've picked it up recently.' John swapped the leather bag he was holding to his other hand. 'I've gone through it again, with fresh eyes so to speak. Some of the mathematical models you developed were, quite frankly, astounding. I'm only *now* seeing similar models in the scientific literature. And even those aren't nearly as ambitious as what you worked on. You had some vision, Daniel. You were way ahead of your time.'

'Is that right? That's good to know… twelve years later.'

John ignored his sarcasm. 'From what I understood, you performed five calculations on fellow students to predict the dates they were going to die.'

A silence elapsed. Finally Daniel said, 'Is that a question or a statement? Look, I'm not going to talk about this. I turned my back on it the day you threw me out.'

'I didn't throw you out, Daniel. I had nothing to do with your expulsion. I was…'

'At the bottom of the food chain. I know. Tell me where in the food chain are you now?'

'I'm a professor.'

'A professor? How about that. Congratulations.'

'Look Daniel, I understand you're bitter but when I look at your entire thesis now, it's pure genius.'

Daniel said nothing as he stared at the professor. A scruffy colleague with a cigarette behind his ear called out as he passed by. 'See you tomorrow, Daniel!'

Daniel waved.

'Do you keep in contact with the five students you did the calculations on?' John asked.

'No. Of course not. I'm a fucking crane operator. I've got nothing in common with them anymore.'

John squinted his eyes, as if trying to see if he was telling the truth. 'So you don't know?'

'Know what?'

'You really don't know?'

Daniel shook his head. 'Know what?'

'One of the predications you made was spot on.'

Daniel looked away, trying to comprehend what the professor had said. 'What do you mean "spot on"?'

'Spot on. The date you predicted in your theory was correct. One of your ex-fellow students passed away and he died on the exact date that you calculated.'

Daniel's heart stopped. He felt the hairs on the back of his neck raise. He swallowed and tried to cover his surprise. 'That's… interesting.'

'Interesting?' John looked around briefly and then pointed to the building construction. 'The architecture of this new building is interesting. Your prediction is more than interesting, trust me. It's… phenomenal. It could be one of those discoveries that go down in the history books.'

'Who was it?'

'Who was who?'

'The person who died.'

'A guy called Brian Nolan.'

Daniel turned and stared in the distance. His mind stretched to twelve years previously.

'Do you remember him?'

'Brian. Yeah, I remember him,' he said as he turned back to John. 'He was a fun guy. Very social. And very bright. He was always top of the class when it came to exams.'

'That's right. That's the guy.'

'Did he have a family?'

'Not that I know of. I think he was one of these people who lived the student life for too long.'

Daniel rubbed his stubble and took a deep breath. 'I can't believe he's dead.'

'I can imagine. It's not particularly nice hearing about an ex-classmate dying, whether or not you kept in touch.'

As he listened to the professor, Daniel rubbed his stubble again. He waited a couple of moments before saying anything. 'How do you know I didn't kill him myself?' he asked eventually. 'I mean just to prove my thesis.'

John smiled as if he was expecting the question. 'I don't. But, judging from his death, it just seems like a tragic accident. I'm sure the police would have looked into it if there was foul play involved.'

'How did he die?'

'In a car crash, on the way home from a party. No surprise there. The alcohol in his blood was three times over the legal limit.'

'When did he die?'

'About four years ago. I only found out myself when I dug out your thesis and did some research.'

An uncomfortable silence rose that Daniel finally broke by shrugging and saying, 'Okay. So what now? What is the purpose of you coming here?'

'To tell you that your predication was correct.'

Daniel waited. He knew there was something else.

'And if you would consider coming back?'

There it was.

'Coming back? Where? To Trinity?'

John nodded. 'To finish what you started.'

'I *finished* what I started.' He raised his voice. 'It's just that you guys couldn't put your stamp of approval on it.'

'Look, I know you're bitter about it, but Jesus, Daniel, don't turn your back on this second chance. It's one hell of a thesis. The impact it could have... on humanity itself. This could lead to big things for you. The Fields Medal even. You don't want to stay in this kind of work all your life.' The professor pointed to the crane. 'Stuck up there, eight hours a day.'

Daniel took off his hard hat and looked at it for a few moments. A little sticker of Ben10 was stuck to the side of it. His son had given it to him for luck. 'When you do something for so long you get used to it.' He looked at John. 'I'm thirty-five years old. I have a wife. A great kid. I lead an uncomplicated life. No maths questions. I go to work. I come back from work. My salary at the end of the month more or less pays the bills, with a little left over for a rainy day. I don't need any complications and false hopes in my equation right now.'

'But this isn't you, Daniel. We both know that.'

'How do you know what is or isn't me?'

The professor pointed towards Daniel's plastic bag of belongings.

'Great book isn't it? *The Power of Mathematical Thinking.* Don't you love the hand-drawn illustrations throughout it?'

Daniel looked down and saw the front cover of his book pressed up against the white plastic bag. He didn't say anything.

'Come on Daniel. I don't think there's a single guy on this building site who reads books like this.'

'It doesn't mean anything.'

'Of course it does. I remember you. The enthusiasm.

15

The drive. I have read your thesis again. It's written by a genius, Daniel.'

Daniel smirked and shook his head. 'My maths teacher in school used to say that there's a hair thickness between the genius and the madman. Maybe I've crossed over. Maybe I'm the madman now.'

'Then cross back over. I know your potential now, Daniel.' John held his hand out in a surrender pose. 'At least meet me for lunch or even coffee so we can talk about it.'

'We're talking about it now, aren't we? The answer is no. I'm not going back to university. I'm not re-visiting that thesis. I'm not going to be rejected again.'

'You won't be rejected. I promise.'

'I know I won't, because I'm not doing it.' He turned away and walked towards the prefabricated buildings to sign out for the day.

'One more is due to die in six days,' John shouted after him.

Daniel turned back to the professor. 'What do you mean by "one more"?'

'One of your Guinea Pigs. One more of your ex-classmates who volunteered in your thesis.'

'Well if it's meant to be, it's meant to be. I'll make sure I have an alibi when he dies,' he said as he turned around and continued walking.

'It's a "she" this time,' John added. 'And from what I remember, she was a past lover of yours.'

02

Sometimes Grace hated Amsterdam, especially when it started raining at the precise moment she left work. Standing at the doorway of Kuhlman International B.V. on Vondelstraat, she glanced upwards and felt the first few drops. It was a battle between a blue sky and dark clouds. The dark clouds seemed to be winning. She sighed. Moments earlier she had checked *Buienradar*, an app on her phone predicting rain in the area. The app had given her the all-clear. *Next time*, she vowed to herself, *I'll just look out the window.*

Checking her watch, she pondered whether to wait for a clearing or just go for it. As she still had to stop off at Albert Heijn to pick up some oregano for dinner, she decided to go for it. She reached in her bag and pulled out a crumpled rain jacket. She hated it, but it was a necessary evil that protected her Ralph Lauren suit. She put the jacket on and went rummaging in her bag again. She pulled out a Converse baseball cap and gently placed it on her head. She then pulled the rain jacket hood gently over the baseball cap. The peak of the cap kept the rain from her face. That too was a necessary evil to prevent her make-up from running. It wasn't so important now, coming home from work, but in the mornings it was essential. The last thing she wanted was to arrive at work looking like Captain Jack Sparrow.

Stepping from the temporary shelter of the entrance to her work, she walked into the rain. Although it was a one-way street, she looked both ways before crossing. She had been living in Amsterdam long enough to know that you could expect a cyclist to jump out of nowhere at any time. Often she felt like the Looney Tunes Coyote crossing a desert road only to suddenly encounter Road Runner. Instead of the *meep meep*, it would be a bicycle bell that would startle her.

Grace's bike was locked to a bicycle rack on the other side of the street. As soon as she unlocked and rolled it onto the street, she realised the chain had come off.

'Shit!'

She wheeled her bicycle back onto the pavement and stared at it. Resisting the temptation to give it a quick kick, she leaned it against the iron fence that surrounded Vondel Park. Afraid of getting oil all over her hands, she looked around for a stick or something similar to use to lift the chain back on.

'Have you lost something, Grace?'

Grace looked up and saw her colleague Rik standing in front of her, holding an umbrella. He was tall, handsome, late-twenties; the kind of guy who had everything going for him. He wore thick-framed spectacles that oozed a modern and stylish aura. Another man could wear the same spectacles and be classed as a geek. Not Rik though. The word "geek" was never part of anyone's vocabulary when it came to describing him.

Like every day, Rik wore a suit and an open-collared shirt. And brown shoes. That was one thing about Dutch men that Grace never understood. The suit-and-brown-shoes look. It's not that it didn't look stylish with certain suits. It did. But sometimes she got the impression that it was some kind of secret Dutch law; every Dutch man above the age of eighteen must own at least one pair of brown leather shoes and wear them with a random suit at least once a week.

She didn't know much about Rik's private life but always imagined him to be Mr Popular. Mr Popular in a nice way. At work he was courteous and responsive. He greeted people in the mornings. He wished them pleasant evenings when he left. Everybody liked him, but few actually knew him.

'Hi Rik.' Although it was still raining, Grace pulled her hood off quickly. 'It's my bloody chain.'

Rik handed her the umbrella. 'Hold this.'

Grace held it over him as he bent down and examined the chain. To fill the silence she started chatting. 'I think I was five-years-old the last time I tried to put a chain back on my bike.'

He stood up and gave the gears on the handlebars a few clicks until they were back in first gear.

'And my bike was much smaller back then. And probably even had stabilisers.'

He looked at her frowning. 'Stabilisers?'

'Yes, you know. The side wheels children use to learn how to cycle.'

He nodded and smirked.

'What?' Grace asked.

'No, nothing. I was thinking of something else,' he said as he looked at the ground and grabbed a disposed lollipop stick.

'What were you thinking of?'

'Nothing,' he said. 'You'll just laugh.' Using the stick, Rik picked the loose chain and placed a section of it on the teeth of the chain ring. Once there, he lifted the back wheel from the ground and turned the pedal.

'No, go on. Tell me.'

The chain slipped back onto the chain ring.

'*Et voila*,' Rik said as he ignored Grace's question.

'Thanks a million, Rik.' She passed the umbrella back to him as he handed her the handle of the bike. 'So what did you think of when I said stabilisers?'

'Nothing. It's silly. Forget it.'

'I like silly.'

Rik laughed. 'Really, it was nothing. I just misheard you and thought of something else.'

'Okay. Well, thanks a million anyway.'

'Have you far to go?' he asked.

'About a twenty-five minute cycle.'

He glanced towards the sky and pointed to some dark clouds. 'There's a huge downpour coming from the north.'

Grace had no clue which way was north and just looked in the direction Rik was pointing.

'Not sure if you're going to make it.'

'Oh,' she said, unsure. 'Well, at least I have my rain gear with me.' She patted her rain jacket, but secretly cursed at just how unglamorous she appeared.

'I live two blocks from here,' he said pointing in the opposite direction.

South, Grace guessed to herself.

'If you want to stop off for a coffee until it blows over, you're more than welcome. It will probably be just a cloud burst.'

'That's awfully kind of you, Rik, but no. I really should be heading back home.'

'I can even cycle your bike,' he said ignoring her. 'You can sit on the back and we'll be in my place within three minutes flat, sipping a hot cup of coffee while the rest of Amsterdam run for cover. You'd actually be doing me favour too.'

'In what way?'

'Otherwise I will have to walk and very likely get caught out in the downpour.'

Grace smiled. Any other girl at work, especially the single ones, would have jumped at Rik's proposal. Instead here she was actually hesitating.

Then she thought of Otto, her husband.

What are you doing? A voice in her head was asking. Or was it her husband's voice? She could hardly do anything without thinking of him first. Otto would expect her to be home by six to prepare dinner.

What's on the menu tonight? Grace asked herself. *Pork with Roasted Peppers and Potatoes? I really don't know if I have enough Oregano.*

She needed to pop into Albert Hein and pick some up just to be safe.

Just to be safe. What have I turned into? She hated herself sometimes. She was sick of being safe. She was tired of being so organised. Why couldn't she be like the person she used to be, before she met Otto?

Rik could sense the hesitation. 'Look, don't feel obliged. I just thought...'

'No, I understand, Rik. You're very kind. It's just...'

To hell with "just to be safe".

'One condition,' she heard herself saying. 'You tell me what you were smirking at when I said "stabilisers"'.

Rik threw his head back laughing. 'Oh my God, you really won't let me away with that will you?'

'Deal?'

He shook his head gently, more in disbelief than anything. Finally, he reluctantly said, 'I thought you were referring to *tranquilisers*. There. Silly isn't it? For a split second I thought children in Ireland cycled around with tranquiliser darts sticking out of their bikes.'

Grace closed her eyes and shook her head. 'You're right. It wasn't funny.'

'I tried to warn you,' he said handing her back the umbrella and grabbing the handlebars. 'Hop on.'

She hopped on the back of her own bike as Rik started to pedal. In the distance she could see the thundercloud approaching.

To hell with Pork with Roasted Peppers and Potatoes.

A storm was on its way.

03

Zoe Geller sat on the sofa with her two feet on the coffee table. She admired the nail varnish she had just applied as they air-dried. *Coronation Street* played on the television and a stench of nail varnish lingered in the air.

She glanced up briefly as Daniel entered the room. 'Did he go to bed okay?'

Daniel nodded. 'Eventually. He insisted that I read *The Big Pancake* with his Gonzo puppet on. Of course I couldn't resist doing the funny things, and he found the antics of Gonzo more amusing than the actual book.'

Zoe smiled as she leaned forward, shook a bottle of nail varnish and proceeded to paint her fingernails. Daniel sat down on the armchair and looked at his wife.

'I don't understand how you don't break those nails when you're kickboxing,' he said. 'Surely there's a rule about how long nails can be.'

Zoe's biggest hobby was keeping fit. And the only way she kept fit was by kickboxing. Daniel wasn't mad about his wife's hobby. Kickboxing left bruises on her body; mostly on her arms and legs, but sometimes on her face. He wondered how many neighbours secretly thought that he was a wife beater.

He wouldn't go so far as to think of Zoe as a fitness fanatic, but she certainly was passionate about it. She usually went three times a week. Every couple of months she had a match, but she didn't take those seriously. She did it for the training. To keep fit. It took her less than three weeks after giving birth to Sean to go back to training, albeit a mild form of it.

'They're not *that* long,' she said as she carefully painted her nail on her index finger. 'And anyway they're protected in the gloves.'

'Not that long? Jesus you're like Freddy Krueger.'

Zoe picked up a copy of the *Evening Herald* and flung it

at Daniel. He blocked it as it fell to his lap.

'You sound like the guys at work.' She put on a nerdy guy's voice. 'Jeez Zoe, how do you type with those nails…narp narp narp?'

Daniel laughed. Zoe worked as a HR assistant in an IT company, and he could picture the kind of guys she worked with.

'Jeez Zoe,' she continued, 'how do you pick your nose without piercing a blood vessel?'

'Yeah right. I'm sure they've asked you that.'

'I'm sure they've thought about it.'

A moment passed.

'How *do* you pick your nose with those nails?'

She shook her head. 'I don't pick my nose at all.' Breaking into a *Little Britain*-esque voice she said, 'I'm a lady, you see!'

Daniel rolled his eyes and admired his wife as she sat there in her tracksuit bottoms and sweatshirt. He was surprised that her clothes actually seemed to fit her. Often she bought clothes that were too big for her but pinned them back or adjusted the sizes with paper clips, elastic bands or staples. When they first met, Daniel called her Stationery Woman, because of all the office stationery he would find attached to her clothes. It wasn't unusual to hear them rotating in the washing machine.

The oversized clothes apart, Zoe was an attractive woman. Blonde shoulder-length hair, beautiful brown eyes, friendly smile. Apart from the nail varnish, she seldom spent time grooming herself, at least when it came to make-up. She still had plenty of beauty products but there was something very natural about her. She had skin that most women envied.

'I need to go up into the attic,' Daniel said, changing the subject. 'Do you need anything?'

Zoe looked up for a moment and then returned to her nails. 'No. Why? What do you need?'

'My thesis. It's still up there, isn't it?'

'The one about predicting someone's date of death?'

'Yes. It's not that I've written a heap of theses... or thesi or whatever the plural is.'

'If you put it up there, then it's still there. There's so much rubbish up there.'

'Are you calling my thesis rubbish?'

She ignored the question. 'Why do you need your thesis all of a sudden?'

He unfolded the *Evening Herald* and glanced briefly over the front page before looking up.

'It's a strange situation. I ran into an old professor from Trinity. He got me thinking about it again.'

Zoe placed the brush back in the bottle. 'How in the name of God did you just *run into* a professor? Your job doesn't exactly give you many opportunities to run into people.'

'He was waiting for me when I came down at the end of the day.'

'Waiting? That sounds a bit...'

She didn't finish her sentence, but Daniel understood what she meant and just shrugged. 'He was actually my old mentor. He has since risen through the academia ranks and is now a professor.'

'Oooh,' she said in mock admiration. 'Good for him. And he just told you to go home and have a look at your thesis?'

'He mentioned that one of my calculations was right.'

Zoe sat upright. 'Really? Meaning what exactly?'

'It means that the date of death I calculated twelve years ago for an ex-classmate turned out to be correct.'

'You're joking.'

'I couldn't believe it either, but that's what he said.'

'So will they give you your PhD?

'I don't know. I'm not sure what he wanted. I walked away.'

'You walked away?'

'The conversation wasn't exactly over,' he looked

towards Zoe. 'I felt the hurt and anger from years ago begin to resurface. I walked away. I needed to clear my head.'

Nobody said anything for a while. A snippet of the *Coronation Street* theme came from the television as it went to a commercial break.

'So why do you want to get your thesis down from the attic?' she asked.

Daniel shrugged. 'Just to have a look through it, see if it still makes sense.'

'Be careful, Daniel. If the pain and anger are still there, as you say, be careful. I don't want to see you getting hurt again.'

'I won't.' He refrained from telling her about the final words the professor had said to him as he walked away.

'One more is due to die in six days… a past lover of yours.'

He would tell Zoe if and when the time was right.

04

Professor John Redmond entered the front door of his home. As his shoes were dirty from his construction site visit, he reached down and took them off.

'I'm home!' he announced. The only sound he could hear was from the television in the sitting room. He placed his shoes neatly to one side, hung his jacket up and walked into the sitting room.

The room was dark. The only light came from the television set. His wife, Claire, lay on the sofa. An empty plate lay on a tea towel on the floor.

TV dinner again.

'Claire, I'm home,' he said softly.

She was fast asleep. He decided against waking her. She looked so peaceful. The light from the television danced and cast shadows on her tranquil face as she breathed deeply.

John's foot hit off something on the floor next to the sofa. He bent down and picked up an empty wine glass. He sighed and shook his head. 'Not again,' he whispered to himself. Reaching down, he placed his hand on the carpet to make sure the wine hadn't spilled. It was dry. Claire had emptied the glass herself well before John knocked it over.

As he walked into the kitchen he switched on the light. He left the wine glass on top of the dishwasher and pulled the blinds behind the sink. He opened the refrigerator and found a dinner covered with cling film: chicken with cashew nuts and rice. On the inside door of the fridge, he spotted a bottle of white wine: Wolf Blass Chardonnay. He lifted it up and saw a trickle at the bottom.

'For God's sake. It's getting worse,' he mumbled as he put the bottle back where it came from and took out the plate with dinner on it. As he closed the fridge, Claire was standing next to him. John almost jumped.

'Jesus! You frightened the shit out of me,' he said.

'You frightened the shit out of *me*,' Claire said. 'I didn't hear you come in. All I heard was somebody snooping around the kitchen. I thought we had a burglar.' She looked down at his feet. 'Why aren't you wearing any shoes?'

'They're mucky.

'How did they get mucky?'

'I visited a construction site. Doing some research.'

Not really interested in his reply, she opened the fridge and took the bottle of wine out.

'Where's the full bottle of Sauvignon Blanc that was there this morning?' John asked.

Claire raised her hand to her head like she suddenly had a headache. 'Stop John. Okay? Just stop. I'm not in the mood today.' Her eyes were glassy and wild. Impression marks from lying on one side of her face were visible. Dried saliva marked the side of her mouth. The chaotic look was something you might get away with on a Sunday morning after a night out. Not on the evening of an ordinary weekday.

'You can't go on like this,' he said as he gently placed his dinner in the microwave.

'You have your way of dealing with things. I have my way.'

'The counsellor said...'

'I know what the counsellor said! You can tell her next time if you like. I'm a disgrace, I know. But I'll get through this my way.'

With the bottle of wine in one hand, she grabbed the wine glass from the counter and stormed back to the sitting room.

Frustrated, John slammed the microwave shut with a bang.

05

There was something very romantic about sitting on the back of a bicycle, while a man pedalled hard through the streets of Amsterdam in the rain. It was something Grace had never experienced with Otto, even during the honeymoon period of their relationship.

As she sat sideways on the back of her own bike she wondered if she was doing the right thing. She couldn't explain the mysterious attraction she had for Rik. How could a thirty-six year old married woman be so attracted to him?

She thought for a moment, and rephrased the question in her head. How could a thirty-six year old married woman *not* be attracted to Rik?

As he cycled over a bump, Grace felt it sharply on her bottom. She grimaced but bit her lip on time to stop her wincing out loud. She made a mental note to pump up her back wheel when she got home.

Rik turned into Westlandgracht, a residential street next to a large canal. At first sight the canal could pass for a lake, but it didn't take a trained eye to realise that it was a man-made creation. Perhaps it was necessary for the inflow and outflow of the city's canals. Its similarity to a natural lake was made all the more legit by the wild water birds living on a small island of rushes in the middle of it.

'Here we are.'

When Grace hopped off the back of the bike she realised that she had her rain jacket on and was holding Rik's umbrella. She looked at Rik. 'I'm so sorry. You're drenched!'

'I'm fine,' he said as he leaned the bike against a lamppost. He took a handkerchief out of his pocket and quickly dried his glasses. 'Anyway, I'm home. I can slip into my pyjamas if I want to. My Tellytubbie ones are my favourite,' he said with a wink.

Grace's perception of Rik's Mr Popular image almost evaporated then and there.

'Lock your bike here. I'll open the front door,' he said as he put his glasses back on and crossed the street to the apartment. A quick flash of light filled the darkening sky in the distance.

Grace placed the umbrella upside-down on the pavement as she quickly locked her bike. Her lock couldn't fit around the lamppost, so she resorted to locking the wheel and the frame of the bike together. The rumbling sound of thunder filled the air. Although it was still some way off, the downpour started. Turning around she saw Rik disappearing into the apartment building. The door was left wide open.

You can still change your mind, thought Grace. She wouldn't be too late if she left now. Maybe she even still had time to pick up oregano before Otto came home - *if* he came home at all. As the key came out of her bicycle lock the decision was made.

It would be nice to have some company. Was there anything wrong with that?

She picked up the umbrella and ran across the street. As she approached the door she closed it and shook it a couple of times before entering the building. Closing the door behind her, she could hear Rik on one of the floors above unlocking his apartment door. She climbed the steep stairway. The umbrella dripped as she ascended the stairs leaving behind a small trail.

Despite wearing her rain jacket and holding the umbrella, she still managed to get wet. Her trousers were soaked. As she got to the top she saw Rik's face poking out of the apartment, as if he was afraid that Grace would miss it.

'This way.'

She left the umbrella standing outside the door and followed him in.

The apartment was small - perhaps a little on the cramp side - but clean. She detected a mild scent that reminded her of a wet dog and suddenly had an awful thought that the smell was coming from her.

'You can hang your jacket here,' he said pointing to a coat hanger next to where he had just hung up his suit jacket. He removed his shoes and flung them on a pile of shoes just beneath the jackets.

'Make yourself at home,' he said as he disappeared into the bathroom.

Grace removed her rain jacket and hung it up. She also followed Rik's lead and removed her shoes and placed them neatly next to the pile.

Rik appeared again drying his hair with a towel.

'You want a towel?'

'Oh no, I'm fine,' she said, as a drop ran down her forehead.

'Are you sure? Don't worry, they *are* clean.'

'Okay. Actually, can I use your bathroom?' she asked, suddenly becoming very self-conscious that she now looked like a drowned rat and smelled like a wet dog. Rik pointed to the room he just came out of.

'Of course. Be my guest.'

'Sorry, were you finished in there? Didn't mean to be pushing you out.'

'Go for it.'

She entered the bathroom. It was like the rest of the apartment; cramped but efficient. A faint din hummed in the background, an extractor fan that was nearing the end of its life cycle. She looked in the mirror. Strands of hair were plastered to her forehead.

'God, what do I look like?' she whispered to herself. She picked up a hand towel hanging next to the sink and gave her hair a quick rub. The sink seemed cluttered. Or maybe her house was just too clean and sterile. Would she have found this messy and cluttered when she was Rik's age? *Probably not*, thought Grace as she continued to dry her hair. She couldn't help but admire his collection of toiletries: Zirh *Face Wash*, Clinique *M-Lotion*, Lab Series *Age Rescue Eye Therapy*.

'This guy has more grooming products than I do,' she whispered to herself. The only item they had in common was the Oral-B dental floss.

A bottle of Jean Paul Gaultier - *Le Male* - caught her eye. That was the scent she detected from him sometimes at work. She picked the bottle up and sniffed the top of it. It brought back so many memories. Not of Rik or even her husband, but of someone else. Someone she used to love.

She glanced in the shower. It was clean and, unlike the rest of the bathroom, or the apartment for that matter, quite spacious.

Plenty of room for two, she thought to herself. She shook her head as if it would help in dispersing the sudden spicy thoughts she was having.

Next to the sink stood a wicker laundry basket. She told herself to stop snooping, but before she knew it, she had lifted the cover. A shirt was the last thing that had been thrown in. The previous day's shirt perhaps. She flung the towel over her shoulder and glanced towards the door. She couldn't remember if she had locked it or not. If she went over and locked it now, it would seem a bit strange. She lifted up the shirt and held it in front of her. She brought it towards her face and took a sniff. There it was again. Jean Paul Gaultier - *Le Male*. It was more natural this time than smelling it from the top of a bottle. It was *his* scent. Fresh, bold, confident. She threw it back in the wash basket and replaced the cover.

As Grace continued drying her hair, she wondered what his reaction would be if she emerged from the bathroom wearing his previous day's shirt. And nothing else.

She giggled to herself. *Jesus, I need to get out more*. After she finished drying her hair, she gave it a quick brush until she looked half-decent again.

As she came out of the bathroom - which she now realised she hadn't locked - Rik poked his head from the kitchen.

'So, what would you like to drink?'

'Whatever you're having.'

'Red wine.'

Grace looked around. 'Wine?'

'Sure, why not?'

'What happened to the nice warm cup of coffee that you suggested?'

'Wine will also warm you up,' Rik continued from the kitchen.

It'll do more than that, she thought.

'Okay,' she agreed as she walked into the living room.

A large window looked out onto Westlandgracht. The rain was now pelting down. As she looked out on the street, she saw two teenage girls carrying hockey sticks cycling like crazy. They were completely soaked. The drops of rain were large. The type that actually bounced back off the street when they landed. It suddenly felt very cosy in Rik's apartment.

'It's really pissing down now,' she said, not really to anyone.

Rik entered the living room wrestling with a corkscrew and a bottle of red wine. 'Are your clothes wet?'

'I'm okay,' she said looking down at her wet trousers.

'I have a tumble dryer,' he said. 'Without wanting to sound like a cheesy Italian porn movie, you're welcome to throw whatever damp stuff you have in it.'

'Right,' Grace said with sarcasm. 'And I'll walk around your apartment in my underwear for the next half hour?'

'Not at all,' he said. 'You can throw your underwear in too.'

Grace laughed.

'Seriously though,' he continued. 'I have clean tracksuit bottoms, T-shirts or whatever you want.'

'Tellytubbie pyjamas?'

'That too.'

'Thanks Rik, but I'm fine.'

He pulled the corkscrew from the bottle but was annoyed by the absence of the pop sound. Looking at the end of the corkscrew he found only half a cork.

'Ah, shit. I hate when that happens.'

'Tea is also fine,' Grace said.

'It's half-opened now. I might as well try to get the other half out.'

'Or half-closed. You can keep it for a different occasion.'

He turned the corkscrew the other way round and pushed the handle into the bit of cork that was still jammed.

'Sorry. I hate doing this to the poor wine, but it's the only way.' The piece of cork came free, only it was inside the wine bottle. Rik retreated to the kitchen, poured two glasses of wine and returned to the living room.

'I picked out any loose pieces of cork. I hope it's okay.'

Grace took the glass and clinked her glass softly against Rik's.

'I'm sure it's fine. Cheers.'

'*Proost.*'

They both took a sip, and continued to look out the large front window, mesmerised by the downpour outside.

'So,' Rik said eventually. 'Do you enjoy working at Kuhlman's?'

'It's okay. Like any job it has its ups and downs.'

'When I first started, what is it, nine months ago now? I could tell you weren't Dutch before I heard you talk.'

'How come?'

'Your eyes.'

'My eyes. What about them?'

'I don't know, they don't look... Dutch.'

'Really? I never realised that you guys had a specific look.'

'I don't know, they seem very… sad.'

She laughed. 'What?'

'Sometimes it looks as if you're carrying all the worries of the world on your shoulders. You look sad sometimes at work.'

'Well,' she said, not really sure what to say. 'I don't know if that's a compliment or an insult.'

'It's not an insult,' Rik said immediately. 'Maybe it's not even a compliment. Just an observation.'

Grace wasn't used to such a direct conversation.

'Listen…' She was stuck for words.

'You don't have to say anything.'

A hurricane of emotions engulfed her. She wasn't sure if she should be happy or sad, angry or embarrassed.

'I'm not sad. Why do you think I'm sad?' she asked, forcing herself to smile.

'Your eyes don't lie. Eyes never lie.'

Grace looked towards the floor. Her heart was pounding. How did he know? How was it so obvious to him? He lifted her chin with his finger. Their eyes met. Grace stared into the mysterious blue eyes hidden behind the designer glasses. There was something so kind and honest about them. Something she wasn't used to seeing. They reminded her of the same person that wore the Jean Paul Gautier fragrance all those years ago. Turning her head away, she said nothing.

'Sometimes I've just wanted to give you a big hug.' Rik shrugged. 'But of course you can't take a shit in the office without half the colleagues knowing about it.'

Grace smirked and turned back to Rik. 'I'm married, Rik.'

'I know. I said "hug".'

'So why are you doing this?'

'What? Offering to give you a hug?'

'No. I mean…' she didn't know what she meant.

'Why are *you* doing this?' he asked with a gentle voice. 'I'm not married. I can do what I like. The question is why are you here?'

'Because you invited me.'

'You could have said no.'

'You could have not invited me.'

He laughed. 'That's not an argument.'

'It's all I have.'

'I just want to let you know that if you want to talk about what's going on in your private life, you can. You won't be judged by me. And it won't reach the gossipers of Kuhlman's.'

'Thank you, Rik.'

He reached towards Grace's face again. With his thumb he rubbed beneath her eye.

'Your mascara has run a little.'

Grace moved closer as his arms opened and wrapped around her. They stood in the middle of the living room in each other's arms. Grace closed her eyes. It felt so comforting. For the first time in a long time, she felt like someone in the foreign country she lived in actually cared about her. The cherry on top was that she could pick up that scent again.

For a split-second she pretended Rik was him.

06

Daniel pushed the attic door open and eased it to one side. As he stuck his head into the attic, he felt a slight drop in temperature. The unique attic stench hit his senses. It was a mixture of dust, damp air and lifelessness. It was a scent that reminded him of his grandfather's house in rural Galway years ago. All that was missing was a turf-burning stove.

He shone the torch around the attic. Not so much to view it, but more as a "warning shot" to any living creature that someone was coming. They could escape now or remain hiding until he left again. Even though he was thirty-six, Daniel feared attics.

Grabbing the edges of the attic entrance and stepping onto the topmost rung of the ladder, he pulled himself upwards. A pile of boxes and plastic bags lay close to the entrance. It was the so-called Lazy Pile; the pile that evolved and grew due to its close proximity to the entrance. It was a result of Daniel and Zoe throwing things in the attic without actually going up there. Daniel was mostly responsible for the pile. Zoe was less hesitant and often went into the attic when she wanted to put something away properly or if she needed something.

He knew for sure that his thesis wasn't in the Lazy Pile. He had placed it in the attic, out of harm's way, as soon as they moved into the house, eight years previously. He had saved it for a rainy day.

I guess it's raining today.

He shone the torch towards the water tank. Behind it he could just make out the silhouette of the box. He stood up keeping his head low and walked across the attic. Carefully, he stepped on one wooden beam after the other. One wrong step and his foot would be through the ceiling of Sean's bedroom, or the bathroom. He stopped suddenly and his hand went quickly to his face to wipe away a cobweb he had just walked into.

'Goddammit.'

He paused to see if his panicky swipes at his face had scared away any spider that may have been attached to the web. Unable to sense any movement on his face, or anywhere else for that matter, he continued. He crept around the water tank until he came to the box. He squatted down on his hunkers and shone the torch on it. Rubbing his hand over the top, Daniel looked at the clumps of dust that had formed on his fingertips.

The box was still sealed with Sellotape. He pulled the tape off and shone the torch into it.

A few notebooks and A4 binders lay inside. The covers of the notebook and binders brought back memories. The colours were so familiar to him at one stage of his life. He pulled them out and saw the thesis. It was a large spiral-bound document of more than 300 pages. On the front it read:

Date of Death
A theory in predicting the date of death of homo sapiens
by Daniel Geller

'Homo sapiens. Christ, what was I thinking?' He took a deep breath as he held four years of his life in his hands. Four wasted years.

As he rummaged through the box and noticed the various binders, floppy disks and hardback notebooks, it brought back bittersweet memories. They were memories of a time when he was excited about his future. It was a time when he truly believed that the mathematical models and formulae he invested so much time in, would amount to something in the end.

How that was taken from him in a flash.

As he picked up a red hardback notebook, a photograph fluttered out of it and landed on the yellow fibreglass that insulated the attic. Daniel picked it up and stared at it. Two young lovers stared back at him. They were students. The photo had been taken in the Buttery; the student bar in Trinity back then. They were both smiling and - judging from the shine in their eyes - slightly tipsy. Their arms were wrapped around each other. A bright future lay ahead. Although one of the lovers was himself, Daniel couldn't help feeling that he was looking at some complete stranger.

An intense ache of nostalgia exploded inside. First love. Was there anything more pure or beautiful? He rubbed his finger on the girl's face. He wondered what she was doing with her life. Was she successful? Married with kids? Didn't they share the same dreams back then? Sometimes Daniel regretted what he had done.

Still, there was always time to redeem himself, wasn't there?

Six days, to be precise, he thought as he folded the photograph and placed it inside his back pocket. He threw his thesis and hardback notebook back into the box.

'I'm not taking any chances,' he mumbled to himself as he lifted the box, still in a crouching posture. 'I'm not going to just wait and see if she dies.'

07

John finished his chicken with cashew nuts alone in the kitchen. He could hear the murmurs of random characters from one of the TV soaps Claire loved so much.

He opened the dishwasher and found it completely empty. They both simultaneously had stopped using it after the tragedy. It wasn't a conscious decision, but one that seemed to have evolved. With only the two of them now, who rarely ate dinner together, it would take too long for it to fill up. And they both knew that there was nothing more wasteful than putting on a half-filled dishwasher.

He washed his dish in the sink. When he finished, he looked around for a tea towel. Nothing. He resorted to drying his hands on his trousers. He then remembered seeing a tea towel in the sitting room. Instead of facing Claire again he decided to get a clean one from upstairs.

As he walked upstairs, he kept his eyes in front of him. Sometimes he just couldn't look at the family photo on the wall. The beautiful brown eyes smiling back at him were sometimes too much to bear. But the thought of removing the photo was a million times worse. That would be as if he never existed in the first place. As if they were trying to forget him.

He opened the door of the hot press and grabbed a tea towel. As he turned around to go back down, he was distracted by the door to a bedroom that was left ajar. His son's bedroom. John threw the tea towel over his shoulder and walked towards it. He peeked inside. Everything remained as it was. Time stood still. An unanswerable question floated within the four walls, like a stubborn stain in a tablecloth. When do you get rid of the belongings of your deceased child? There *has* to be a time.

But when?

A blue schoolbag lay on the floor next to his desk.

Ready for the school day. A school day that never came. His Manchester United duvet covers were creased again. John knelt beside the bed, placed his hands on the duvet and smoothened the creases. Closing his eyes, he inhaled softly through his nose, trying to capture any remaining scent from his son. Nothing. At least nothing obvious. Nothing strong enough to trigger a memory or bring him closer to his son, even if it was just for a nanosecond.

On the floor next to the bed, he spotted an elastic hair band. He picked it up and allowed it to slip onto his index and middle fingers. It had obviously fallen from Claire's hair. He suspected that his wife lay there in the middle of the day. Maybe she even slept there. Often he would straighten the covers and smoothen the creases, like he was doing now, only to find them messed again the following day.

John noticed a dark patch on the pillow right next to the little red devil emblem. He placed his hand on it and discovered that it was still damp. Was it from tears or drool? He hoped it was drool. It broke his heart to imagine his wife lying on their son's bed in the middle of the day crying. All alone.

Did she cry herself to sleep?

He stood up.

When would it end?

The tea towel on his shoulder reminded him of why he came upstairs in the first place. As he looked around the room he fixed his gaze for a moment on the bigger red devil at the centre of the main duvet.

How many times had he watched a football match with his son? John couldn't recall a single one that he watched from beginning to end. Not one single football match. Sure he had walked in the sitting room *during* a match. Or sat reading the newspaper while there was a match playing in the background. But to sit down with him and give a match his devoted attention?

Not once.

John sighed. The realisation stung like hell. He felt a stirring emotion inside him. He blocked it off. He would not cry now. He had to be strong. He would save this for his next "crying session". Maybe at work. Maybe in the car. Maybe at night when he was busy in his study and Claire was asleep.

As he left the bedroom, he felt a buzz come from his Blackberry. He took it out and glanced at the message. It was an email. He was surprised to see that it was from Daniel Geller with the subject "Call me". He clicked on Open.

John,

I got your e-mail address from the TCD website. I've been thinking about our conversation today. Please call me on 028 9018 0452.

Regards,
Daniel

08

Grace awoke. Her head spun. A feeling of nausea crept from her stomach. She swallowed hard to try and make it go away. It didn't work. She strained her ears, listening for the sound of breathing beside her. Nothing.

Did Otto even come home last night? she wondered in a daze. Her mind wandered, searching for the reason her husband wasn't beside her and why she felt so bad. Reliving the previous day she remembered leaving work, returning home…

Her mind retracted. There was no recollection of returning home. The image of Rik popped into her head and caused the floodgates to open. Her eyes shot open as it all came back. It was still dark but she now knew why Otto was not in the bed, next to her.

Oh God, I'm still in Rik's house.

She wondered if she was even in a bed. Rolling over she fell to the floor.

Nope. Sofa.

The floor was wooden and foreign. Looking around the room she spotted a digital clock on some electronic gadget. She still had her contact lenses in; they seemed to have dried up. Unable to read the actual time, she blinked several times. Eventually the digits came into focus.

5:34am

'Shit!'

Her heart started to race.

Otto's going to kill me.

She stood up and went looking for the bathroom. Although she badly needed to pee she was more concerned about her nausea and watering mouth, sure signs of the inevitable.

She had taken only two steps when she hit her shins off something. It was the coffee table.

'Shit!'

The room started to spin.

Not good.

As her eyes became accustomed to the dark, she hobbled towards the hallway. Her hands felt the walls for a light switch. *Any* light switch. Nothing. Something fell to the ground. She was trying desperately to recall the layout of the apartment when her hands came to a door handle. Was it the door to the bathroom?

The queasiness took control. As she pushed the door open, Grace fell to her knees and threw up on the floor.

Please, God, let this be the bathroom.

Another surge of vomit rose through her body and splashed onto the floor in front of her. The stench of her own puke made her stomach revolt more, sending another bout of vomit upwards and out. As she gasped for breath in between the spasms, a light came on. Grace squinted. Through her dried-up contacts, she looked up and saw Rik lying in his bed right in front of her.

'Well, that's one hell of a wake-up call,' he said sleepily.

'Oh God, Rik. I'm so sor-' Grace's stomach retched and she looked down at the mess she had already made. All she wanted now was the world to swallow her up.

Rik got out of bed. 'Bathroom?'

She nodded as she turned her head downwards both in shame and to observe the damage. To make matters worse, it seemed she actually puked on something that was lying on the floor.

'This way,' he said as he helped her up and guided her towards the bathroom. As soon as Grace saw the toilet she pounced at it like a cat on an oblivious mouse. She dropped down heavily on the tiled floor, hurting her knees in the process. They were the least of her worries though. Her head reached the toilet bowl just as another hurl of vomit erupted.

'You want help?' Rik asked.

She shook her head as she coughed and spluttered,

waving him away with her hand.

'I'll make some tea, perhaps.' He backed off and went to the kitchen.

Grace stared at the toilet bowl through eyes that now seemed not to be so dry anymore. A stream of saliva hung from her lips. She hacked and spat, and hacked again.

Jesus, how did this happen?

Her stomach retched and she gagged again. This time nothing came out. Just fresh streams of saliva.

She thought back to the previous night. She remembered that Rik had opened a bottle of wine. The atmosphere was so pleasant, relaxed, like it was the most normal thing in the world. Then another bottle of wine appeared. The atmosphere became more pleasant. Even more relaxed. She had a flashback of sitting back and curling up on Rik's sofa. Did they have any physical contact? Apart from the hug? She searched long and hard. All she could think of was the wine. The thought of which made her stomach retch again. Nothing more than strings of saliva came out. She wasn't sure which was worse, throwing something up or having to go through the same actions with nothing coming out.

She reached up and flushed the toilet. By doing so, by taking assertive action, she hoped her body understood that she was now finished and it was time to move on. She then pulled on the toilet roll and gave it a quick tug. The quick tug wasn't sharp enough to rip the sheets from the roll. Instead the roll just rotated a few more times making the strip of toilet paper even longer. She straightened up, held the roll with her free hand and this time managed to rip off the tissue. Scrunching it up, she buried her face in it, wiping her chin and blowing her nose. She hacked again and spat into the toilet bowl. She wiped her chin one more time, dropped the paper into the toilet and flushed again.

It wasn't a full flush as the cistern was still re-filling. But it was enough to flush the toilet paper away.

A tear fell down Grace's cheek. It wasn't from crying

but more as a physical reaction from all the throwing up. Leaning her back against the wall she looked towards the ceiling and took some deep breaths. Flakes of loose paint hung from the ceiling. It reminded her of peeling skin, the after effects of too much sun. The ceiling swayed a little through her vision.

She moaned and turned her attention to the white tiled wall in front of her. It wasn't completely white though. She noticed that every fourth tile was beige. An unfortunate choice of colour that made the design appear as if it was based on the image of cigarettes.

Her gaze moved to the lid of the bin. She could see a layer of dust on top of it and a stray piece of dental floss hanging from the side. Covering her face with one hand, she closed her eyes, shutting out the dull world that surrounded her.

It was only then that she noticed a constant high-pitched hum in her head. It was the dilapidated extractor fan that worked in partnership with the light. It sounded like one of those remote-controlled aeroplanes flying around the park on a Sunday afternoon, or perhaps one that had crashed too many times.

Grace tried to ignore it as her thoughts wandered.

I did text him, didn't I? she asked herself. *I did text Otto to tell him I wouldn't be home?*

She had no recollection. Where had she left her mobile? Probably in the living room.

'How did I end up like this?' she moaned, holding up her head in between her two hands. She wanted so much to stand up and leave, to order a cab and just get back home. She would have to face the music, suffer the consequences. But the thought of even standing up was too optimistic.

Grace's eye caught the colour of the top she wore and realised that it wasn't hers. It was a blue T-shirt at least two sizes too big with the words:

"IF ALL ELSE FAILS: CTRL-ALT-DELETE"

She shook her head. She was unable to comprehend either the writing on the T-shirt or why she was wearing it in the first place.

'You thought it was hilarious when I gave it to you last night.' Grace looked up to find Rik standing at the door, holding a cup of tea.

'Seriously?'

'Yes. Well, you said you wished you could do it in real life.'

She pulled the T-shirt and glanced down.

Silence.

'I don't wear it anymore,' Rik admitted. 'Actually, I never wore it. It was one of those presents that you think is nice at the time and then just toss it to one side.'

'Until strange women decide to sleep over?'

'More or less.'

She stood up and took the cup of tea. No milk. She was used to that by now, the Dutch never adding milk to their tea. She blew it and took a sip. It was still too hot. She poured a little into the sink and replaced it with cold water.

'Sorry. I wasn't sure how you like it.'

She shook her head in a way to say, *how were you to know?* She took a big mouthful to wash away the taste in her mouth, and spat it down the sink.

A cold sweat came over her. She wasn't ready for tea. Pouring it down the sink, she turned the tap on and filled the cup.

'Sorry. I think it's just water I need for now.' Her hands shook. She knocked back a cupful of water. Rik noticed the trembling getting worse. She took a deep breath as she bent over the sink. She tried to place the cup on the sink but misjudged the space available. It fell to the floor with a smash, startling her.

'Shit!' She tried to take a deep breath. 'Sorry,' she groaned. Pain exploded throughout her chest. All she could manage was a short shallow breath.

Christ, she thought. *What's Otto going to think when I get home? He's going to kill me.*

Rik approached her side. His foot hit a piece of the cup sending it sliding across the floor.

'Are you okay?'

She waved him away. She didn't feel like puking. It was something else. A film of sweat formed on her forehead.

'What's wrong, Grace?'

'I don't know,' she said. 'I feel... lost.'

'Lost? What do you mean?'

She grabbed hold of the side of the sink. Suddenly she took a deep breath like she had just emerged from deep underwater. A look of panic shot through her eyes.

Rik caught hold of her arm. 'What do you mean "lost", Grace? Do you know where you are?'

She shook her head. 'I dunno... I dunno. I feel...,' she said in between shallow breaths.

'You want some more water?'

She ignored him, concentrating on trying to breathe.

Rik looked around. The tiny window above the shower was already opened. There wasn't much more he could do to increase the oxygen in the house.

'Do you need to breathe into a paper bag or something?' he asked feeling completely useless. Isn't that what they did in these situations? His mind raced. If she nodded he would have to think fast on where to find a paper bag. It wasn't as if they were lying around the apartment.

I wonder if an unused hoover bag would do?

Grace didn't respond.

'Grace, tell me what you want me to do.'

She continued breathing quick and short. 'Just... give me... some time,' she said in between breaths. A drop of sweat trickled down her face.

Just when Rik thought she couldn't get much paler, she seemed to have turned ghostly white. Turning her back against the cigarette wall, she slid down onto the floor where she sat moments earlier. Her mind kept throwing images at her. Images of her husband.

'Why?' she said. Her arms shook uncontrollably.

Rik looked at her. 'Why what?' he asked. 'Why what?'

She shook her head.

'Do you have epilepsy?' he asked looking confused, desperate for answers.

She continued to shake her head. He wasn't sure if it was a reply to his question.

'You want me to call someone?'

'Goddammit!' Grace screamed. She continued to shake her head. 'I want my life back!'

Instinctively Rik took a half-a-step back, and then moved forward and got down on his hunkers closer to her.

'Grace?' he said. 'Seriously Grace. What do you want me to do?' He could see another drop of sweat trickling down her face. She ignored him and stared at the wall with an empty expression.

'I can't keep living like this,' she mumbled. 'I want my life back.' She started to sway. Rik caught hold of her to stop her from banging her head. She pulled away suddenly as if she had received an electric shock from him.

'Grace. You have to help me out here. I want to know what's wrong.'

An intense dizziness exploded in her head. 'I want my life back…' she mumbled again, before falling sideways. Rik tried to catch her but was too late. She had already passed out as her head hit the tiled floor with a hollow thud.

09

It was just starting to get bright when Daniel arrived at Bewley's Café on Grafton Street. Although the shops weren't yet open, the street was gradually coming to life.

Daniel found Professor Redmond on the first floor of Bewley's by the window looking out onto the infamous shopping street. He was reading the *Irish Times* and sipping Earl Grey tea. John folded the newspaper when he saw him approaching. He stood up and offered his hand. This time Daniel took it.

'Daniel, I'm glad you could take the time to meet me,' he said as they shook hands. With the folded newspaper in one hand, John gestured to the chair opposite. Daniel pulled it out and was about to sit on it. He stopped and glanced at John's newspaper.

'Can I borrow that?' he asked pointing at the newspaper. Unsure, John gave it to him anyway. Daniel gave the chair a sweep with it and handed it back to John.

'Crumbs. Lots of them. I'm guessing a child.'

'Indeed.'

He sat down and observed John as he quickly shook his newspaper and placed it on the window sill next to them.

'I would like to know where Grace lives,' Daniel said, getting straight to the point. 'Do you have her contact details?'

John nodded. 'I can get them.' He leaned forward. 'Can I ask why?'

'Isn't it obvious? To tell her she might die in a few days.'

John said nothing and thought about Daniel's words for a moment.

'Here, have some tea. I have an extra cup.' John poured some tea into a clean cup that stood next to his newspaper.

As he placed it before Daniel, he pointed to the sugar, milk and half a lemon standing in a small tray.

'Help yourself.'

Daniel poured a drop of milk and a sachet of sugar into his tea and gave it a quick stir.

'So,' John said. 'You're going to just turn up on this woman's doorstep and tell her to watch out on the date you predicted?'

Daniel pressed a fingertip to the table and picked up some random sugar granules that had fallen from his sachet. 'More or less. I suppose it depends on where she lives. I mean I'm not going to fly to Sydney or Los Angeles. But if she's living in a house in... I don't know, Malahide, I'm sure I can manage to drop by.'

John nodded. 'So you never kept in contact with her?'

'Would I be here now if I did?'

'I thought you were pretty *close*.' He used a different tone when he said "close" but they both knew what he meant.

'Yes. I was,' Daniel said as he rubbed his finger with his thumb and let the sugar granules fall again to the table. 'We were. Past tense. I tried Googling her. Nothing obvious came up. Nothing on Facebook or LinkedIn. Either she's dead already or, more likely, she got married and changed her surname.'

John shrugged not giving away anything. 'What if you didn't tell her? What if you just don't do anything and see what happens?'

Daniel said nothing. He glanced out the window, his jaws working as if they were chewing on something invisible. Eventually he shook his head. 'I have to tell her.'

'Why?'

'It's private. We were *close* after all.'

'Yes. *Were*. Past tense as you rightly pointed out. Why not just let it go?'

Daniel shook his head.

'Listen, Daniel. Imagine if you do nothing and she just

dies on the date you predicted. That would be two deaths that you predicted. *Two*. Based on your mathematical formulae. I mean this would reopen your thesis. You would receive your PhD immediately. That'll be only the start of it. You will be nominated for the Fields Medal without a doubt. Probably even win it.' He paused for a moment to let it sink in. 'That's like wining a Nobel Prize or an Oscar for a mathematician.'

'Trust me. I still know what the medal is.'

'It doesn't get much better than that.'

Daniel took a sip of his tea. 'How driven do you think I am? Do you think that would mean anything to me if I could have stopped one of the deaths?'

John sighed, frustrated at Daniel's refusal to budge. 'Just say you didn't know. Say you forgot or...'

'But I do know. And I want to try and warn the person. End of discussion. Are you going to help me or not?'

'Come on. Think of the prestige of winning -'

'I don't want it.'

John rolled his eyes and leaned back in his chair. 'That's bullshit. You spent four years working on this? Even more if you consider the years you spent as an undergraduate leading to this thesis. You *believed* in it.'

'Yes "believed". Past tense again. You guys ruined every shred of belief I had in this. Now I'll do anything to disprove it.'

An awkward silence rose between the two. Daniel glanced outside. A small elderly man with two Jack Russells stood waiting for someone outside *Awear* on the corner of Grafton and Lemon Street. He held the leads of the dogs in one hand and a flimsy bunch of flowers in the other. Daniel admired the guy who looked at least seventy-years-old. How considerate he appeared with the bunch of flowers. He looked nervous, glancing up and down the street every couple of seconds. Daniel wondered if he would be so considerate when he reached that age? Would he even reach that age?

'I'm sorry you feel that way,' John said eventually.

Turning his attention back to John, Daniel said, 'Do you have Grace's contact details or not?'

John fidgeted in his seat before placing his hand on the table and drumming his fingers once. 'I can help you if you can help me. I want you to do me a favour.'

Daniel raised an eyebrow, immediately curious how he could help the professor. 'What kind of favour?' he asked with scepticism.

'I want you to predict a date of death using your thesis.'

Daniel sat back on his chair and looked at the professor as if he just asked him to smuggle cocaine into Indonesia.

'You're joking.'

He shook his head.

'Whose?'

'My wife's.'

'Your wife's?'

John nodded. 'I need to know, Daniel. I need to...'

'I can't do it. I don't know how to do it anymore. Why would you assume I could still do it after all these years?'

John smiled. A fake smile. 'You don't expect me to believe that, do you?'

'I don't care if you believe it or not. I just can't do it. I don't even have all my notes, all the formulae. I checked in the attic last night. I have some, but...'

'I do,' John added quickly. 'I kept them safe since the day you left.'

Daniel took a deep breath, inhaling through his nose. Despite the Earl Grey tea in front of him, the aroma of fresh coffee was all he could detect. He scratched his forehead wondering if he could do what the professor was asking him.

'Listen, Daniel. My wife is not well and I just want to know when it will end.'

'Then take her to a doctor.'

'Mentally I mean, she's not well mentally.'

'Take her to a psychiatrist. Sorry, I don't mean to be

rude, but you need to find *help* for her. Not just find out when she's going to die.'

John remained silent for a moment, unsure how to continue. Daniel went back to picking up sugar granules with his forefinger. A little quicker this time.

'Do you have children, Daniel?'

Daniel frowned, unsure of the change in direction. He nodded. 'One.'

'How old is he…or she?'

'Six. He's a boy.'

John smiled. 'Nice.'

Daniel frowned as he rubbed his fingers again and let the sugar granules fall. 'What's that got to do with anything?'

John looked down towards the spilled sugar. He swallowed. 'I had one too. Or should I say *we* had one. My wife and I. A boy. Max. He was ten years old. A fantastic little boy. So full of life and getting up to mischief. Just a normal boy.'

He kept his eyes downwards as he spoke. Daniel braced himself for what was coming. The use of the past tense told him enough.

John looked up to meet Daniel's gaze. 'He died eight months ago.'

10

Rik bent down and lifted Grace's head up.

'Grace, wake up.'

No response. He gave her a few taps on the cheek with his hand. 'Grace.' Her head flopped to one side.

'*Godverdomme*. Grace, can you hear me?'

Not wanting to leave Grace on the cold hard floor, he decided to move her out of the bathroom.

'Grace? Can you hear me? I want you to stand up.'

Still nothing. She was out cold. As much as he wanted to just pick her up in his arms like a superhero, Rik knew he didn't have the strength for it. Instead he pulled her to a sitting position. He then grabbed beneath her armpits and lifted her upwards. It was a struggle, but, by using the wall for support, he made progress. As he pushed her upright with all his strength, her head flopped to the side like a rag doll's.

As soon as he had her high enough, he quickly ducked his head beneath one arm and took her onto his back, like a fireman rescuing a victim. As he swung around, he felt her legs hit some toiletries and send them flying across the bathroom.

'Shit.'

No time to worry about that now. He was about to carry Grace to his bedroom, when he remembered the pool of vomit on the floor and took a sharp left to the living room. Again her feet hit something, but this time he didn't hear anything fall.

He laid her down upon the sofa, on top of the messed sheets that still lay there. She had insisted sleeping there the previous night, despite Rik offering his bed.

Once he believed she was comfortable, he bent down and positioned his ear close to her mouth. He was relieved to hear her breathing at least. Gently he patted her cheek to see if he would get a reaction now.

'Grace?'

Still nothing. He stepped back and scratched his head.

Should I put her in the recovery position?

Placing the pillow beneath her head, he turned her on the side. He wasn't sure what to do with the inner arm, the one that now held all her body weight.

'Shit.' Would the weight on her arm slow down her blood circulation? Rik mentally kicked himself for never having enrolled in a First Aid course at some stage in his life. He promised he would soon, to avoid these dilemmas in the future.

Grabbing her arm from under her, he pushed it further towards her head. He then placed her hand beneath the same pillow where her head was. He moved her legs into a position that he thought was the most comfortable.

'There.' He stepped backwards and admired his work. He was almost tempted to brush his hands off each other, like a sculptor who had just finished his latest masterpiece. Satisfied with her position, he placed the sheet on top of her. Only her head was visible. She seemed peaceful.

He couldn't understand what brought on the anxiety attack.

What was all that about?' I want my life back.'

Without thinking, he moved closer to his patient and caressed her pale cheek. He brushed a loose strand of hair behind her ear.

'You'll be fine in a little while.'

As he was about to stand up, Rik noticed a trickle of blood escaping from her head. He used the bed sheet to clean the blood. He moved the sheet upwards to the source of the wound.

'Grace. Wake up, you're bleeding.'

The anxiety attack was one thing, but now the bang to the head and the blood, Rik was on the verge of his own panic attack.

'Grace. Please wake up. Otherwise I'm calling the

ambulance.'

He pulled the sheet back and saw a red gash on the side of her head. The bleeding didn't seem to slow down. He realised that the alcohol still in her blood system was not helping.

Something didn't seem right.

'Fuck it. I'm calling the ambulance, Grace. I'm sorry.'

He spotted Grace's mobile on top of the coffee table. He looked at her and then back at the phone. She was still out of it, breathing more heavily now as she fell into a deeper sleep. Rik kept the sheet on her wound and picked up the mobile. There were six missed calls, three voicemails and four text messages. Sliding the scroll bar across, Rik was surprised to see the phone jump to life. No PIN request.

He dialled 1-1-2, the emergency services. In Dutch he explained the situation he found himself in and was reassured that he did the right thing. The operator announced that they would send an ambulance, and he should keep her comfortable until they arrived.

He hung up. Before placing the mobile back on the coffee table he opened one of the text messages. It was from Otto.

"WHERE THE FUCK ARE YOU ?!!"

That was it. Nothing more. Rik scratched his chin. He contemplated deleting it, but decided against it. There was little point in trying to protect her from the verbal abuse that she was probably used to.

As he was putting the mobile back onto the coffee table it suddenly started vibrating. "Otto" flashed on the screen.

'Shit.'

He picked it up again and stared at the name for a while.

'Why are you calling at six in the morning?' he whispered to the vibrating phone in his hand. He figured that Otto probably received an alert when he read the text message seconds earlier.

Bloody control freak.

It kept on ringing.

Rik answered it but said nothing.

'Grace, where the fuck are you?'

Rik remained silent.

A moment passed. He could hear Otto breathing. He kept his own breathing under control.

'Grace. If you are there, can you please just say something so I know that you're okay.'

Like you give a shit, Rik wanted to say. Instead he remained silent. He didn't know what to say anyway. It would be a lie if he told him that she was okay. At the same time he didn't want to worry him or give him a reason to come to his apartment before the ambulance got there.

He took the easy option and hung up. He continued to look at the mobile for a few moments wondering what other abuse was in the text messages and voice mails. Deciding not to investigate further, he placed the phone gently on the coffee table. It was only then that he realised that his hand was shaking. As he took a deep breath, it dawned on him the kind of life Grace was living. The verbal abuse was probably just the tip of the iceberg.

11

The buzz of a street cleaner could be heard from the first floor of Bewley's as it slowly moved up Grafton Street. The brushes at the front pulled in any piece of rubbish it encountered.

Daniel closed his eyes and shook his head. 'God. That's terrible, John. I'm sorry to hear that. I really am.'

'Thank you.'

Daniel remained silent, unsure how to proceed. The din from outside receded, as the street cleaner continued towards St. Stephen's Green. Daniel thought of Sean, the one person in the world he hoped he would never see dead.

'I was the one who found him.' John took a deep breath. 'Which in hindsight I suppose was a good thing. I don't know what Claire would have done if she found him. He was lying in his bed, stone cold. Stiff. Lifeless. Since then, every day is a living hell. Claire is like a zombie. I don't think she'll ever get over it. I don't think *I'll* get over it. Well, who does get over the death of their child?'

John took a sip of his tea as he let the question linger in the air.

'But I can handle it,' he said as he placed his cup back on the table. He closed his eyes for a few seconds, as if he wanted to sleep. 'I can block it out when it gets too much.' He opened his eyes again. 'I can put the grief away and take it out when I need to. Or when I have the privacy I need. Claire on the other hand… well, it's like a disease. It's eating her alive.'

He stared straight at Daniel. 'I need to know when she's going to die, Daniel. I just need to know. I need to know when her pain will stop, and this living nightmare ends. For both of us.'

Daniel met John's stare but remained silent. Nothing

he could think of seemed appropriate to say. He hated these situations. His eyes fell to John's fingers and he noticed that the top half of one of his thumbnails was black. Like he had banged it on something weeks earlier, and it was gradually growing out.

'But predicting her date of death, that's absurd.'

'It wasn't absurd twelve years ago.'

'It was a test twelve years ago. On five random people. A theory. I didn't want to know their dates of death so I could decide how to live my life.'

'I know. Look, there are really two reasons I want you to predict her death. Jesus, I sound like Monty Python's Spanish Inquisition now.

Daniel smiled. It was a welcome piece of comic relief in the serious conversation they were having.

'I want to see if you still have it in you. The mathematical ingenuity to use your thesis and predict someone's date of death. And I just want to see when my wife will die. Obviously if it's in thirty years from now I'm going to need a different approach to deal with our situation. I mean, she's getting through at least two bottles of wine a day. She is slowly killing herself anyway. I feel like I'm drowning, and up to now, there has been nobody around to throw me a life line.'

'Up to now?'

'I seriously think you have a life line you could throw to me. It might not pull me in the right direction, but it will pull me in *a* direction. It will pull me from the rut I'm currently in.'

John looked down at the table. His voice seemed to drop in volume. 'Sometimes it feels like I'm her life support machine. But I can't go on like this forever. Sooner or later I too need to pull the plug. I'm not saying knowing her date of death will fix anything. I just want to know. If there's a possibility of knowing, then I want to know.'

John took another sip of his tea. 'I still love her. And

maybe I just want her to die soon so she doesn't have to continue with this unbearable pain.' He paused for a moment as he placed the cup back on the saucer. 'It would also be a test for you. For both of us, really.'

'A test? What do you mean? What kind of test?'

'A mathematical test. A moral test. I get to see if you still have the passion and ingenuity from all those years ago. You get to ask yourself if you still have feelings for Grace and if you're willing to give up this second chance of being a renowned mathematician for her.'

Daniel smiled. 'Whether I have feelings for her or not is irrelevant. If I have the power in me to stop someone from dying or warn someone that they might die, then I will do it.'

'Okay. Well, you do have that power. I don't want it to sound like some kind of blackmail, but if you agree to predict my wife's date of death, then I will give you Grace's contact information and you can do what you like with it. Plain and simple.'

Daniel glanced out the window and sighed. John looked towards his folded newspaper. The headline on the back was something about Manchester United and a player called Van Persie. He looked up and stared at Daniel again. Daniel returned his gaze and saw the pain creeping back into the professor's face.

'He loved Man United, you know,' John said. Daniel smiled, and reflected on his own son who was also a big fan.

'He used to watch all their games.' His voice became quivery; an obvious sign that he was fighting to hold back the tears. 'I never watched one bloody match with him,' he said holding up his index finger, as his voice cracked. 'Not one. I mean, I paid a fortune to get the Sports channel. That was the easy part. Spending money. But as for spending time with him and watching a match together? That was too much to ask me.' He looked out the window and cleared his throat. After taking a deep breath he regained control of his voice and looked back to Daniel.

'Do you want to know what the funny thing is?'

Daniel doubted that there was *anything* funny about this.

'Guess how many games I've watched since he died?'

He could guess, but he decided it was more polite to remain silent. John's eyes glistened in the morning light, like the streets below.

'All of them. I haven't missed one match. Not one fucking match. Crazy, eh?' A tear escaped suddenly down John's cheek. He quickly brushed it away. Daniel felt even more uncomfortable. 'They're top of the bloody Premiership and Max isn't here to see it.'

Daniel swallowed hard. He reached for his cup but then decided against it. He couldn't keep hiding behind a cup of tea.

'I'm sorry to hear that.' It sounded insincere, but he meant it.

'What?' John asked. 'Sorry to hear that Man U is top of the Premiership?' He forced a smile. His attempt at humour didn't do much in reducing the tension of the sensitive conversation they were having. Daniel offered a polite smile in return.

'It's as if ... I'm making up with him,' John admitted.

'What do you mean?'

'I don't know why else I watch the matches. What else is there to do? I'm watching the heroes my son had. It's as if I'm watching them so I can give him a recap, should he show up at our front door any of these days.'

Daniel turned and glanced at the old man outside with the two Jack Russells. The flowers seemed to have withered in the past few minutes. Was it the rain? Or could they somehow sense the pain John was feeling?

John grabbed a paper napkin and blew his nose. 'Do you know what else?' he asked as he wiped his nose. 'He never threw away the cardboard insides of toilet rolls. He used to always leave them on top of the tank of the toilet.'

Daniel failed to see the link between Manchester

United and used toilet rolls.

'I used to give him such a hard time about it. It's amazing what you argue about when you don't realise how little time you have left. Do you think I would have argued about insides of fucking toilet rolls?' He looked down and stirred his tea.

'Don't do this to yourself,' Daniel offered.

'Do you think I would have missed *any* football matches if I knew my son was going to die at ten-years-old? Christ, if I knew he was going to die, I would have taken him to Old Trafford for every game. Why do we assume that we'll all live to be seventy or eighty? Why do we assume that our children will outlive us?'

'I don't know,' Daniel mumbled. 'I suppose life is a gamble. You just never know when your luck runs out.'

'Exactly, Daniel. Exactly. Until now. You broke the code. Now we *do* know when our luck runs out. In gambling they say the house always wins. But not anymore. You're on the brink of the most important discovery of all time. You can't turn your back on that. I will do anything to support you.'

'I can't stop people from dying.'

'No, but if you can predict when you're going to die, then you make more use out of the time that is given to you.'

'Shouldn't we be doing that anyway? Seizing the day? *Carpe Diem* and all that shite?'

'Yes, of course. We *should* be. But even so. All the stress and responsibilities in our day-to-day routines make us forget about it. But knowing the day you're going to die, that's a different story. It's like getting a bucket of cold water thrown over you every day. Forcing you to realise just how precious life is and the time you are given. Your thesis could be this cold bucket of water we need. Your thesis could mean that no other parent has to go through this pain. This awful feeling of not having spent enough time with someone they loved and treasured more than

62

anything else in the world.'

John's dark protruding eyes met Daniel's once again. Daniel realised that they were the same eyes that witnessed something terrible. They were the very same ones that had found their dead child. An image that was no doubt burnt into his memory forever.

A moment passed. A middle-aged woman drenched in cheap perfume passed their table and sat in the corner. As if on cue, Daniel and John turned their heads in her general direction, like the two Bisto Kids picking up the scent of gravy. When they realised they were both giving her attention, they turned back to one another and smiled. It was enough to cut some slack in the conversation they had been having.

'Listen, Daniel. You don't have to come back to Trinity or defend your thesis if you don't want to. I can't make you do it. But you would be doing me a huge favour if you predicted my wife's date of death. In return I will tell you how to find Grace.'

'John,' Daniel said with a tone of concern. 'I don't think I can do it. Seriously.'

'Please,' John begged. 'At least try. If I know Claire will die in the near future, life might become bearable. I know it's a horrible thing to say, but I can't do this anymore. Right now it feels like I'm carrying all the burden. I'm afraid to cry in front of her in case it sets her off. I need to support her. I need to be strong for her, but I can't do this forever. I need to know there's a light at the end of the tunnel.'

'Meaning her death?'

'Anything.'

'Look, I'm not a counsellor, but isn't there professional help out there that you can both attend?'

'We've tried. We're still trying actually. Every fortnight.' John shook his head slowly. 'It's not working, Daniel.'

Daniel took a slurp of tea. 'Where does Grace live?' he asked.

'Will you try to predict Claire's death?'

'It's not as easy as just popping some values into a formula and Bob's your uncle.'

'Trust me Daniel, I know that. I've seen your thesis. Some of it hardly makes any sense to me. If it did, I would have tried to predict the date of death myself.'

Daniel glanced in mid-air as a distant memory came back to him. 'I remember adding some unnecessary information to some of the theorems so nobody else could use it.'

John seemed somewhat relieved. 'That explains it. I didn't know where you got some parts from. A true sign of a genius.'

Daniel wasn't buying that and returned to the prospect of doing another prediction. 'There's a biological theorem in it. A blood sample needs to be taken from her for a range of sixteen genetic tests. This was a big pain in the ass twelve years ago, but probably isn't a big deal these days.'

'Already taken care of. My cousin is a Lab Manager at the Mater hospital. I've sent blood samples to him a few weeks ago. His team has performed all the tests outlined in your thesis.' John pointed to his bag. 'I have the reports here with me.'

'Seriously?'

John nodded.

'Now that's what I call thinking ahead.'

'Like I said, I was going to try and do it myself but couldn't make head nor tail out of some parts of it.'

'There are other unusual data I need. Like her response time. I use this as an indication of how quick she reacts to sudden external stimuli. This has an impact on her chances of survival.'

'Those tests were done by the doctor a while ago when she was hospitalised a few days for depression. I have all her doctor reports.' He held up a conference bag with *European Congress of Mathematics: Stockholm, Sweden* printed on the front.

'All your old information is there.' He unzipped the top. 'Also in a separate folder are doctor reports, genetic reports. I think you'll find all the information you need. If not, let me know and I'll get it for you.'

Daniel stared at the bag for a moment and then reached over and took it. It was heavier than he thought.

'Can you get me access to the library?'

'Trinity library?'

Daniel rolled his eyes. 'No the mobile bus library that passes through Glasnevin twice a month. Yes, of course Trinity library.'

John smiled. Not so much at the joke, but at the sudden enthusiasm Daniel seemed to have for the project. A sparkle appeared in John's eyes. 'Consider it done.'

'Along with unlimited access to internet while I'm there and possibly access to a printer and photocopier.'

John took out his wallet and handed him a credit card sized card.

'Take mine. Unlimited access.'

Daniel took the card. Apart from a magnetic strip on one side it was completely blank.

'Don't worry. It works. The idea is that if it gets lost, nobody would know what the card was for.'

'Okay,' he said. 'I'll have a glance through my notes and the thesis itself, but I can't make any promises.'

John nodded. 'Okay. That's all I ask.'

Daniel continued to flick through some documents while they were still in the bag. He recognised his own handwriting. He was amazed at the amount he actually wrote back then and suddenly felt old.

'Grace's details are in the front pocket of the bag,' John said.

Daniel's heart skipped a beat. It was the reality of seeing Grace after so long that made him nervous.

'I have a friend working in the Trinity Alumni department and managed to get her address. She's living and working in Amsterdam,' John continued. 'As a Risk

Assessor in some insurance company.'

'Amsterdam?'

'Yes. I suppose she married some Dutch guy, as her married name is Visser. Grace Visser.'

Despite it being so long since Daniel and Grace were lovers, he couldn't prevent a sharp ache inside at the mention of her being married. What had he expected?

'I'm not sure what you're planning to do,' John continued. 'I'm sure she'll love to get a call from an ex-classmate to say she is about to die in five days.'

'Five days?'

'Listen. It's up to you. You can just do nothing and see what happens. If your predication is correct, I mean...' John didn't know how to complete his sentence. 'I mean it would just be a miracle. It would prove that you really are on to something and this could be the most important discovery in generations. If not, ever.'

Daniel knocked back his tea. 'I'm a different person than I was twelve years ago. I will do anything to make sure she doesn't die on the day I predicted.'

12

Grace felt dazed. She could hear the beeping of a machine and a mild drone in the background but couldn't visualise where she was. Her mind was a labyrinth of questions. Where was she? What had happened?

Her mouth was dry. She wanted to open her eyes but decided to wait a while; try and assess her surroundings before letting her environment know that she was conscious again. Grace tried to recall what had happened.

She stayed in Rik's place.

Or did she dream it?

No, she didn't dream it.

Her memory of wine and *gezelligheid* filled her memory. Such a lovely atmosphere. Rik was so easy to talk to; especially after a few glasses of wines. Good company was something she sorely missed.

She remembered waking up with a hangover from hell. Or was it really a hangover? Maybe it was that point when drunkenness metamorphosed into having a hangover. The point where the worst elements of each collided. Most normal people slept through it.

Not me, thought Grace. *Trust me to wake up and embarrass the shit out of myself.*

A flashback of puking came back to her. She remembered Rik's silhouette hovering over her. Embarrassment spread inside to every cell of her body - like Aspirin dissolving in a glass of water.

What kind of impression did I leave?

She recalled that he was trying to help. But then nothing. Had she gone back to bed? No memory.

Grace heard a cough. Someone was sitting next to her. Possibly watching her. Analysing her for signs of life; signs of waking up. Maybe Otto was there. Staring at her with his beady eyes. Wanting to know why she didn't come home last night. Waiting patiently so he could pounce on her with his razor sharp tongue when she was most vulnerable. Wondering where his Pork with Roasted Peppers and Potatoes were. Disappointed with the frozen dinner he had to eat. Or the take-out. Alone. Or did he even come home?

Another beep from a machine nearby.

Jesus, am I in a hospital?

It was time to wake up. If anyone had been analysing her close enough, they would probably have noticed that she was now awake.

Okay, thought Grace. *Time to face the real world again.*

Slowly, Grace opened her eyes. Bright. She closed them again and rubbed them. She yawned and turned her head towards the direction of the cough. She strained her eyes. Rik was sitting in the chair.

'Hi there,' Rik said.

'Hello,' Grace mumbled sleepily. 'Where am I?'

'Sint Lucas Andreas.'

'Hospital?'

'Yes,' Rik smiled. Grace looked around. It was a large ward with seven other beds, all of them occupied. Most of the other patients slept.

'I didn't know what else to do but call an ambulance. I don't know what happened to you. What *did* happen? Do you remember?'

Grace rubbed her eyes again. 'I puked. In the middle of the night. I remember that much. Maybe because I drank too much.'

'Yes. That part I could diagnose myself. But after that? You were trying desperately to breathe. And then just passed out.'

Grace scrunched up her face, and then relaxed it. Despite the rough night she had, her skin radiated in the soft morning light.

'The paramedics believed you had an anxiety attack.'

'An anxiety attack. Really?'

Rik nodded. 'Do you normally get them?'

Grace looked in the distance, trying to think. She shook her head. 'No. Never.'

A silence rose as she became lost in her thoughts. 'I remember not being able to breathe all of a sudden. And a horrible feeling around my chest. Like I was trapped in an air-tight container or something.'

'You were shouting something like you wanted your life back.'

Grace shuffled a little as she sat upright. 'Really? ...I don't remember that.'

Rik noticed Grace touch her wedding ring. She didn't look at it, but just touched it. Softly. She rotated it around her finger several times and then let it go as if she was winding up a clockwork toy.

'He's been calling, you know,' Rik said.

Grace looked in the opposite direction, making him wonder if she heard him. The woman in the bed opposite her caught her eye. She was young. Maybe nineteen or twenty. Her arms were covered in tattoos and one of her ears was full of studs and some spikey things that must have been particularly painful to get done. The girl browsed through some trashy gossip magazine. What Grace would do to be nineteen again. She tried to recall: where was she at that period of her life? In Trinity. Studying Maths. Falling in love for the first time.

Grace looked back at Rik. 'Did you bring my mobile with you?'

He cringed and shook his head. 'I wasn't thinking. I'm sorry. I saw it on the coffee table, but when I left I just quickly grabbed some stuff'

'My handbag?'

'It seemed kind of expensive and didn't want the risk of it being stolen so I just brought your wallet. I figured your insurance card would be in there. I also quickly gathered your rain jacket, trousers and high heels.'

'Shit.'

'What?'

'I'm not wearing any lenses. It's not your fault. I could do with a fresh pair right now. I usually have a spare pair of daily disposables in my bag. Right now everything is a bit on the blurry side.

'I didn't know you wore contacts.'

Grace smiled. 'That's the whole idea.'

Rik grinned. 'I suppose.'

Grace looked down to see what she was wearing. A hospital gown. *At least they removed the geeky T-shirt,* she thought. Turning back to Rik she said, 'Thanks for taking care of me anyway.' She reached over and touched his hand.

'Well I didn't do much… obviously.'

'You called the ambulance. You're here when I wake up. I'm grateful for what you've done, Rik. Really, I am.'

'Listen,' he said, changing the subject, 'they contacted your husband.'

Grace's facial expression changed.

'They were obliged to do it legally when I told them I wasn't your husband. And he is officially your next of kin.'

She sat upright.

'Don't worry,' he assured her, 'they only called him fifteen, twenty minutes ago.'

'Shit. I wonder if he's on his way.'

'I assume he is. Isn't that what husbands do when their wife is in hospital?'

'You don't know Otto.'

A nurse arrived at the bedside. Her wrinkled face said she was close to retirement, and her kind eyes radiated years of caring experience.

'Hoe gaat het met u?' 'How are you feeling?'

'I feel fine actually. A little bit hung…' Grace trailed off, reluctant to let the nurse know of her drinking the night before. Unable to come up with anything suitable to say instead, she decided to continue.

'A little bit hungover to be honest. But other than that

I'm fine. Don't think I should be taking up a bed here.'

The nurse glanced at the board at the end of her bed, and wrote something. 'I'll have the doctor come by within the next hour or so and he'll speak to you. There doesn't seem to be any major complications according to this.' She tapped on the board. 'But he will make a decision whether to keep you overnight or let you go this afternoon.'

'Oh, I can go this afternoon, I think.'

The nurse nodded. 'I'm sure you can too, but let's wait until you have spoken with the doctor, shall we?' she said as she moved onto the next woman.

'You were bleeding as well, do you remember that?' Rik asked

'Bleeding? No. Where?'

'On your head.'

Grace put a finger to her head and felt the scab straight away.

'Don't touch it, in case you disturb the scab. I think your head hit off something sharp on the drainage pipe beneath the sink. Or a piece of the broken cup on the floor.'

'Jesus. I don't remember that at all.'

'Well, strictly speaking, it happened after you passed out,' he said. 'You really freaked me out, you know.'

'Sorry. I don't know what to say.' Grace took a deep breath. She felt something foreign on her wrist. She looked down and saw the hospital wristband. In addition to her name and date of birth, it had a barcode. Beneath the barcode there was a unique number, and although she knew its purpose perfectly well, she couldn't help feeling like a prisoner wearing a number.

'I guess I just felt like a prisoner,' she said as she stared at the wristband.

'A prisoner? That's a bit heavy, isn't it?'

She shrugged her shoulders. 'I think I just need to readjust to society again. I need to readjust to having my own friends, a social life, my own time.' She touched the wristband again. 'I remember reading a news article years ago about research into ex-prisoners. Those that were sentenced to life and got out after, say, twenty years. They usually find it nearly impossible to readjust to society.' Grace continued to fiddle with the wristband. She twisted the part with her details on it around so the blank underside was facing upwards. A clean slate. 'Maybe it's the same with me. I'm just trying to readjust to society again. I don't want to be a prisoner anymore.'

Rik was unsure what to say, so he said nothing. Grace looked at the tattooed woman next to her. Again she reflected on the time of her life when she was of a similar age. She turned back to Rik.

'Do you ever have a feeling of utter happiness, but not sure if it's going to last?'

He shook his head. 'I'm not sure what you mean.'

'Forget it,' she said smiling. 'I'm not sure what I mean either. Maybe I'm still drunk. By the way, how many bottles of wine did we drink?'

'More than one each,' he said as he glanced at his watch. He seemed nervous suddenly.

'What's wrong?'

'I was thinking of going to work, but I don't want to leave you if you need support.'

'Thanks, Rik. Don't worry. I'm a big girl. You've done enough. The truth is I've been unhappy for a long time. I guess it took you to notice it and get me to talk about it. The eyes don't lie, eh?'

Rik's eyes dropped downwards. Was he responsible for her anxiety attack? Had he opened an emotional can of worms?

'I'll be okay,' Grace continued. 'I don't need you to look after me. I'll sort this thing out. There's nothing here you should be ashamed of. We both know you did nothing wrong. I don't want you to get involved.'

He looked at Grace. 'Maybe I want to be involved.'

She smiled and touched his hand again.

'That's sweet. But seriously…'

The nurse came in.

'There's a man here to see you,' she said to Grace. 'He says he's your husband.'

13

Rik looked at Grace. The expression on her face said it all. 'Don't worry, I'm going,' he said.

'I'm sorry. I just don't want you to get involved so soon.'

He got up and handed Grace his business card. 'I wrote my personal mobile number on the back of it. Call me when they release you.'

'Okay.'

'*Sterkte*, okay? Be strong.' He squeezed her hand.

Grace smiled. 'I'll be fine.'

'I might use the bathroom first,' he said pointing to the ward's toilet. 'So I don't pass him while I'm leaving.'

'Probably a good idea.'

'Just ignore me when I come out.'

'Will do,' she said as she buried Rik's card beneath the mountain of pillows behind her.

The nurse sensed that something was going on. Although she didn't want to interfere, the patient's welfare was always her first concern. She had seen it all before.

'If you don't want to see your husband, that's okay. I'll tell him. I'll make up a story.' The nurse winked at Grace.

'No, it's fine. But thank you anyway.'

The nurse left the ward as Rik disappeared into the toilet. Grace took a deep breath. Although her heart was beating like crazy, she appeared very calm.

Otto walked in with large confident strides. He was a tall man who dressed well. He wore a solid gabardine three-button suit from Armani. His hair was combed to one side, not a single hair out of place. Grace had to hand it to him, he had a dress sense that made most women weak at their knees. Unfortunately the wedding ring on his left hand was nothing more than a dress accessory to his attire. An accessory that he removed when required. He was a perfect picture of a successful married businessman. Or unmarried businessman when he needed to be.

The Adidas sneakers however were a different story. Otto never drove the car wearing shoes. As he strode across the hospital floor, it was the first thing Grace noticed, despite her blurred vision. She wondered if he forgot to change his footwear when he parked the car or if he just didn't care.

'Grace. Oh my God, I was so worried,' he said loud enough for half the ward to hear. Grace rolled her eyes. It was his public act, using words and a tone of voice that were never used behind closed doors. 'What happened, darling? No answer on your mobile.' He bent down and kissed her on the cheek. 'I was worried. I called the police. They hadn't a clue. I hadn't a clue until the hospital rang me just a while ago. What happened?'

Grace looked up at Otto clearly unimpressed by his theatrical entrance. 'You can have a seat now if you like,' she said nodding to the empty seat beside her bed.

Otto sat down. He raised an eyebrow like he just noticed something, but continued with his performance. He took her hand in his. As he did, he quickly glanced at his watch.

'I was worried, baby, seriously.' His head moved to one side, observing her. 'You look pale.'

She ignored him. 'I think we should get a divorce.'

Otto let go of her hand and straightened up. Eventually a smirk broke in his face. And the tone of his voice became more sober. More realistic.

'What are you talking about, baby? You're not feeling well. What happened?'

Grace could feel her blood starting to boil. She hated the way Otto could just brush aside something she had to build up so much courage to say in the first place, something she wanted to say for years.

'I feel fine.'

'Good.' He lowered his voice. 'What are you talking

about divorce for? This isn't the time or place to discuss it. Let's get you feeling better first.'

'There's never a good time or place to discuss it, is there?'

He looked around. His gaze paused momentarily on the tattooed teenager next to Grace's bed and then beyond her, a middle-aged woman with a headscarf - an *allochtoon*, foreigner. He turned back to Grace.

'Why aren't you in a fucking private ward anyway? I pay enough insurance. You shouldn't have to mingle with this riff raff.'

'Keep your voice down, for goodness' sake. And I pay my own insurance,' she said.

'Relax. It's not as if they understand me. Even if I was speaking *Dutch*, they probably wouldn't understand me.'

Grace closed her eyes and took a deep breath. 'Why did you come here, Otto?'

'I wanted to know that you were okay.'

'Well, I am. Surely the hospital told you that. I can probably leave this afternoon. Are you happy?'

'What happened?'

'I had an asthma attack,' Grace lied.

'And you couldn't send me a text or something to let me know?'

'My battery was down.'

'Bullshit. Who answered your mobile this morning? And where's all your stuff ?'

'What stuff?'

'Your clothes, for a start,' he said pointing to her hospital gown. 'I'm assuming you didn't wear that to work yesterday.'

Otto opened the narrow wardrobe next to the bed. Her rain jacket hung next to her Ralph Lauren pin-striped trousers. The blue T-shirt that she wore to bed hung next to that.

'What the fuck is that?'

'What?'

He turned the T-shirt towards him and read it. '*If all else fails: Ctrl-Alt-Delete*. Oh that's very good,' he said with sarcasm. He let go of the T-shirt and turned to Grace. 'Since when have you started wearing geeky T-shirts?'

'None of your business, Otto.'

He closed the wardrobe and leaned forward. 'You're fucking someone, aren't you?'

'Jesus, Otto…' Grace trailed off. She didn't know where to start.

'He was here, wasn't he? Just before I arrived.'

Secretly she was startled but acted like she didn't know what he was talking about. 'Who was here?'

'Whoever you're fucking,' he said. 'I'm not stupid. The seat is still warm.'

Grace massaged her temples. She wasn't sure how much more she could take of this. 'Is that the real reason you checked the wardrobe? To see if he was hiding there? Why stop there? Why don't you check underneath the bed while you're at it?'

Otto sniggered. 'So you are fucking someone else? You admit it?'

'Like you said, this isn't the time or place to be discussing it.'

Just then, in the corner of her eye, Grace could see Rik come out of the toilet. Although Rik didn't look towards her, he managed to catch Otto's attention. Otto frowned as he gave Rik the once over. He pointed at him and looked at Grace.

'Is that him?'

She looked at Rik as he walked through the ward. She turned back to Otto.

'Is that who?'

Otto's gaze followed Rik like a hawk.

As if Rik could feel Otto's gaze on him, he took an incredible chance. Without hesitating, he walked over to a woman who was still fast asleep. He stood there for a moment before leaning forward and kissing the woman on the forehead.

Please God, don't let her wake up, Grace thought. *He'll be arrested for harassment.*

She even noticed him whispering something to the woman. Grace smirked, and figured maybe he should have been an actor. The woman continued to sleep as Rik walked out the ward.

Grace felt suddenly relieved. Although she wasn't having an affair with Rik, she knew that even an innocent friendship was something Otto found unacceptable.

'So,' she said, 'you're going to be thinking I'm sleeping with every guy you see from now on?'

Otto leaned back on the chair. He rubbed his clean-shaven face. For someone whose wife had been missing all night, he didn't look like he lost much sleep.

'If you're fucking someone else, you won't get a single cent out of me,' he threatened. '*Capisce?*'

Grace couldn't help laughing. '*Capisce? Capisce?* Where the hell did you get that from? Have you been watching *Godfather* movies again?' She giggled again. It was a forced giggle but anything to cover the fear she was feeling. To downplay Otto's threat. 'And why do you make it sound like I rely on *you* for my money,' he added. 'I have my own job. I have my own money. *Capisce?*'

Otto didn't say anything. Grace looked at him. For a second his face contorted with pure hatred.

'I'm just saying,' he said calmly.

'Go to work, Otto. Time is money. You're wasting money sitting here.'

Otto stood up. He bent down to kiss her. She turned away. Otto grabbed her by the chin. He whispered, 'If you try and divorce me, you'll see what happens. You'll need every fucking cent to pay for a good bodyguard.' Unable to look away she stared into her husband's menacing eyes. She knew immediately it was not an empty threat. The grasp seemed to be tightening around her chin. She reached up and dug her nails into his hand.

'Yeah. Of course,' she managed to say through the tight grasp as she dug further into his skin with her nails. He let her chin go with a sharp clip.

'See you later *schatje*.'

Otto walked away with the same large confident strides he entered. Grace blinked rapidly and took a deep breath. As soon as Otto disappeared from the ward, she covered her face and broke down crying.

14

Claire lowered her eyes as she passed the cereal aisle in Superquinn. If there was one section of the supermarket that reminded her of Max, that was it. She couldn't bear the look of the Coco Pops' monkey or Sugar Puffs' Honey Monster. The endless colour of bright boxes brought back too many memories. The name of the cereal never really mattered to Max, but the one with the newest toy, the free prize, the bonus. It was marketing at its best. Or worst, depending on your viewpoint.

Claire picked out a packet of oatmeal without looking at the other boxes. Blurred colours sat on the edge of her peripheral vision, as if waiting for the chance to pounce.

Not today.

When she reached the end of the cereal aisle, she looked up and took a deep breath. It was as if she just crawled from a burning house. Suddenly she realised she had forgotten to pick up tomatoes and made her way back to the fruit and vegetable section.

She rummaged through the tomatoes and pressed them for ripeness. She pulled off a plastic bag from a roller and looked for the opening. With her fingers, she rubbed two sides of the bag together on one end. Unsuccessful, she turned it around and did the same on the other side.

Come on.

She shook her head and turned it around again. Finally the plastic bag opened. She placed five tomatoes into the bag. Turning around abruptly she hit off another shopper. The bag fell and all but one of the tomatoes rolled across the floor.

'Shit!'

'Sorry,' the passer-by said. He was a man in his late fifties, carrying a basket. He was taken aback by Claire's reaction. 'Relax. They're only tomatoes. I'll get them.'

'Leave them.'

The man laid his basket on the ground and bent down to pick them up.

'Leave them!' she said, louder this time. Two other shoppers glanced at Claire.

The man had already picked up two which he placed back in the tomato box. 'I was only trying to help. You knocked into *me*. Maybe you should learn some manners.'

He picked up his basket and continued shopping. Claire bent down and picked up the bag and the remaining tomatoes. She did what the stranger had done and placed them back into the tomato box. Reusing the bag that had fallen, she rummaged for new tomatoes. She took a deep breath. Since when had she become so rude to strangers? Never in a million years would she have shouted at a stranger who was only trying to help. She suddenly felt like shit. Tying the bag tightly, she turned around and placed the new tomatoes in the shopping trolley. She glanced ahead and saw the man disappearing to the left as he reached the end of the aisle.

Claire pushed her trolley forward.

Maybe I should apologise...

She continued shopping. Pushing her trolley down the coffee aisle, she picked out a packet of her favourite coffee beans. Another memory of Max crept from within. One where Max was about five-years-old and had sprinkled coffee beans on the dining-room floor pretending he had seen a rabbit, and the beans were the rabbit droppings. For a split-second she had believed him.

She was about to push the trolley onwards when she caught sight of the man again at the end of the aisle. Claire contemplated for a second whether to do a U-turn and go back up the aisle she was in. She rolled her eyes at the thought.

She could imagine the conversation he would recite to his family later in the evening.

I was out shopping today when someone bumped into me and

dropped her vegetables. I bent down to help her and she just screamed at me. Can you believe that? She bumped into me and then screamed at me when I tried to help her. What is this country coming to?

She knew her reaction was out of character. She needed to apologise. The man stopped at the tea section further up the aisle. Claire continued to look at the man and then turned to look at the bottles of wine that were in her trolley. One of them was a screw top. It was tempting. Just a mouthful.

No! Stop!

How much lower would she have to go? Was she really thinking of knocking back some unpaid wine just to get through the shopping? She pushed her trolley towards the man. He was still scanning the tea. She wondered if he could see her approaching, but refused to look up. She cleared her throat hoping that it would attract the attention of the stranger, but was drowned out by the intercom:

'Collette Byrne to check-out please. Collette Byrne to check-out.'

Once the message was finished, Claire said, 'Excuse me.'

The man looked towards her. His warm facial expression changed as he saw Claire.

'I'm sorry for being rude just now,' she said.

'That's fine,' the man said coldly and went back to analysing the tea.

Claire looked down at the handle at the front of her trolley. The seat was folded in. All she could see was a euro coin protruding out the front. As Max grew old enough to wheel the trolley back to the collection points around the car park, she used to let him keep the euro each time. Everything she touched or saw seemed to throw memories at her.

'I'm not usually so rude,' she said.

The man picked up a box of Barry's classic blend tea and turned to her again. His facial expression remained neutral.

'I think I'm falling apart because I lost my ten-year-old

boy eight months ago. I don't know why I am telling this to a complete stranger but it might give you some understanding...to...' Claire wasn't sure what she wanted to say.

The man's facial expression became warmer. She saw pity coming from the man's eyes. It was almost tangible.

'I'm sorry to hear that.'

'Thank you. And thank you for offering to help pick up my tomatoes. I shouldn't have been so rude.'

The man continued to look at Claire. A silence rose. But it wasn't uncomfortable. It felt very natural. Finally, the man asked, 'What was your son's name?'

Claire was caught off guard. Remaining silent for an instant she was unsure if she wanted to go down that road. She decided she would, for now.

'Max.'

The man placed the box of tea in his basket. He stepped towards her, closer than she would normally have liked for complete strangers. There was something very different about this man, however.

'Tell me something. What would Max say if he could see you now?'

She stared into the man's eyes. They were blue like the deepest part of the ocean. They were a beautiful shade. She felt she could jump into them and never come out, away from all the pain. She wasn't quite sure how to answer the question. Should she be sad or mad for him asking such personal questions?

'I-I don't know,' she stuttered.

'You really don't know?' The blue eyes narrowed slightly. 'Well, would he be happy to see you like this, falling apart, as you say?'

She shook her head. 'No, I suppose not.'

Without warning, the man placed a hand on her arm. It felt warm and welcoming. How did she feel so calm around this stranger? He was like a long-lost beloved uncle she had never known.

'I lost a loved one too,' he said. 'Ten years ago, my wife passed away.'

'I'm sor-'

'You don't have to say anything,' the stranger said. The man's eyes twinkled in the fluorescent light above. 'She meant everything to me. She was my life. I was devastated and yes, I often lay in bed thinking how nice it would be to join her. But it was the easy way out. Suicide?' the man shook his head. 'It's taking the short-cut in the race called life. It's cheating.'

Claire continued to stare at the stranger and admired his openness. It was as if he had an invisible ability to see deep within her thoughts, almost caressing her soul.

'You have the same look that I had a few of years ago,' the man continued. 'I know that look. It's like a sixth sense. You're someone who is going through the grieving process with absolutely no end in sight except the ultimate one.'

She shifted her weight and swallowed hard. His words were striking a nerve.

'One day,' the man continued, 'I was in my kitchen and started to pretend that she was there.' The man held up his hands like he was under arrest. 'Now, I'm not one of these paranormal people who believe in ghosts and all that codswallop. I just decided to use my imagination and I asked her how she thought I was doing.' He stopped and smirked.

'You can bet she wasn't impressed. In fact we had a bit of an argument that day in the kitchen. But it was refreshing. I knew her so well that I could guess what her answers would be. She gave me a bollocking, telling me to look at myself, to get my act together. I told her that I missed her and that I didn't like my life anymore without her. You know something? I actually imagined her rolling her eyes to that.'

Claire smiled, rubbing the euro coin at the front of the shopping trolley.

'She was a bit ruthless but it made perfect sense, as she did when she was alive. I think when you're living with someone for so long, part of them enter your soul, wherever that may be. Like I said, I'm not that spiritual or anything. I think part of her really does live within me.'

She said nothing for several moments, almost dumbfounded that someone would be so open with her. She wasn't buying all of it though.

'With all due respect,' she said, 'as much pain as it has caused you, I don't think that you can compare losing your spouse to losing a child. Someone who you've cared for since before they were even born. Someone who had given so much joy and who had the potential to continue to do so until the day *I* would die.'

The man nodded his head. 'Maybe. But it's not up to you to quantify the grief or loss someone feels when a loved one dies. Statistically the mother-child grief is no doubt the worse. But I'm sure there are other mothers out there who couldn't care less if their child dies. An extreme minority no doubt, but they still exist. On the other hand, there are people who go through the grief that you're currently going through with their pet dog.'

The man could see by the look in Claire's face that she thought he was joking.

'Seriously. I remember reading about a couple in the US who committed suicide after their dog died. The grief was too much.'

A young business woman carrying a laptop bag politely excused herself as she squeezed in between Claire and the stranger and picked up a pack of Lyon's Green Tea. The woman continued up the aisle.

'Look, I'm not an expert at this,' the stranger admitted. 'And I'm not going to comment on the six bottles of wine you have in your trolley.'

Claire glanced at the bottles and suddenly felt embarrassed.

'You might be having a party, for all I know. What I do

know is that you can't go on the way you're doing now. This downward spiral. Go home and listen to what your son says.'

She took a deep breath and looked away. At the end of the aisle she saw a teenager stocking biscuits. He dropped a packet, looked around and pushed it to the back of the shelf he was packing. It was something like Max would have done.

'I can't.' She shook her head. 'He's everywhere. I'm trying to block him out, not invite him in. Everywhere I look. Everything I see, he's there. Christ, I even started coming *here* instead of my local supermarket because of the memories I have in the old place.'

The man looked down at his basket and then at his watch. 'What kind of smoothie do you like?'

Claire was taken aback. 'Excuse me?' She glanced down at the stranger's basket expecting to see a smoothie.

'There's a smoothie bar just out around there on the right.'

'Yeah, I know. I just didn't...'

'Don't get it wrong. I'm not asking for a date, just that we both finish our shopping and have a little smoothie.'

She tried to think of a reason not to. She had no other plans that afternoon, or for the entire month for that matter. She smiled. 'Okay. Why not?'

'What flavour would you like? I'll order ahead.'

'How do you know I won't be finished before you?'

The man shrugged his shoulders.

'I have a basket. You have a trolley. Go figure.'

She mentally slapped her forehead.

'Okay then. Order something with kiwi fruit. Just a small or medium sized one.'

Claire turned her trolley around and walked back in the direction she came from. When she was just a few metres away, she turned back.

'What's your name, by the way?'

'Edward. And you?'

'Claire.'

Edward stood still.

'Well, fancy that.'

'Fancy what?'

'That was my wife's name.'

15

Grace was released from hospital in the late afternoon. She wore her high-heels, pinstriped trousers, the blue geeky T-shirt and her rain jacket. From her waist down she could pass for a professional businesswoman, from her waist up she looked more like an eccentric. It would be just her luck to run into Trinny and Susannah, the fashion makeover experts from TV, Grace thought as she left the hospital. They would have a field day.

Without her bicycle she felt somewhat lost. Although an excellent spiderweb of trams covered the city, she had no clue which trams went where. She decided to go for the easy option and jumped in one of the two taxis that were parked at the taxi rank outside the hospital.

'Amsterdamseweg, nummer 23,' she informed the driver in perfect Dutch.

'*Zeker*,' the taxi driver replied as he pulled out onto Jan Tooropstraat and took a right onto Jan van Galenstraat. The taxi driver was of foreign descent. Grace guessed Surinam, the former Dutch colony.

'This might be a strange question,' she said to the driver, 'but I didn't have my mobile when they brought me into the hospital. Would you mind if I borrowed yours to make a quick call to a local mobile?'

Without hesitation the driver disconnected his device from the mobile holder beneath the dashboard and handed it over his shoulder to her.

'*Alstublieft.*' 'Here you go.'

'Thank you. Don't worry. I'll keep it short.'

As the driver made his way onto the A10, the ring road around Amsterdam, Grace called Rik on his mobile. She tried to imagine his mobile tune.

What was it again? The Muppet Show theme?

The first time she had heard his ringtone at work, she

couldn't help but smile. She half expected a bunch of muppets to dance into her office announcing that it was time to put on make-up.

Rik picked up on the second ring. '*Met Rik.*'

'Hi Rik. It's me, Grace.'

'Hello. How are you?'

She noticed that he spoke in a very neutral, professional tone. The kind of tone you would use when talking to a bank manager. It then dawned on her that other colleagues were probably within earshot.

'Can you talk?'

'Just a moment,' he said. Grace could hear him walk through the hallway, (probably) looking for an empty room. She heard a door shut. A few moments later he was back on.

'How did it go with whatshisname?' he asked, more casual this time.

'Fine,' she lied. 'That was some stunt you pulled off.'

'You liked it?'

'Kissing complete strangers. What next?'

'Yeah, I know,' he said. 'I saw your husband from the corner of my eye. He was all over me. I just assumed that he kept watching me when I had my back to him.'

'You should have been an actor.'

'Not going to give up the day job just yet. Where are you? Do you want me to collect you?'

Grace anticipated that he would offer to pick her up but the frightening vision of her sitting on the back of his bike encouraged her to go with the taxi option.

'No, it's fine, thanks. I'm in a taxi on the way to my house. I'm going to get some stuff and...' she was unsure how to finish the sentence. She played with the idea of staying in a hotel for a few nights or maybe even Rik's apartment but she had no idea how to bring it up. Rik saved her the trouble.

'You want to stay at my place?'

She smiled. She caught a glimpse of the taxi driver's

eyes in his mirror. Either he was checking her out or just checking the traffic behind them.

'Would that be okay with you?'

There was a silence that Grace wasn't sure what to make of.

'Of course it's okay with me,' he said eventually. It sounded like he had more to say but didn't dare say it. Did he wonder where they were going with this relationship? Or if you could even call it a relationship? It could hardly be the beginning of something serious.

Could it?

'They're wondering where you are at work. You didn't call in sick.'

'Oh shit. You didn't tell them?' She had asked the question before she realised how obvious the answer was.

'There's no reason for me to know your whereabouts. I don't want rumours to start, if you know what I mean.'

'I know. I'm sorry. I wasn't thinking. I'll call them as soon as I get off the phone.'

'Well, you can give it a few minutes in case anybody sees me hang up and then straight away sees a call from you come through.'

'Sure. I'll call from home.'

'Sounds good. Will I meet you at my apartment around six? I should be home by then.'

'That would be great. I really appreciate this, Rik.'

'I know. See you later.' The line went dead.

Fifteen minutes later the taxi pulled up outside a beautiful three-storey house on Amsterdamseweg in Amstelveen, one of the upmarket neighbourhoods around Amsterdam. The taxi driver had obviously heard and understood some of Grace's conversation.

'Would you like me to wait for you?' he asked.

She handed him the fare plus a generous tip. 'That won't be necessary, thanks.'

As soon as she entered the house, she ran to the alarm key panel and entered the security code. At least Otto wasn't home.

She placed her wallet on the small table in the hallway and entered the kitchen. It was a mess. She raised her eyes to the ceiling. Frustrated. Disappointed. One night away and the place had turned into a student flat. Otto obviously had better things to do and kept the dirty dishes as a welcome home present. Even placing them in the dishwasher was too much to ask.

'Idiot,' she muttered with zero intention of tidying up. She felt sorry for Klara, the Polish cleaner who visited once a week. It would ultimately be her task.

As she went upstairs, the house phone rang. Tempted as she was to answer it, she resisted, mainly out of fear that it might be Otto. Who else could be calling in the middle of the day? Except for maybe a company with a survey? Grace used to try to get out of those calls by pretending she didn't speak Dutch, only to be met with the option: 'That's okay. We can do it in English.'

The phone continued to ring as she pulled out a Samsonite suitcase from beneath the bed. She filled the suitcase with random clothes from her wardrobe and drawers. Coordinating her clothes in a fashionable way would come at a later stage. Grace grabbed a pair of boots from the shoe pile and threw them on top of the clothes. She briefly considered throwing her brown bunny slippers into the suitcase, but thought against it. It wasn't something she should subject Rik to right now. Maybe at a later stage. If there was a later stage.

She entered the bathroom and started packing her wash-bag. Suddenly she heard the front door open. She froze.

'Honey, I'm home!' Otto called from the entrance. She heard the door close.

16

Claire arrived at the Smoothies Juice Bar wheeling her trolley full of groceries. The queue was long, keeping a constant pressure on the young immigrant workers behind the counter. It reminded her of her summer in Cape Cod when she was a student. She worked two jobs, earning dollars to get her through another year at DCU. It was hard work, but she remembered still having plenty of energy to have fun. Life seemed so simple back then.

Edward stood next to the smoothie bar holding two plastic glasses with straws. His bag of shopping lay on the floor between his legs. He handed Claire a smoothie.

'Shall we sit down there?' he said pointing to the fountain close to Debenhams.

'Okay.'

'Here, if you carry both of them,' he said as he handed Claire his smoothie too. 'I'll throw my shopping bag in your trolley and wheel everything.'

'Okay,' she said as she took his smoothie. She looked at both of them. 'If that's the medium, I'd hate to see what the large one is like.'

'They're kiwi fruit and banana. I hope it's to your liking.'

'You have the same?'

He nodded. 'I usually go for something with strawberry and banana, but kiwi is also nice.'

She could see that he had already taken a few mouthfuls from his. As they approached the fountain, she sat next to two uniformed schoolgirls who were deep in conversation, oblivious to anyone around them. Edward took his smoothie back from her and sat down next to her.

The afternoon shoppers were out in full force. A mix of mothers with young children, workers out for lunch, unemployed people who had nothing better to do and school children. A fresh, cool atmosphere hung in the air created by the water fountain streams.

Claire took a mouthful of her smoothie. 'Mmm, not bad.' She turned to Edward. 'You seem to be a smoothie connoisseur?'

He smiled. 'They taste good. They're full of vitamins. What is there not to like about them?'

She smiled. 'Nothing. You're right. I just never really got into them.'

They both took another sip of their drinks. 'This is strange, isn't it?' she asked.

'What? Having a smoothie with a strange guy?'

'Yeah. Don't you think?'

'I suppose so.'

'I mean it's innocent of course, but...' she was unsure how to finish her sentence.

He waved his hand in a dismissing manner. 'Don't worry. I know what you mean.'

She glanced into the fountain at all the coins lying there. She remembered once or twice giving Max a coin to throw in and make a wish. Often she wondered what his wish might have been. Max being Max never said.

She turned towards Edward. 'So your wife died ten years ago?' *Way to go, Claire, with your delightful topics of conversation.*

'It will be ten years this November.'

She reflected on his reply for a moment. 'That's a long time.'

'I suppose you can say that, yes.'

'And is it true what they say?'

He tilted his head to one side. 'And what's that?'

'That time heals all.'

He took a deep breath. 'Honestly, I don't know.' His grave silence that followed was so prolonged that she thought he had said all he wanted to on the matter.

'I'm not sure if it's *time* that heals,' he said finally, 'or if it's the fact that every day brings you closer to the day that you too will die. Maybe it's *that* thought that makes life easier to deal with. Knowing that one day we too will die. This probably depends on your religious beliefs though and whether you believe you will meet again.'

'And do you?'

'What? Believe that I will meet Claire again?'

She nodded.

'I think I have to. The thought of never seeing her again in whatever form, doesn't help.'

'I know how you feel.'

'And if I'm wrong, I won't know until I'm dead and by then nothing really matters.'

Claire slowly glanced at the coins again. She would throw everything she owned into that fountain if the wishes actually came true. Everything. Even if she could just hug him one more time and smell his hair. She pushed the thought away and looked at her new friend with a slightly scrunched up nose. It was her "something is not right" look.

'It's funny, isn't it?' she asked.

'What?'

'Drinking smoothies and talking about death.' She held up her plastic glass. 'I mean smoothies are so colourful and alive.'

He smiled. 'We could change the subject to rainbows and bunny rabbits if you like.'

She shook her head. 'No, it's okay.' She rubbed the thin film of condensation outside her plastic glass.

'You know, there are a lot of aspects to one's death nobody ever tells you about,' Edward announced looking down at his hand.

Claire nodded slowly.

'For instance, nobody ever told me when I was supposed to remove my wedding ring.' He glanced at her. 'I mean, when *are* you supposed to remove your wedding ring after the death of a spouse? Is there a rule? Even an unwritten one?'

'Good question,' she agreed. 'I have no idea.'

He glanced at his hand once again as if he wasn't sure what was there anymore. There was no sign of a wedding band.

'I guess everybody is different. There is no right or wrong answer to that.' He squinted, like a stray splash of water had gone into his eyes. He blinked rapidly and continued. 'I guess the answer is blowing in the wind. You know, like that song.' He rubbed his chin. 'Or maybe that was before your time?'

Claire grinned. 'Bob Dylan. I love Bob Dylan.'

She glanced at his hand. His nails were long for a guy, but clean and well-shaped. A subtle shine came from them and she wondered if they had been professionally manicured. She almost envied his nails.

'I see you have removed yours anyway.'

'From my finger, yes.' He pulled at a silver chain that was around his neck and let it hang outside his shirt. Two gold wedding rings hung next to his chest.

'I feel a bit like an overgrown hobbit, but here they are. I keep them close to me.'

She smiled. 'That's sweet.'

'She meant the world to me.' He popped them back inside his shirt. 'They will stay there until the day I die.'

'Even if you marry again?'

'I don't think I can marry again.'

She wasn't buying it. 'And if you do?'

'Then we'll cross that bridge when we come to it. What about you?'

'What about me?'

He took another mouthful of smoothie, unsure whether he ought to continue. He decided to go for it. 'Would you ever have another child?'

Claire took a deep breath. Nobody asked her that since Max died. She knew it was a question that passed people's mind, including her own. Eventually she shook her head. 'No. I don't see myself starting from scratch again. I'm too old. I don't have the energy to go back to the start.'

'Too old. You must be joking?'

She smiled. 'Don't get all flattering on me now. I'm forty-two. I already had enough difficulties conceiving with Max. And it wasn't exactly a smooth pregnancy. Fast forward ten years, I might as well forget about it.'

The two schoolgirls next to her stood up. The school bag of the closest one brushed off Claire's head. She looked at them but said nothing as they walked away, still deep in conversation.

'I mean the ideal situation would be just to have a child. Already walking and toilet-trained.'

'Adoption?'

'In an ideal world, yes. That could be an option. I would love to. But it's such a lengthy process with so much stress and costs involved. I'd probably be close to fifty before we would get anywhere. In the olden days, or even still now, fifty-year olds are becoming grannies, not mothers.' She took another sip of the smoothie. 'Also, my track record as a mother doesn't look good.'

'Don't be too hard on yourself.' He waited a moment and then changed the subject. 'What about Max's bedroom? How was it cleaning it out?'

Her expression turned to one of sadness. It was as if an invisible blanket of pain landed on her head. 'His bedroom,' she said finally 'is still the way it was the day he died.'

He nodded as if he was expecting that answer. 'That's tough. Especially if you don't need the space.'

'Of course we don't need the space. It was his space. What could we possibly put there? And what do we do with all his stuff?'

'Charity.'

She closed her eyes for a moment. She opened them and looked at Edward. 'Is that what you did?'

He nodded.

'I'm not sure if I could do that. What if I see a boy with

the same football jersey as his? Or the same shoes? I'd be wondering the entire time if they used to belong to Max. I would probably try and follow the boy and try and touch him, to feel warm flesh wearing the jersey once again.'

'What about an African charity then? Or any other charity that ships the material abroad. That way you really won't ever see them again.' He paused for a brief moment. 'Unless you *go* to Africa.'

She smiled as he continued.

'Even then, you would have to beat some pretty high odds to run into a little boy wearing a jersey belonging to Max.'

Claire looked towards her shopping. How few items she bought now with one less person in the household. What an appetite Max had.

Edward sucked on his straw until it gave slurp noises, announcing the end of the drink. He looked at it as if expecting more to come from it.

'You drink them fast,' Claire said.

He tapped on his forehead with his knuckles. 'Ouch. Brain freeze. I always do that. I don't know why.'

'What, drink cold things too fast?'

'Yep.' He looked at his watch. 'I have to be getting back to work.'

'Of course. Don't let me delay you any longer.'

He looked at her with his warm blue eyes. 'You're not delaying me. It was wonderful to meet you.'

Claire was a little taken aback by how sincere the man beside her sounded.

'It was nice meeting you too. I appreciate your advice.'

'I'm glad you do. If there's one piece of advice I want you to take is to talk to him. Go home, have a little conversation with him and move forward.'

'I'll do my best.'

He placed his hand on her shoulder.

'That, Claire, is all anyone can ask. I know that you're stronger than you think you are. You've hit "The Wall" in this marathon we call life. But you will get through it.'

'Thank you.' She didn't know what else to say.

Edward picked up his bag out of Claire's trolley. As he walked off, she couldn't help wondering if she would ever see him again.

17

'Shit!' Grace whispered to herself. There was little point in pretending she wasn't there. The alarm was switched off and her wallet was on the table in the hallway. She threw her wash-bag beneath the sink in the bathroom and tiptoed into the bedroom. She closed over the suitcase without zipping it shut and lifted it onto the floor. With a quick shove it disappeared beneath the bed.

'Grace!' Otto called as he made his way up the stairs. Grace flung off her trousers and jumped into bed. With her heart racing she closed her eyes. It was difficult to act calm and sleepy, but she gave it her best shot.

Otto entered the bedroom.

'Hi,' he said with a fake grin. 'You're home.'

Grace rubbed her eyes.

'Why didn't you call me when you were discharged?' He sat down on the side of the bed.

Grace made a half attempt at yawning and ran her hand through her hair. 'After what you threatened me with, before you left the hospital? You're the last person in the world I would call.'

He touched her face in a futile attempt at affection.

'I'm sorry, baby. How are you feeling?'

'Tired,' she said coldly, as she pushed his hand away. 'And don't give me any of this caring shit. You make me want to vomit.'

Otto narrowed his eyes and a look of extreme hatred seemed to flow from them.

'That look doesn't scare me anymore,' she said trying to act as casual as possible. Inside, her heart was racing. Was it wise to provoke someone who was so unpredictable?

A fake smile came to life on Otto's face. 'Where were you last night? You still didn't tell me.'

'Out. Getting my social life back.'

He tutted like a school teacher. 'You don't get it Grace, do you?'

'Get what?'

'We belong together. We...'

'Oh, shut up. We don't belong together. We haven't belonged together for a long time.'

His fake smile disappeared. He took a deep breath but said nothing. Was this the calm before the storm?

As Otto stood up, his foot hit part of the suitcase that was still protruding from beneath the bed. Without thinking, he shoved it further beneath the bed with his foot. Then he stopped. A penny dropped. He looked at Grace for a reaction. She closed her eyes trying to give the impression that she wasn't bothered. The truth was, she was the total opposite.

He bent down and pulled the suitcase from under the bed. He pulled back the cover to find the pile of random clothes and the pair of boots.

'Are you going somewhere?'

Grace sighed. She said nothing

'Answer me.'

'What do you want me to say? I mean, really? After what you said to me in the hospital. The way our relationship is going. Come on, Otto, don't act so surprised.'

He raised a finger. 'You're not leaving me.'

'Is that a threat? Are you threatening me with something?'

She pulled back the covers and hopped out of bed. 'What are you going to do? Chain me to the bed?' She wasn't sure if she should be giving him ideas. She picked up her striped trousers from the floor and put them back on. Otto stepped back and remained still as he watched her. When she was finished with her trousers, she lifted the suitcase from the floor onto the bed again. This time she zipped it closed.

Otto moved forward and took hold of her arms.

'You're not leaving me, I said.'

'Let go of me, Otto!' Her heart was pounding. Her adrenaline spun into overdrive. She was not going to be bullied anymore.

'I won't let you leave me,' he said, deadly serious.

'It's not a question of you letting me,' she said as she pulled away. 'I *am* leaving.'

Without any warning, her husband elbowed her nose and then slapped her across the face with his other hand. She felt the pain before she even realised he had raised his hand. The force of the slap made her lose balance, and she found herself sitting on the bed. One side of her face stung like hell. Blood trickled from her nose, ruining the T-shirt she still wore and the silk bed sheets instantly. She touched her nose. Was it broken? She didn't think so.

She stood up and faced Otto. She could feel the blood flowing down her throat. Wiping away the blood from her mouth she reached for a handful of tissues from the bedside locker.

'Happy now?' she spluttered through a mouthful of blood as she wiped it away. Her eyes watered. The adrenaline flowing though her body added to the speed at which the blood was exiting her nose and flowing down her throat.

'I'm sorry, baby.' Otto moved towards her and then stopped suddenly. Grace wasn't sure why but figured it was from fear of getting blood on his Armani suit.

She looked at him while holding the tissues to her nose. Her eyes squinted. Although her heart raced frantically, she was surprised how calm she suddenly felt. Was it because she was through it before? Was it because there was nothing else for him to do to her?

At least this time, she thought to herself as she pinched the bridge of her nose, *there's no baby growing inside me*.

18

Daniel chewed hard on his salami and cheese sandwich. At home they were down to the last slices of bread, so both of his sandwiches comprised of one heel and one regular slice. He had been tempted to call into Spar on the way to work to pick up a readymade sandwich, but he would have felt guilty for the rest of the day if he did. After Zoe going to the trouble of actually making his sandwiches, the last thing he wanted to do was to discard them and eat a sandwich made by a stranger wearing a hair net.

It took a lot of chewing to get it down, but he got there in the end with some mouthfuls of Diet Club Orange. Like most lunch times, he ate his lunch sixty metres above the rest of his colleagues. It was too far to go all the way down just to eat a sandwich and talk shit to his colleagues. They were good blokes and he got on well with them, but he found it hard to *really* relate to them. Often he would sink to a certain vulgarity to blend in but he wasn't being himself. He often told jokes that he didn't find funny but knew his colleagues would. Sometimes he wondered if everybody was in the same boat and just had a foul mouth for the amusement of others. Maybe in reality, when everybody went home, they would play chess and discuss to what extent the political revolutions at the end of the 18th century had cultural origins.

Daniel enjoyed the privacy his cabin offered. Particularly today. He had brought with him the bag that John gave him earlier that morning so that he could read through his old notes in between manoeuvres. It was like getting reacquainted with an old friend, the first time in twelve years.

Inside the bag there was a binder full of notes and calculations and a larger hardback notebook. He was a little astonished by the amount of detail he had gone into.

The theories, the theorems, the mathematical models. Some calculations went on for over twenty pages. It wasn't straightforward, that was for sure. Some parts were more familiar to Daniel than others. These were the sections that had kept him awake at night all those years ago, the sections that he lived and breathed for weeks.

As he read through the thesis, it reminded him of watching a movie he had seen hundreds of times as a child, and now watching it again as an adult. Certain scenes came back to him like it was yesterday. He placed the binder and notebook on a small storage shelf to his left. As he rummaged further in the bag he found a smaller A5 hardback notebook. A *Garbage Pail Kid* sticker was attached to the front saying "Dental Daniel." It was a comical cartoon of a kid brushing his teeth with the toothbrush going right through his cheek.

'Jesus, I remember that,' he said as he held it up. A couple of coffee stains marked the front, indicating that it was used for more than writing in. 'This was my first notebook when I started the thesis.' As he flicked through the notebook he came across the Feather Theorem.

'The Feather Theorem. Of course. This is what started it all.' The introduction was written in his handwriting. It seemed to be much neater than his current handwriting.

"Every day we make hundreds, even thousands of decisions. Some conscious, many sub-conscious, but we make them. They all have consequences. If we combine the decisions with external forces, external likelihoods, I believe you can package these thousands of daily decisions into formulae. I believe you can use mathematics to determine the ultimate consequence, i.e. death. I believe you can calculate the likelihood of dying every day in the next seventy to eighty years. The result is a most-likely value. My original idea came from simply watching a feather land on the ground.

Feather Theorem.
Feather; all the bristles are the decisions; the internal factors; the

genetics. When I drop it from a certain height at a certain angle I know roughly where it will land.

Only roughly.

However, when I use all the physical characteristics such as size, quantity, density and angles of the bristles I am able to predict the landing spot much more accurately.

That is within a controlled environment, however, with minimal external forces acting on it. If I know the external factors such as wind velocity, direction, strength, I can also predict the likelihood of it landing on a certain spot.

I believe anything in a controlled environment can be predicted. So the real question is: can you take the outside world and model it into a controlled environment? In other words, pretend it is a controlled environment based on all the data accumulated over so many years from all the scientific literature available. That is the concept behind the Feather Theorem. That is what I want to prove here."

Further down the page something attracted his attention. It was different handwriting and made him laugh.

"Daniel smells of poo-poo"

It was Grace's handwriting. It was written there to break up the monotony of formulae and notes that filled the notebook, to add some badly-needed comic relief to his otherwise dull observations. A human touch.

Daniel's mobile started to vibrate on the dashboard, dragging his thoughts away from the thesis. He looked at the display panel for a moment before answering.

'Daniel speaking.'

'Hi Daniel. It's John.'

'Why am I not surprised to hear from you?'

'Well, I'm just checking up to see how the calculation is going.'

'Seriously? I haven't started yet. But I *am* becoming familiar with an old friend,' he said looking down at his notebook.

'Really? You got in contact with her already? Did you

tell her the date?'

Confused, Daniel took a moment before realising the professor had misunderstood him.

'No, I meant the thesis was my old friend. Not Grace. I haven't had contact with Grace yet.'

'Oh. Right. Of course,' he said. 'And? Is it coming back to you?'

'Slowly. I'm quite impressed by how smart I was back then,' Daniel said with a pinch of sarcasm.

John laughed. 'And still are, I bet.'

'Let's hope so.'

A silence arose. Since John was the one who called him, Daniel resisted in filling the pause.

'Look,' John said eventually, 'I didn't just call to see how things were going, but I wanted to thank you for listening to me this morning.'

'Listening to you?' Daniel asked. 'Well, you're welcome... I think. It was a sad story. Not sure if I was much help. I can't imagine the pain you and your wife went through.' He quickly corrected himself. 'And are *still* going through, of course.'

Another silence unfolded. He could hear John take a deep breath.

'Are you okay?' he asked. 'You sound a bit...' He searched for the correct word. 'Down.' He cringed at the choice of word. 'Of course you have every right to be.'

'It was good to talk to you this morning. I mean it was good for *me* to talk to someone.' John gave a small cough as if clearing his throat. 'I think it was the first time that I really did.'

Daniel raised an eyebrow, surprised that John had obviously been bottling up everything.

'It felt like a huge weight was lifted from my chest after we met. It was a very strange feeling. Strange in a good way.'

'Really?'

'Yeah...' he spoke slowly as if he wasn't sure what his

next word would be. 'It's usually me trying to keep composed and calm. I let Claire do all the talking… and crying.'

'That's probably not good John,' Daniel offered, certain that it was redundant advice. 'I'm no expert, but you need to let it out. You need to grieve properly.'

'I know.'

A strong gust of wind passed through the crane causing it to shake. Daniel picked up the can of Diet Club Orange, just in case it toppled. He took a sip of it while it was in his hand. Turning his attention back to the call, he waited for John to reply. Was he hinting at something? He decided to find out.

'Do you want to do it again sometime? Meet up and talk?'

John let out a laugh mixed with a sigh of relief. 'To be honest, yes, I think that would be good for me. Deep down I think I was hoping you would offer.'

'What? Offer to meet again?'

'Yes. It's not the kind of thing that I can just blurt out and ask.'

'Why not?'

'Well, you know. We don't exactly have a good history.'

Daniel saw where he was coming from. And he hadn't exactly been overfriendly when John approached him at the foot of the crane the previous day.

'I know,' Daniel said. 'But you're not the only one who screwed up. I made some mistakes too back then.'

A foreign voice echoed through the crane cabin as Daniel's walkie-talkie came to life. *Daniel, are you finished lunch?*

'Excuse me for a second,' he said to John and grabbed the walkie-talkie. 'Give me five minutes,' he shouted into it and turned down the volume.

'You've got three,' came the almost immediate response.

'Asshole,' Daniel said beneath his breath, resisting the temptation of pressing the Push-to-Talk button. He could hear John laughing as he placed the mobile back to his ear.

'I assume he didn't hear that?' John asked.

Daniel laughed. 'Not this time.'

Listen, I don't want to keep you from your work.'

'Don't worry. They'll wait. They don't have much of a choice. So when and where would you like to meet?'

'Good question. I guess just a pub or something.'

'Sounds like we're having an affair.'

John laughed. 'That's all my wife needs now, a husband who is having an affair with another man. I'm sure Mary will like that too.'

'Who's Mary?'

'The overpaid counsellor we're going to.'

'I see. Well let's set a day for now. We can come up with a venue in the meantime. Say, Thursday evening?'

'Sounds good.'

'We need the steel barrier moved on top of the east scaffolding, Daniel,' came the same voice through the radio. Daniel threw his eyes to heaven.

'Okay, I gotta get back to work.'

'Don't forget, the offer is still there, Daniel.'

'Okay,' he said without realising what John was talking about. He scratched his head. 'What offer?'

'To finish what you started. Get your PhD and do something with your life.'

Daniel stared out across the Phoenix Park to the Dublin Mountains. It was so beautiful. There was something so simple and natural about the life he now led. Yet the thesis was once all he lived for. It used to be the first thing he thought of in the morning, and the last thing he thought of at night. Or early hours of the following morning, which back then was often when he went to bed. The thesis was such a part of him for so long. But could he really go back?

'I don't know, John,' he said eventually. 'I don't think I have it in me anymore.'

'I'm not going to discuss it now. You need to go back

107

to work. But I think you do. It's part of you. I think it's like asking a fish to go back into the water. It's in your nature.'

Even though John couldn't see him, Daniel shrugged and continued with John's metaphor. 'Maybe I've evolved into a land creature now. I'm afraid I might drown if I go back into the water.'

'At the end of the day it's up to you. But the offer is still there.' He paused for a moment. 'It will always be there'. And he hung up.

19

Grace sat patiently on a park bench across the street from Rik's apartment. She looked out over the water. A small island of wet grassland in the middle of the water served as a nesting area for herons, ducks and other urban wildlife. It was completely isolated from dry land. A refuge. A safe haven. Grace looked down at her suitcase beside her and then over her shoulder to Rik's apartment block. Was this to be her refuge for now?

To the east of the water she noticed a couple of tower cranes that stood erect, slowly assembling a new apartment block. An apartment block that would soon be full of young couples, families, retired couples, singles, new beginnings. The building would have no history, no scent from previous owners, no lines on the wall monitoring the growth of children, no random spots of Blu-Tac, no dirty fingerprints. The apartment would only really be complete when people started living there.

She watched one of the tower cranes moving slowly. It was carrying a large piece of concrete. She often thought about Daniel when she saw cranes. When she heard that he had become a crane operator all those years ago, her heart had sunk, just as it sank now. It wasn't that she had anything against crane operators, but she knew first-hand how passionate Daniel had been about mathematics and his thesis in particular. It saddened her immensely to find out that he had thrown away everything he had worked for.

But then anger swept the pity aside, as it always did, when she thought about how their relationship ended. It was as if his love for mathematics was inseparable from his love for her, if he ever loved her. And when one died, the other died with it.

'Hey there, stranger!'

Grace swung around with a start and saw Rik approaching. As usual he was dressed in a suit, but he decided to go for black shoes today. Grace wondered if she had brought up her whole brown shoes rant the previous night when the wine was flowing.

'Hey,' she said, giving him a quick wave. 'I was a million miles away.' She stood up and grabbed her suitcase.

'Let me get…' Rik was about to pick up the suitcase, but stopped in his tracks when he noticed dried blood around one of her nostrils and a faint purple shade on the bridge of her nose.

'What happened, Grace?' he asked with a deadly serious expression.

She let go of her suitcase and told him about the blow to the face. Rik's face turned pink with anger. When she noticed this, she tried to trivialise the event.

'It was good to get it over with, to be honest,' she said. 'After he hit me, he went downstairs quietly. Two minutes later I heard him leave the house.'

'You should press charges. Have him charged with assault. Seriously.'

She shook her head. 'What's the point? His lawyer friends would get him off before this has even healed,' she said, pointing to her nose.

'So what are we going to do?'

Grace smiled. 'We?'

He nodded and put on a French accent. '*Oui.*' He picked up the side handle of her suitcase and began wheeling it towards his apartment. 'I just want to help.'

Grace followed. 'I know you do. And I really appreciate it.' They both stopped at the edge of the pavement as a Dutch *bakfiets* with at least three children in the front carrier, passed by.

'I will file for a divorce. We'll split everything.' They crossed the street as she continued talking. 'We both pay half the mortgage, so I'm entitled to half the house. He'll have to buy me out if he doesn't want to sell it himself.

And that's it. End of story. He's out of my life.'

'But he's a violent man, Grace,' Rik said as he rummaged for his key. 'He almost broke your nose. I assume he has done something like that before?'

Whether it was a *rhetorical* assumption or not, she avoided it. Her eyes moved towards the ground. 'I don't want to talk about it now.'

Realising that he had hit a nerve, Rik took his key out and opened the front door. Before he went inside, he tried to meet Grace's eyes. 'But you don't want him to do it with other women, do you?'

'Of course not,' she said looking at him, 'but what are you suggesting we do?'

'Give him a taste of his own medicine.'

She stared at him and shook her head. 'Don't even think about that, Rik.' Her thumb rubbed against her wedding ring on the same hand. It was as if talking about her husband forced her to make contact with the ring. *When am I going to remove the damn thing?* she wondered. It wasn't just the removal of a piece of precious metal, but a whole segment of her life.

'I have a friend who might know the kind of people who could help out. Just a few smacks to the head. Nothing serious.'

'A few smacks to the head? Jesus Christ, Rik! What is that going to solve?'

'I'll tell you what it will solve,' he said, 'The next time he raises his hand to a woman, he might think twice before swinging it.'

'He will know that it was me who arranged it. It will spiral out of control. You don't just get beaten up out of the blue.'

'Sure you do. It happens all the time. We can request that his wallet is stolen while they're at it, to make it look like there's an alternative motive.'

Grace sighed and placed her hand on his arm. 'Listen, I really appreciate what you're offering to do. But it's not going to help. I won't let you do it.'

'But it'll be just...'

'Rik,' she cut in again. 'I'm pleading with you, do not do anything. Promise me you will not do anything. Let's just leave it. I will get him where it really hurts. Not his head, but his bank account. The house. Forcing him to split everything will cause him more pain than any slap on the head.'

Rik remained quiet.

'Promise me,' she asked

He stood for a moment without saying anything. 'Okay. I promise. For now. If he does something like this again, then I'm going to do something about it. Okay?'

'We'll deal with it if and when that happens.'

Rik went inside and carried her suitcase up the stairs. Grace was about to follow him when the tower cranes caught her eye again. The thought of Daniel came back again, and a sadness flowed through her body. She shook her head as if that helped in dispersing the thoughts of him. *I need to stop thinking of the guy,* she told herself as she followed Rik inside. *I haven't meant anything to him for so long.*

20

The kitchen was a mess. Random papers were scattered all over the table. Folders and notebooks were dispersed on the chairs and floor around Daniel. It was like his student room from twelve years previously. It was only the random children's books, pieces of Lego and a drawing of a dinosaur chasing a red car on the refrigerator door that confirmed he was at a different stage in his life.

He tried to recall the last time their kitchen was in such a mess because of his mathematical studies but couldn't recall exactly. Then again, didn't he throw his mathematical life away before he settled down with Zoe? And yet he had a fuzzy memory of doing a couple of calculations when they first moved in together.

'I did two more didn't I?' he mumbled as he looked around all the paperwork. 'Yeah, I remember now, while it was still relatively fresh in my mind...' He flicked through the notebooks and folders that lay on the table. Everything was related to his original research and the predictions of the five classmates. In the back of his mind, there was something about the results of the other calculations that made him toss them aside. Either the results were dates in the past or maybe he was just so fed up with maths by then that he hadn't really given it the same effort as the original five.

He turned his attention back to the prediction on hand. Among the documents and notebooks were Claire Redmond's doctor's reports and genetic test results. There was so much personal information. It served as a glimpse into her genes, her psyche. Daniel knew so much about this stranger whom he had never met and maybe never would.

He looked up and studied the drawing on the refrigerator door. It wasn't very good. He would be the first to admit it, but that was so not the point. It came from a beautiful boy, a boy that he had helped create. Amazing, when you thought about it. How could he even begin to imagine what Claire was going through? The complete shock to the system. A tsunami, earthquake and volcanic eruption rolled into one.

As he turned his attention back to the documents in front of him, he wondered if all these reports really captured what was going on in her mind. He wondered if it would even be possible to predict her date of death after so many years. So much time had passed where he hadn't even picked up a calculator to do some simple algebra. He felt like a onetime boxing champ entering a ring for a big comeback. Only something wasn't right. He hadn't trained for it. Without training he had a feeling that he would need to go the distance before completing the calculation. There would be no shortcut. There would be no knock-out.

While he went through the paperwork, it dawned on him why John would pick up his thesis again after all these years. He tried to imagine what went through his mind. If the thesis was approved twelve years ago, or even just published or publicised somehow, it might have been accepted by now. More research might have gone into it. Maybe himself and other mathematicians throughout the world would have built on it. And who knows, John might have known the date of death of his son. Maybe once or twice he would have watched a Manchester United match with him. The guilt of not being a good father that was currently eating him alive like a parasite would simply not be there. Or at least not be so strong.

Zoe entered the kitchen wearing her dressing gown and slippers. She took one look at the mess and shook her head. 'It's getting late,' she said, as she went over to the kettle, checked the water level and switched it on.

'I know,' he said as he finished scribbling some calculation on a random page. 'Listen. There's something I've been meaning to ask. I need to go to Amsterdam this weekend. I know that...'

'You're joking,' Zoe said, cutting him off. 'It's Helen's hen party this weekend. I'm going to London.'

'I know. Relax. I'll ask my parents to mind Sean.'

'What do you need to go to Amsterdam for?'

Daniel bit his thumbnail. 'It's to do with my thesis. It's complicated. But I need to meet someone who was involved with my thesis years ago.'

'Can you not go next weekend?'

He shook his head. 'I'm sorry.'

'Your parents aren't exactly full of life, Daniel. Are you sure they can watch Sean for the whole weekend?'

'Of course. They'll be fine. They'll love it.'

Daniel's parents were Sean's only grandparents still alive. Zoe's parents had passed away. Her father died when she was eight, and her mother three years ago after a sudden brain tumour. As for Sean's uncle and aunt situation, it wasn't much better. Daniel was an only child and Zoe's younger sister, Liz, lived in the suburbs of Auckland in New Zealand. She never really kept in touch and, in fact, had never even met Sean in person. It wasn't much help when it came to last minute childminding.

'Did you call your parents?'

'Not yet. I'll do it tomorrow.'

'But if they can't do it...'

'Then I'll take him with me!' he snapped.

Silence. Zoe turned around and grabbed a mug from the cupboard and a tea bag. Daniel continued to scan through some pages and then stopped. He stood up and walked over to Zoe.

'Sorry. I didn't mean to snap at you.' While she still had her back towards him, he placed his arms around her waist and held her. 'I just need to do this and get it over with. I don't plan to go back to university and I don't plan to quit my job. We're doing okay. We're happy. There aren't going to be lots of changes.'

Zoe turned around. Her face shone in the kitchen light.

She had gone through her pre-bedtime beauty ritual with face exfoliating, cleansing, moisturising and other actions with overpriced creams.

'I don't want to see you get hurt, Daniel. I saw how hurt you were all those years ago. You were almost suicidal, for Christ's sake.'

Daniel and Zoe had both worked as waiting staff in The Winding Stair restaurant in the city centre. Daniel worked there in the weekends. Zoe worked there full-time still trying to figure out what she wanted to do with her life. When Daniel's thesis was rejected he had confided in Zoe. Their friendship took a new turn, and although neither of them knew it at the time, foundations of a future together were put in place.

'Oh, come on. I was never suicidal.' His hands dropped down and found themselves in Zoe's large dressing gown pockets. 'I'm not that kind of person. I was really upset but I would never have killed myself over … that.' He nodded in the direction of the mess on the table.

Zoe leaned forward and kissed him on the cheek. 'If you get hurt, it will hurt me. It will hurt Sean. I don't think...'

'How am I going to get hurt? I'm just doing this one little calculation for someone and that's it.' He could feel scrunched-up tissue in one pocket and a small tube in the other. Perhaps a cream of something that she hadn't got round to applying yet.

'It might get your hopes up again. They might...' She trailed off and looked down. 'Do you want to take your hands out of my pockets?'

He pulled her closer. 'Not really. It's cosy.'

She rolled her eyes, and continued what she was saying. 'They might give you a reason to submit your thesis again. And then just reject it again. You were devastated, Daniel. I don't want to see that again.'

'I promise you it won't, okay? My life is you and Sean. Back then I had no one. I had only the thesis.'

Deep down, he knew it wasn't completely true. But he couldn't tell his wife about Grace. Not now. And although he had zero intentions of cheating on Zoe, he was going to Amsterdam to meet the one person that meant something to him back then. How could he explain that? Zoe would never understand.

'How long will you be?' she asked as she turned around, forcing Daniel to remove his hands. She placed a green tea bag into a cup and added some boiling water.

'Two nights. Leave Friday, come back Sunday.'

'I mean with the calculation.'

He scratched the back of his head. 'I'm not sure. It's a bit tricky. It's been a while and I kind of coded some of the thesis so no one would steal the formulae. I will take a day off tomorrow and work on it.'

'Daniel. You said it wasn't going to interfere with your life. Or with us. Don't let it take over your life again.' She dabbed the tea bag a couple of times with a spoon and then lifted it out and threw it in the sink.

'I won't. I promise. It's just this one thing. I'll have a result by tomorrow and then, after that, the trip to Amsterdam, and that's it.'

'I'll believe that when I see it.' She took a sip of her green tea. It was as if the tea contained some magic formula, as her tone of voice changed to something softer. 'Look, I'm not against your maths and your thesis and everything. I'm against the hurt it caused you before. If you really have the chance to get your PhD and do something you really wanted, without the same devastation as before, then that's fine. But you have to be careful.'

He nodded. Zoe turned around and left him in peace.

Daniel stared at the picture of the dinosaur chasing the red car again. The simplicity of a child's imagination. He remembered back to when he was that age. The dreams he dreamed. The ambitions he had. He wanted to be an astronaut, a film star, a soldier like Rambo. As he grew older, his ambitions metamorphosed into something less childlike. He wanted to become a mathematician, and not just an ordinary one. More than anything, he wanted to make a difference and leave his mark in the mathematical community.

How all that changed overnight.

Was he truly happy being a crane operator? What if this was his second chance? His *last* chance to do something with his life. To make his dreams come true. Was he true with himself when he told others that he was content with what he had? The simple life?

The truth was that if he searched deep within him, there was an instinct that longed to get out; a desire that wanted to prove that he was the most brilliant mathematician in the modern world.

What if Michelangelo had never picked up a paint brush? Or Archimedes had taken a shower instead of a bath? How many geniuses have come and gone without having had the chance to bloom? People who took their potential to their graves. Could he really do that?

Was he even one of them?

He sat back down on his chair and looked at the mess on the table. His eyes jumped between the different formulae. The different calculations. The complexity of it all. A twinkle in his eye appeared and he smiled. This is what he truly loved.

21

'Feeling better, Grace?' Cynthia asked, as Grace walked into the reception area of Kuhlman International B.V. Cynthia was an attractive woman with round green eyes, in her mid-twenties.

'Yes, thanks.' Grace said. She walked to the corner where the postal trays stood. 'I think it was one of those twenty-four hour bugs.'

'I had one of those a couple of months ago,' Cynthia said, as Grace opened her tray and removed her mail. 'My God, I thought I would not stop vomiting. My throat was killing me, and my stomach was completely empty. I mean, so empty it felt I was puking the acids from my stomach. You wouldn't believe it.'

Grace stood still, not sure if she should be listening to such a story so early in the morning. Or at all, come to think of it.

'Sorry to hear that, Cynthia. Glad it's over now,' she offered as she passed the reception desk and ascended a flight of stairs to her office.

'Well, it was like you, I suppose,' she called out. 'It was gone in twenty- four hours.'

Cynthia was the only person in the world that Grace had no trouble walking away from mid-conversation. During her first few weeks, she had got trapped many times by her babbling. She was too polite to interrupt her or to excuse herself. It wasn't until one of the clerks told her that she needed to just walk away if she kept talking. Everybody in the office did it. They had to if they were to get any work done. Cynthia suffered from ADHD – Attention Deficit Hyperactivity Disorder, which often caused her to talk non-stop about nothing, really. The clerk assured Grace that Cynthia didn't take it personally if someone walked away.

'Is she a suitable person to have at reception then?' she had asked, not out of malice, but more out of curiosity of why you would put someone with ADHD at the front of a small company like Kuhlman International B.V.

The clerk had smiled. 'On the contrary, she's fabulous at reception. There's no fear of uncomfortable silences when she's around. Many of our regular clients love her. And as for the new clients, once they get to know her behaviour, they usually grow to like her too. Oh yeah, and she works damn hard.'

It wasn't just the clients that had grown to like her. Every employee loved her too, Grace included. Who wouldn't love a colleague whom you could just turn away from when you have had enough and not upset them?

Kuhlman International was located in an old building on Vondelstraat. It was a red brick building, four stories high that looked onto Vondel Park. The building housed three companies. Kuhlman International was situated on the ground and first floor, a creaky floor at that. Grace, whose office was on the first floor, often wondered if it bothered her colleagues below.

In the basement there was an IT company that did things that Grace didn't understand, or if she was honest with herself, didn't want to understand. The company above them coordinated the releases of new independent films in the major cities of the Netherlands and Belgium. Their floor didn't creak. At least she never heard a thing from their office.

All three companies shared the same canteen on the top floor. They hardly ever mingled though.

Grace shared an office with Martin, a Senior Actuary Manager who led all the technical actuarial projects, such as embedded value reviews, audit support, modelling, M&A and financial reporting. He had a receding hairline and wore trousers that were too short for him. Or maybe he just pulled them up too much. Either way, Grace couldn't help smirking when she walked behind him. It was as if someone gave him a wedgie and he never noticed. She often wondered if someone ought to tell him.

'Morning, Grace.'

'Morning, Martin.'

'The files from the THH project are lying on your desk,' he said, straight down to business as usual.

'Okay, thanks. You want coffee?' she asked as she switched on her computer and logged in.

Martin shook his head. 'I have a conference call in two minutes. I'll get some on my way to the meeting room.'

Grace went to fetch coffee from the machine in the hallway while her computer warmed up. Dirty cups still lay on top of the dishwasher, despite the dishwasher being wide open and half full. She couldn't understand why people didn't put their cups in the dishwasher. She found a clean one, placed it in the coffee machine and clicked on *Café au Lait*. The servings were so small that she clicked on it again for a second one. In some of the mugs you could actually fit three servings. As for espressos, rumour had it that you could fit eleven servings into one of the mugs. Although why anyone would want to do that was a different story.

She returned to her room and glanced at the file on her desk. 'Did you have a look at them yourself?' she asked Martin.

'Yes, my feedback is written in red.'

She opened the file and scanned through it. His feedback was indeed in red. Sometimes it felt like she was back in school.

'Did you grade it too?'

Martin smiled from behind his screen but didn't look up. 'B minus.'

'Not bad, eh?' she said as she sat down and took a sip of her café au lait.

Martin continued to tap on his keyboard, with his two index fingers, before poking his head up and looking over his screen. 'Is everything okay?'

'Yes, why?' She opened up Microsoft Outlook and waited for the influx of emails.

Martin stood up and closed the door. 'Your husband called your direct line yesterday morning, early.'

'Oh.'

'I answered it of course, as it wouldn't stop ringing. He kind of pretended to be a customer, but after all these years I know what your husband sounds like.'

An email alert announced the first of many emails to Grace's inbox. She muted the sound of her computer.

'You don't have to say anything, Grace, but if there are problems at home and you want to discuss them, I'm here, okay?'

She nodded, but couldn't imagine a least likely colleague she would share her problems with than Martin.

'Thank you. I'd rather not go into it now.'

'No problem.'

She turned back to her computer but was wrong to assume the conversation was over.

'When Joyce and I divorced three years ago,' he continued, 'I didn't want anyone to know.'

She wasn't sure if this required a response. She continued to look at her screen as the emails continued to flow in. Fifty-four so far.

'It was my fault of course,' he added. 'It's only after she's gone that you realise that it was probably for the best.'

Grace was confused. 'For the best? What do you mean?'

'Well, yes if it's not working, it's not working. For instance, say you have a broken car. I mean you can go on for years trying to drive it. You can get it fixed every now and then, and then after a while it breaks again. Sometimes it's best just to trade it for another model.'

'Or a *younger* model you mean?' she said, unable to believe that Martin was comparing a husband-wife relationship to a driver and a car. 'You had an affair with a student you met online.'

He smiled almost proud of the fact. 'Nobody's perfect.'

'I'd appreciate it if you didn't compare my situation with yours.'

'I'm not. I don't even know what your situation is.'

'Let's just keep it that way for now, okay?'

'Sure.'

He picked up some files, along with his mug which had an image of the Canadian maple leaf on it. 'If anyone's looking for me, I'm in The Sunflowers having a conference call.' The three meeting rooms at Kuhlman's were named after famous Dutch paintings, the other two being The Nightwatch and The Milkmaid.

Grace nodded. Martin left the room, leaving the door ajar. As she read through her emails, she saw at the corner of her eye someone appearing at the door.

'You left while I was in the shower,' Rik said.

She looked at him slightly annoyed. 'Can you say it a little louder? Maybe Cynthia downstairs didn't hear you.'

He looked behind him and dismissed her sarcasm with a wave. 'Relax. Hardly anybody's in yet,' he said as he walked towards her desk carrying a file.

'I brought this,' he said holding up the file in his hand. 'In case someone enters and we need to change the subject quickly.'

'Good thinking,' she said relaxing a bit as she took a sip of coffee. 'But from which subject do we need to change?'

He looked around the office. His eyes fell to a clear space on the desk. He decided to chance it. He half sat and half leaned on the desk.

'Go ahead and sit on my desk,' she offered as she leaned back in her chair with her mug cupped in two hands.

'I wanted to check if you didn't leave early because of something I did or didn't do.'

Grace's mouth moved to one side, clearly thinking of something to say. Unsure whether to take the humorous route or the serious route, she decided for somewhere in between.

'No, of course not. But we can't arrive at work at the same time holding hands.'

'Of course not. I perfectly understand…,' he trailed off. 'Why would we be holding hands?'

'Forget it. It was a joke.'

'So that was the reason?'

'The reason for what?'

'For leaving while I was in the shower? So it doesn't start rumours?'

'Yes, more or less.'

'It wasn't anything I did?'

She shook her head. 'No. Why would you think that?'

A photo frame next to Grace's screen caught his eye. It was a picture of Grace and Otto taken five years previously during a weekend in Barcelona. She noticed Rik looking at it but said nothing. She often contemplated removing the photo, but it would have raised too many suspicions around the office, so she left it there, collecting dust.

'When are you going to collect your stuff?' he asked.

'I'm not sure. Right now my head is overloaded. Between work and my private life, I can't think beyond today.' She glanced at her screen as the messages in her in-box came to a stand-still. 124 unread.

Could be worse, she thought.

'I'm more than happy to help you, but this weekend doesn't look good as I have that hockey weekend away with the team.' Rik said. 'You can come with me if you want. The rest of the team are bringing partners. I don't mind if you came… as a sort of friend.'

'*A sort* of friend? Jeez, thanks. Is that a compliment?' she said, teasing him.

'No, I mean you are more than welcome,' He tried to clarify, '…you know. To get away for a few nights and just forget about things here. It's in the Ardennes. Belgium.'

'You just want to get me drunk again and take advantage of me.'

Rik decided to play along with her light-hearted comments. 'Exactly. It didn't work the other night. So second time lucky.' He let a moment elapse and continued on a more serious tone. 'Of course not. I just thought it might be a nice break. You get to meet some new people.'

'I know what you're trying to do, and I appreciate it,' she said. 'But to be honest, I think this weekend would be a good time to clear my head. I need to think what the next steps are for me.'

'File for a divorce. Move in with me,' he blurted out.

She wondered briefly if he was still being serious. Judging from the sincerity in his eyes, she realised he meant every word of it. She tried to make light of the suggestion without offending him.

'Do you have any idea of the amount of shit I own? It would fill every cubic inch of your apartment from floor to ceiling.' She shook her head. 'No, I probably need to find my own place.'

He glanced at the photo one more time. 'Well, I guess you won't be going to your husband's notary firm to do the purchase agreement when you buy a new place?'

She shook her head. 'I guess not. Assuming I buy a place.'

'I guess renting is also an option.'

She placed her mug on her desk on top of a pad of Post-Its. 'I'm not even sure if I want to stay in Holland.'

Rik looked at her as if she had just tugged a rug from beneath his feet. 'Seriously,' he said, with a weak smile. 'You're thinking of leaving?'

She glanced quickly towards the door and considered touching his hand. She changed her mind at the last second.

'I'm keeping my options open, Rik. As much as I love it here, the person I moved here for turned out to be a bastard. Maybe it's best to start somewhere new.

Somewhere with no memories of me and Otto.'

Rik looked at her but said nothing.

'I don't know what I'm doing right now, Rik. I really appreciate your kindness and generosity. But I'm not ready for a fling right now. Or any kind of serious relationship. I'm going through a difficult stage and I want to take it one step at a time.'

He swallowed hard and looked behind Grace. On the magnetic whiteboard behind her hung various photos and flyers, even the occasional postcard. On the corner of the board there was a random drawing of some lines, squares and an arrow. It was a drawing that no doubt had an explanation accompanying it when it was drawn. Perhaps it was meant to show directions. Perhaps it was a piece of IKEA furniture. It reminded Rik of a kid's drawing; a simple, innocent, line drawing. His focus went back to Grace.

'Children. You want children, don't you? ' he asked. 'You're at that age when you want kids, but have just realised you've married the last person in the world whose genes you want to pass to your offspring.'

Grace looked away and took a deep breath. She picked up a random pen that was lying on her desk and clicked it. 'You're not completely wrong, Rik. I wouldn't want any child to have genes from that man. But to be honest... '

'I want to have kids too, you know,' Rik blurted out before she could finish her sentence. 'I mean some day. I want to have them. The sooner the better, I guess. If you gave us a chance, then maybe… it could work.'

Grace looked up at him. She searched for any sarcasm in his expression, but found none. It dawned on her that he was being deadly serious.

'Oh Rik,' she said. This time she did touch his hand. It was their first intimate moment since Monday night. At least the first one she could remember. 'That's sweet, assuming you're serious. But you have your whole life ahead of you. Trust me. You do not want to be tied down with the responsibility involved in having kids. Enjoy your life while you're still young.'

He smiled. 'Are you trying to say that people who have kids don't enjoy their lives?'

She shook her head. 'No. That's not what I'm saying at all.' Looking up at him again she continued. 'It's just that you're young. Ten years younger than me, maybe. I'm not the...' she trailed off trying to think what way to put it. 'I'm not the right long-term partner you need. Even if you don't realise it now. Sooner or later a nice younger girl will come by.'

'And if she doesn't?'

She moved her hand from Rik's as she spotted a stray hair on the desk. It was one of hers. She picked it up and let it fall to the floor. Eventually she said, 'When I was your age, I went out with a wonderful guy. A truly wonderful guy whom I shared a lot of time and experiences with. One day he just walked out.' She stopped. She reviewed her sentence mentally and wondered if she should give more information on why he walked out. Deciding against it, she moved on. 'Although it hurt at the time, and in a way it still hurts when I think about it, I don't regret one moment we spent together.'

Rik wasn't sure where she was going with her story. As if reading his thoughts she clarified what she was trying to say.

'My point is that you will meet someone like that. A young girl with lots in common. Someone with whom you can share your dreams.' She realised she was touching on a level of sentimentality that she was just not accustomed to. 'Or share your wild sexual fantasies with,' she added trying to spice things up a bit. 'Someone special. I know you'll meet her. And it will be someone who would fit right in when it comes to a weekend away with your hockey buddies. Not someone who's just *couch surfing* for a few nights.'

'That's another thing. I don't want you sleeping on the

sofa...' He suddenly stopped as he saw Grace's eyes shoot to the door. He stood up as Grace thought of something to say quickly.

'Well I would just run it by the Financial Officer at the company and compare it to their previous life assurance policy. That's the only way we can really make ground.'

Martin was back from his conference.

'The UK is an hour behind, aren't they?' he muttered under his breath as he placed the file he was holding on his desk.

Rik and Grace smirked at each other, out of Martin's comments and the quick cover-up Grace had managed to come up with.

'Okay, I'll run it by him,' he said, and gave her a quick wink.

A minute later she received an email from him that made her smile.

You're not such a bad actor yourself!

22

The silence that governed the house since Max died was unbearable. Claire sat on the sofa with a mug of wine in her hand staring at an empty television screen. Even with the ridiculous amount of channels they had, she couldn't think of anything remotely interesting that she wanted to watch.

Her thoughts turned to the meeting with Edward at Superquinn the previous day. Was she glad that she had met Edward? Did she even meet him or was it her imagination?

It was real.

'Talk to him?' she whispered. 'That is so fucked up.' She took another sip of wine. 'I just want to *be* with him.' Her hand caressed the arm of the sofa. It was becoming threadbare. They always agreed to buy a new sofa when Max was old enough not to spill food or drink on it. How many times, like a comic book superhero, had Max climbed onto the arm of the sofa and jumped from it?

She took another mouthful of wine, easing the pain inside her. She noticed that it was taking more and more to ease the pain. The alcohol was like a drug and she was becoming more tolerant to it. How many glasses of wine did she drink per day? It reached the stage that she now counted in bottles. Was it one? No, definitely more now. One and a half, sometimes two per day. The worst thing about it is that she stopped using wine glasses. They spilled over too easily with their long stems. She wondered what eejit could have invented such a ridiculously shaped glass. If there was a mishap during a dinner, nine times out of ten it was the wine glass falling over.

Not for Claire though. She now used a mug. It was less likely to topple over. It had the extra advantage of hiding its contents. From the distance it could be a harmless cup of tea.

It reminded her of her days of being a student in DCU. She shared a house on Ballymun Road with four other female students. Usually before going out they would have other students drop by. It wasn't long before the three resident wine glasses were taken. Then the normal glasses were used. And finally the mugs. By the time she got round to pouring a glass of wine, it would be into a mug. Still, it served its purpose.

Back then it was social drinking, everybody having a bit of *craic*, a bit of fun.

What was it now?

It wasn't even drowning sorrows. Drowning sorrows was when your team lost a match, you have a bit of drink and then next day everything is back to normal.

Nothing would ever be back to normal.

She wanted the pain to go. She wanted to feel numb. That was it. The wine helped her feel numb. But no matter how much she drank, no matter how drunk she became, deep inside her, it remained.

The pain. The memories.

'It's always there,' she whispered.

Go home, have a little conversation with him and move forward.

'I can't. I don't want to move forward.'

What was she afraid of? Deep down she was afraid that moving forward would mean she would forget about him? That the memories would fade? She didn't want her memories to fade. If anything, she wanted them to become stronger. To have new ones of things she had long forgotten about.

She sighed deeply. 'Goddammit.'

She glanced at her mug. It seemed to be getting bigger. Or perhaps the contents inside were diminishing. How many more would she have to drink today to feel numb? She grasped the handle stronger. She could hear Edward's voice again:

What would Max say if he could see you now?'

'I can't do this anymore.' She brought the mug to her lips and then stopped.

One more sip.

'No.' A tear fell. 'I can't keep doing this.'

She stood up. Dizziness swept over her. She walked slowly to the kitchen. She moved to the sink and stopped. Slowly she tipped the mug over and watched the wine disappear down the sink.

'I'm sorry.' She wasn't sure who she was apologising to. Herself? Max? The wine itself?

Maybe all three.

She rinsed the cup and left it on the draining board. Next she opened the fridge and removed two chilled bottles of white wine, one already opened, one unopened. She tipped the remains of the opened one down the sink first, followed by the full one. She couldn't trust herself anymore. Opening the cupboard beside the sink, she placed them next to the other empty bottles. She would bring them to the bottle recycling container soon.

Looking in the sink she saw the wine slowly disappearing. Rice that was stuck in the plug hole from the previous evening was slowing down its progress. She continued to stare at the wine.

She vowed that next time she would drink wine it would be in a normal wine glass, in a social environment. No more drinking alone. No more drinking from mugs. No more drinking to numb an indestructible pain.

23

Daniel entered the Stag's Head just off Dame Street and looked around. He spotted John in the corner, reading. As he crossed the floor; he pulled the headphones from his ears and wrapped the wire around his iPod nano.

'Well, here we are again.' John said as he shook Daniel's hand. Daniel looked around taking in the leather chairs, stained glass windows and big mahogany bar with its red Connemara marble top. It was often considered as Dublin's best preserved Victorian pub.

'God, this place hasn't changed a bit. I used to come here a lot when I was in Trinity.' Daniel pulled up a stool, placed his iPod on the table and looked around.

The after-work crowd started to gather in their dribs and drabs, along with students and the occasional shopper. The early evening sunlight filtering through the stained glass window seemed to add colour to random faces as they entered - a natural rejuvenation.

'I think that's what makes this place so special. The fact that it doesn't change.' John nodded towards the mosaic marble tiled floors. 'Think of the all the people of Dublin's past who have walked on that floor.'

Daniel looked down almost expecting to see a *Hollywood Walk of Fame* type floor. Thankfully, he was met with the same mosaic marble tiles that he remembered as a student. They hadn't changed in decades - maybe centuries.

'Do you want a pint?' John asked.

Daniel looked at his watch. It was 5:48pm. 'Are you having one?'

'Sure, why not? Do you not drink until after midnight or something?'

'To be honest, I try not to drink on weekdays.'

John laughed. 'So you were checking the day of the

week when you looked at your watch?'

'I don't know what I was checking.' He waved his hand in the air. 'Ah, feck it, give us a pint then.'

John raised his eyebrow. 'You sure? I don't want to be a bad influence on you.'

Daniel just smiled as John went to the bar.

The barman, probably a student himself, worked briskly behind the bar. He picked up a dishwasher tray of steaming glasses and plonked it down on the bar with a great clank. Obviously he had done it hundreds of times previously and wasn't afraid of smashing them. He left the glasses to air dry and nodded at John for his order.

Back at the table Daniel picked up a journal that lay open on it. John was in the middle of reading an article entitled: *Global stability of multi-group epidemic models with distributed delays.* Using his finger as a bookmark, Daniel flipped through the journal and scanned the articles. Looking at the various mathematical equations, he got a funny feeling inside. It was as if a door to a past life was opening before him. The mathematical equations and symbols almost called out to him.

Hey, where have you been, Daniel?

They were like old friends. He turned the issue to view the front cover. *Journal of Mathematical Analysis and Applications.* He didn't recall the name. But then again why would he? There were so many journals back then. Even more nowadays, he was sure.

John arrived back at the table. 'The barman will bring them over.'

Daniel flicked back to the original page and placed the journal back down on the table.

'I see something caught your interest,' John said

'Yes. It's just funny looking through a journal after so many years.'

'How do you feel about it?'

He shrugged. 'A bit strange. It's like being reacquainted with an old friend.' He pointed to the publisher's logo at the top of the article. 'Even the little Elsevier tree logo brings back so many memories.'

John looked at the journal and back to Daniel. 'So you're tempted to come back?'

He shook his head. 'I don't know, John. I just don't know.'

'It wouldn't be for long, if you did want to try it out. Even if you came back part-time. You could submit your paper for publication, defend your thesis, receive your PhD.'

'And then go back to being a crane operator?'

'Entirely up to you.'

Daniel picked up a Bulmers Pear beer mat that had been lying on the table and started fiddling with it. 'Can I ask you a question?' he asked, as he pulled a strip from the beer mat and wrapped his chewing gum in it. As there were no ashtrays on the table anymore, since the introduction of the smoke-free laws, he just laid it on the table. 'And feel free not to answer it if you think it's too personal, but I'm just curious.'

John frowned and then his expression turned neutral. 'Sure. Go for it.'

'Why did you pick up my thesis after so long?'

The barman arrived with the two pints. 'Here you go, guys.'

Daniel slid his beermat to a better position on the table so the barman could place the pints down with ease. John handed him a tenner and told him to keep the change. He then turned to Daniel and gave a cautious smile, as if he was expecting that question sooner or later. He reached over and picked up the chewing gum that Daniel had just wrapped up. 'This is the reason.'

Daniel frowned and shook his head but said nothing. He had no clue what he meant.

'This is what triggered everything.'

'I don't understand.'

John remained silent for a while. 'I never told anyone

how I found him. My son.' He took a mouthful of Guinness and quickly wiped away the inevitable moustache. 'I never even told Claire in any great detail. Perhaps it's time to get it off my chest.'

24

'Did you wake Max up?' Claire shouted from downstairs.

John was shaving. 'Not yet,' he cried as he wiped the condensation from the mirror in front of him. 'Relax. We'll be on time. I told you that I'll drop him off at school before I start.'

John rinsed his face with the foamy water and wondered briefly why he was shaving in the first place. As he patted his face dry, he put it down to routine. He had taken the day off work on the garden furniture, which was something they had been putting off for far too long. When John and Claire had bought the house nine years previously, they had also purchased an expensive handmade oak furniture set. It consisted of a beautiful solid table and four chairs. Over the years the Irish weather had given them a fair beating and it was time to restore them before it was too late.

The previous weekend John had sanded the table and chairs. Now it was a matter of cleaning them and applying several coats of varnish. They had visitors coming for a barbeque the following weekend so it had to be done before then. Claire couldn't stand the fumes from the varnish and asked John to do it. As he didn't have any lectures or meetings planned, he decided to work from home and take time off to apply the coats of varnish that were needed.

Picking up a bottle of Clinique post-shave healer he rubbed it into his freshly shaved face.

'Time to get up, Max. Are you awake?' he shouted towards his son's bedroom. The door was still closed.

No answer. He threw the towel over his shoulder and crossed the landing to Max's room. As he opened the door and poked his head in, he could immediately hear a faint din. His son lay still, with his headphones on.

'No wonder you can't hear me,' he said as he entered the room and walked towards the bed. As he approached he got a sense that something was wrong. Max lay face down looking to one side.

'Max,' he said raising his voice to beat the volume of the music. 'Wake up, Max.' He waited for movement. He placed his hand on Max's shoulder. It didn't feel right.

'Max. Wake up,' he said in a nervous voice. Slowly he moved his hand to the cheek of his son. It was like an electric shock. He pulled away quickly. Cold. His son was cold. His first thought was that the window was left open, but he quickly dismissed it. He got down on his knees and stared at his son's face. His eyes were closed. But his tongue was sticking out.

'Jesus Christ!'

John froze as he stared at his son. Slowly he picked up Max's iPod and fumbled. He tore the headphones out. The music ceased. He prayed that this would cause Max to stir. He begged that this would cause his son to jump to life, to grumble, like he had always done when he was annoyed. *What are you doing, Dad?! I was listening to that.* He was never afraid to speak his mind.

Nothing.

He placed his hand on Max's face again. It felt surreal, like the skin of an uncooked chicken when you remove it from the refrigerator.

'I'm going now!' came a cry from downstairs.

John jumped with a start. Claire was calling from below.

'See you later!' she shouted.

He got up and ran to the landing. He stopped.

Say something. Say something.

'See you later.' John said and took a deep breath. He covered his face immediately with his hands. His hands shook. He spoke softly into his hands.

'Tell her. Tell her. Tell her. Don't go. Please don't go.'

'Is he getting up?' she asked.

John pulled his face away from his hands.

'Yes,' he shouted without thinking. Trying to remain calm, he hoped that she wouldn't hear a difference in his voice.

He heard the front door opening and closing. Taking a deep breath, he walked softly to the master bedroom. He pulled the curtains slightly to one side and saw Claire getting into the car. He would never forget the look on her face. Calm. Confident. Content. The look of a woman who had never experienced real loss. Real pain.

'Don't go,' John whispered. His vision became blurred. He blinked and felt the first tear trickle down his cheek.

'Don't go,' he mumbled. It wasn't too late. He could run downstairs and stop her. But something stopped him. What was it? Why couldn't he move?

'Don't leave me alone. Don't make me go through this by myself.'

The car reversed out the driveway and took off towards the motorway. He was alone in the house with his son. Half naked with a towel on his shoulder. His dead son in the bedroom, next to him. He collapsed on the floor with a hand to his mouth, muffling the hysterical roar that he let out.

*

John had finished his pint by the time he had recounted the worst day of his life. Daniel was only half way through his.

'After Claire left I just walked back into his bedroom and lay beside him. I tried to hold his hand but it was impossible because of the rigor mortis. It was a very surreal experience. Someone who was normally so full of life just lying there. Stone cold. It was awful. I don't know how long I lay there with him, fifteen minutes. Maybe half-an-hour. He had choked on chewing gum during the night. It just completely blocked his windpipe. He died peacefully in his sleep. Or so the coroner said. It was a horrific accident. Nothing more. Nothing less.' He looked towards the stained glass window. 'If your thesis could have predicted that, however absurd it might sound, well, what more can I say? That was the reason I picked it up again after all these years. To give it a second chance and see if we can get it out there into the mathematical world to develop further. To prevent another parent from going through what I did.'

25

Daniel stared at the final result and shook his head. 'It can't be.'

The kitchen was a mess again. Scraps of paper lay scattered on the kitchen table. Some of them even lay on the floor. He had been busy with the calculation all day, pausing only for dinner. With the kitchen table being temporarily out of bounds, they had bent the rules of the house and ate dinner in front of the TV. Sean loved the idea and wished that his dad worked more often on the kitchen table.

Daniel walked over to the counter and poured himself a cup of tea from the teapot. As he took a sip, a look of distaste went through his face. 'How in the name of God is it so cold?' he asked himself, thinking that he just made it ten minutes ago. He looked at the clock on the microwave oven. It was 2:23am. He had been so engrossed in the calculation he lost track of time. Zoe and Sean were long gone to bed.

He wondered for a moment if he had read to Sean earlier in the evening? No. He couldn't remember. Everything seemed like a blur, like he had just come out of a coma. *Is that a good sign?* he wondered. He became so preoccupied with the work that his world existed of just himself and the thesis. It was a similar situation to many years previously.

No. There was also Grace back then.

With the cup in his hand, he walked back to the kitchen table and sat down. The date stared back at him. It was an eight digit number. The day, the month, the year.

'This is really strange,' he muttered.

He had already gone through the entire calculation twice. It was too late to do it a third time. His brain really needed to rest. But there was something at the back of his mind that was nagging at him. What was it? There was something about his thesis. Was he forgetting something?

He rubbed both his eyes with his thumb and forefinger and yawned. 'Jesus, I can't do this anymore.'

He remembered back in university that sometimes he had worked through the night, hardly realising what the time was. It was only when the sun started to break through the slits in the blinds that he knew it was time to sleep.

A certain loneliness hung in the air when it came to staying up all night. Or being still awake when everyone would soon be coming out of their deep sleeps. Daniel took satisfaction in the fact that, at least now, the sun wasn't beginning to rise yet.

Picking up a pen, he wrote the result in a correct date format. The number, followed by the actual month and the year. He then drew a circle around it. As if a circle would protect the date from the consequences it had in real life.

From the corner of his eye, he noticed the door opening slightly. He looked up and saw Sean peeking through the gap in the door. Daniel pretended to be startled when he made eye contact. This made Sean giggle as he pushed the door open the whole way. Daniel's startled look transformed into a warm smile when he saw his son standing at the doorway in his Transformer pyjamas. One of the legs of his pyjamas was caught above his knee. The other leg had a toothpaste stain on it. His hair was messy and his eyes were squinted, as he still got used to the bright kitchen light.

'Hey mister, what's up?' Daniel asked.

'I'm thirsty,' Sean said as he walked slowly into the kitchen. Daniel got up and walked with him towards the sink.

'You're in your bare feet, pet. Aren't your feet cold?'

Sean shrugged. Daniel opened the dishwasher expecting to be hit in the face with a cloud of steam. But the dishwasher had finished its cycle so long ago that the steam had gone elsewhere. He pulled out the top rack and took a glass. It was still a little warm. He placed it on the counter.

'You want some Ribena?'

Sean stopped in his tracks and scratched his unkempt hair. 'Does it mean that I have to brush my teeth again?'

Daniel smiled as he reached for the Ribena bottle in the cupboard next to the cooker and placed it next to the glass.

'No, you're alright,' he said. 'I won't tell Mammy if you won't.' They were about to shake on it when Sean pulled away in the last minute.

'Biscuit too?'

Daniel retracted his hand as well and placed his hands on his hips. He looked towards the kitchen door that was now left ajar.

'Are you sure Mammy is asleep?'

Sean nodded eagerly.

'Did you hear snoring?'

'Yeah or ...' Sean thought for a moment. Daniel could almost hear his brain working. 'Mammy doesn't snore. You snore.'

'Oh yeah?' He grabbed Sean in a friendly headlock. 'What makes you so sure that Mammy doesn't snore?'

Sean burst out laughing. 'Daddy! Let go!'

Daniel tried to quieten him. 'Ssh! Quiet. Mammy will hear you and then we'll both be in trouble.'

'Well, give me the biscuit and I'll go,' he said in between jolts of laughter. He tried to wriggle free but Daniel was too strong for him.

'Okay, I'll let you go,' Daniel announced. 'But you have to eat your biscuit and drink your Ribena quickly.'

'I can't breathe!'

'Do we have a deal?'

'Yes.'

Daniel let him go. His hair was even more muffled than before. And his face was red with laughter. He wiped away a piece of saliva that had landed on his chin during the headlock. He stood in front of his father, put his hand out, closed his eyes, and said, 'Ribena and biscuit please.'

'Cheeky fecker,' Daniel snorted.

'Mammy said not to use that word.'

'Which word? Cheeky?' he asked, challenging his boy.

'No. The other word, beginning with "F".'

'Is that right now? Mammy also says to keep a glass of water beside your bed at night. I don't suppose you did that now, did you?'

The boy walked towards the kitchen table and sat down where Daniel had been sitting.

'Well, I did actually. But Ribena is yummier.' He looked around the table, with all the papers and mess. 'What are you doing here anyway, Dad?'

'Something for work.'

'Homework?'

Daniel nodded. 'Something like that.'

Sean picked up one of the many scraps of paper and analysed it.

'Do you want a hand with it?'

'No, thanks.'

'You help me with my homework. Maybe I can help you with your homework?'

'Well, to be honest, I think I'm kind of finished.'

'Do you have to hand it in tomorrow?'

'I suppose you could say that. I have to hand it in as soon as possible.'

Daniel poured a little Ribena into a glass and topped it up with water. He opened the cupboard and took a digestive biscuit.

'Ah, Daddy, can I not have something with chocolate on it?'

'Are you joking me? At this time of night?'

Sean realised that Daniel wasn't going to budge on that debate.

'Ah, well. It was worth a try,' he admitted, as he laid the

143

scrap of paper back on the table.

'Was it now?' Daniel brought the biscuit and drink over to him.

'That looks complicated,' Sean said staring at all the calculations in front of him. 'It's like lots of sums.'

'That's right. It *is* lots of sums.'

'Lots and lots of sums.'

'A whole lot.'

'Did you get the right answer?'

Daniel smiled at the innocence of the question. 'I don't know yet.'

'Isn't the answer at the back of your book?'

He shook his head. 'If only. It would have saved me a lot of work.'

'Is this your answer?' Sean asked pointing to date with the circle around it.

'It sure is.'

'It's a date?'

Daniel nodded.

'Oh that's easy. We did dates at school. We have to write them on the top right of our page if we start a new exercise.'

'Good. That's good practice.'

'I hope you get it right.'

Daniel remained silent, not sure how to answer it. How could he tell his son that he hoped the opposite?

'We'll see.'

Sean ate his digestive biscuit for a while in silence. He took a swig of his Ribena and glanced at his Ben10 watch. He pressed a button a couple of times and then looked at the date on the table. He then turned towards his father. It was clear that he was trying to figure something out.

'Hey, that date you wrote down. That's in two days, isn't it?'

Although Daniel had realised it already, it was as if Sean saying it out loud made it even more real.

'Yes, it is.'

26

John woke with a start. He had been lying on the sofa watching Prime Time when he nodded off. Looking around he noticed that the current affairs program was over and some awful American sitcom was now contaminating his TV screen. He placed his hand over his head to grab the remote control he had left on the arm of the sofa. He misjudged its position and ended up knocking it to the floor. It landed with a clank, and the batteries scattered across the room.

'Shit.'

As if on cue, laughter from the sitcom audience could be heard from the TV. He stretched his arms and rubbed his eyes. He wondered what made him wake so abruptly anyway. He reached to the ground and felt around for his mobile. He always left it on the floor while lying on the sofa. There was something about keeping it in his pocket while sitting or lying on the sofa that he disliked immensely, especially on this sofa. John often joked that it was designed by the Artful Dodger. It seemed you only had to sit on it for a second and the contents of your pockets would disappear.

He pressed a random key on his mobile and the display panel lit up. Long enough to tell him that it was 2:31am. On the corner of the display, the "message received" icon was visible. Maybe it was the receipt of the text message that woke him up. He unlocked the keypad and scrolled to the incoming message.

The sender was Daniel.

"Hi, John. Can you call me if you're still awake? Otherwise, I'll talk to you tomorrow. I have a result. Daniel."

John sat up, suddenly wide-awake. It was as if someone had thrown ice-cold water over him. His foot hit off one of the batteries from the remote control and sent it flying across the floor. Again, an over-the-top sound of laughter resonated from the TV. Instead of wasting time gathering up the batteries from the remote control, he got up and switched off the TV on the device itself.

He sat back down on the sofa and called Daniel.

'Hi, John,' Daniel answered. 'Sorry for contacting you so late. I hope I didn't wake you with my text?'

'No, not at all,' he lied. 'Well, actually you did, but it was a good thing you did. I was just dozing on the sofa. I might have spent the whole night here otherwise.' he admitted. *And it wouldn't have been the first time*, he thought to himself.

'Well I have a result, John.' He paused. 'I don't know if it's right. It has really been tough. You see, I remember I put something in the formula as a deliberate error, but now I don't know if I left it there or not in the final thesis.'

John was confused. 'What do you mean exactly?'

'I was a bit overprotective and I guess naïve. I didn't want anyone stealing my ideas.'

'I remembered you mentioned something like that the other day in Bewley's. You remind me of Da Vinci sometimes.'

'What do you mean?'

'In order to protect his ideas from being stolen or abused by others, Leonardo left some information out of his designs.'

'Oh. I didn't know that. I remember doing something like that while I was working on it, but I can't recall if I left it there or decided to take it out before submitting it.'

'I assume you would have taken it out. Submitting a thesis with deliberate misinformation contained in it would not have been the wisest thing to do. Not that the reviewing committee even got that far with your one.'

'You're right. Come to think of it, I must have removed it before submitting.'

There was silence on the line. Finally John asked, 'So what's the date and how sure are you of it?'

Daniel bit his lip. 'I went through it a few times and as long as there isn't some misinformation in it, then I'm pretty certain of it.' He waited for a short moment before proceeding. 'The date I calculated is this coming Saturday.'

John stayed deathly still and silent.

'John?'

'Yes, I'm here,' he said. 'You mean Saturday the tenth? This weekend?'

'Correct.'

'The same date as Grace?'

'Yes.' With his little finger, Daniel swept the crumbs of Sean's biscuit together into a tiny pile. 'I hope I'm wrong, John, I really do.'

'And if you're right?'

Daniel didn't understand the question completely. 'What do you mean if I'm right? If I'm right it means your wife is going to die on Saturday.' He ran his hand through his hair. 'I thought you understood?'

'I meant if you're right, what are you going to do about your thesis?'

Daniel let out a sigh. 'I don't know.'

'Will you come back?'

'Back?'

'Back to university.'

He closed his eyes and shook his head. 'Listen, I'm tired. I need to go bed.' He took a deep breath, unable to fully comprehend John's question. 'I just told you the date your wife might die and you're more concerned about me coming back to defend my thesis. What are you doing?'

'You're right, Daniel. I'm sorry,' he admitted. 'I'm really tired too. I'm not thinking straight.'

They both remained silent for several moments. Daniel looked at the mess he still needed to clean up. Would everything go straight back to the attic? He took hold of the corner of a random page and flicked through the thesis. It was more out of affection than anything else. Years ago, the folder in front of him had been his baby.

Now that it had come back into his life, what was the right thing to do?

'Are you still there,' John asked.

'I'm still here.'

'What am I going to do, Daniel? I will miss her.'

'Well, then don't let her out of your sight on Saturday. Do you hear me? If possible, don't let her leave the house. Just for that day. Forget about my thesis. I don't give a shit about it.'

'I don't think you mean what you're saying.'

Daniel was about to reply when the line went dead. He listened to the tone for some moments before hanging up too.

Looking at the mess, he wondered if he *did* mean what he just said. He lowered his head onto his arm. Resting. Exhaustion had snuck up on him. His eyelids became heavier, almost as if tiny invisible anvils were attached to each.

Did I mean what I said?

His mind was too disorientated.

Forget about my thesis. I don't give a shit about it.

He was exhausted.

But you do, Daniel, a voice in his head told him. *You do. And in a few months you could be the biggest name in mathematics.*

That was his last thought before he fell asleep.

Part II

To lose one's wealth is sad indeed,
To lose one's health is more,
To lose one's soul is such a loss
That no man can restore.

Robert H Smith

27

Although the autumn weather was gradually moving in, and the temperatures were back to single digits, Claire decided to hang out the washing on the clothesline anyway. There was something about letting Mother Nature dry clothes that she loved. The breeze seemed to add a layer of freshness to the clothes that tumble dryers or radiators just couldn't. Or maybe she was too much influenced by the washing detergent commercials with the big white sheets blowing in the wind. Either way, she never understood people who constantly used tumble dryers when they had the option to hang the clothes outside.

She returned to the utility room next to the kitchen with the empty washing basket. As she placed it on top of the washing machine, she heard something fall behind it. Moving the basket out of the way, she bent forward and scanned the back of the washing machine. She could see the little plastic ball used for washing detergent jammed at the back.

'Shit.' Placing the basket on the floor, she leaned on top of the washing machine and slowly reached her arm down the back. Because of the tight fit against the wall, she was unable to look and reach at the same time. She could hear creaks coming from the top of the washing machine as it gradually took her weight. It was too tight to place her hand all the way down. She stood upright. Grabbing a front corner of the washing machine and the diagonally opposite back corner, she crouched down and pulled. She managed to move it out a few centimetres. It would be sufficient for her to reach her arm all the way down. At least that's what she hoped.

Again she leaned on top of it and reached down behind it. This time she was able to stretch all the way down.

Although she was still unable to see what she was doing, she knew that the plastic ball wouldn't be too difficult to find. Suddenly she felt something soft. It wasn't the plastic ball, but at the same time it wasn't something that belonged at the back of the washing machine. She pulled it up. When she saw what it was, she slowly removed her weight and stood upright. The plastic ball would have to wait.

It was a stray sock, an old football sock belonging to Max. As she held it up in front of her, she wondered how long it had been there. A collection of dust and fluff were stuck to it. She blew at it and watched some of the fluff flutter to the top of the washing machine. Although she was tempted to sniff it, she decided against it at the last moment. A wave of intense sadness came over her. She took a deep breath.

'Come on, Claire,' she said to herself. 'Get a hold of yourself.' She unfolded the sock and held it out with two hands. She could imagine the scrawny smelly foot that went into it. Another sharp surge of pain rose from within her. She swallowed hard and tried to remember the words of advice Edward had given her. She closed her eyes.

Go home and listen to what your son says.

Claire opened her eyes again. She wasn't crying. Were there any tears left to shed? She decided to give the stranger's advice a go.

'You were looking for this a while ago, weren't you?' she asked. It came out more as a whisper.

Silence.

'Oh this is ridiculous,' she said. 'Who am I talking to?'

She heard Edward's advice again. *'I think part of her really does live within me.'*

She looked at the sock for a few more moments. She noticed some black rubber granules stuck to it, reminiscent of the artificial pitch on which the last game was played and this sock was worn. She decided to try again.

'Will I throw it away? I suppose you won't be needing

it?

Suddenly she heard his voice, in her mind.

'No, Mammy, I won't.'

Although it was her mind that created the voice, it felt kind of real.

'Is it smelly?' Max's voice asked.

'I haven't sniffed it yet,' she answered. 'I'm afraid to.'

'Why?'

'In case I smell you.'

'Mammy, it has been lying at the back of the washing machine for the past eight months. Even longer. You should be surprised if you smell anything other than fluff and dust.'

Claire wasn't sure what to say. Finally she said, 'I miss you, you know.'

'I know. I miss you too.'

'Am I going crazy?'

'Because you're imagining my responses?'

She nodded.

'No, you're not.'

'You're biased,' she said.

'Of course I am, but let me ask you something. Does it make you feel better?'

'I don't know yet. Maybe.'

'Well then. What's the problem?'

'I'm hearing voices.'

'You're not hearing voices, Mammy. You're just imagining what I would say if I was there, because you knew me more than anyone else. You knew me as much as I knew myself.'

'How am I going to continue?'

'With this conversation or with life in general?

She smiled, shaking her head.

'Still as cheeky as ever,' she whispered. She took a deep breath. 'With life in general?'

'That's the question, isn't it? You need to be strong.'

She picked up the washing basket and placed it back on the washing machine. 'Oh, this is ridiculous.'

'No, it's not. As long as you have memories of me, then in a way

I am still alive.'

'You really believe that?'

'It's not a question if I believe it or not. It's whether you believe it.'

Claire said nothing.

'Mammy?'

'Yes.'

'Why don't you give my stuff to charity? It's just collecting dust. You know it's what I would have wanted.'

'It's hard, pet. It's just so hard. But I'll try. I promise I will.'

'Well, you can at least start with that filthy sock.'

Claire burst out laughing.

28

Staring out of the window of tram number 5 from Amsterdam Central Station, Daniel got a fabulous view of the old Dutch architecture. Looking at the seventeenth and eighteenth-century gabled houses gave him the impression of it being one of the most historical intact cities he had ever visited. Not that he had visited a whole lot of historical cities in his life. Paris, Prague and Lisbon were about it. But it still gave him that great sense of being somewhere *foreign*.

Cyclists were out in full force utilising the endless network of bicycle lanes winding through the city, a grave difference to the scarce bicycle lanes in Dublin. Daniel suspected that Dublin Corporation had employed magicians to plan and construct the bicycle lanes. One would be cycling on them when all of a sudden, poof! They'd vanish.

As he looked at the Amsterdam cyclists from the tram, it reminded him of a scene from The Wizard of Oz where Dorothy's house is swept away by the hurricane. She looks through the window at her nasty neighbour, Miss Gulch, who later becomes the Wicked Witch of the West, cycling away. The bike is decrepit and old-fashioned. As Daniel stared onto the streets of Amsterdam it occurred to him that he was in a world of Wicked Witches of the West. Everybody seemed to cycle bikes from the 1950's. Racers and mountain bikes were almost non-existent, the ethnic minorities of the Dutch bicycle population.

Daniel checked into his hotel, The Green Tulip, that was situated on one of the central canals, Herengracht. It was an old gabled house that had been modernised into a small two star hotel. The modernisation was reasonable, but not enough to obliterate completely the feeling of staying in an historic building, which wasn't necessarily a negative thing.

The hotel room was small and cramped. It didn't really have enough space for the double bed. It was positioned with one side against the wall, so that if two people were sharing it, they would both have to climb into it from the same side. It didn't really bother Daniel, but he knew that if he was with Zoe, she would request another room.

As he glanced into the bathroom, he was surprised to see an actual bathtub. The silver mosaic-designed shower curtain scrunched to one side meant that it doubled as a shower. The bathroom seemed disproportionately bigger compared to the bedroom.

A sticker about saving the planet and re-using towels was stuck to the wall next to the mirror. It was beginning to peel. Two plastic cups wrapped in plastic stood on a small shelf just above the sink. Next to them there were small bottles of unbranded toiletries, enough for a stay of two or three nights. It was sufficient for Daniel. He had travelled very light. All his toiletries were also in small containers so that he could get through airport security without having to check-in luggage.

A strange dog-like stench lingered in the room. Remnants of the countless occupants, and their dogs, that had stayed there before him.

He walked to the window and looked out. He was slightly below the street level due to the structure of the building. From the reception he recalled that he had walked down a few steps. It wasn't a complete flight of stairs, and it wasn't as if he was in some kind of basement. It was just slightly below the street level. As a result, he was now looking up at passers-by.

It seems apt, he thought, *while staying in a country that is below sea level.*

He sat down at the end of the bed and wondered if he would make his contribution to the stench as he undid his G-Star trainers. He didn't know what it was about flying but it made his feet sweat like he had just ran a marathon through Bangkok. Peeling his socks off, he placed them one after the other on the end of the bed.

As he let his feet air dry, he went rummaging in his bag. By the time he found a pair of clean socks, his feet were dry. He put them on and lay back on his bed. How the little luxuries in life made all the difference.

Any feeling of luxury was short-lived. The mattress he lay on was hard and uncomfortable. Again if he were here with Zoe, she wouldn't put up with it.

We probably wouldn't have booked a two star hotel in the first place, he thought.

Closing his eyes he decided not to let it bother him. He figured the bed was probably good for his back.

His thoughts turned to Grace. Would *she* still recognise him after all these years? Had he changed much? Had she changed much?

Sitting up, he pulled out his wallet. He flicked through a selection of cards before coming to his old student card. He always carried around his final year student card as a memento, a sort of reminder of a period in his life where he had done so much and yet had so little to show for.

That, and also to try to get student discounts where he could.

The face of a younger Daniel looked back at him. He seemed to be a completely different person. Scruffy dark hair. Smoother skin. His eyebrows more pronounced than they were now. He couldn't recall when he started plucking his eyebrows, but was thankful that he did or he would look like Martin Scorsese by now.

The photo he had found in the attic was hidden behind his student card. He unfolded it and held it up. Looking at Grace his heart fluttered at the thought of seeing her soon. He wondered how much she had changed. He focussed on her face, especially on her eyes.

He often wondered if there was a time in life when happiness *peaked*. True happiness, without the complications associated with adulthood. A time without mortgages, bills, tight schedules, traffic jams. A time when worrying about the future would be postponed to one day in the future. Back then, wasn't there always a sense of enjoying life? Seizing the day? Even smoking cigarettes back then was enjoyable and nothing to worry about. It would be easy to give them up some day in the future. Wouldn't it? Let's just enjoy the day and see what tomorrow brings.

Did happiness reach a certain point and then slowly subside?

He rubbed his finger against Grace's face, reliving the intimate moments. She continued to smile back at him. It was the same smile that had been trapped there for more than twelve years, frozen in time.

Like the smile, he wondered if his feelings for Grace also froze. From the moment he walked out on her, did he somehow bury them? Were those feelings now slowing thawing, creeping back out from somewhere within, like an air bubble rising though the water? And would that air bubble grow in size as it reached the surface?

He suddenly felt guilty thinking about Grace the way he was. He loved Zoe. And Sean, of course. There was no doubt about that. He was very happy. But there was just something *different* with Grace. Perhaps it was a typical case of always wanting what you can't have. A feeling of the grass being greener on the other side. He was certain that if he had stayed together with Grace and had a child with her, his feelings would be different to what they were now.

What *were* they now?

Was he, in a strange way, still in love with Grace? Or was he in love with the *time* in his life when they had a relationship?

That was it, he thought. It was the time and place that he loved more than anything. The feeling of having the future ahead of him. A bright future.

He stood up and walked to a full length mirror by the door. He saw that he was no longer a teenager. He wasn't even in his twenties. Where had the time gone? The only feeling he had now was that the future was slowly overtaking him, and it was gradually becoming the past.

After Daniel had settled in and unpacked his few belongings, he threw some items into a shoulder bag and left his room. He stopped at the reception. The lady behind the desk was a short overweight lady of Indian descent. She seemed to have side-burns which Daniel found distracting. She was too engrossed in her mobile to notice him approaching.

He cleared his throat. 'Excuse me.'

The woman stopped what she was doing and looked up. 'Yes sir, how can I help you?'

He laid out the address that the professor had given him. 'I'm looking for this address here. Is this close?'

The receptionist moved her head to one side and said something in Dutch which Daniel assumed was the equivalent to 'mmm, let's see.'

On closer look, he realised that the woman didn't have side-burns, but strands of hair hanging around her ears where her side-burns would have been if she were a man. They were nevertheless disturbing. He turned his attention away from the woman's hair and back to the subject at hand.

'I also have this if it's any good.' He showed her a printout from GoogleMaps with a couple of circles marked on it.'

'Let's have a look.' The lady had a glance and shook her head. 'No, that's not that great, to be honest. It's not very detailed.'

She studied the address for a little while longer before she said, 'Okay, I think you need to turn left when you come out of the hotel and walk all the way down to Rozengracht and then left again until you come to Dam Square. From there, just jump on a Tram 5 and it should lead you in the right direction.'

The receptionist squinted her eyes as she studied the

map one more time.

'I think you need to get out at Benelux Baan and then just maybe ask someone.'

'Okay. Thanks very much.'

As he walked out of the hotel a cold gust of wind hit his face, a sharp bite. Although the weather was brighter than in Dublin, it was certainly colder. He walked in the direction the receptionist suggested. He looked at his watch. It was 3.31pm.

I probably have at least an hour and half to get there before she finishes for the day.

29

John was unable to concentrate at work. He had postponed an afternoon lecture on logarithm theorems to the following week. He sat alone in his office with the blinds shut staring at his computer screen, but couldn't focus.

How is Claire going to die? The question scared him. He didn't really want to lose her. Deep down, he still loved her, despite the widening gap between them. Despite the drink problem that was apparently growing out of control. It was impossible not to have noticed the collection of empty wine bottles in the cupboard next to the sink. Claire wasn't even trying to hide the problem.

Would things really get better if she died?

For her, maybe, thought John. *For Claire the pain would cease. Who was it that said 'Death was the cure of all disease?'*

But what about me? It was the first time he really gave it some thought. He would be left with nobody. Only memories. Memories of two wonderful people who made his life complete. He took a deep breath and rubbed his forehead. The question remained in his head.

How is she going to die?

On the computer screen in front of him was an article from ScienceDirect entitled "Fatal Unintentional Injuries in the Home in the U.S." According to the article more than 30,000 people died annually from unintentional injuries sustained at home during the period 2000 to 2008. John found it difficult to comprehend.

30,000.

It was twice the number of students registered at Trinity College.

He picked up a hair clip lying next to his laptop. He had no idea how a hair clip ended up there. Maybe the cleaners had found it and placed it there. Maybe it actually belonged to one of the cleaners and had fallen out. He pushed the clip out and back in again, making a 'click' sound, in and out as the question kept coming back to him. How was she going to die?

He couldn't think of a possible way. Would she die in the house or somewhere public while running an errand?

If she left the house, anything could happen, of course. She could get knocked down, or end up in a car crash. *But what if she just stayed in the house?* he thought. Would she get electrocuted? Would she cut herself with a carving knife so deeply that she would bleed to death? Would the fridge suddenly topple over and kill her?

It seemed ludicrous to even imagine these different scenarios. All these ways of dying suggested that she was some kind of clumsy individual, a character from a Loony Tunes cartoon. But she was nothing of the sort. She was the most careful person John knew. She was careful in every sense of the word. It was the way she would rotate the handle of a pot with hot contents around, even when Max was old enough to know not to touch it. The way she would run the cold water tap for a few seconds in case it still had hot water in the pipes. Even the way she would save an email before sending it, in case something crashed before she clicked on "Send".

The causes of home injury death based on the article in front of him were poisonings, falls, fires and burns, choking and suffocation, drowning... The list went on. Nothing seemed likely when it came to Claire. She was no fool. It was highly unlikely that her death would be a direct result of her action only.

He suddenly dreaded the thought that came to him. Would he have to do it himself? Now that he knew her date of death, was it up to him to actually pull it through?

Shaking his head suddenly like he had a twitch, he dispersed the ridiculous thought. He laid the hair clip back down on the desk and observed it wobbling from side-to-side. His thoughts went back to Max finding a hair clip in the local library once, and using it as a bookmark for his copy of *James and the Giant Peach*. He also remembered how he had told him off, saying that it was dirty and he should throw it away.

'Jesus, did I ever say anything nice to the boy?' he wondered out loud. 'Instead of admiring his innovation, I just complained.' He sighed heavily as he looked again at the hair clip.

'Or did I just care too much? I mean I just didn't want him getting lice.' His gaze remained fixed on the hair clip.

'Seriously though,' he thought to himself, *'how often was there a lice outbreak at school during Max's life?*

He couldn't think of a single occurrence.

'Why was I such a prick to him?'

He glanced around his cold, quiet office. A collection of mathematics journals lay in a chronological order on a mahogany bookshelf close to the window. Some of the journals contained articles he had written. He stood up and walked over to the bookshelf. He picked up one of the journals with a pink Post-It protruding from it. He flicked through it until he came to the page with the Post-It. It was bookmarking an article he had written four years previously.

'How many late nights did I spend in this room to get this submitted on time?' He shook his head with dismay at his own rhetorical question.

'Now all I have to show for it is a lifeless article, instead of a warm memory of doing something with Max. Playing football, painting a picture, reading a story...'

He walked back to his desk with the journal still in his hand. He removed the Post-It, crumpled it up and threw it in the waste paper basket beneath his desk. Carefully he slid the hair clip onto the opened page, and clicked the clip closed.

'Thank you, Max, for your innovation.'

He closed the journal and left it lying on the desk in front of him. He rubbed his day-old stubble. The same question came creeping back. How was Claire going to die?

He couldn't really do it. Could he?

What if they were both meant to die this coming Saturday? Why hadn't he asked Daniel to predict his own date of death too?

So many questions.

He lowered his head and covered his eyes with his hand. His mind was like a night's sky hit with a meteor shower. A million and one thoughts echoed throughout his head. Which meteorite would land in his conscience?

He lifted his head. The thought returned to him. If Claire made it through the day without dying, should he take it upon himself to end her life? Or even to end both their lives? To put a stop to the suffering of his beloved wife and prove that Daniel was one step closer in proving his mathematical theory, even though this calculation would be undocumented.

But did he have it within him to end both their lives?

30

Daniel had a horrible feeling as he got out of Tram 5 on Benelux Baan and walked down Catharina van Clevepark towards the circle on his map. The address that John had given him was that of Grace's house, and not her work. He glanced at his watch. It was 4:30pm. Did she finish work early on a Friday?

Maybe she didn't even work on Fridays, Daniel thought. Since he was almost there, he decided to give her home address a shot. If nobody was home he would just go for coffee somewhere and come back in a while.

Grace's house was on Amsterdamseweg. It was a beautiful three story red-brick building dating back to the 1930's. A blind was pulled down on the single window on the top floor, and curtains were drawn on each of the two windows on the middle floor. The window on the ground floor offered a view to the large living room. Daniel resisted the temptation to stare in.

As he walked towards the front door, he looked around and was impressed by the state of the front garden. Either Grace, or her husband, had very green fingers. Or they earned enough money to hire a gardener.

A silver BMW was parked in the driveway. *A good sign,* thought Daniel, *unless they both cycled to work... which isn't unrealistic considering the city I'm in.*

He rang the bell. As he waited, he noticed a sticker on the letterbox with a red "Nee" and a green "Ja" on it. He assumed it meant "No" and "Yes", but the small white text explaining it in more detail was literally Double Dutch to him. A flyer protruded halfway out the letterbox. He was about to push the letterbox inwards, so the flyer would fall all the way inside, when it disappeared, sucked inwards as someone on the other side beat him to it. A few seconds later a tall man with untidy hair opened the door and stared at him.

'*Kan ik u helpen?*' he said looking at Daniel and then at the flyer he had just snatched from the letterbox. A whiff of alcohol exploded on Daniel's face. He resisted the urge to wave the stench away.

'Sorry to bother you. Does Grace live here?'

The man suddenly straightened up as if a policeman had just asked him to take a breathalyser test. Despite the attempt to appear more alert, the man swayed.

'Who wants to know?' he asked with distaste.

Daniel almost looked behind him, half-wondering if it was a trick question. 'Me. I'm an old friend of hers.' He put his hand out. 'Daniel Geller.'

Otto refused to take it. Instead he swayed and stumbled as he tried to lean against the door. Daniel wasn't sure if it was from the drink or the shock at the possibility of Grace having an old friend call round.

'Well, what are the chances?' the man asked, as Daniel lowered his hand.

'The chances of what?'

'She leaves me for someone else and a random stranger drops by.'

Daniel started to get the feeling that it was not good timing.

'She… left you?'

Otto nodded. 'Yes, she did.'

Daniel took a deep breath and looked down at the crumpled Google map printout he held in his hand.

'I don't suppose you know where she…'

'No, I don't have a fucking clue where she is. Nor do I care.'

Daniel's heart started to sink. He glanced at his watch. It was still office hours. Maybe he could get to her work if…

Shit, I have no clue where she works.

'Do you know the best way to get to her work from here?' he asked, trying not to sound too desperate.

Otto sniggered. 'From here?'

Daniel nodded, wondering if he would help.

'Let's have a look at your map.'

He gave him the map and took a step closer, expecting Otto to show him the best route. Instead he ripped the map in two. And then in fours and threw it on the ground, together with the flyer he had in his hand. Daniel reached out immediately to catch the fluttering pieces of paper but was caught off balance. Otto pushed him from the steps. He fell to the concrete pathway and banged his head on the ground.

'Get the fuck off my property!'

Daniel looked up from the ground holding his head. Otto's looming figure took a step forward. He braced himself.

'And if you see her, give her this from me.'

Otto spat at him. Daniel felt some of the spray land on his hand, but most of it either landed on his clothes or missed him completely. He heard the front door slam shut. He was gone back inside.

Daniel's heart was beating like never before. The adrenaline that shot through his body was something new. The urge of picking up the biggest stone he could find and throwing it through the front window was overwhelming.

Taking a couple of deep breaths he tried to regain composure. Finally he picked himself up, readjusted his bag on his shoulder and wiped the spit from his hand. For what they were worth, he picked up the pieces of the Google map. He needed to stay focussed. He needed to find out where Grace worked as soon as possible. If he missed her before she left work, then he was in big trouble. There was a real possibility that he wouldn't find her on time.

31

Daniel walked quickly out of the driveway and onto Amsterdamseweg. He felt lost and shook up. A teenager wearing large Bose headphones stood on the pavement. He wore pale green combats and his hair was spiked with what seemed to be extremely powerful gel. Daniel could almost see a shine coming from each and every spike. His head looked as if it would immediately burst a football if he tried to head one. The teenager pulled one side of the headphones from his ear and said something in Dutch.

Daniel shook his head. 'Sorry. I don't understand.'

'Are you okay? I was passing by and saw the man push you to the ground.'

'Oh that,' Daniel said, playing it down and rubbing the back of his head. 'I'm fine.'

The teenager saw the pieces of the Google map in his hand. 'Are you lost? Do you need help finding somewhere?'

Daniel looked at the scraps of paper in his hand and realised how useless they were now.

'I need to find someone, but I don't even know where to start...' he trailed off. He suddenly realised that he had never googled Grace himself since finding out her new surname. He had searched once using her maiden name but didn't get very far. That was before John had given him Grace's contact information. Now that he knew her surname, he wondered if there was information online that could tell him where she worked.

'Do you have internet on your mobile?' he asked.

The teenager laughed. 'Yeah, of course,' he said as he pulled the headphones down around his neck. A faint din of the music he was listening to could still be heard.

'Could you google someone for me? I need to find out where she works. All I know is that she works for some insurance company in Amsterdam.'

The teenager took out a Samsung smartphone from one of the many pockets on his combats. His headphones were still attached to it. The device looked much bigger than a normal smartphone, so much so Daniel wondered if it was a small tablet rather than an actual mobile. *At the end of the day*, he thought, *I couldn't care less as long as it has internet.*

The teenager pulled out an electronic pen from somewhere within the device, tipped the screen a couple of times and looked at Daniel. The din from the headphones stopped.

'Shoot,' he said as he held the pen like a waiter about to take his order.

'Grace Visser. Amsterdam.'

The teenager typed in the words, tipped something on the screen and showed Daniel the results. The first few results were from Facebook. The fifth result down was from LinkedIn.

'Can you click on that one?' he asked pointing to the LinkedIn hyperlink.

The teenager did so. They both waited for the page to load. After a few seconds a page appeared showing Grace Visser's public profile.

'Shit. There's no photo,' he said. 'I wonder if that's her. Can you scroll down?'

The teenager did so. Daniel caught sight of the words "Trinity College" and knew immediately.

'That's her!'

'Okay. Good.'

'Scroll back up. What's the name of the company she works for?' he asked as he frantically searched for a pen in his shoulder bag. He found one, took hold of one of the scraps of Google map, and dropped the rest to the pavement. Now it was his turn to pose like a waiter about to take an order.

The teenager read it out: 'Kuhlman International B.V.'

'Can you spell the first word?'

The guy spelled it out while turning his mobile towards

Daniel so he could get a better look at it.

As he scribbled it down he asked, 'Is that far from here?'

The teenager laughed. 'I have no idea. It's not exactly the ING House.'

'The what?'

'The ING... I mean it's not a well-known company or building.'

'Of course. You're right. But it's in Amsterdam?'

'According to LinkedIn, it's in the Amsterdam area indeed.' The teenager copied and pasted "Kuhlman International" and did another quick Google search. 'Vondelstraat 45. That's pretty central. It's close to Vondel Park.'

Daniel scribbled down the street name and looked up at the guy. 'Thanks a million,' he said patting him on the arm. 'You have no idea just how helpful you have been.'

The teenager smiled as he touched the screen with the electronic pen and turned the music back on. 'No problem.'

Daniel threw his own pen back in his bag and started looking around for a taxi. After five minutes of brisk walking back in the direction of the city, he managed to flag one down. The traffic was very congested around Amstelveenseweg and Overtoom. As he helplessly watched the endless flow of bicycles that overtook the cab, he realised why cycling was such a popular mode of transport. He arrived at Vondelstraat just before 5:20 pm.

Kuhlman International B.V. was a white brick building, four stories high, that looked onto Vondel Park, the main park in central Amsterdam. The windows at street level had a frosted window film, preventing passers-by from looking in, (or perhaps preventing workers from looking out). At the same time, they allowed plenty of natural light inside.

The building could have passed for a large residential house if it wasn't for the brass plaques bolted to the wall next to the front door, with the names of the companies that were housed in it. Daniel scanned them. The second one read:

Kuhlman International B.V.
Sinds 1905

He tried pushing the door but it was locked.

'Shit.' He glanced inside. The first thing that caught his eye, just inside the door, was a bicycle pump. He wondered if every establishment in Amsterdam had a pump for visitors and workers alike. Much the same way hotels offered umbrellas to guests.

A make-shift sign hung on the door announcing something in Dutch. He couldn't understand it. He cupped his hands around his eyes and stared inside looking for any signs of life.

A receptionist was busy looking through some papers. Daniel pressed the doorbell. Cynthia looked up, frowned and pressed something. He heard a buzz which he took as his cue to push. As he entered, he almost fell over the step at the entrance. Gently, he closed the door behind him.

The interior smelled fresh and clean, almost lemon-like. Looking down he could see why. The grey marble floor had just been cleaned. To the right he caught sight of the cleaning lady pushing an electronic floor polisher into another room.

The receptionist said something in Dutch. Daniel shook his head. 'I'm sorry. I'm afraid I don't speak Dutch.'

'That happens quite often with visitors,' the receptionist said pointing to the step at the entrance. 'I think we need to do something about it before someone breaks their neck.'

He glanced back at the door and nodded his head in agreement. He turned back to the receptionist and pointed at the floor.

'Am I allowed to come in?'

The receptionist stood up slightly, so she could see over the higher part of the front desk. 'Oh sure. Should be almost dry by now. Just don't slip on it.' She let out a laugh. 'First the step and now a wet floor. It's like an obstacle course here!'

He smiled as he tip-toed across the floor; a futile manoeuvre as he left foot marks all the way across.

The front desk was small and pokey. It reminded him of the old video store he used to go to when he was a child. Back then, however, it was a middle-aged man with a receding hairline and yellow fingertips that would greet him. The woman behind this desk was more appealing to the eye. She was in her twenties, and she had a friendly smile. She wore huge earrings that were the same size as her bracelet. Her nails were long and perfectly manicured.

'Hi, I'm looking for Grace Visser.'

The receptionist nodded. 'She has already left, I'm afraid.'

Daniel's heart sank.

'I can take a message if you want and give it to her on Monday?'

He shook her head. 'I need to reach her before Monday. Do you know where she's staying?'

A look of confusion came over the young woman. 'Staying? You mean living?'

He realised that Grace's private situation with her husband wasn't something she had necessarily shared with her colleagues. 'Yes, living I mean.'

'Well, to be honest we're not allowed to divulge that kind of information to strangers. I'm sure you understand.'

Daniel scratched his head. 'Of course.' He didn't really know what to ask. When he thought about it, he didn't even *want* her home address. The bang on his head acted as reminder of the nutcase she was married to. The question was where she was staying?

'Is there any way I can get in contact with her? Maybe a mobile number?'

The receptionist shook her head. Her earrings continued to dangle for a short time after. 'That

171

information is also private.'

He tried to turn on his charm. Unsure if he actually had any, he leaned on the ledge of the higher part of the front desk.

'Listen Miss...', he paused. 'Sorry, I don't know your name.'

'That's okay. You don't need to know it.'

He shifted his weight and glanced briefly across the desk. Next to a small plate with melon pips and a knife, he saw a pile of folders with a Post-It on top. It read "Cynthia", followed by an instruction in Dutch. He decided to chance it.

'Listen, Cynthia. I'm an old friend of Grace.'

The receptionist smiled. 'How do you know my name?' She looked around the desk to see if there was anything obvious. She didn't see the stack of folders.

He felt he was on a roll and continued to play it cool. Casually he tried to raise an eyebrow. Unfortunately he didn't have such good control over his eyebrows and he raised both of them, giving the impression that he was surprised at something. Quickly he stopped trying to move them and gave a neutral expression.

'Seriously, how did you know?' She asked again.

He ignored her and removed the old photograph from his wallet and showed it to her.

'This is Grace and me about twelve years ago. We go back a long way. I would really appreciate it if you can help me get in touch with her.'

She took the photo. 'Wow. She was quite pretty back then.'

He frowned. 'What? She's not pretty anymore?'

'No, that's not what I meant. It's just...,' she paused for a moment. 'I've never seen her like this. Young and... happy.' She looked at Daniel and scrutinized the photo again. 'Were you her boyfriend?'

'One time, yes. A long time ago.'

'You make a nice couple.'

'Made.' He corrected the tense of her sentence. He held up his hand and pointed to his wedding ring with the thumb on the same hand. 'Not anymore, I'm afraid.'

'That's too bad. *Her* husband is an obnoxious prick.'

His eyes lit up. It was a view they had in common. 'You've met him?'

'We had one of those annual days out, where partners could come along. Which by the way I think is really shit.' She turned her hands in a way that showed she had nothing to offer. 'I mean partners don't know anybody else, and it makes people who don't have partners, like *moi*, feel really shit. Anyway, this guy came along and you would think that he was the most important guy there was. The way he spoke to people, even to Rob, the director of Kuhlman's. My God, I felt sorry for Grace. I think she was quite embarrassed.'

'I can imagine,' he said, recalling the encounter with him less than an hour earlier.

There was a moment of silence before Cynthia continued. 'But still, I can't give you her number.'

Daniel sighed. He turned towards the humming of the floor polisher, as the cleaner pushed it out of one office and crossed the hallway to another. He raised a finger as an idea popped into his head.

'How about *you* call her and tell her that I would like to talk to her. That way, you're not breaking any rules and she can give you the greenlight to pass the phone on to me or not. Once I'm talking to her, it'll be fine, I promise.'

Cynthia looked to the side, reflecting on the idea. 'Sounds reasonable.'

'Great.'

She picked up the phone, pressed a few numbers.

He was impressed. 'You know her number off by heart?'

She shook her head. 'I just type in her surname and it dials the number automatically.'

'Oh. That's handy.'

'Certainly is,' she agreed as she held the receiver to her ear. He was impressed at how she didn't get an earring caught on the earpiece.

They both waited in anticipation as the phone rang. 'Will I put it on speaker?'

Daniel suddenly felt very nervous. He took a deep breath and tried to remain cool. 'Yes. Okay.'

32

Grace sat back on the sofa and wiped her fingers on a paper napkin. Rik sat next to her. He had already given up trying to finish the Thai takeaway that stood before them. Spring rolls, fried prawns in red curry sauce and chicken with cashew nuts. The portions were just too big. Each white plastic container contained leftovers, to serve as someone's snack another time. Next to the containers lay some scrunched-up used napkins. The room was rich with the scent of Thai spices.

'I hope I'll be able to play hockey after all that,' Rik said, patting his stomach and then taking a swig from a bottle of Singha beer.

'You're not playing already this evening, are you?'

'No. There are a couple of games already for the local teams. But our pool starts tomorrow morning.' He looked at his watch. 'A friend is picking me up in about an hour and we'll drive there in about three hours, if all goes well. So we avoid the mad rush hour.'

'I'm sure you'll be fine. It will be well digested by tomorrow morning,' she said as she hit him gently on the belly. 'You're as fit as a fiddle.'

Rik jumped like he had just received an electric shot. A splash of beer fell onto the coffee table.

'Whoa!' Grace said, 'you're jumpy.'

He wiped away the beer from the coffee table with one of the napkins. The beer disappeared, but some brownish marks from one of the sauces remained. 'You would not believe how ticklish I am, Grace. Seriously, it's disturbing.'

She leaned forward and took a mouthful of her own Singha. 'I'm sure you're exaggerating.'

He shook his head. 'Nope.'

As soon as Grace placed her bottle back on the coffee table, Rik reached towards her and tickled her. She screamed with laughter before sliding off the sofa and landing on the floor with a thud. Trying desperately to recover from her seizure, she brushed back stray strands of hair that were covering her face and shot Rik a dirty look.

'If you don't want any serious damage to your apartment I advise you not to do that again.'

'Relax. I have tickle coverage in my insurance,' he said, as he gave her a look as if it didn't worry him.

She rolled her eyes. 'Of course you do,' she said and remained sitting on the floor looking absently at a Chinese Evergreen plant in the corner. She noticed, even from where she sat, a film of dust on the leaves.

Rik sat back on the sofa and patted the spot were Grace had been sitting, like a dog owner allowing his dog to jump up. 'I won't tickle you again. Come on. It was cosy. It was *gezellig*.'

'Nope.' She pointed to the plant. 'Do you ever dust your plant?'

'Don't change the subject. Come on. This time tomorrow you'll be home alone with nobody to talk to.'

She looked at him. 'What makes you so sure? Maybe I'll have a whole line of ex-boyfriends queuing up outside with less ticklish stomachs than yours.'

He nodded his head and rubbed his chin feigning interest. 'Of course you will.'

She reached forward and took another mouthful of Singha.

'That reminds me,' he said. 'Yesterday you mentioned briefly a wonderful guy that walked out on you. What was so wonderful about him? It's kind of a contradiction, isn't it? If he was so wonderful, why did he walk out?'

She looked down at her bottle of beer and started scraping at the top corner of the moist label. 'It was a bit more complicated than just walking out of a relationship so to speak.'

'In what way?'

'Well, we studied together at university and then we

both went on to do PhDs together. He worked on a very...' she searched quickly for the correct word to use. 'Let's say alternative thesis.'

'How alternative?'

She looked down at the mystical golden lion on the beer bottle. 'Basically, he was trying to predict the date of death of people.'

Rik sat up right. 'Seriously? Predicting someone's date of death? How the hell can you do that?'

'Lots of complicated maths equations.'

'Sounds pretty alternative, alright.'

She nodded. 'Well, the Mathematical faculty at our university thought so too. They thought it was more than just alternative. His thesis was rejected.'

'Rejected as in...?' He waited for Grace to clarify.

'As in dismissed. His work was not recognised to merit a PhD.'

'Ouch. That must have hurt.'

She continued to pull at the beer label. She managed to tear a small piece away and let it fall to the coffee table. As she went back to the beer label and scratched some more, a wave of sadness seemed to come over her. Rik could see that it was a sensitive topic for her.

'I guess you can say that,' she said quietly. 'The poor guy just turned his back on everything. He was super intelligent, and okay, fair enough, the subject of his thesis was unconventional. But he had a really bright future ahead. He just turned his back on everything. University, friends, future.' She tore another piece from the Singha beer bottle and rolled it up in her fingertips. 'And me.'

Rik placed his hand on her shoulder while she was still sitting on the floor.

'Sorry to hear that. It is kind of strange though. I mean why throw away everything because of one rejection?' he asked. 'It must have been a tough break up.'

She turned her head to look at him. 'You know, usually a break up involves a two-way conversation or argument.

Some form of communication where you both agree to go your separate ways. Or one throws the other out. Or something *happens*. There is some interaction between the two parties involved, for better or for worse.' She shook her head slowly and turned her attention back to the bottle. 'Not this break-up. The day of his rejection I tried to find him. He was nowhere to be found. I came back to my apartment and all his stuff was gone. It was if it had disappeared into thin air. It seemed like he kind of blamed me for what had happened. I don't know why.'

She bit on her bottom lip before continuing. 'In a way, it was like he died.' She paused for a few moments. 'I suppose, in way, part of him did.'

Rik listened intently. Unsure what to say, he decided to take another swig of his beer.

'Still. After all this time. Not one word,' she admitted.

'Weirdo.'

'The strange thing is we were a perfect match,' she continued. 'We laughed so much. Our personalities fitted together so nicely. I have no doubt that if we got through that patch, then we would have made it. Up until that point, I thought he was the one for me. And that's what I meant yesterday when I told you that you will meet someone like that too. Except of course, hopefully she *will* be the one for you.'

'So what's he doing now?'

'The last I heard is that he was working as a crane operator on a building site somewhere.'

'A what?'

'A crane operator. You know, operating those big huge yellow things that lift heavy loads from one point to another.'

'That's one hell of a career change.'

'Tell me about it. It saddens me to think of him throwing it all away. Our relationship was one thing, but his bright future? What a waste.'

'You still have feelings for him?'

Grace remained silent for a moment, trying to choose the right words that would convey her feeling.

'Honestly?' she shook her head. 'I don't know. I mean what was his reason for just walking out on me with not so much of a note? If he had an explanation for that, then maybe I could answer the question. But right now, I can honestly say I don't have any feelings for him. It's like my heart froze in time. If I could find out why he left me, I can at least thaw it out and choose to hate him or forgive him or even love him again, who knows?' she shook her head dismissing the scenario. 'My feelings for him are in limbo. I don't have any feelings for him, good or bad. Does that make sense?'

Rik nodded.

Grace's mobile that was lying on the coffee table suddenly leaped into life with a tune from Snow Patrol. It snapped her away from the conversation she was having. It was actually the first time she had spoken to anyone about Daniel. She stood up and bent over to pick up the phone. She looked at the display panel. 'For God's sake.'

'What is it?'

'It's the bloody office.' She turned towards him. 'Will I bother answering it?'

33

Cynthia looked at Daniel. 'Doesn't look good. She probably sees that it's the office trying to call and…'

Grace answered the phone on the sixth ring.

'Grace speaking.'

'Grace, it's Cynthia here at the office.'

'Hi. Is everything okay?'

'I'm sorry to be calling you on a Friday evening, but I have a visitor here and he wanted to get in contact with you.'

'A visitor?'

'He's here. You're on speaker.'

Daniel took that as his cue. 'Hi Grace. It's Daniel here.'

There was a silence. A long silence. Daniel was about to ask if she could hear him, when Grace spoke.

'Daniel Geller?'

'Yes.'

Another bout of silence filled the line. Eventually she said, 'Wow. That's a blast from the past.'

'Yes. I know.'

'What are you doing here?'

Daniel was lost for words. Although he had rehearsed some kind of conversation in his mind, it all seemed to have gone out the window. How could he tell her what he was really doing here? 'Um…,' he hesitated. 'I'm here for the weekend. I knew you lived in Amsterdam. So I thought I would look you up.'

'How did you look me up exactly?'

'I googled you.'

Daniel could hear some music or the television in the background.

'I'm married, Daniel.'

'I know…' He glanced at Cynthia and shrugged his shoulders. 'I didn't get in contact with you for *that* reason.'

'No, I mean I'm married. My surname changed seven years ago. What exactly did you google?'

Cynthia interrupted. 'Look, maybe I'll take this off the speaker and you guys can have a private conversation and swap contact details if you want. Okay?' she said while looking at Daniel. She then turned to the phone. 'Grace, for the record, I haven't given him any of your contact details. I'll leave that up to you if you want to exchange numbers.'

'Thanks, Cynthia. Talk to you soon.'

Cynthia clicked a button on the phone and handed Daniel the receiver. 'Here you go.'

'Thanks a million for your help,' he said with his hand over the mouthpiece. He turned around and lowered his voice. 'Okay, we're off the speaker.'

'Great,' Grace said. It was a cold tone of voice.

Daniel decided to come clean. 'I got your details from Professor Redmond. John Redmond.'

'From Trinity?'

'Yes.'

'Why?'

'Look, Grace, I don't feel comfortable catching up like this, over the phone, after so long.'

'This is really bad timing, Daniel.'

'I know.'

'How do you know?'

He didn't want to tell Grace about his encounter with her husband while Cynthia was still listening.

'I don't want to go into it over the phone.'

Another silence engulfed the lines.

'Daniel, you completely shut me off after your thesis was rejected. You could have sworn that it was something I did wrong.'

'I know, Grace. I'm sorry. I was angry. I wanted to break away completely. From everything that had anything to do with Maths.'

'We had a relationship, Daniel. Maths or no maths, we

181

had a relationship and you walked out with not so much as a goodbye.'

'I'm not proud of what I've done or how I treated you, but...,' He was running out of ideas. 'I want to meet you. While I'm here.'

'What for?'

'To say I'm sorry.'

'You can say it over the phone.'

'It's not the same.'

'Is that the reason you came to Amsterdam?'

He bit his bottom lip. 'Kind of.'

'Kind of?'

'Grace, I need to see you tomorrow. Or tonight even.'

He could hear a muffled sound. He could picture her covering the mouthpiece and speaking to someone. After a few seconds she was back on.

'Not tonight, Daniel. Tomorrow is okay.'

'Morning.'

'Why so eager? Especially after twelve years?'

He ignored her response. 'Is the morning okay?'

She remained silent for a moment. 'Okay, why not? Where?'

'Your place. I mean the place where you are now.' He could see Cynthia's head raise in curiosity. She didn't look at him though.

'How do you know that I'm not...? Never mind. Is Cynthia still there with you?' she asked.

'Yes.'

'Give me your mobile number. I'll text you the address.'

Daniel gave her his mobile number.

'Got it,' she said. 'Shall we say around ten?'

'How about eight?'

'My God, you are eager.'

'It's important.'

'Okay, let's say nine then.'

Reluctantly, Daniel agreed. 'Okay.'

'See you tomorrow then,' she said.

'You won't forget to send the text message?'

'No, I won't. Relax.'

'Thank you.' There was an awkward silence, before Daniel mustered up the courage to say, 'I'm sorry, Grace, for what I've done.' But the line was dead before he had finished saying it.

34

John woke up early on Saturday morning. It was still dark outside. He squinted to see the clock-radio on the bedside locker.

6:42am

His neck cracked as he twisted his head towards Claire. She slept soundly. A small stream of drool escaped from the side of her mouth forming a damp stain on the pillow. She looked so peaceful. He wondered what she dreamed of these days, or if she actually had dreams anymore.

Gently he pulled the duvet to one side and sat up on the side of the bed, careful not to disturb his wife. The thought of what could happen today made his heart beat faster. Taking a deep breath, he stood up. His head spun slightly. Tip-toeing out of the room, he made his way across the landing to the bathroom. As he switched on the light, the explosion of light forced him to shut his eyes. He grabbed onto the sides of the sink, like an elderly person holding a Zimmer frame. Gradually his eyes became accustomed to the light. Staring into the mirror, he leaned closer to it. He could see bags beneath his eyes and a stray hair protruding from his nose. He picked up a tweezers from Claire's toiletries and, with utmost precision, pulled the hair out. He placed the tweezers down and continued to stare at his reflection in the mirror. Memories of the morning that changed his life flooded him. The morning he went to Claire's work and told her the news.

*

Claire worked as a graphic designer in Interactive Blue Ltd, a small advertising company on Harcourt Street. The office was in a large Georgian building overlooking St Stephen's Green. It was spacious, but draughty. The windows were yet to be replaced with double-glazing. Claire insisted on having an electric heater when the temperature within the building dropped below 17 degrees Celsius. And it often did.

It was a small company with one general manager, one secretary, three graphic designers and a video editor. Claire had been working there since it started up, thirteen years previously. Everybody worked hard. There was good team spirit in the office. The work was flexible, which was important when Claire became a mother. She often had to take time off to look after Max when he had fallen ill. She never felt comfortable asking John to take time off. After all, he was on the road to becoming a professor. And then he *became* a professor, which meant that he had even less free time.

On that morning, Claire had popped out to Lifestyle Sports in the Stephen's Green Shopping Centre during her coffee break to pick up new football socks for Max. His old ones had more holes than a chunk of Swiss cheese. Claire could visualize his teammates laughing at his socks in the changing room. Boys will be boys. Still, it wasn't a pleasant thought for a mother. Although he had a back-up pair of football socks, one of them had gone missing recently. And it wasn't that they couldn't afford them. It was just something that she kept forgetting about. She had asked John to do it, but he obviously kept forgetting too.

She had just sat down at her desk when Rebecca, the secretary, came to tell her she had a visitor.

'John's here to see you.'

'John?' she asked with genuine surprise. 'My husband?'

'That's the one. He's in the meeting room.'

'Why don't you just show him in?'

Rebecca didn't make eye contact. 'He's waiting for you.'

Full of curiosity, she walked to the meeting room. When she saw John standing next to the oval-shaped desk, she knew something was wrong. Deep down maybe she knew straight away. A blanket of confusion and worry came over her.

'John. What are you doing here? Did you start varnishing the garden table?'

'Close the door, Claire. We need to talk.'

She could see he wasn't himself. He looked untidy. His shirt was hanging out. Millions of thoughts shot through her mind. One of them was the idea that John was having an affair. His mistress had become pregnant and it was now time to break the news. It couldn't be about Max? Max was at school.

Wasn't he?

Claire closed the door. Her hand trembled as she took her hand from the door knob. She remained facing the door for a short while. Bad news was coming whether she liked it or not. How bad would it be? Part of her screamed at her to leave the room, to run away from the news that her husband was about to tell her. But that would be putting off the inevitable. She turned around to face the music.

'What is it, John?'

He took a deep breath. 'It's Max.'

On hearing her son's name she closed her eyes briefly. She would have bargained anything, even her own life, for John to say something else. News of an affair would have been music to her ears.

'What about him?'

He remained silent, summoning the courage to say the words. The words he couldn't bear to hear himself.

'Max's dead, Claire.'

It was as if John had spoken Chinese. A look of utter confusion came over her as she shook her head. John stepped closer to his wife and stopped. Their eyes met. The same eyes that met when Claire announced she was pregnant. What joy there was back then.

'Claire?'

Her eyes were full of fear now. Confusion. Pain.

'Where is he, John?'

John held her arms. 'Max's dead. He died during the night. It was a horrible accident. I found him this morning.'

She took a step back. Suddenly she slapped John across the face. 'How dare you!'

'Claire.' He rubbed his face. 'Claire, please.'

'He was getting up this morning! You told me. How dare you pull this stunt? Is this some kind of sick joke?'

'He choked on a piece of chewing gum during the night. They believed he suffered a heart attack.'

She shook her head. Details. Those were the details. A shot of authenticity that turned the sick joke into a living nightmare. Staring at John, her eyes pleaded with his.

Tell me it isn't true.

'I'm so sorry, Claire. He's gone.' He started crying. 'Our baby is gone.'

He wrapped his arms around his wife. He could feel her struggling. Trying to break free from the nightmare she was entering. Shaking. Finally, she buried her face into John's chest. It helped muffle her sobs.

'No,' she cried. 'He can't be!' Tears streamed down her face.

'I'm so sorry,' he cried.

The sobs grew louder. She lost the strength in her legs. John took her weight, as he lowered himself to the floor, keeping hold of his wife. They both sat on the floor.

She peered out from her husband's shirt. She could smell his deodorant. It was a scent that, from then on, she would always associate with death. A feeling of utter desperation covered her. It was like an invisible film clung to her body, covering her from head to toe, suffocating her.

'Where is he, John?' She mumbled. 'Where's my baby?'

'Temple Street.'

Claire caught sight of a pen beneath the table. It had probably fallen during a past meeting. It was a simple Bic

187

pen. A blue one. She knew immediately it belonged to her as its top was chewed. She remembered that day when Max had to write 500 lines for Ms Jackson.

I must not use a pen as a pea-shooter.

Max had removed the inner tube of the pen. He moistened small scraps of paper and placed them inside the pen barrel. He fired them at his friends. His friends fired back. It was fun. He got caught. He received punishment.

'John. This isn't happening. Where is he? I never kissed him goodnight last night.'

'Ssh, don't do this. It's not your fault.'

'I want to kiss him goodnight. Let me kiss him goodnight.'

'Don't do this to yourself.'

She pulled away from John and picked up the pen.

'He wasted at least an hour writing those goddamn lines!'

John stared at Claire.

'What are you talking about?'

'He had to write 500 times "I must not use a pen as a pea-shooter". I helped him, John.' The tears streamed down her face. 'I helped him. You were working late. I knew you wouldn't have agreed. I copied his handwriting. We turned his punishment into fun. Why couldn't I have stuck up for him? Why couldn't I have made my own pea-shooter and shoot that bitch. How dare she make my son write so many lines? Wasting an hour of his precious life.'

'Ssh. Claire.'

'How could we let it happen?'

John closed his eyes. A tear ran down his cheek. 'I don't know,' he murmured. 'I don't know.'

'Choking on chewing gum. This can't be happening. Is there anything they can do?'

John was silent as she continued to examine the pen. Slowly he took hold of her wrists.

'Is there anything *who* can do?'

Claire looked as if she had just aged ten years. She was pale. Her hair was a mess.

'He's gone, Claire. He's dead. Do you understand? He's not in intensive care. He's not on a life support machine. He's dead. There's no coming back. There's no second chance.'

'He can't be, John. HE CAN'T BE!' She buried her face in John's shirt again. Together they huddled on the meeting room floor, crying in each other's arms.

A sharp bang pulled John from his thoughts of the past. He was now in the shower. A shampoo bottle had fallen to the floor making the bang. He raised his face to the streaming water. It was only then that he realised he was crying. He didn't mind crying in the shower. The tears were washed away immediately. He looked towards the door of the bathroom, hoping that Claire wouldn't appear. She was sleeping so soundly. He would feel bad if he had woken her up.

He dried himself, put on a pair of jeans and a black polo shirt. Although he could do with a shave, he decided to give it a miss. He went downstairs to a silent kitchen and living room. Saturday mornings were the worst for him. The TV should be on by now. Cupboards should be opening and closing. Milk should be spilling. The kitchen and living room should be a mess. Now it was spotless. Silent. Like a morgue.

John needed to get out of the house. The silence was suffocating him. He needed to go for a walk. He put on a jacket and left the house.

A cold air blew in his face as he walked down the driveway.

Was today a good day to die?

35

Daniel woke up several times during the night. It was the shouting of drunken tourists on the street outside. It was the foreign smell of the bed sheets. It was the hard mattress. It was the million-and-one things that were on his mind. By 7:00am he decided to stop trying to go back to sleep. It was time to get up and face the music. It was time to meet the woman he once loved and do everything in his power to make sure nothing happened to her today.

He showered and put on a fresh pair of clothes - a black pair of Levis and a V-neck pullover from Mexx. He didn't shave for the simple reason he had never packed his razor. He was half-afraid that it wouldn't be allowed in his carry-on luggage. At the back of his mind, he was pretty sure they were allowed, but since he was only going to be away for two nights, he figured that there was no point to it.

Taking a croissant and cup of coffee from the hotel's breakfast buffet, he sat down in the dining area. About seven other tables stood in close proximity to each other. All of them were empty. A beautiful black and white photograph of an Amsterdam canal with a church in the background hung on the wall on the far side of the room. It was crooked which seemed to add to the old neglected effect. He wondered if it was an effect the hotel was trying to create on purpose or if it really was somewhat neglected.

Daniel's poor appetite meant he was unable to get full value of the breakfast buffet that was on offer. A young Japanese couple arrived and walked along the buffet searching for anything that would wet their appetite. When they came across something they didn't recognise, they pointed and giggled. The small puffy pancakes, *poffertjes*, seemed to attract most of the attention.

As Daniel left the hotel, he headed south towards Westermarkt. It was a sunny autumn morning. A blue sky gave Amsterdam a light setting he failed to see the previous day. It was like someone had pulled over a curtain to let the sun in and lighten up the streets and buildings. The cyclists were already out and about. A group of three swans made their way gracefully along the canal. It was a beautiful sight. He regretted not bringing his camera.

Some tourists were already queuing outside an old building. It was only after he passed it that Daniel noticed a sign saying "Anne Frank Huis" pointing back the way he came.

When he reached the tram stop on Westermarkt, he tried to get his bearings and glanced on the map next to the timetable. He scanned both the map and timetable for Westlandgracht but couldn't find it. He eventually asked a teenage girl who was in sports gear and carrying a hockey stick. She took one look at the address.

'You need to go further that way,' she said pointing towards the city centre. 'Just behind the Palace you'll find another tram stop. Jump on a tram 2 and that should bring you to Westlandgracht. It's probably about 10 or 15 minutes with the tram.'

Daniel thanked her and continued on his way. It didn't take long to find the tram stop and not much longer before a tram came along. How he loved public transport in European cities. Unlike the miserable Dublin buses, these trams actually adhered to their timetables.

Jumping off at the Westlandgracht tram stop, he double-backed a little before he came to the actual street called Westlandgracht. Once there, he kept an eye out for the numbers on the doors. He kept walking until he came to number 29. Grace had mentioned in her text that she was on the second floor, and that the name plaque outside would have the name Rik. When he came to the door he glanced at the name plaques. The third one up said "Rik

Bergman".

He closed his eyes and took a breath. 'Here goes,' he said to himself. There was no turning point once he pressed the buzzer. He swore to himself that, no matter what happened, he would tell her the truth, the real reason he was there.

36

John expected the fresh morning air to clear his head. Instead it seemed to clog his mind even more with random thoughts. They were a mixture of fears of what was supposed to happen today, memories from the past that would never be matched, and a genuine sadness of what would become of him should his wife really die. If he thought the house was quiet now, he hadn't even considered what it might be like should Claire die.

But how would she die? And would it be just her? It occurred to him again that maybe they were going to die together.

But how? The question gnawed on him like an intense headache, only no painkiller would diffuse the sensation.

As he strolled up Beechpark Lawn he looked towards the sky for answers. It was still dark enough to see the stars. As the first signs of daylight appeared to the east, the dark blue sky became lighter and stars started disappearing. It reminded John of Magnetic Doodle, the magnetic drawing toy Max had owned. Soon the entire sky would be a blank canvas once again as the increasing light became the sliding eraser bar.

The grass was wet from the night's chill, as was the exterior of his Audi Q5 which stood in the driveway. The windows of the car sparkled in the light of the streetlamps. He wiped his finger along the back window to make sure it wasn't frozen. It wasn't. Not yet. Another couple of weeks and he would need his ice scraper again.

He felt something crunch below his foot and knew immediately what it was. Looking down he kicked any remains of the snail towards the hedge on the side. Snails were not uncommon in his garden. He could see a whole network of glistening dots interwoven on the driveway like Aboriginal artwork.

Standing in the driveway, John looked up to the front

room. The curtains were still drawn. No light appeared from inside. Downstairs there were also no signs of life. Without entering the house to see if Claire had gotten up, he removed his keys and pressed a button on one of them. The doors of his Audi unlocked with a soft thud and the alarm gave a quick beep to say it was turned off. He climbed into the car and reversed out the driveway.

If it happened tonight, if he was also going to die, he wanted to ensure someone could easily continue with his work at Trinity. He wanted to file all his documents in a way that made it easy for his successors to find everything on the network, whether it was his research, presentations, workshops and the like.

The Saturday morning traffic in Dublin was light. It would become busier when people finished their lie-ins and decided to go out and about. He loved driving through the Phoenix Park in the morning when it wasn't busy. Getting the glimpse of the wild deer in the distance and the Dublin mountains in the background always gave him a warm feeling. For a few seconds each morning he could be miles away, in a National Park on a different continent.

He stopped at a roundabout at the corner of Chesterfield Avenue and Ordnance Road. A young boy crossed with an elderly man, probably his granddad, and an enthusiastic cocker spaniel. The dog tugged like crazy on the leash, delighted with the fresh air and all the smells and scents that went with the park. The granddad waved at John, thanking him for letting them cross. John acknowledged his wave with a nod.

The boy was younger than Max had been. John thought that he looked familiar but couldn't say why. He continued to look at them as they continued down Ordnance Road. What was it about the boy?

Headlights of an approaching car in his review mirror snapped John from his daze, and he continued towards the city.

37

Daniel pressed the doorbell. He couldn't hear anything and assumed that the bell could only be heard inside the apartment, two floors high. Instinctively he stepped back. He looked up to see if there was any movement from any of the windows above. His heart skipped a beat when his eyes met Grace's two stories above. Twelve years suddenly evaporated. It was as if he had just seen her yesterday. She didn't smile or give any sign of recognition. Daniel waved and immediately cringed inside. He felt like an awkward teenager visiting his girlfriend for the first time at her parents' house.

Although Grace was quite high up, he could see a sort of sparkle in her eye. Perhaps his awkward wave was enough to break down the barrier that time had built and allow her expression to soften. It was as if she was thinking: *It's good to see you again, Daniel.* At least he hoped she was thinking that and tried to convey the same feeling to her.

After several moments, he hunched his shoulders and pointed to the front door. The international sign language for "Aren't you going to open the door?"

She nodded her head, before disappearing from the window. Maybe it was his imagination, but Daniel thought he had seen her smile just as she turned away.

The door buzzed after a few seconds, and he pushed it open, careful not to trip over any step this time. The entry hall was tiny. An expensive-looking bicycle blocked the hallway. He turned to the side and crawled past it like a crab, avoiding the handlebars by a matter of centimetres. He walked up two flights of steep stairs before arriving at the landing of Grace's apartment. There was only one door, which was left ajar. Slowly he walked towards it. As he got closer, it opened slowly. Grace stood at the doorway.

'Hey there, stranger.' Her voice was soft and friendly. She looked older than she did from the pavement. That's what close-ups did to a person. Daniel had little doubt that, to her, he too looked older. The sparkle in her eye was still there, however. He smiled, unsure what to say. She met it with a smile of her own. He slowed down as he reached the doorway.

'It's good to see you again, Grace.' He offered her his hand.

Grace rolled her eyes. 'Jesus, since when did you become so formal, Daniel?' she said as she moved forward and gave him a friendly hug. Taken aback slightly, Daniel took a split-second to reciprocate. He forced himself to relax and embraced her with the same warm gesture. The two ex-lovers stood at the doorway with their arms wrapped around each other.

'Or would you prefer if I called you Mister Geller?'

It was a sharp contrast to the vibe he got from the phone call the previous evening. She smelled good. He couldn't tell if she wore the same scent as the university days, but it was pleasant nonetheless.

Grace, who initiated the embrace, was also the one who initiated the pull away. 'So how have you been?' she asked.

'Not bad,' he answered. The small talk had to start somewhere. Twelve years of catching up still had to start with the usual pleasantries. 'And you?'

She smirked. 'To be honest, Daniel, I've seen better days.'

He could see in her eyes that she had been through some hardships. She looked tired. Her crow's feet were more pronounced.

'Come in.'

'Is your friend here?' he asked, not really sure what kind of affair he was gate-crashing.

'Rik? No, he's gone to a hockey tournament down in

the Ardennes.'

'The what?'

'The Ardennes. Belgium,' she clarified. 'He'll be back tomorrow evening.'

Daniel noticed that Grace was in her bare feet. 'Do I need to take off my shoes?'

'If you want to.'

He didn't really want to, but did it nonetheless. The knot on one of his laces became stuck, so he decided to pull off his runner with the laces still tied instead. He would deal with the knot later. He left both runners on a pile in the hallway.

'Is he the new fella?' he asked as he went inside.

Grace offered him a sour look. 'He's a colleague. He's helping me out until I get my life back in order.' She walked into the kitchen and looked at the coffee machine. 'You want coffee?'

He followed her. 'That would be nice,' he said looking around. 'So life isn't going so well?'

'No, it isn't actually, Daniel,' she said. 'But at the end of the day, do you really give a shit?' She opened the top of the coffee maker and glanced inside. The aroma of fresh coffee beans met her senses.

'Of course. I mean...' He trailed off. It sounded fake and he knew it.

'Oh, don't give me that crap, Daniel. You walked out.' She clicked her fingers. 'Just like that. You'd swear that you were the first person who had their thesis rejected.' She opened the lid to the water reservoir of the coffee maker. Taking a cup from the draining board, she filled it with water and poured it into the coffee maker.

Daniel looked down, unsure what to say. He noticed his socks already had some sweat patches from his short journey to the apartment. He looked up at Grace as she poured another cupful of water into the coffee maker and said, 'You have every right to be angry with me.'

'I do?' she asked as she took a step back from the

197

coffee maker searching for the ON button. 'Well, thank you. That's nice of you.'

'That's it there, isn't it?' he said pointing to a switch on the side of the apparatus. Grace pushed the button as he continued. 'Seriously. What I did was wrong, and if I could go back in time, I would do some things differently.'

The kitchen was suddenly filled with the grinding noise of coffee beans.

'Well, that's mighty nice of you, Daniel,' she said, raising her voice so she could be heard over the coffee machine. 'And what would that be exactly? What would you have done so differently? Would you have *called* to say you were leaving me? Would you have sent me an SMS or an email?'

He shook his head. 'You know what I mean.'

Grace took some milk from the fridge, laid it down on the counter and turned around. 'Twelve years, Daniel. Twelve bloody years. I mean, why now?'

The coffee machine started spurting out fresh coffee. Daniel noticed that there weren't any cups beneath the spout where the coffee was coming from. He pointed to it. 'Shouldn't we stick a cup there?' Grace picked up the cup she had used to fill the reservoir, and placed it beneath the spout.

Daniel turned his attention back to the conversation, as the smell of freshly brewed coffee filled the kitchen.

'Do you remember Brian Nolan?' he asked.

'From our class? Of course. I heard he died a couple of years ago.'

'That's right. He died in a car accident.'

'Don't ask me how I heard about it,' she said, 'but these things find their way to me.' The first cup of coffee was ready. She took a clean cup from the cupboard next to the fridge, placed it beneath the spout and pressed the button again. The coffee grinding restarted.

'Brian was a volunteer in my thesis.' Daniel said. It was now his turn to raise his voice so he could be heard over the coffee grinding. There was no other way to say what he wanted to say without just coming out with it. The coffee grinding stopped, almost on cue as Daniel continued.

'Grace, the date that Brian died was the date that I predicted years ago.'

A cold chill ran up her spine. She managed to resist a shiver. Glancing at Daniel, she almost expected him to be smiling, joking.

He wasn't.

Next to the microwave hung a Salvador Dalí calendar. *The Persistence of Memory* was the current month's painting. She looked at it. Daniel wasn't sure if she was looking at the actual days or the painting itself. She turned back to what she was doing. 'I was also a volunteer,' she said, almost as a whisper to herself. Daniel heard her.

'That's right, you were,' he continued. 'And that's why I'm here.'

The second cup of coffee was ready.

She swung around. 'If you're here to tell me the result of the prediction you made years ago, that my date of death is approaching, I don't want to know,' she said, raising a finger.

He was surprised at her reaction. He persisted nevertheless. 'You have to know, Grace.'

'Is that why you're here, Daniel? Seriously?'

'Don't act this way. I need to tell you.'

'No, you don't. We all agreed. Everyone who took part in your...' she searched for the right word. 'Experiment. We all knew that you would never be able to tell us. If we knew, it could change the result. It could warrant your thesis useless.'

He smiled, impressed that she remembered his hypothesis. 'Correct. That's what I thought back then. And, who knows, maybe it's true. But it doesn't matter, Grace. Don't you see? I don't give a shit about my thesis.' He paused. 'You're more important.' This time it didn't sound fake. This time they both knew Daniel was telling the truth.

'I don't want to know,' she insisted.

'You have to know.'

'I don't have to know. You being here is already too much. You obviously think it's soon. Goddammit, Daniel. Goddammit. This is all I need at this stage of my life.'

He stepped forward and held Grace by her arms. Their eyes became glued to each other. Suddenly they both felt something from all those years ago. Their eyes served as a window into the past for each other, a reminder of a feeling they once had, or maybe still did. Could love remain dormant for so long?

'Grace,' he said, his heart pounding. He swallowed and said, 'Today is the date I predicted for you. According to my thesis, you will die today.'

She pulled herself away from Daniel's grip. 'I don't believe you're doing this. I just don't believe this. That thesis. It was once all you had. It was your life. You believed in it.' She raised her arms in the air out of desperation. 'You're just screwing it up for yourself. Jesus Christ. Why did you tell me? Why couldn't you just let me get on with my life and observe from a distance? That's what real scientists and mathematicians do.'

He shook his head. 'Human nature is more complicated than any mathematical problem. I know you probably don't believe me after so much time but I *do* have a conscience.'

'Your so-called conscience is destroying your own mathematical models. For what? We have nothing anymore. Why do you give a shit if I live or die?'

He stood still. The words were like a slap in the face, only more painful. He deserved it, though. He lowered the tone of his voice. 'Maybe it's my way of saying sorry.'

'By destroying your own hopes and dreams?'

'Those hopes and dreams are long gone, Grace.'

'Just like me.' She shrugged. 'I apparently evaporated from your life when these hopes and dreams were ruined.'

He ran a hand through his hair. 'I'm here now.'

'For all the wrong reasons,' she said shaking her head. She turned back to the coffee.

'Say what you want, Grace. But I am not letting you out of sight until midnight tonight.'

She smiled. 'Really? My own personal bodyguard,' she said as she added a splash of milk to the cups of coffee. 'And what if I said "No. I don't want you here"?'

'I would wait outside and just follow you for the day.'

She said nothing for a moment, lost in the prospect of a past lover following her around as she ran some errands.

'You really believe it's possible that I die today?' She reached for the sugar and scooped two teaspoons into one of the cups. She stirred and used the same spoon to stir the one with just the milk.

'I don't know. All I know is that one of the dates so far was spot-on. I couldn't believe it myself when I found out. I'm not chancing it with you.'

'You're a fool, Daniel. You shouldn't have done this.'

'I guess it's too late.'

She turned around with the two cups of coffee. 'You still want some coffee?' she asked.

'More than ever.'

'White, Two sugars?' she asked.

'You haven't forgotten. I'm impressed.'

38

John entered his office. Despite it now being bright outside, he switched on the light anyway. His office never received a lot of daylight. A mild chill lingered, so he decided to leave his jacket on.

He began tidying up his desk. Not too much though, as he didn't want to make it look like he had planned anything, which, come to think of it, was the truth. He wasn't really planning anything.

Post-Its were stuck around his monitor to serve as countless reminders. As he scanned them, he realised many of them were old and no longer served their purpose. His Outlook calendar now synchronised with his Blackberry anyway, making the Post-Its obsolete. He started pulling them off one by one, giving them each a once over to make sure they were no longer current. He stopped suddenly when he came to one at the bottom of the monitor. Slowly he pulled it free. It read:

New football socks - Max

Holding it up, a whirlwind of emotions erupted inside. Unable to recall buying football socks for Max, a sharp pain shot inside like an arrow going right through him. A vague memory revisited him. He remembered that Max indeed had asked for new football socks. One of them had gone missing. John remembered that he had volunteered to go out at lunchtime to pick them up. But that's as far as it went. Something must have come up during that lunch break and then…? He completely forgot. Why hadn't Max reminded him? Had Claire bought them instead? Did he find the missing sock? He couldn't recall. How did he not see it stuck to his monitor all this time?

Gently, John placed the Post-It down on the desk in front of him. Closing his eyes, he took a deep breath. He could sense a bubble of emotion rising inside. Sorrow, anger, loss, regret.

Regret. That was the predominant one. He wanted so desperately to have a memory of coming home. He longed for a recollection of interrupting Max as he was watching television or doing his homework and announcing, 'Hey buddy! Look what I bought in town today.' He would have held up a pair of black Manchester United socks.

But it wasn't there. There was no such memory because it never happened.

The bubble of regret suddenly exploded to the surface. John reached forward, grabbed the computer monitor and threw it. A loud bang echoed in the cold room as it crashed to the floor. He turned around and kicked his chair. It just rolled a few metres to the side. Suddenly he felt very out of breath.

He turned back around and stood over the screen trying to catch his breath. How many hours had he spent staring at that screen? Reading, writing, researching, when he should have been at home with his wife and child. His family.

As much as he would have loved to tear the room apart, he took some deep breaths and regained his composure.

What's happening to me? Is this what it feels like to be falling apart?

The electrical cable attached to the monitor had knocked over a photo of Max. It was facing down on the desk. He picked it up and sat back on his chair. The glass pane on the front of the frame had cracked. One single crack going diagonally across Max's face.

'What kind of father was I?' he asked the brown-eyed boy staring back at him. A teardrop fell from his cheek and landed on Max's forehead. He touched the tear and slowly spread it around Max's beautiful face, inadvertently cleaning the small film of dust that had accumulated on the glass itself.

He couldn't believe that he failed to find time to buy

socks for his son. Looking out the window, he tried to think of the nearest sports store.

Wasn't there even a Champion Sports store on Grafton Street? A five, maybe eight minute walk from here? He shook his head as the anger within him transformed to disappointment, extreme disappointment in himself.

He turned his attention back to the monitor lying on the floor. He wondered if anyone below him had heard the crash and were now on their way up to investigate. Quickly he regained his composure and wiped away any tears from his face. If anyone came to the door, he would just say it fell over.

Likely story.

Picking up the screen, he placed it neatly back on his desk. He noticed that it didn't actually look damaged. Maybe it even still worked. He took comfort in the fact that at least it didn't look like it had been thrown to the floor. It was sturdier than it appeared.

Connecting his laptop to the computer screen, John was amazed when he saw the screen come to life. He plugged in the network cable to the back of the laptop as it started up. It was only when the home page appeared on the screen that he realised that a cluster of pixels on the top left were no longer working. He would request a new one from IT next week. *If I'm still around*, he thought to himself.

He started copying all his current files onto the network. Although he was sure someone would still go through his laptop for anything important, he was confident that by putting them on the server himself, he would be saving someone from cursing him later. The Window's message told him it would take 2 hours, it then jumped down to 8 minutes and back up to 21 minutes and stayed there.

While he was waiting, John turned his attention to the office plant that stood next to his desk. He never really noticed it before. He never watered it and interestingly enough, never saw anyone else water it. Suddenly he had doubts if it was real. Reaching over, he tore a piece of the leaf. It tore easily. He held it to his nose. It didn't smell of anything special, but it did smell real, alive. He flicked the piece of leaf onto the floor.

It was strange the things he noticed now, first the football socks reminder that failed its job and now the plant. These things had been in his office for months, even years, and he had been oblivious to them.

He felt somewhat like the Post-It reminder that had failed its job. He was supposed to be a father first, everything else should have come after that, but he failed. It hurt him when he felt that he was not a good father. What did Max really think of him? As for Claire? He was pretty sure that she thought that he was a terrible father.

Rubbing his forehead he felt some dry skin fall onto his desk. He felt suddenly tired and drowsy. He was happy that he hadn't bumped into anyone, colleagues or students. Normally if he worked on Saturdays, which was quite often, he would pop into the Buttery for lunch or a sneaky pint. Sometimes he would meet students or fellow lecturers. It was pleasant to meet them at the weekend, away from the tight timetables of a weekday.

As the files and presentations continued to transfer to the network, John got up and strolled to the window. Looking out he could see the rugby field in the distance. A small group of students were already out training.

'Now that's what I call dedication,' he muttered to himself, reflecting briefly on his stint as a rugby player. It lasted a couple of years at UCD where he had studied. Often he had been too hungover or busy to really focus on it. But it was always a game that he enjoyed watching and was something he was looking forward to teaching Max when he was older. He had wondered though, with Max's small build and gentle character, if he would have taken to it. Max definitely had his mother's genes in great abundance. He recalled the few times that he had taken

Max out to play ball, when he was much younger. Max would sometimes lose interest and pick some daisies for his mother. He would often ask his daddy to mind them until they were home. John would put them in his pocket and forget about them. Days later he would find them in his pocket during a lecture. Not remembering what they were, he would take the withered flowers out of his pocket, smile and place them back. The students must have thought he had some kind of random flower fetish.

Although he was a confident lecturer, deep inside, he hated speaking in public. When he found the scrunched up three-day-old daisy or dandelion, he gained strength from it.

He walked back to his desk and surfed the web for a while. When the file transfer was complete, he closed down his laptop and switched off the monitor. The football sock Post-It lay on the table. Not really sure why, he picked it up, folded it in two and placed it in his wallet. Next, he picked up the photo frame and glanced briefly in Max's eyes.

'Maybe see you sooner than you think, little fella.'

He placed the damaged photo frame face down on the desk and left the room.

39

Grace knocked back the final drop of coffee and looked at Daniel. They had spent the last ten minutes going back over old times. He told her about his marriage to Zoe and their son. They touched briefly on what other ex-classmates were doing with their lives. Who had children, who didn't. Who worked abroad, who didn't. Although there was so much more catching up to do, Grace started to become restless.

'So, what now?' she said placing her cup on the counter. 'If I decide to leave the house, what are you going to do? Just follow me?'

Daniel shrugged like he had no other choice. 'Yes. I suppose so. But to be honest I would prefer if you didn't leave the house today,' he said with a serious expression.

'Not leave the house!' She threw her head back in mock laughter. 'Do you see the size of this apartment, Daniel? Do you really think I'm going to stay locked up in a stranger's apartment for the day?'

He suddenly looked interested. 'So he's a stranger, is he?'

She walked to the sink and rinsed her cup. 'Well, he's not somebody I've known for years if that's what you mean.' She placed the cup on the draining board and turned to check the coffee machine. Sliding out a tray from beneath it, she removed a container that collected the old used coffee.

'What's his name again?'

'Rik.'

'And he's a colleague?'

She nodded. 'Have you finished your coffee?' she asked, more in an attempt to change the subject than really wanting to know. She threw the coffee dregs in the bin and put the container back in the machine.

Daniel looked down at the drop remaining in his cup and knocked it back. 'Yes.'

'Okay, I'm going out for a walk to the park. You can walk with me, walk behind me, you can even walk in front of me like a real bodyguard and monitor my path for danger. Either way, I'm leaving this apartment.'

He raised his eyes as he left his cup on the counter. 'I see you haven't lost your stubbornness over the last decade.'

Grace flung a threadbare tea towel at him which landed directly on his face. He removed it immediately. His stern look transformed into a smile. 'Okay, I'll walk with you. Just don't do anything stupid today, that's all I ask.'

She took his cup and rinsed it in the sink too.

'And by stupid you mean what exactly? Some people would regard talking to an ex-boyfriend who never had the courtesy to break up properly, extremely stupid.'

'True,' he admitted. 'The stupidity category I'm talking about however is along the lines of jumping out on a street when a lorry is approaching.'

She placed Daniel's cup on the draining board next to hers. She said nothing for a while as she dried her hands, clearly reflecting on something. 'You know what this actually reminds me of?' she asked, putting her hands in her pockets. 'When I was in school, I once wrote my name on a copybook with a ruler. I measured out the letters and did it so neatly. It took me probably twenty minutes or something. When I sat back to admire my work, I realised that I had spelled my surname wrong. I had left out one of the R's in "Farrell."'

Daniel wasn't sure what she was getting at. He gave her a look to continue.

'My level of concentration in drawing the letters with the ruler was so high that I ended up screwing up the simple task in a different way. If I just wrote my name the regular way, I wouldn't have spelled it wrong.'

'So what you're saying is that now that I have asked

you to be more careful today, you're afraid that you're going to concentrate so much that you end up screwing up anyway?'

'Exactly.'

'So let's stick to my initial plan of not leaving the apartment.'

She shook her head. 'I'm not staying inside today, I'm sorry.' She pointed to the back window. An orange glow from the early October sun shone through it. 'Look at the weather, for God's sake. Trust me when I say that the sun is just as scarce in Amsterdam as it is in Dublin.'

Daniel knew she had a point. Deep down he didn't want to stay inside either. It wasn't a particularly pleasant apartment for two ex-lovers to be confined to for a whole day. It would also be nice to see some of Amsterdam, he thought.

'Okay,' he agreed. 'Just no BASE jumping or cave diving,' he said. 'And if you see street performers asking for a volunteer to throw knives at, please move towards the back of the crowd.'

'Deal,' she agreed.

They walked along Westlandgracht, up by Theophile de Bockstraat before coming to a pedestrian bridge. Once over that, it was downhill and across Amstelveenseweg to the back entrance of Vondel Park.

'I live on this street, you know,' she said as they crossed Amstelveenseweg.

Daniel looked confused. 'I didn't realise we were so close to your house. My sense of direction is such a mess.'

'Well, we're not really close to it. This is like one of those streets that go on forever. But, if you stay on this street, it eventually leads onto the street where I live,' she said pointing to the right. 'Or lived, I should probably say.'

It was turning out to be a wonderful autumn's day. Vondel Park was already a hive of activity. Cyclists, joggers, mothers pushing buggies, fathers pulling kids on rollerblades. Daniel and Grace walked in silence for some of the way, lost in their separate thoughts. How do you really catch up after so long? Some small talk had been covered in the apartment, but when would they get to the interesting stuff?

'So what's the story between you and Rik anyway?' Daniel finally asked as they walked along a path next to one of many large ponds in the park.

'We're colleagues. We're friends. He wants something more, but I'm just not ready for that yet,' she admitted openly.

'Okay, so it's just a non-sexual fling you're having?'

'A non-sexual fling? Is there such a thing?'

He shrugged. 'There is now.'

'Yes, I suppose you could put it that way. I'm having a non-sexual fling with my colleague. Rik's just there at the right time. What is certain is that I had to end it with Otto.'

'So you just moved out recently?'

She nodded. 'Literally a couple of days ago. Although the word 'moved' sounds a bit planned and organised. It was more like I just had enough. To be honest, it's something I should have done a long time ago.'

'Are you getting a divorce?'

'Eventually I guess. But at least start with moving out, lock, stock and barrel. So far all I have is a hastily packed suitcase.'

They followed the path along a pond. The sun glistened in the water. An Asian woman with black flowing hair played with a collie dog and two poodles. An unlikely combination. Maybe she was a professional dog walker.

The pathway that they walked on led to a statue surrounded by a flower bed.

'Who's that?' Daniel asked pointing to the statue.

'No idea.'

As they arrived closer, the name became clearer.

'Joost van den Vondel,' she said eventually.

'You know him?'

'Well I guess he's the guy the park is named after. Vondel Park.'

'I could have guessed that myself. You'd make a great tourist guide,' Daniel said sarcastically.

'Okay, smart ass. Who is Saint Stephen then?'

'Saint Stephen?'

'As in Saint Stephen's Green in Dublin. Surely you know who he was and why the park is named after him?'

He raised his hands in a surrender posture. 'Fair point.'

As they continued towards the statue of Joost van den Vondel, Grace pointed to the flowerbed that surrounded the memorial. It was encircled by a small stone wall. 'Shall we sit down there for a while and enjoy the sunshine?'

'Sounds good.'

'Not too dangerous?' she asked teasingly.

He gave her a soft thump on her arm. 'You tell me, is Amsterdam renowned for statues falling on people?'

She shook her head. 'The statue-falling season is over. It lasts from June to September,' she added with a deadpan expression.

Daniel couldn't help giggling like a schoolboy. It was this dry stupid humour that Grace possessed that made him fall in love with her in the first place. They had laughed so much together in the past.

As they sat down on the edge of the small flowerbed, he looked behind him and gave the statue a once over. It stood tall looking down at them and was surrounded by what looked like four small angel-like statuettes. Next to one of the statuettes, a man was on all-fours doing some maintenance. His jacket hung on the head of one of the statuettes.

'So where did you meet Otto?' he asked, turning his attention to the park in front of him.

Grace looked in the distance and then at Daniel.

'Edinburgh,' she said. 'I was doing a post-doc that didn't really work out. He was doing a year-long international business course that *did* work out. We met in

211

a student's bar. One thing led to another. You know how these things go, right?'

Now he was sure it was a dig at him. He and Grace met each other in The Long Stone, one of the student bars in Dublin.

'After he finished his course, he asked me to move back to his hometown of Amsterdam with him. It's the typical story, the kind you read in gossip magazines on famous celebrities' lives gone horribly wrong. At first it was like a fairy tale. He was really your perfect gentleman. Then sometimes I noticed that when he would smoke a joint and combine it with alcohol and God knows what else...' She shook her head. 'I don't know... something weird happened.'

'Weird. As in violent?'

Grace looked towards the ground before continuing. A pansy from the flower garden behind her lay on the ground. Someone, probably a child, had picked it and dropped it there. She picked it up and then looked up across the park.

'One night I was having a bath. It was a Friday night. It had been a pretty hectic week. I was shattered. I knew Otto was out with the lads and I wasn't expecting him back until later. I was just enjoying the soak. I had lit a couple of scented candles and had relaxing music playing in the background. You know, the works. I never heard him come in. I had my eyes closed, lost in myself. I opened them and he was standing over me. I almost leapt out of the bath with the fright. It was like something you see in a horror film. Just standing there. He frightened the shit out of me.' She paused for a few moments and swallowed before continuing. 'I think I splashed his suit. He was smiling though. I could see in his eyes that he was drunk and stoned. I thought for a second he was pleased to see me.' She started picking the petals from the abandoned flower she held in her hand.

'"So, who were you expecting?" he said.

"No one," I said, still recovering from the fright.

"Come on," he said, "who were you expecting?"

I didn't need those accusations after such a week. I kind of lost it and shouted, "I'm having a bloody bath in peace. Fuck off!"

Suddenly, without any warning, he dragged me out of the bath by my hair, banged my face on the sink and threw me down on the floor. He kicked me a couple of times in the stomach.'

Daniel's heart sank as he heard Grace tell her story. As he looked at her he could see a tear roll down her cheek. She continued.

'He shouted something, but I don't remember what. It was probably some abuse in Dutch. I looked up through blurred vision and just saw spit flying from his mouth. It was horrible. I've never seen so much hate in a person's eyes. He walked out again. I lay there crying. I was cold. I started drying myself, afraid that if I got back in the bath, it would trigger him to return. I pulled the plug and blew out the candles. The strawberry scent was replaced by extinguished candle scent. My stomach ached. A lot of shampoos and toiletries lay scattered on the floor around me. He had broken a shelf. It was disgusting. I felt absolutely sick. As I dried myself I noticed the blood. At first I thought it was from my face. Then I realised it was…'

She trailed off for a moment, continuing to pick petals from the lost flower.

'The blood was coming from between my legs. I couldn't recall when my period was due, but I found it too much of a coincidence that it would start straight after having been kicked in the stomach. I placed a sanitary pad in and got dressed. The pain became unbearable. I went downstairs holding my stomach tight. Otto was in the living room watching Top Gear, acting as if nothing had happened. It's funny the details you remember, like what programme he was watching. I remember so clearly the images of Jeremy Clarkson and the other two guys on the TV screen. I told Otto I was bleeding. He got up suddenly, all concerned. He was like a different man. Sometimes I think he was. He said straight out that he was too drunk to drive, but called a taxi. Five minutes later we were sitting in the back of a cab on our way to A&E. He made sure I told the doctors that I had slipped getting out of the bath. They did a scan and found that I was pregnant.' She took a deep breath. 'They took me into theatre to have a curettage.'

Grace paused again for a moment. The flower in her hand was now bare. She allowed the last petal to flutter to the ground.

'Right before the procedure I heard them say "twins". I've been haunted every day since.'

40

Daniel said nothing. What could he say? How could someone pull a defenceless woman from a bath and beat the living shit out of her? Grace didn't seem to mind the silence. She let the bare flower drop to the ground, next to the petals.

'You know the funny thing about all this?' she asked. Daniel took it as a rhetorical question and remained silent.

'It was like it never happened. The weeks after the incident, he was so kind. And I know, I've read the stories and seen films of stupid women who stay with violent men. I could never understand it until it happened to me. I don't know what it is. Either it's a fear of being alone or deep down still loving someone. When you get married you promise to stay with them in sickness and in health. And that's what I did, because I think he was very sick.'

'But not anymore?'

'What? I don't think he's sick anymore?'

'No. You don't believe in staying with him in sickness and in health?'

'I don't believe men can change. Or let me put it another way. I don't think it's possible for any *woman* to change a man. And the sooner women realise that, the better. We can change our attitudes towards them, but I don't think they change, unless they want to themselves.'

Daniel nodded in agreement.

'So what I know for sure now is that I can never change Otto. I can only change my attitude towards him. And quite frankly, my attitude is, to hell with him. I can't stand him.'

'What about the *through sickness and in health* promise?' he asked, challenging her.

'If he came to me and asked for my help. If he admitted that he was sick and needed help, then I would, or at least back then, would have helped him one hundred percent.' Grace started blinking rapidly as if a fly or piece of dirt went into her eye. She continued, despite the irritation. 'But Otto is too proud to ask for help. He is too pig-headed to admit that he has a problem. Maybe he just doesn't realise and doesn't want help. Quite frankly, I couldn't care less anymore.'

A tear fell from her eye. Daniel was unsure if it was from the irritation in her eye or from the story she was telling.

'Not a day goes by that I don't think what might have been.' She glanced in the distance and saw a mother jogging and pushing a stroller at the same time. 'If I see twins in the street I turn away. It upsets me too much.'

The mother in the distance stopped and took a bottle of sports drink from a pocket on the front of the stroller. After she knocked back a few mouthfuls, she placed it back in the pocket. Before she got on her way again, she stuck her head under the hood to check on the baby.

'After that incident,' Grace said, taking her attention away from the jogging mother, 'I was unable to have children.'

Without thinking, Daniel placed his hand on top of Grace's.

'I'm sorry to hear that, Grace.'

She said nothing for a while, enjoying his touch. 'Thanks,' she said eventually, as she wiped away the tear falling down her cheek. 'Shit, I've got something in my eye,' she said while rubbing her watery eye. She turned towards Daniel. 'Do you see anything?' she asked trying her best to open her right eye.

Daniel removed his hand from hers. He could indeed see that the eye in question was much more watery and bloodshot than the other. Bending forward he stared into her eyes. 'Keep it open.'

'I'm trying.'

'Are you wearing contacts?'

Grace nodded. 'Daily disposables.'

'It might help if you take out the one from that eye, so I can have a proper look.'

She stopped moving as she thought of something. 'Shit.'

'What?'

'My glasses. They're still in my house.'

Daniel frowned. 'Which house?'

'My house. Otto's house. The thought crossed me briefly this morning,' she continued, 'but then I forgot about it. I thought I had enough daily disposables in my handbag to last me a few days, so I wouldn't have to go back to the house until next week, when Otto would be at work. But this morning I didn't see any extra ones except the two I'm wearing now.'

'Oh. That's annoying.'

'Just have a good look in my eye and see if you see anything.'

He stared into her eye. Gently he pulled the lower eyelid downwards. He nodded. 'Just next to your tear duct there's a little flea or something.' He pulled a tissue from his pocket and rolled up the corner of it, so it looked like a kind of a pipe-cleaner. He turned back towards Grace, lowered the eyelid again and gently inserted the makeshift cleaner into her eye. She moved her head back suddenly due to the sensitivity.

'Sorry,' he said. 'I think I can push the flea towards your tear duct and then let your eye's natural resources take over.'

'Okay.'

He repeated his original action. Grace stayed still, as he pushed the flea towards the tear duct. The flea became attached to the tissue, and he pulled away immediately.

'Got it.' No sooner did he pull the tissue out than the flea fell and disappeared.

'Thanks.' She blinked rapidly, gaining equilibrium in her eye. Daniel, unable to see any near-by bin, stuffed the tissue back into his pocket.

She turned towards him. 'I need to go back to my house and get my glasses.'

He shook his head. 'You're joking, right?'

She searched her handbag for something. 'I need them. I don't have enough lenses.' She pointed to her eyes. 'Once I take these lenses out, I'm blind as a bat. I completely forgot them the other day, as I basically wanted to get out of the house quickly.'

'But is Otto usually home on Saturdays?'

'Usually, yes. But normally up in his study doing work or God knows what.'

'I don't think it's a good idea.'

'We'll drive. I'll run in. I know exactly where they are. I probably won't even meet him. It's not as if he's going to chase me out of the house with a shot-gun.'

'That's debatable,' he said, reflecting on his encounter with the guy the previous day and the story he just heard. 'Can we not just go to Specsavers and get new glasses or a few contacts to keep you going?'

Grace withdrew a tissue from her handbag and dabbed her watery eye. 'I'm not buying new glasses just because I'm afraid of going back into my own house. I pay half the mortgage.'

'You just spent the last five minutes telling me how violent he is.'

'When he's drunk or stoned. He's not going to be drunk or stoned in the middle of the day. Not unless he has sunk to a new low.' Grace decided that it was best not to mention her encounter with him two days earlier and the bloody nose when he was sober. 'Are you with me or not?' she asked.

Daniel turned his attention to something else. 'What's the drive like? Driving is, statistically speaking, the most dangerous thing you can do today. Probably more dangerous than entering the house of your violent husband.'

'Well, you can drive if you want.'

'Yeah, right. Driving on the right hand side is bad enough without having to worry about the million-and-one bikes in this city.'

'Look, I'm going anyway. If we get there early enough, he might even still be in bed,' she said, looking at her watch. Under her voice she continued, 'Assuming he even made it home last night.'

'Oh, he was home all right. The scrape on my head can vouch for that.'

'What scrape on the head?'

Daniel gave her a quick recap of his encounter with her husband the previous day.

'I'm sorry you had to experience that, Daniel.'

'Don't worry about me. I'm sorry that you married him and experienced a lot worse.'

Satisfied that her eye was more or less back to normal, she placed the tissue back in her handbag.

'So, are you with me?' she asked, touching him on the shoulder. 'I could do with your support.'

'My goal of keeping you locked up and safe today has now resulted in us driving to your violent husband. Are you sure you don't have a bungee jump planned for later as well?'

Grace smiled. 'And increase the chances of losing my contacts? No way. At least not until I have my glasses in my possession.'

41

Claire decided today would be the day. She would do something with Max's room. Or at the very least discuss it with John. Too many awkward silences filled the house. It was time to put a stop to it. After she showered and dressed, she had a quick bowl of muesli and yoghurt, and jumped on bus number 37 to the city centre.

Hopping off at Lower Ormond Quay, she walked around the corner to Capel Street. After a five minute walk, she reached the entrance to the St Vincent de Paul charity shop. It was a small pokey building with a large sign saying simply "Vincent's". Faceless male and female mannequins stood in the window, showing off the latest fashion in second hand clothes. Surprisingly enough, the clothes they wore seemed to be in mint condition.

Taking a deep breath Claire entered. A musty scent that differed from regular shops hung in the air. A scent of a hundred households intermingled under one roof. A melting pot of family aromas. It was like walking into someone's garage or attic, or the house of a grandparent who had stopped throwing things away fifty years previously.

She scanned the shop. It was long, stretching back a good twenty metres. It was bigger than it looked from the outside. A cashier counter stood midway, behind which there was a woman scribbling something on a piece of cardboard.

The shop was predominantly full of clothes. To the right, Claire could see the children's section; a combination of clothes of all shapes and sizes. There were also shelves full of toys and random games. She recognised some of the games from her own childhood: *Hungry Hungry Hippos, Fibber, Operation.*

Her eye fell on a red football jersey hanging in the kids'

section. Walking closer to it, she could see the small yellow Manchester United emblem. The main letters on the front said: AON. She had no clue what "AON" was. She turned it around and saw the name "Giggs" printed on the back, just above the number "11". She had heard of Giggs, but couldn't picture the player. The jersey was in good condition; a little faded, but would easily do a little boy for a year or two. Yes, it would have easily fitted Max.

I've got to stop doing this to myself.

She continued wandering around the shop. She walked by a clothes rail of men's suits and jackets. Some of them were like the one in the front window - almost mint condition and actually quite modern-looking. Others were more shabby and just begging to be bought. They would probably be snatched up at Halloween by those who wanted to dress up as Jack the Ripper or some other morbid character. These were the types of suits that you wouldn't actually mind throwing some fake blood onto, or spilling beer down the front, depending on the time of night.

Out of curiosity, she felt the material of one of the modern jackets. She picked up the sleeve and glanced at the price tag.

Twenty euro.

Not bad, she thought. Maybe she should send John here next time he was in need of a suit.

She walked towards the counter. The lady behind the counter looked up from what she was doing. Her hair was fuzzy, like it had been blow-dried one too many times. She wore heavy mascara. Claire estimated her to be in her mid-forties.

'Mornin',' the woman said, with a bright smile and a strong Dublin accent. It was a rough voice, like she had sandpaper caught in her throat. As Claire drew closer, she couldn't help but notice that the woman was drenched in perfume. She wondered if it was an attempt to dilute the stale aroma that hung in the air. Tempted as she was, she refrained from taking a step backwards.

'Is there a procedure or something for donating items?' Claire asked, returning the polite smile.

'No, not really. Ye just bring them along, and we'll take them from ye. The items we think are sellable we'll try and sell. Other stuff we give away for free to schools or community centres. And in some cases we throw it away. Ye'd be surprised what some people give to charity.' She glanced towards the door, at the constant stream of people passing by. 'Especially since the fecking city council started charging to dispose bags of rubbish. People started leaving their rubbish outside the shop! Feckin' gobshites.' The woman realised she was wandering off the topic of conversation and observed Claire for a moment. 'What kind of items are you thinking of donating?'

Claire nodded towards the children section. 'Children's stuff. Clothes, games, toys, you know.'

'Of course,' the woman smiled. 'Don't talk to me about it. They grow out of them so quick, don't they? And the clutter. My ones are always suspicious when they see me going to work with a plastic bag full of stuff. They're like "Ah, Ma, what are ye givin' away now?" Is your place cluttered too?'

Claire hesitated for a moment and then smiled. 'In a way.'

'Well, I can give ye some plastic donation bags and ye just throw everything into them, and bring them here. Or if ye wish, we can have someone call out and collect them directly from your home. Whereabouts do you live?'

'Castleknock.'

'Ah, we can send someone around no problem if ye want. Are there a lot of items?'

'Quite a few, yes.'

The woman handed her a flyer. 'Here we have all the contact information ye need. Web address, phone number. Also, ye can see a list of what we take and what we don't.' The woman glanced at the door again and then back at

Claire. 'I once had someone come in with a bag of grass.' She lowered her voice. 'I mean the grass you smoke,' she said winking. 'He was wondering if I wanted to buy it for half the usual street price. Can you imagine that? I told him to feck off before I call the bleedin' guards. Can you imagine the cheek of him?' The woman held out her hands in front of her about twenty centimetres apart. 'It was a fairly decent sized bag, I tell ye. I'd feckin' die if I smoked it all. Anyone would.'

Claire just smiled and took the flyer and glanced over it. 'Thank you.'

Suddenly she looked up.

'Just as a matter of interest. What happens to all the stuff? I mean in general, where do they end up?'

The woman looked a little confused. She made a wide gesture with her hand for Claire to look around.

'Well, like I said, we sell them here if we can.'

Claire stared at the Manchester United jersey.

A silence rose between them. Claire glanced back at the flyer. She remembered Edward's advice on not being afraid to speak about Max.

'I'm getting rid of my little boy's stuff. He passed away a few months ago.' Claire could see a look of concern on the woman's face, as another moment of silence rose between them. It was a silence that was no stranger to the charity shop, with precious few visitors in the mornings.

Slowly, the woman cupped Claire's hands in hers. 'Ah, my dear. I am so sorry to hear that.'

Claire was taken aback by the warm physical gesture. Unlike the lady's voice, her hands were warm and soft. She looked at the woman, gaining strength from her tenderness.

'Thank you. I've been putting this task off for so long.'

The woman shook her head. 'No, you're not. Some people don't even try to get rid of their loved ones' belongings. The fact that you're in here is further than some people can even begin to imagine. So don't be too hard on yourself. Getting rid of loved ones' belongings is a task that nobody wants to do. But at the end of the day you're helping people who are...,' the lady trailed off for a moment. 'I won't say less fortunate than ye, because nobody can be less fortunate than someone who has lost a child. But people who are experiencing different hardships than you. Such as poverty or some kind of abuse. Make no mistake. What you are doing or at least thinking of doing is *very* generous.'

The woman let go of Claire's hands.

'Thank you for the warm words,' she said eventually, wondering if the woman was actually finished.

'I remember me Da took me dog Sooty to the vet to be put down,' the woman continued. 'He was such a beautiful dog. A golden Labrador. I know you would think a dog called Sooty would be black. Anyway, I didn't talk to me Da for a month afterwards. I thought he did it to hurt me. I thought he did it because he was sick of having a dog. As you grow up you realise he did out of pure love. Sooty was already fourteen years old. He was so slow. He had arthritis. He had a bladder infection. He was really quite sick, actually. It was the best thing anybody could have done for him. But it was one of those decisions, one of those unwritten rules that nobody tells you about.'

The woman picked up from below the counter a roll of thick yellow plastic bags with the St. Vincent de Paul logo.

'Here. Take these. Fill them up when you are ready. Then call us. And we will pick them up. They will go to new homes. They will raise money for people living in poverty. They will go to deprived schools. Even though he is no longer with us, your son will help people.'

'Thank you.'

'But don't be afraid to keep some of his stuff. There's nothing wrong with having reminders of him around the house.'

'Of course. I'll keep that in mind.'

'Take care, love.'

Claire smiled and walked out of the shop. A certain weight from her shoulders was gone. Although there were many more steps of recovery to come, she knew she had made an important first step. Just by entering the charity shop and taking some plastic bags with her, she stepped in the right direction. It was time to move forward. It was time to talk to John.

42

The Saturday afternoon traffic in Amsterdam was very busy. Grace weaved her Ford Fiesta gracefully between trams, cyclists and scooters.

'For a city renowned for its bikes, you have plenty of cars all the same,' Daniel said.

'Tell me about it. I normally wouldn't dream of using my car unless it was completely necessary. I use my bike for almost all the trips I make within the city.'

They pulled up across the street from the house Daniel had visited less than twenty-four hours earlier. The silver BMW still stood on the driveway.

'Well, he's home, that's for sure,' Grace said.

'How do you know that?'

She looked at Daniel and then back at the BMW.

'Maybe you're the one who should be visiting Specsavers. Do you not see the car in the driveway?'

'Maybe he's gone for a walk or out on his bike. You just told me that you use your bike almost all of the time.'

'Yes, *I* use my bike a lot. You don't know Otto,' she said, turning off the ignition. 'If his car is in the driveway and it's daytime, then he's in the house. Simple as that.'

She waved to a woman carrying two large bags with pictures of a cartoon hamster on each of them and the words *Albert Heijn Hamster Weken*.

'She's a neighbour,' Grace said. 'I wonder what she's thinking, seeing a strange guy in the car with me.'

'Close neighbour?'

'Two doors away.'

'I mean "close" as in, are you friends with her?'

'I just know her to say hello to. I called around to her when she had a baby a couple of years ago,' she said as she gave her own house a once over, looking for any signs of life.

'So what's the plan?' Daniel asked bringing the topic of conversation back to the subject in hand.

'There's not much of a *plan*,' she pulled the keys out of the ignition. 'I'll go in, find my glasses. They're in the drawer in the hallway, I think. Normally, they're the last thing I take before leaving the house.' She took a deep breath. Despite trying to act brave, he could see that she was a little nervous.

'Well, judging from that plan, if you're not out in five minutes, I should come and get you, right?' he asked.

She thought for a minute, then shook her head. 'Let's say if I'm not back in twenty minutes to come and get me. Who knows? I might run into him and we have a sophisticated conversation. The last thing I want is an ex-lover ringing on the doorbell. No offence.'

'Fair enough. But how do I know he won't be beating the shit out of you while I'm sitting here twiddling my thumbs?'

'I'll scream or throw something through the window.'

'Oh right. Should I be on the lookout for anything specific coming through the window?'

'Shut up. Who's taking the piss now?'

'I do that when I'm nervous. I don't think you should be going near that house at all. Especially today of all days.'

Grace re-entered the key into the ignition, turned it slightly to connect, and pressed the windows to go down. She took the keys out again.

'Just keep your ears… peeled,' she said. 'Or whatever the phrase is.'

'*Eyes* peeled, ears… to the ground.'

'Exactly,' she said, as a large truck drove by, drowning out her words.

Daniel smirked. 'Oh sure. I'll hear plenty in this racket?' he said pointing to the traffic going by.

She winked. 'I'll be fine. I'm a big girl now.' She got out of the car and pushed the door shut behind her. She crossed half the street and waited in the middle, as an oncoming Citroen went by. She crossed to the other side and entered her driveway.

Daniel could see her slowing down as she approached the front door and ascended the couple of steps, the same steps that he was pushed from.

A sudden movement in a window on the second floor caught Daniel's eye. When he looked at it directly, he couldn't see anything. The curtains were drawn with just the slightest gap visible. He closed his eyes fully and then opened them focussing on the window. Had he seen something or was it just some light reflection on the window? Was he too nervous himself to trust what he saw from so far away? He scanned the other windows quickly to see if there was any other movement. Nothing.

He couldn't help feeling like a getaway driver parked outside a bank during a heist. Only he felt completely useless, with no key and zero intention of doing any driving, even if he had it.

He monitored Grace as she slipped the key into the front door lock. Turning the key, she opened the door and slipped inside.

43

Otto had been getting dressed and checking his email on his Blackberry in the master bedroom when he saw the blue Ford Fiesta pull in across the street. Immediately he placed his Blackberry on the windowsill and drew the curtains, leaving a small gap in them so he could still see outside. He took a couple of steps back so that he wouldn't be visible from the street. Tempted to retrieve his binoculars from the study, Otto decided against it. He wasn't completely sure where they were. His eyesight was good enough to recognise the car and the driver immediately. It took him a few moments more to recognise the passenger.

'So you found her, did you?' he whispered looking at Daniel. 'You found your long-lost friend, eh?'

Otto continued to dress himself quickly as he watched them talking to each other in the car. Finally, Grace climbed out of the car and crossed the street. He picked up his Blackberry that was lying on the windowsill. This caused the curtain to move slightly. He remained still. He moved backwards very gradually and then ran to the bathroom. He quickly turned on the tap in the shower and pulled away before he got wet. Next he went back to the bedroom, grabbed his shoes and sat down on the landing to put them on. As he did so, he listened for the front door.

Eventually he heard his wife creep in like a mouse. He could picture her standing in the hallway, straining to hear what he was up to and pick up any clues that would tell her where he was. Or where he was pretending to be. Otto was certain that she would be able to hear the shower, and that she probably relaxed a little. He finished tying his laces.

Will she come upstairs? he wondered. After a short

moment, he could hear her light footsteps moving towards the kitchen. He peeped his head over the stairs and saw the back of her as she entered the kitchen. He decided to stay put. Pulling away from the stairway, he stood still, straining to hear what she might be up to. Unable to hear anything at all from the kitchen, due to the shower and extractor fan in the bathroom, he just waited. After about a minute, he could hear her light steps again walking towards the front door. He could now imagine her looking up the stairs. He didn't move.

Faintly he heard the front door open again, and closing a second later. He poked his head over the stairs again. The hallway was empty.

Quick as a flash, Otto ran back into the bathroom and turned off the shower. He then descended the stairs and put his face to the front door to look through the peephole. He could see his wife walking down the driveway with her back to him. She held a little box in her hand. From the peephole, he was unable to see the parked Fiesta. He ran to the front room and drew the curtain back a smidgen. He saw Grace climb into the driver's seat and place the box on the lap of her companion. They both put on their seat belts, and when a gap in the traffic came, Grace pulled out and joined the influx of cars.

Otto knew that if they had come from that direction in which they pulled up, they would have to do a U-turn at some stage to go back the same way. Amsterdamseweg was blocked off further up. He ran to the front door, opened it and slammed it shut behind him. He pressed the central locking button on his car key and jumped into his BMW. Slouching down, he placed the keys in the ignition. He readjusted the rear-view mirror so that he could view traffic passing on the street behind him while still in his slouching position. No sooner had he adjusted the mirror than he saw the Ford Fiesta pass behind him, heading back towards Amsterdam. Not wasting any time, he reversed out of the driveway. Slowly at first, but when he noticed there were no pedestrians or oncoming traffic, he put his foot down and swerved his car in the direction that his wife's car had just passed. He quickly accelerated to match the speed of the afternoon traffic. He glanced ahead. Three cars separated him from the Ford Fiesta. Otto eased off the gas now. The last thing he wanted was to be spotted by Grace.

44

'He was in the shower?' Daniel asked as they made a U-turn at the end of the street.

Grace nodded.

'I thought I saw some movement coming from one of the upper windows after you left the car.'

She shrugged. 'Maybe he was pulling over the curtains before he got undressed or whatever. Who knows? But basically I didn't run into him. And as far as I could hear, he was in the shower.'

As they drove by the house heading back towards Amsterdam, Daniel glanced at the front upstairs room again. If he hadn't been so obsessed by the movement he saw moments earlier, he might have noticed Otto's hands reaching up to readjust the mirror from within his BMW.

'Happy now?' Grace asked.

'What do you mean?'

'That I didn't come running out of the house dodging bullets or with a big Indiana Jones-style boulder chasing me down the driveway.'

'Delighted,' he said. 'But I will be even more delighted once you drive back to the apartment safely.'

Grace glanced into her rear-view mirror and then her side mirrors. When she was happy there were no obstacles nearby, she made a little "out of control" swerve. 'Whoa.'

Daniel wasn't impressed. 'Oh, very funny.'

'Relax. Don't statistics show that most accidents occur a couple of kilometres from your home?' She glanced at her speedometer. 'And now that we're almost a couple of kilometres from *my* home, you can relax a bit.' She glanced briefly at Daniel. 'Didn't you enter that into your "Date of Death" calculations?'

'I put something on road death statistics in it alright, and the likelihood of being in a fatal road crash.'

'So do you want to have dinner tonight?' Grace asked changing the subject.

'Takeaway. In your apartment. With the door locked. Wrapped in bubble wrap.'

She rolled her eyes. 'Come on, Daniel. Loosen up. We've almost done the two most dangerous things that we're going to do today. It's all downhill from now on.'

She eased off the accelerator as a cyclist came off the bicycle path. The cyclist manoeuvred around a truck that was double-parked and flashing its hazard lights. Once the cyclist was back on the path, she overtook him.

Daniel smirked as he glanced at the cyclist. 'I would probably have killed that guy if I was driving.'

'You get used to it. It's all about anticipation. I saw that lorry double-parked. I saw the cyclist. The cyclist did exactly what I would have done.'

'Seriously? You would have just pulled out?'

Grace shrugged. 'Probably.'

Daniel wasn't sure if she was teasing but decided to go with it. 'Okay, let's add cycling to the list of dangerous things to avoid today.'

45

Claire got off the bus early on her way back from the charity shop and picked up some groceries at the Castleknock Village Centre. It was her first time visiting her local supermarket since the tragic event. It was the same supermarket that she had brought Max to countless of times.

As she carried her bags up Castleknock Road, she thought to herself, *Well, at least I didn't scream at any strangers. I must be improving.*

Opening the front door she called out, 'John, I'm home!' It was probably the first time that she announced her homecoming for a long time. When she didn't receive any response she glanced back to the driveway and realised his car wasn't there.

'I wonder where he is.' she muttered to herself as she lifted the shopping bags inside and closed the front door behind her with her foot. Taking the roll of charity bags and a 4-pack of toilet roll out of one of the grocery bags, she placed them on the stairs to remind her to take them up later.

As she picked up the shopping bags and walked towards the kitchen, she took an intelligent guess that John was at work again. Anything to keep his mind off real life. She placed the bags on the kitchen table and decided to let John have the time to himself. There was no point in calling him on his mobile and asking him to come home. He would be home soon enough. The conversation that she wanted to have with him had to be face-to-face. So much had been swept under the carpet for too long. It was time to pull back the carpet and face the challenges ahead. It was something she should have done a long time ago.

After she put away the groceries, she stepped out to the back garden. Although it was early autumn, the garden had been pretty much neglected since the tragic day eight months earlier. The far corner of the garden was completely overgrown with weeds. It was supposed to be the vegetable patch, although very few vegetables grew there. Stalks of rhubarb and scattered patches of mint were the only useful plants remaining. Next to the back wall grew some Boston Ivy which displayed wonderful red and yellow autumn colours. The rest of the vegetable patch was made up of weeds.

Pulling out one of the garden chairs, Claire sat down. As her hand rubbed against the arm-rest of the chair, she realised it was smooth. *Very* smooth. She placed her hand on the table and realised that too was frictionless and much cleaner than what she remembered. It dawned on her that John had sanded the furniture months ago.

Of course, she realised. *Didn't he take the day off to varnish the furniture? Hadn't he sanded the furniture just the weekend before…*

Sitting back on the chair and examining the furniture, she gave herself two choices. She could wrap the furniture in the large grey tarpaulin in the shed that was used every year to store it for the winter. Or she could do what they had originally planned and varnish the furniture before storing it for the winter.

It didn't take her long to decide on the latter. She was going to varnish the furniture herself. It would be another way in which they could move forward. It dawned on her that it must have been too difficult for John to do it.

It must bring too many painful memories back to him.

Claire got up and walked down to the shed at the back of the garden. Stepping inside, she couldn't get over the amount of clutter that seemed to have duplicated since the last time she had visited it. On the workbench stood three tins of varnish. Next to them lay two different sized paintbrushes, some torn-up old T-shirts to be used as rags, and a bottle of turpentine.

John had prepared everything for the job. It seemed

like yesterday he had come home from Woodies DIY store and placed them in the shed, ready for his chore.

She rubbed a finger along the top of a tin of varnish. A line appeared in a thin film of dust. She rubbed the dust that accumulated on her finger in one of the rags that lay on the workbench. Picking up the same rag, she gave all the lids a quick rub.

Glancing around the shed, her eyes fell on a screwdriver rack hanging over the workbench. She would need one to open the lids of the varnish. Reaching over, she grabbed a large flat-headed screwdriver. 'You'll do nicely,' she said shoving it, handle first, into her front pocket.

She threw one of the rags over her shoulder, picked up a tin of varnish and a paintbrush and walked back to the garden table. Touching the surface of the table, she realised that although it was still smooth, some dirt had accumulated since it was sandpapered all those months previously. Dirt, fallen leaves, snail trails and the occasional dead insect.

Before she started with the varnishing, she cleaned the garden chairs and table with warm water and soap. Stopping for a cup of tea and a snack, she didn't start the actual varnishing until just after midday.

It was soothing work, with no need to use the brain. The woodwork absorbed the varnish like some kind of parched living organism. With every brush stroke the table gave off a faint glint, like a twinkle in the eye to show its appreciation.

Even though Claire was not fond of the smell she figured being outside made it less aggravating. She doubted she would actually get high.

After she had applied the first coat to the table and chairs, she stepped back and admired her work. The pieces of furniture looked like new. She decided to wait until they were dry before applying the second coat.

Two coats would be sufficient.

It suddenly occurred to her that the rag used wasn't an old T-shirt of John's. It had been Max's. A very faint picture of *Dora the Explorer* and a monkey with red boots waved at her. At least, the boots used to be red. The colour of the boots was now a very pale pink.

Be strong.

The pain was there again, sharp, knifelike. It felt like root canal surgery. She took a deep breath. The pain subsided. At least a bit.

Be strong.

She closed her eyes. More in a meditation manner than in a sorrowful way. She didn't cry. Not this time.

46

Grace reversed the Fiesta into a free place on Westlandgracht opposite Rik's apartment. It was a tight spot. After numerous forward and reverse manoeuvres, she switched off the ignition and turned to Daniel.

'Thank you for coming with me.'

'No problem. Thank you for not crashing,' he said, handing her the spectacle case that he had been holding. 'Are you finished parking or are you just taking a break?'

'Smart ass,' she said as she snatched the box from him. 'So, since we're stuck together for the rest of the day, how about taking in some of the sights?'

'Some sights?'

Grace nodded. 'When is your flight?' she asked getting out of the car.

'Tomorrow afternoon.'

'So you have time to see some of Amsterdam.'

'I suppose so, yes,' he admitted, unsure if it was a question.

'Or were you purely on a *Saving Private Grace* mission?'

He nodded. 'To be honest, yes. I didn't even think about doing any touristy things while I was here.'

Grace walked a few metres towards a parking machine and fed it with coins until she was satisfied it was enough. She pressed a green button, and moments later the machine spat a ticket out the bottom.

'Let me be your tour guide for the rest of the day and you can be my bodyguard,' she said as she went back to the car and placed the parking permit on the dashboard. She shut the car door and looked at Daniel.

'Okay.'

'Let's pop into the apartment for a minute,' she said as she locked the car. 'I need to change my shoes.' She raised her finger as she suddenly thought of something. 'You

238

know what? Maybe I can find the key to Rik's bicycle and you can borrow it.'

Daniel stopped in his tracks. 'No way. Did you not hear me in the car? Cycling has been officially added to the list of dangerous activities to avoid for the day.'

She placed a hand on his arm as they crossed the street. 'Maybe you're right, given the day that's in it.'

To any onlooker, they looked like the perfect couple. They entered the apartment building and closed the door behind them.

Neither of them saw the silver BMW that pulled into a free parking spot further down the street. Otto remained in the car, not really sure what to do. At least now he knew where she was staying. A surge of jealously diffused to every cell in his body, as he watched his wife cross the street holding onto this stranger's arm. It was as much the physical aspect of it as her happy appearance.

He was about to get out of the car and check the building number when two uniformed parking attendants caught his eye in the rear-view mirror. Slowly they made their way up Westlandgracht. Otto looked around. The closest parking metre was outside the apartment Grace had just entered. Not wanting to risk being spotted, he started the engine. He pulled out and drove by the apartment, quickly turning his head to see the house number.

29.

He turned left at the end of the street onto Heemstedestraat and disappeared into the flow of traffic.

47

Daniel and Grace managed to fit a lot in for an unplanned sightseeing day. By 3:00pm, they had visited the Anne Frank House and the Van Gogh museum. Luckily for Daniel, Grace was unable to find Rik's bicycle key, so the mode of transport for the day was tram. Not that it was a unanimous decision. Grace had still pushed the idea of cycling.

'You can always jump on the back of my bike if you want?' she had suggested.

Daniel couldn't understand her infatuation of getting him onto a bicycle. 'You have a perfect network of trams, why do you want me to risk my life?'

'It's quicker. It saves money. More flexible,' she had said. 'Will I go on?'

'I'll pay for the tram tickets, okay?'

And so tram it was.

'Shall we go to one more museum,' Grace asked, 'then we'll call it a day?'

'The Rijksmuseum?' Daniel suggested while reading through a random tourist leaflet he had picked up somewhere. 'After a ten-year refurbishment, it's now open again to the public.'

She shook her head. 'You need a whole day for that, even more if you want to see it properly. Do that when you come again.'

'And what makes you say I'll be returning?' he asked smirking.

'Because you haven't visited the Rijksmuseum yet.'

He frowned, but accepted that there was logic somewhere in her answer.

They walked for quite a bit, catching up further with old times. They passed the busy Dam Square and before they knew it, they were strolling along quiet streets once again. Daniel assumed they were walking aimlessly around the city.

'So are we actually heading somewhere?' he asked.

'How about the Hermitage Museum?'

Daniel remained silent for a moment, clearly thinking of something. 'I'm no museum connoisseur,' he said eventually. 'But isn't that in Russia?'

She nodded. 'Yes, it is actually. The main one. But they also converted an old folks home into a museum to show exhibitions from the original Hermitage. It's a beautiful building too. I've had dinner there once or twice but I've never actually visited the various exhibitions.'

He shrugged but was happy with the choice. 'Sure, seems safe enough.'

She rolled her eyes at his constant reference to safety.

On their way, they stopped off at a small cafe on the corner of Staalstraat and Zwanenburgwal.

'This is a lovely family-run cafe,' she told Daniel as they sat at one of the small round tables on the narrow pathway. 'It's a wonderful place to watch Amsterdam pass by. The pedestrians, the cyclists.' She pointed to the street next to them and then towards the canal running parallel to Zwanenburgwal. 'Even the boats.'

A waiter, a man in his fifties with a bushy moustache and wearing glasses, came out of the restaurant. *'Goedemiddag.'*

'Hoi.' Grace said. She turned to Daniel. 'You want coffee?'

'Sure, with sugar, and maybe a little snack or muffin to go with it.'

The waiter started scribbling on his pad.

'We don't have muffins,' he said, 'but maybe I can offer you some nice sandwiches or a croissant.'

'A croissant should do the trick,' Daniel said.

The waiter turned to Grace.

'En voor mij, graag een koffie verkeerd en een broodje gezond.' A cafe au lait and a ham, cheese and salad sandwich.

The waiter smiled politely and went back inside. The

heaters above them managed to keep the autumn chill away. Nevertheless, they both left their jackets on.

Two policemen on scooters zoomed by on the bicycle path. Daniel grinned. 'In the past four hours I've seen a police boat, a police car, police on top of a horse, police on mountain bikes, and now police on scooters. All the modes of transports! It's hilarious.'

'And your point is?'

'If a criminal makes a getaway on a scooter, are the police pursuing him only allowed to do so on a scooter too?'

She raised her eyebrows and stared at him with a deadpan expression. Eventually she just agreed with him. 'Yes, they can only be pursued on scooters. It's all down to fairness. As you know, Holland is very tolerant and criminals have the right to a fair getaway.'

'I might rob a bank and make my getaway on a unicycle just for the laugh. Can you imagine the amount of hits on YouTube if I uploaded a video of me flying down the streets of Amsterdam with six policemen on unicycles in hot pursuit?'

Grace just closed her eyes and shook her head, trying to get rid of the mental picture that he had painted. She failed and burst into a fit of laughter. Daniel joined her and they both giggled like school children, reliving the same type of enjoyment they experienced when they were a couple.

'In one way, you haven't changed a bit,' she said as the laughter receded. 'You haven't lost your crap sense of humour. That's for sure.'

'I take that as a compliment.'

She touched his hand. 'It is. And I'm happy to see that you haven't changed much at all.'

The waiter arrived with the two coffees and the snacks.

'I'll get these,' Daniel offered, as she removed her hand.

'You don't have to pay now,' the waiter said. 'Unless you want to?'

'Sure, why not? It will save us from bothering you again later.'

The waiter did a quick calculation in his head.

'Ten euro, fifty-seven.' The waiter shook his head briefly and corrected himself. 'Seventy-five, I mean.'

As Daniel opened his wallet to pay, something fell to the ground. Grace bent down immediately to pick it up while he continued to pay.

'Do you want a receipt?' the waiter asked.

'No, thanks.'

Daniel turned to Grace to see what she had picked up. She was practically glowing as she looked at it. 'Where did you find this? What a cute photo!'

He mentally slapped his forehead for leaving the photograph of both of them from years earlier in such an obvious place in his wallet. He felt his cheeks turn pink. He tried to act like it didn't bother him by opening a sugar sachet and emptying it into his coffee.

'Where did you get this from?' she asked again.

'I had it,' he said quickly, clearly annoyed that she had seen the photo. 'Can I have it back?' he asked with his hand outstretched.

Grace noticed the annoyed look on him and after a few seconds handed it over. A few moments of silence elapsed as she bit into her sandwich and Daniel stabbed his croissant and put some jam on it. Eventually it was Grace that gave in.

'Why are you carrying a photograph of me in your wallet?'

A minute went by. Daniel continued to eat his croissant, and drink his coffee.

'Daniel?'

He placed his cup sharply on the table. 'It's not a photo of you. It's a photo of *us*.'

'Okay, why do you have a photo of *us* in your wallet?'

'What do you want me to say, Grace?'

'Say whatever you want to say.'

'I found it among my notes last week when I went rooting in the attic. Maybe I carry it now to remind me what happiness was like.' He closed his eyes, not really sure if that's what he meant to say.

Grace waited several moments before asking, 'You're saying you're not happy now?'

He shook his head sharply. 'No, that's not what I'm saying either. It's just, I don't know... a different *type* of happiness maybe. Is it even possible to categorise happiness?' He picked up some flakes of croissant that fell on the table. He was unable to make eye contact with her.

'I was really happy with you,' he admitted, placing the croissant flakes on the plate again. 'And there isn't a day that goes by that I don't think about the time we spent together.' He raised his head and took a deep breath. 'There. I said it.'

She met his eyes for a moment but then looked into the distance. 'All very nice, Daniel, but why couldn't you have told me that before. Years ago?'

A couple of policemen passed by on mountain bikes. Although they both noticed them, it failed to reignite the humour from moments earlier. Daniel took a bite of his croissant and a sip of his coffee. Grace signalled at him that there was something at the side of his mouth.

'Thanks.' He wiped his mouth, realising that it was jam. He searched for a napkin and cleaned it properly.

'So what do we do now?' Grace asked.

'I thought we're going to the Hermitage?'

Her eyes shone. 'I mean...never mind. I suppose you want to drop the subject?' she asked.

'Look,' he said, 'I could talk about it for the next week and still not truly understand it myself.'

'Understand what?'

'Everything. Why I walked away from everything. Why I walked away from you.'

48

Claire felt lucky with the day. It remained dry and a mild breeze blew; ideal conditions for a spot of garden furniture maintenance. She managed to give the table and chairs two thorough coats of varnish. In between coats, waiting for the furniture to dry, she worked in the vegetable patch in the corner of the garden. She pulled weeds, trimmed overgrown plants and used the hoe to agitate and tidy the soil around the plants. It didn't take long before the garden turned into something that looked like it belonged to an *occupied* house again.

Once the furniture dried, she pushed the chairs in under the table and covered everything with a large tarpaulin. It was the same cover they had used for years. A few small rips were spread throughout it, as well as a couple of splatters of dried-in bird shit from the previous winters. She threw a thick cord around the bottom and tied a tight knot so the wind wouldn't blow it off during the winter months ahead.

Taking a step back, Claire admired her work. It was ready for hibernation. She wondered how the furniture would look in springtime. Or whenever the weather became warm enough to sit outside.

Knowing Ireland, she thought to herself, *it might not be until the middle of August.*

She collected the varnish-covered paintbrushes and rags and placed them in the Woodies DIY bag. Looking down, she wondered if she should try washing the brushes.

'Forget it,' she said to herself. 'They probably just cost a euro or two anyway.'

She tied the bag well so the fumes wouldn't stink up the house and threw them in the rubbish bin in the kitchen. The bin was almost full. Contemplating on whether to take the bag of rubbish out already, she decided to do it after dinner instead.

She washed her hands and turned her attention to preparing the evening meal. By the time she prepared a relatively simple dish of pasta, salmon and stir-fried vegetables, she was ravenous. She was about to pour herself a glass of red wine, when she stopped. Didn't she promise herself that the next time she would drink wine it would be in a more social environment?

Dinner alone. Not very social.

Instead she took a can of Lipton Ice-Tea from the fridge.

Where's John?

Deciding not to wait for him any longer, she started the dinner without him. Eating alone was one of the tough parts that she was forced to get used to since Max's death. In the weekdays John still worked long hours. Instead of having Max to keep her company, she had to be content with the Six-One News. It was already quite late and the Six-One News was already over. Today she had a Scottish presenter with long hair discussing the coasts of Britain and Ireland to keep her company. She had seen the programme on numerous occasions just by flicking around. It was the aerial shots (and Scottish accent of the presenter) that always caught her attention. It was an easy programme to watch. No conflict or worries.

After dinner, Claire felt exhausted and decided to go upstairs for a bath. In the hallway, she saw the roll of charity bags and the pack of toilet rolls on the stairs. She picked them both up but her attention remained on the charity bags.

'What now?' she asked herself. She decided not to do anything until she discussed it with John. This would be one of many topics of conversation she would have when he came home. She glanced up the stairs as if expecting to find someone to encourage her.

Nobody.

She climbed the stairs, slowly. Her muscles ached all

over from the gardening and varnishing. The door to Max's bedroom was ajar. Leaving the toilet paper on the landing, she pushed Max's door all the way open and looked around. She walked over to the window and pulled the curtains across. Every morning she would also pull them back, to allow light into the bedroom. If any neighbour across the way noticed this, they would think that it was an occupied room. Claire didn't do it for the neighbours, however. She did it for herself, to let more light in during the day. And for a split second every morning to imagine that Max would be getting out of bed any moment.

Looking around the room, she noticed a football card had fallen from a wall chart hanging over Max's desk. She picked it up and looked at the name. She placed it back on the chart, under the Spanish flag.

'Well done, Mammy.'

She could hear her son's voice again.

'What do you mean "well done"?'

'I didn't think you knew what nationality Xabi Alonso was.'

She smiled.

'It was the only blank spot on the wall chart.'

She held up the roll of charity bags.

'I got these.'

'To give my stuff to charity?'

'That's right.'

There was a silence. She wondered how stupid she must look. Luckily the curtains were drawn.

'Well, about time.' She could hear a sarcastic tone in her son's voice.

'Don't be cheeky. I just need to discuss it with Daddy.'

'That's fine. Where is he?'

'Your guess is as good as mine, sweetheart.'

'Is he okay?'

She looked towards a picture hanging on the wall next to Max's desk. It was a photo of the three of them on the *Big Thunder Mountain* in Disneyland Paris. John had his arms wrapped tightly around his son who, in turn, had his arms in the air and was screaming with laughter. Both his two front teeth were missing. Claire was next to Max with her hair blowing backwards and holding on for dear life.

'I don't know.'

'You need to talk to each other.'

'I know.'

'You're growing apart.'

'I know.'

'I don't want you to grow apart.'

'I know.'

'I don't want to have been the only reason that you guys stayed together.'

Claire swallowed. 'Okay.'

'Promise?'

'Promise what?'

'That you'll move on together? That you'll stay together? You need each other. More than ever before.'

'I promise.'

She looked around. She suddenly felt stupid. And exhausted. Emotionally and physically. Placing the roll of bags on the floor, she sat down on the edge of the bed. As she went to lie down, her feet hit off the roll of bags and they rolled gently beneath the bed.

She took a deep breath and reflected on all the stories she had read to her son in that bed. She also reflected on all the times she had told him not to bounce on it. In his imagination, the bed had been an aeroplane, a pirate ship, a space ship, a magic carpet. Anything and everything that filled a boy's fantasy world.

Claire curled up and closed her eyes. The fond memories gradually faded away as sleep took over. She fell straight asleep. And for the first time in eight months, she dreamed.

49

Daniel stopped at a painting entitled Baubo. It was an oil-on-canvas. He read the description next to it.

BAUBO by Romana Strynclova - Asia Minor, 5th century BC: symbol of the female sexuality, Boar: symbol of fight, courage and wildness. "The maid who amused The Goddess Demeter with her belly dance and bare crotch, while she mourned her daughter Persephona."

It made absolutely no sense to him. There was indeed a picture of a Boar behind a red female figure on the foreground. What caught his eye, though, were the two symbols on the top left. He turned to Grace, and pointed with a big smirk.

'Do those symbols bring back any memories?'

The sensitive atmosphere of their earlier conversation at the café had gradually changed. They agreed to drop the subject and enjoy the rest of day together.

Grace frowned as she looked at the painting and took a step closer towards the painting. It took a moment, but Daniel could see that they triggered the same memories as he just had. She placed a hand up to her mouth and gave him a friendly push with the other.

'Shut up. I can't believe you're reminding me of that,' she said as she stared at the two symbols; the male and female symbols. 'I assume you're referring to the *wrong toilet* incident?'

'Of course the wrong toilet incident. Have you had other incidents regarding these symbols?'

'No,' she said as she removed her hand, smiling now. 'Where was it again?'

Daniel shrugged. 'Can't really remember. One of those newish bars back then. The Zanzibar or something like that.'

'God, I've never forgotten it. I was so drunk. I never

even saw the urinals when I went in,' Grace said reliving the event. 'Just went straight into a cubicle.'

'At what stage did you realise?'

'I suppose I should have put two and two together when I saw the graffiti on the back of the door. I can't remember exactly, but it was a level of vulgarity you just wouldn't see in a lady's toilet.'

'Right,' Daniel said with a sarcastic tone. 'You girls are perfect.'

'I remember sitting there and two guys came in for a pee. When I heard one of them talk, the first thing that crossed my mind was *Jesus, that woman has a deep voice.* Then when I heard the other guy reply the penny dropped. I remember waiting for them both to leave, but when they switched on the hand dryer I lost track if anyone new had come in. So I just flushed, opened the door and walked towards the sink as if it was the most normal thing in the world. There was a guy at the mirror fixing his hair. Bloodshot, drunk, swaying. As soon as he saw me he said "Jaysus, sorry. I didn't realise this was the ladies'." I just smirked and raised my shoulders as he stumbled out. A few seconds later when I left the men's toilet, I saw him coming out of the ladies' with a big red face and the sound of laughter behind him. I avoided eye contact but he must have been the most confused guy in the world.'

Daniel shot a glance at the symbols again while giggling and shaking his head. 'I remember your face when you returned. Priceless. You just had this big grin. I mean, you weren't embarrassed at all.'

'Trust me, I *was* embarrassed. I just did my best to hide it.'

They both stood looking at the painting and enjoying the trip down memory lane.

'To be honest,' she said, 'I never forgot your explanation of the symbols afterwards.'

'Really? Which was?'

She stepped closer to the painting. 'This one,' she said

pointing to the male symbol, 'is like a shield. And the arrow pointing north-east is like a sword, which reminds you of a warrior, or, of course, a man. And the other one with the cross at the bottom looks a bit like a hand mirror, which is, of course, mostly associated with women.'

Daniel nodded clearly impressed. 'You're a good student. I wouldn't have been able to remember that myself.'

'What I don't get is why so-called trendy bars and restaurants use those symbols on the doors of their toilets. They're just asking for trouble when it gets late at night and people find it hard enough to walk, never mind determine which toilet is theirs to throw up in. I've seen it a few times myself here.'

As they left the Hermitage, it was already getting dark. They walked across the Walter Suskind bridge and continued along the Amstel until they came to Waterlooplein. In the middle of conversation, they came upon a stall selling pink ribbons. The volunteer, a short woman in her fifties with large spectacles, overheard them speaking English.

'Would you like to support the fight against Breast Cancer?'

'Certainly,' Grace said without any hesitation. 'I'll have one, please.'

'Make that two,' Daniel said and took out his wallet.

'That's three euros,' the woman said.

Grace held a hand over Daniel's wallet. 'I'll get these. I don't want any more photos fluttering out of your wallet.'

He smiled. 'Smartass. Are you sure?'

'It's three euros, for God's sake. I'm not a student anymore.'

'I meant are you sure you don't want any more photos of us fluttering out of my wallet?'

Grace handed over the money and accepted the two ribbons. The volunteer thanked them and continued to ask other passers-by the same question in Dutch. As Grace handed Daniel his ribbon, she asked, 'Why would I want any more photos fluttering out of your wallet?'

He shrugged as they continued walking along the Amstel. 'You seemed to enjoy the awkward moment from earlier.'

'What do you mean I "enjoyed" it?'

He stopped walking as he stared at the pink ribbon.

Grace walked for a bit before stopping too. She repeated her question but saw that Daniel was suddenly lost in his thoughts.

After a few moments, he said, 'These are for breast cancer research, right?'

'The money collected goes towards that, yes. Why?'

He continued to stare at the pink ribbon. Something tugged at his mind. He caressed the soft material as if it was an injured bird. 'Breast cancer,' he mumbled to himself. He looked out over the water flowing in the Amstel.

'What is it, Daniel?'

Although a breeze blew directly in his face, he felt his cheeks flush. 'I've done it wrong…'

Grace moved her head to one side, not fully understanding. 'What do you mean?'

Turning towards her, he said, 'I've done a calculation recently, based on my thesis.'

Her eyes widened. 'You have?'

'I'm not sure if I did it right, though.'

'What do you mean?'

'I based it on an old calculation. Brian Nolan's calculation. Since that one came true.'

'Okay. And?'

'And I never included the Breast Cancer Theorem.'

She scrunched her face. 'The what?'

'If I'm predicting the date of death of a woman, there's a Breast Cancer Theorem in my calculations,' he said as he ran his hand through his hair. 'It's related to the genetic make-up of a woman. But I didn't use it in my calculation for Claire.'

'Who's Claire?'

'She's...' he lost track of what he was saying. 'I screwed up the calculation, Grace. I never used the Breast Cancer Theorem, even though the information I needed was in the medical reports that John gave me.'

Try as she might, Grace still wasn't getting it all. 'I'm sorry, Daniel, I'm not following you.'

'When I calculated your date of death, I had certain tests run on your BRCA1 and BRCA2 genes. These are two genes that, if there are mutations present, could increase the chances of breast cancer or ovarian cancer. And ultimately death.'

'Okay. Aren't those the genes that Angelina Jolie found mutations in?' she asked as she began to understand what he was talking about.

'Exactly. She found a mutation in BRCA1 so decided to undergo a double mastectomy. Why? Because she had an 87% of getting breast cancer and she wanted to reduce that. It's all down to mathematics.'

'So with this Claire woman, you just have to recalculate it and include the Breast Cancer Theorem.'

The blood ran from Daniel's face. He took a deep breath. 'The thing is that I predicted her death to be today.'

'Today?'

He nodded.

'The same as mine?'

Shrugging his shoulders he said, 'It's not unusual to share the same birthday with someone. Why is it unusual to have the same date of death too?'

'Just seems like a coincidence.'

'It had crossed my mind too.' He remained silent for a moment. 'I think I even came across something like that in the past when I first attempted in predicting your dates. In this case though, I couldn't, for the life of me, detect where I went wrong.'

'Until now,' Grace added.

He nodded as he glanced at the ribbon and then at his watch. 'I need to call him.'

'Who?'

'John. Professor Redmond.'

'You predicted *his* date of death? I thought we were talking about a female here?'

'His wife's. I calculated his wife's date of death.'

Grace remained silent for a moment as she processed the information and finally asked, 'Why?'

'It's a long story. The short version is that their son passed away a few months ago. I think John is curious just how much longer his wife needs to suffer. Or he wants to help prove my thesis so other parents don't have to go through the same.'

'Oh, my God. That's terrible.'

'Tell me about it.'

'How old was he, the boy?'

'Ten,' he said as he took out his mobile. He called John's number but it went straight to his voicemail.

'Shit! It's turned off.'

'Do you have his landline number?'

He shook his head. 'No.' He tried calling again. It went once again directly to John's voicemail. This time he left a message.

'John! Daniel here. Please call me back when you get this. I think I made a mistake in the calculation.' He hung up and took a deep breath. He placed the mobile back into his pocket. Facing the Amstel again, he grabbed hold of a handrail that ran along the river. His hand rubbed against some dried bird excrement. Although none of the bird shit came off, Daniel rubbed his hand against his trousers.

'You look pale, Daniel,' Grace said as she stepped forward and placed her hand on his arm. 'Try to relax.'

'I don't know what I'd do if...' his words became trapped in his throat. In the distance, he caught sight of a group of tourists on a pedal boat. One of them wore a bright orange life jacket. He wondered if it had a whistle and a light for attracting the attention of a rescue crew. He felt like he could do with one himself. A life jacket. A rescue team. Someone to pull him aside and tell him everything is going to be alright.

'Why are you so worried, Daniel? I mean if he thinks his wife is going to die today and she doesn't, that can only be a good thing, right?'

'I'm half afraid that he might do something to trigger it off. You should see the pain in this guy's eyes when he talks about his son or wife. Coming to terms with a depressed wife. Coming to terms with a dead child. Is there anything worse? Maybe my prediction was the greenlight he needed. The tipping point on the scales.'

'There's nothing you can do about it.'

'I need to talk to him. At least if he knows I made a mistake, then he won't do anything stupid. Have you got internet access on your mobile?'

'No.' She shook her head. 'I mean I do have internet on my mobile, but I didn't bring it with me.'

'Can we go back to the apartment?'

She shrugged her shoulders. 'If you're so worried about it. Sure.' Pointing to Daniel's phone, she continued. 'You don't have internet on that… thing?'

He held up his old scratched Nokia 1100. 'Are you joking? I'm not even sure if the internet was invented when this baby was released.'

Grace rolled her eyes, as they made their way towards the nearest tram stop.

50

It was dark by the time John stumbled in the front door. He popped his head in the sitting room and was surprised to see that it was empty and the TV was off.

He continued to the kitchen and switched on the light. A strange smell hit his senses almost immediately. What was it?

Paint?

Turpentine?

It reminded him of some DIY chore. He shrugged his shoulders and opened the microwave. There, like usual, he found his dinner waiting for him. Just to be sure, he moved his head close to the microwave and sniffed. He was glad to discover that the strange smell wasn't coming from the food. Reaching towards the plate, he tore off a little chunk of cold salmon and ate it.

'Mmm, not bad.'

He timed the microwave on high power for a couple of minutes and sat down at the kitchen table. He got up almost immediately when he felt something beneath him. The Evening Herald was still sticking out of his back pocket. Standing up, he grabbed it and placed it on the table.

After leaving Trinity earlier, he had gone to Paddy Powers on Fleet Street to see what kind of odds they were offering for one of the day's matches, Chelsea versus Manchester United. It was 21/10. He decided to put fifty euros on Manchester United to win. He went down to the Auld Dubliner to watch the match and got talking to a couple of English guys who were over for the weekend. They bought him a pint before the game had started. By half-time they were taking turns in buying rounds like old friends. After the game in which Manchester United won 2-1, "one for the road" turned out to be "five for the road".

Paddy Powers was closed by the time he left the pub, so he kept his betting slip safely in his wallet. With the amount of alcohol in his blood stream he didn't even contemplate driving home. He bought the Evening Herald while waiting for the 37 bus. Being able to read it was wishful thinking. The motion of the bus combined with his blurred drunken vision meant that he could only read the headlines.

The movement of the double-decker bus as it manoeuvred its way through Dublin traffic to Castleknock also made him sleepy. He dozed a little but managed to wake up before his stop. As he walked up Auburn Avenue, a cool breeze on his face freshened him up. A rumble in his stomach told him that the Guinness he drank all day was no substitute for solid food.

Now, as he sat listening to his evening meal splatter and hiss in the microwave, he looked at the newspaper. Still too drunk to really focus on the small print, he pushed it away.

It didn't take him long to devour the food. Every so often he would stop to remove a fish bone from his mouth. Although he was drunk, there were some things he just never let his guard down to. Fish bones were one of them, no matter how small they were and how drunk he was.

Tossing the remains of the fish into the bin he got a strong whiff of the paint-like scent. He looked down at the bin, which was essentially full, and wondered what Claire had thrown in it. Shrugging his shoulders, he shook his head a little with drunken despair. It was more out of how full it was than the smell. He had no inclination to replace the bag.

Not now.

Swaying a bit to the side, he took a couple of steps back to the table and grabbed the unread Evening Herald. Using the newspaper to protect his hands, he pushed the contents of the bin downwards, making enough space to last until tomorrow.

If tomorrow came.

Leaving the now soiled newspaper lying on top, he closed the lid.

He wondered where Claire had disappeared to. Had she already gone to bed? Had she even gotten out of bed in the first place?

Of course. How else could she have made the dinner?, his drunken mind concluded. *Or filled the room with that smell?*

He went upstairs. The door to Max's bedroom was ajar. He pushed the door open further and saw her fast asleep on their son's bed. Although he always suspected that she slept there, this was the first time he had seen it. The sight of her curled up in front of him almost literally broke his heart. Immediately the tears fell, helped on by the alcohol.

'Oh, Claire,' he whispered. He made no effort to wipe away the tears. It felt liberating to let them flow. A cloud of emotions seemed to expand to every part of his body. Walking over to his wife, he looked down. A flashback of finding Max in the same spot all those months ago shot through his mind. Claire lay close to the wall. Even if there was little space left on the bed, he managed to climb onto it and wrapped one arm around his wife. She felt warm.

At least she's still alive.

He closed his eyes.

Let's just make it to the end of this day, he thought to himself. *I was really overambitious expecting Daniel to be able predict her death after so long.*

It didn't take long before he slept soundly.

51

Daniel and Grace hopped off the tram at Heemstedestraat. Still being new to the area, Daniel glanced briefly at Grace for confirmation on which way. She pointed towards the direction in which he was heading anyway, Westlandgracht. They crossed the street, and he quickened his pace.

'I can't keep up, Daniel,' she called after him, despite quickening her pace.

He slowed down and looked behind. 'We're almost there.'

'I know, but come on. A few seconds isn't going to make a difference.'

'Famous last words.'

They walked side-by-side on the pavement. As they reached Rik's apartment, Grace took out the key, but the front door opened just as they reached it. Rik's neighbour, a woman in her thirties wearing black lipstick and a biker's jacket, appeared holding a plastic bag of empty bottles. She saw that Daniel and Grace were intending to come into the building, so she held the door open reluctantly. Grace could see from the woman's face that she was waiting on some kind of confirmation that they were legitimate visitors.

She greeted the woman in Dutch, '*Goedeavond*,' she said as Daniel caught the door and entered. '*Wij zijn vrienden van Rik.*' 'We are friends of Rik's'. She held up the keys to the apartment as additional proof that they were entering the apartment even if she hadn't opened the door.

The lady smiled, satisfied with the answer. The bottles in her bag clanked as she walked away.

Grace closed the door after her and walked up the stairway. 'I've got the key, Daniel, I don't know why you're running ahead.'

He was standing outside the door of the apartment as she appeared. 'You're like a little child bursting to use the toilet,' she said as she unlocked the door.

'Where's his computer?' he asked as he shot inside.

She pointed to the living room. 'That way.'

He found an old Dell Inspiron laptop lying on the coffee table. He wondered briefly if it was older than his Nokia. He quickly opened it and pushed the power button.

Glancing around the room, he could tell from a mile off that the place belonged to a guy. A single guy at that. The navy curtains didn't match the brown carpet whatsoever. It was as if whoever picked them out was colour blind.

The coffee table before him was a colour of oak stained grey. Its surface looked like children used it to practice woodwork skills. Chips and scratches were in abundance. *Maybe it's supposed to be like that*, he thought. *Modern arty furniture.*

A couple of coasters, the same shape and size as the old floppy disks that were once the norm, lay scattered on the table. He picked up one to inspect it. It was indeed a coaster. He threw it back on the coffee table and took a closer look at the laptop in front of him. There was no internet cable connected to it.

'I assume this guy has wireless,' Daniel shouted to wherever Grace had disappeared to. 'Is there a modem or something that has to be switched on?'

She poked her head around the corner. 'The guy's name is Rik. And honestly? I have no idea.'

The welcome screen appeared eventually and showed two profiles to choose from: "Rik" or "Guest". He clicked on "Guest" hoping it wouldn't ask for a password. It didn't. As the computer warmed up, he got up and searched around the room. He found a modem lying on the floor next to the sofa and switched it on.

'Do you want some wine?' Grace called out from the kitchen, clearly not joining Daniel in his urgent state.

'No,' he cried. 'Not yet, anyway.'

As he waited for the Wi-Fi to connect, he tried calling John's mobile one more time. Still nothing. Once the browser was running, he quickly googled "Telephone directory Dublin". Seconds later he was looking at the online Eircom phonebook. He typed in John Redmond, Castleknock and hit search.

Could not find the exact search term that you entered, appeared on the screen.

'Shit.'

He looked at the top of the page and reviewed what he had entered. His name was spelled right. Beneath it was a choice between Business and Residential. The Business option was ticked as default. He clicked on Residential and searched again.

His eye immediately saw Prof John Redmond, 9 Beechpark Lawn.

'There you are,' he mumbled as he pulled out his mobile and dialled the number, remembering to dial the international code first.

It was ringing. He glanced at his watch. It was 8:30pm. After several rings Daniel grew impatient.

'Come on,' he whispered. 'Someone please pick up the phone.'

52

Claire never felt so relaxed lying in bed. Something was different though. She felt an arm wrapped around her and a body next to her. It felt warm. Comforting. The sound of breathing added to the relaxed state she was in. It was a pleasant feeling. A feeling she hadn't had for such a long time. Any desire to wake up evaporated as the foreign breathing sent her back to sleep. Back to whatever she was dreaming of…

In the distance she could hear the phone ringing.

Not now. Please not now…

Why was the ringing so faint? If it were the phone right beside her bed it would be louder. Much louder. Was she dreaming of the phone? Was she in such a deep sleep that it felt so far away?

It continued to ring.

Or maybe she wasn't in her bed?

No, of course not. Reality flooded back to her as she slowly awoke. Wasn't she in Max's bed?

Then who was lying next to her? Surely not…

She opened her eyes and turned around slowly in a state of confusion. There, she found her husband sound asleep. A strong scent of alcohol hit her almost immediately, pulling her completely out of from the land of nod. The disorientation stayed with her, though.

A flashback shot to a day, years earlier, when she was studying for her Leaving Certificate. She had taken a break from her work and laid back on her bed to listen to a Kate Bush album. She remembered falling asleep during *This Woman's Work*. The stereo cassette player on which she had been listening to the album automatically flipped sides at the end of the tape. This happened twice. When she woke up about an hour later it was dark outside, and the same song was playing. It took her literally a whole minute to realise where she was and how she was listening to the same song.

She always thought back to that moment any time she felt completely disorientated. Like now. Sometimes she still felt she was asleep on her bed prior to her Leaving Cert listening to Kate Bush, and one day she would wake up and everything would have been a dream.

The phone continued to ring. Someone was desperately trying to contact them. It wasn't a dream. Just like that day years ago, it was dark outside. The main difference was a glow-in-the-dark *TRON Legacy* poster, now piercing the darkness.

She tried to shake the disorientation away. She yawned. How long had she slept? How long had John been lying next to her? Slowly she pushed John's arm aside and climbed out of the bed. Her muscles ached. John didn't budge. He was dead to the world.

The phone stopped ringing. Claire walked towards the master bedroom in case it started again. As she crossed the landing, she smelled something strange. She froze in her tracks as she sniffed again.

'Jesus.' She looked downstairs and saw smoke coming from the kitchen.

53

Grace arrived in the room with two glasses of wine. 'Any luck?' She asked as she placed the wine on the geeky floppy disk coasters. Slipping off her shoes she collapsed on the sofa. She folded one of her legs beneath her bottom and faced Daniel by resting her shoulder on the back of the sofa. He glanced towards her and quickly back to the laptop screen, as he tried to hide what he was suddenly thinking, *you look extremely sexy.*

Remembering her question, Daniel shook his head. 'No, not yet.' After a few more rings he hung up. 'This isn't good. I don't have a good feeling about it.'

'Relax. What more can you do?' she asked as she took a sip of wine.

He bent forward. After a few clicks with the mouse and some tapping on the keyboard, he ended up in his Google mail. Ignoring the unread mail, he quickly typed a new message:

John,
Can you give me a call as soon as you read this? I think I made a mistake in the calculation. Thanks, Daniel.

He typed his phone number just in case John had lost it. He clicked on *Send* and lay back on the sofa.

'What now?' Grace asked.

'We wait, I guess. I've sent him a text as well. I will try calling him again later.'

'Have some wine,' she said pointing to the glass on the floppy disk coaster.

He picked up the glass of wine and took a sip. 'Thanks. Not bad.'

'Shall we get some takeaway?' she asked.

It was as if Daniel's appetite was in hiding up to then.

On hearing the word "takeaway" he suddenly heard his stomach rumble and realised just how hungry he was. 'Sounds like a great idea.'

'There's a nice Indian place nearby,' she said as she leaned forward, moved the laptop in her direction and googled something. In a few seconds she had a menu opened on the screen. 'Are you still a big fan of Biryani?'

Daniel said nothing for a moment, as if distant memory rose slowly in his mind. 'To be honest, I haven't had Indian for so long.'

She stared at him. 'Really?'

He shrugged his shoulders as if it wasn't such a big deal. 'Zoe's not mad about it. She says the food smells like big sweaty guys.' He took another sip of wine. 'I don't know where she gets that idea from. She obviously had a bad experience.'

'I guess food that reminds you of sweaty guys doesn't help. So you feel like Prawn Biryani?'

His face lit up. 'That would be nice.'

'Naan bread?'

'Garlic,' they both said together.

'Just like old times,' Grace added as she scribbled down the order and the telephone number.

54

Claire's eyes widened as she ran downstairs, two steps at a time. With her sleeve, she covered her mouth and nose as she pushed the kitchen door open.

She felt the heat on her face before she realised the severity of the fire before her. The bin had caught fire and was burning in full force. The flames had reached high enough to set the top cupboard alight.

'Oh my God!'

She knew straight away it was too much to try and tackle herself. She would need a lot more than a jug of water. Not only the heat, but the fumes were getting stronger too. She could see black smoke rising to the ceiling and turning around, back into the kitchen. It was building up with no escape. No ventilation.

Quick as a flash, Claire ran over to the back door, unlocked it and swung it open. The smoke that rose to the ceiling suddenly changed direction like a flock of birds and escaped through the door.

Only one thought consumed her now. John.

She ran back through the kitchen and shut the door behind her. Running back up the stairs, she nearly tripped over the pack of toilet paper that she had left on the landing earlier. She darted into Max's bedroom and made straight for her husband.

'John! Wake up!' she screamed as she pulled at him. He rolled onto his back still fast asleep. 'There's a fire!' She slapped his cheek a couple of times. His eyes rolled to the back of his head.

'John! Wake up!' she shouted as tears ran down her cheeks. She was unsure if they were out of desperation or from the fumes she had just encountered. With John showing no signs of waking up, she reached for her mobile and called 999.

'We have a big fire in the kitchen. My husband is upstairs and won't wake up,' she said through floods of tears. 'I can't get him out of the house. He's too heavy. Please help us!' She gave her address. The operator told her a fire brigade was on its way and if her husband didn't wake up, she must leave the house.

After she hung up, she turned to John. 'There's no way I'm leaving this house alone.'

She continued desperately to try and wake John up. His head flopped from one side to the other. Saliva fell from both corners of his mouth. He was out for the count.

How much did he drink?

'Wake up, John!' she screamed. 'Please!'

After several minutes of screaming and tugging, she gave up. She glanced towards the door. The blaze below was no doubt getting bigger. Despite the backdoor being opened, she could see the smoke reaching the landing.

Calmly she walked to the bedroom door and closed it. She turned back towards John and climbed onto the bed. She wrapped her arms around him and closed her eyes. The smell of alcohol didn't bother her anymore. She just wanted to hold him. Feel his heartbeat. Smell his hair. Touch his skin. For the last time.

'I'm sorry, John,' she whispered. 'I'm so sorry.'

As the flames grew stronger below, the two parents lay together in their dead son's bed.

55

Plates with remnants of Prawn Biryani and Lamb Korma lay next to the laptop that was now closed over, but still switched on. *The Frames* played from the loudspeakers connected to the laptop. A second bottle of red wine stood open, the cork still tightly attached to the corkscrew lying next to it.

'Is this dangerous?' Daniel asked.

'What?'

'This. Us. Here. Alone.'

'Can you say that in a full sentence now?' Grace asked teasingly.

'You know what I mean. Here we are, getting drunk in a stranger's apartment.'

'I wouldn't call three glasses of wine getting drunk.'

He looked at her with glassy eyes. 'This is our fourth, sweetheart,' he said holding up the glass. 'Or maybe even our fifth.'

Something caught Grace's attention. She leaned towards him. 'Go like this: Eeeee,' she said pulling a fake smile.

He did what he was told. 'Eeeeee.'

'You always had that problem.'

'What problem?' he asked frowning.

'Your teeth get all stained when you drink red wine.'

'Yeah. No shit, Sherlock,' he said as he closed his mouth and rubbed his tongue along his front teeth. 'It's the red wine.'

'I can understand *some* staining, but then there's that,' she said pointing to his mouth. 'You're like Jaws from that old *James Bond* movie. I always remember that about you. The black teeth.'

'What a nice thing to remember me by,' he said, grinning briefly before becoming self-conscious of his teeth, and hiding them once again. 'You don't remember me for being generous or making you laugh, but for my black teeth after drinking a bit of wine. That's great.'

'Didn't you say once that you were going to invent a sort of sticky film or tape that you could put over your teeth and then just be able to pull it off after a night of wine drinking?'

He smiled. 'I talked a lot of shite in my student days.'

They both remained silent for a moment. A floor lamp standing in the corner caught Daniel's eye. It reminded him of a plant. Two lights protruded from the main stand in opposite directions. The hanging switches dangling from each light reminded him of dewdrops falling from the leaves. He turned towards Grace.

'You want to know why I had the photo in my wallet?'

She blinked slowly, almost in slow motion, and looked at him. 'If you're willing to tell, sure.'

He took a sip of wine and cleared his throat. 'When I went up to the attic and found the box with my thesis and all the notes with it, the photo fell out from one of the notebooks.'

He laid his glass of wine on the stool next to the sofa. 'It's funny how quickly time goes by,' he said as he went rooting in his pocket. He pulled out his wallet and removed the photograph. 'It just fluttered out of nowhere.'

Grace shuffled closer to him to view the photo once again.

'It's funny,' he said, 'looking at it now.'

'In what way?'

He rubbed his fingers over the two faces. Two strangers with hopes and dreams looked back. 'I get an ache inside. It feels like a sort of homesickness, a sort of longing. I get a really strong nostalgic feeling. But it's more than that.' He looked at Grace for a moment before turning back to the photo. 'I was definitely in love with you. But I was also in love with the whole period of time. It was a time when the future seemed so far away. Where dreams seemed ...' He trailed off for a moment. 'Attainable, I suppose. Strange, isn't it?'

Grace shrugged her shoulders.

'I don't know. I don't think so. I also loved that period of my life. I also have the same warm feeling when I see photos from back then. But life has to go on. Everyone moves on through the different stages of life. For better or worse. There's no going backwards.'

Daniel looked at her. 'What was the turning point for you to finally leave Otto?' he asked. 'Was it when he beat you?'

She sipped her drink and thought for a moment. 'No. Strange as it might sound, that wasn't it.' She bit on her lip slowly before letting it go. 'I think the turning point was just last week actually. When I was at work.'

'So recent?'

She nodded.

'What happened?'

She rubbed the stem of her wine glass with her thumb and forefinger. The whole glass turned slowly clockwise as she twisted it. And then counterclockwise.

'You know the way things build up in your handbag?' she asked eventually.

Daniel sat motionless with a deadpan expression. 'Can't say I do. No.'

'I mean you know what a woman's handbag can be like? You can compare it to a drawer in your house that you keep throwing all kinds of shit into, until it's time to clean out.'

'Of course, yes.'

'I tend to gather these bits and pieces of random junk too. Anyway, I was searching for my lip balm the other day when I found an old leaflet advertising a local window cleaning service.'

Daniel wondered where this was leading and whether she understood his original question.

'I thought to myself "why would I keep an old leaflet of

a window cleaning service in my handbag?" I turned it around and found a list on the back of it.' She left her wine down and spoke softer. 'It was a list I had made maybe a year earlier.'

'What kind of list? A bucket list?

She shook her head. 'No. It was a list I had made before Otto beat me up that time. It was divided in two. On the left: girl's names and on the right: boy's names. I had made it when we half-decided to try for a baby. If I would ever become pregnant, then at least I had a preliminary list ready. To start discussing names.' She took the photo from his hand. 'I felt so sad that day. I left my desk and disappeared into the toilet. I looked at the list and I cried. I cried for the twins I lost. I cried for all the *time* I lost. I cried for my inability to have children.' She remained silent. She rubbed her finger softly over Daniel's smiling face. 'For some reason I thought of you. I don't know why. I think I even cried for you, Daniel. Can you believe that? It was a strange day. A strange realisation.'

Daniel was taken aback. 'Why did you cry for me?'

'I don't know.' She looked at him. 'It was as if you died and I never got to say goodbye.'

He placed his hand on her knee.

'I'm sorry, Grace.' He frowned and slowly shook his head. 'Sorry for what I've done. Or for what I didn't do. I know how crap it sounds twelve years later but...' he trailed off as Grace leaned her head on his chest and wrapped her arms around him.

'I missed you,' she said.

Daniel felt dizzy, not sure if it was from the wine or the millions of thoughts that were rushing to his head. He could smell her hair. The same scent from twelve years previously. Reviving many more memories. Memories of wakening in the middle of the night to find himself in a face-full of Grace's hair. He would tip her on the shoulder and she would automatically move her hair to one side so that he could snuggle up next to her, and still be able to breathe. Still be able to remain beside her warm body.

'Why did you do it, Daniel?' she asked with her arms still wrapped around him.

He relaxed. He placed one arm around her and began gently caressing hers. 'I needed to just go. Get away from everything. I felt ashamed. I felt embarrassed. All my dreams were in that Godforsaken thesis.' He rubbed his forehead with his other hand. 'Talk about putting all your eggs in one basket. They teach you a lot of things at university but the one thing they don't teach is coping with failure. Coping with rejection. I mean, I had serious dreams of winning the Fields Medal , for Christ's sake.' He paused for a moment. 'I even had dreams of asking you to marry me during my acceptance speech.'

Grace propped her head and stared up at him. 'Yeah, right,' she said, full of scepticism.

He nodded slowly. 'Yes, I did. Just don't vomit on me please.'

'Really...? what do you mean vomit?'

'Well, it's a bit of a soppy idea.'

'No, it's not. It's sweet.'

'I was a sweet guy.'

'You had a second chance, you know?'

'Of what? Marrying you?'

'Of winning a Fields Medal. Of getting your thesis accepted. Of becoming Doctor Daniel Geller.'

'A second chance?' he asked. 'How?'

'If you didn't come here and just waited to see if I died, you could have been one step closer in realising your dream.'

He reflected on what she said. 'I suppose I did. I suppose I screwed it all up by coming here and warning you. Honestly, I'd rather give my second chance to someone else.'

Grace ran her hand through her hair and looked at him. Their faces were very close. He could smell her perfume.

'Do you truly think I would be dead if you didn't

come?' she asked.

He stopped caressing her arm. 'Are you doubting my thesis?'

'I have never doubted your thesis. Ever. I think *you're* doubting your thesis,' she said.

'Maybe.' He glanced at his watch.

11:23pm.

'There's still thirty-seven minutes left you know. You're not out of the woods yet.'

They continued to hold each other. With her head on Daniel's chest she could hear his heart beating. Daniel rubbed his chin against her head. A stray strand of her hair got stuck in his mouth. He picked it off with his other hand. While his hand was in the vicinity anyway, he decided to caress Grace's head gently.

'I remember those,' she said, after a few moments.

'What?'

'Those head massages.'

Daniel said nothing.

'I never met another guy, who was able to give such good head massages.'

'This isn't an *official* head massage. It's a more of a head...' he searched for the correct word. 'More of a little head scratch.'

'Good enough. I'm still getting the same goose bumps I used to get. My goose bumps missed you.'

He moved his hand that was rubbing her arm down to her hand. Their fingers interlocked. He noticed her hands hadn't changed much, except for an extra ring or two. And her nails were varnished, which was something she never used to do in her student days. Other than that, they were exactly as he remembered them.

Grace however did notice a change. 'Your hands are much rougher than before.'

'*I'm* much rougher than before.'

She rolled her eyes. 'You're not rough, Daniel. You never were and you never will be.'

He thought briefly of Zoe and how she was getting on with her Hens Party in London. What would she think if she saw him drunk and in the arms of his past lover?

56

John wasn't sure what was happening. A vague sense of obscurity echoed through his semi-woken mind. He could hear murmuring coming from somewhere distant. It felt like he was underwater and someone was calling out to him from above.

'John!'

Disorientation pumped through his veins. He took a deep breath to try to gain some kind of composure. A strong smell of smoke assaulted his senses. *I must be still alive,* he thought.

'John!'

It was a voice he knew. But where was it coming from? He felt that he was trapped in a dark room with no doors or windows. His hands felt for an exit, but found nothing. Even the wall felt like it wasn't there. Was he imagining it?

'Where are you?' he wanted to shout, but nothing came out.

He heard crying in the distance. It was Claire. Was she in the next room? He tried to open his eyes. Nothing. A grey blanket. Had he opened his eyes and just not seen anything? Or could he really not open his eyes? This disorientation was something he had never experienced before. Was this part of the process of dying? If so, wasn't his life supposed to flash before his eyes? All he felt was a burning sensation from his lungs.

Strangely though, he wasn't panicking. In fact, he felt the complete opposite. A bizarre blanket of serenity fell over him. *This must be part of the dying process*, he thought. He felt calm. A kind of relaxation that spread to every cell in his body. Was he doing the right thing? Remaining in such a relaxed state.

'John! Wake up!'

There it was again.

This time he forced himself to open his eyes. But nothing came of it. It was as if his eyelids were glued shut. Then suddenly, out of the grey nothingness, he saw a face.

A boy.

It was Max.

But it wasn't the real Max. It was the photo in his office at Trinity. The one he turned down. The photo began to blur, to disappear into the grey blanket that engulfed his mind. Why had he turned the photo down in the first place? Suddenly he felt the need to go back. He needed to go back and lift the photo upright. To see his beautiful face again. Just one more time.

He heard coughing. Was it him? He couldn't tell. The burning in his lungs subsided briefly. The coughing continued for a short while and then stopped. Silence.

John felt movement at his head. The disorientation came back. Where was he? What was the last thing he remembered?

A moment passed. Why couldn't he remember? Another moment passed. *How long were these moments in real time?* he wondered. His last thought was turning down his son's photograph. Did that mean he was still in his office? How did that explain Claire's crying? Was she there too?

Again he tried opening his eyes. This time it worked, barely. He felt stinging in his eyes. The stinging sensation seemed to make him more alert. He forced his eyes open more. The greyness still lingered but he sensed movement within the dull cloud. He blinked several times. Each blink made him more aware of what was going on around him. Then he saw them. Silhouettes. Shadows looming above him. Human figures. At least two. What were they wearing on their faces? Masks. Oxygen masks. They also wore helmets. Yellow helmets. Were they firemen? What are they doing here? His eyes closed over once again.

John's mind raced for answers. Suddenly it came to him. It was like getting an ice bucket of water thrown over him. Everything burst into his mind at once. It was like waking up. Dreams and reality swapped roles once again. He knew where he was now, and he didn't like it.

Jesus, he thought to himself. *What have I done?*

A splurge of adrenaline shot through his body. Was it enough to get him up and alert? He knew the burning sensation in his lungs was not good and he had to leave the house quickly. He had to face the reality that he had thrown himself into. He opened his eyes. There they were again. The dark figures. This time he could make eye contact with one of them.

'Can you hear me, sir?' the figure asked.

He tried nodding his head but wasn't sure if he had moved enough for the fireman to notice. He tried to mutter the word "Claire?" but no sound escaped past his vocal chords. He tried again. Even if there was sound coming from his throat he wondered if it would be heard through all the chaos.

'Can you stand up?'

He opened his eyes again. He tried moving his body. Nothing. Slowly he closed his eyes and shook his head. It felt good to close his eyes, but knew he had to get the strength from somewhere to continue.

'How many people are in the house?' the figure asked. The sound seemed further away this time. It was only when John heard Claire's voice he realised the question wasn't meant for him.

'Just the two of us.'

An overwhelming feeling of relief spread in his veins. She was still alive. However, she needed to get out.

'Come with me,' one of the firemen asked. 'Can you climb down the ladder?'

'I can't leave him.'

'We're not leaving him, you need to go.'

'He's not waking up!' she sounded more desperate.

'He is conscious. Come with me.'

'How is he going to get out?'

'We'll carry him if we have to.'

'He's heavy.'

'We do this for a living. Come on now.' A sense of urgency rose in the fireman's voice. 'Let's go.'

John opened his eyes to let Claire know he was okay. The disorientation returned. He had no idea where she was. One of the firemen wasted no more time and picked John up abruptly onto his shoulder. John could hear a muffled cry coming from the fireman as he stumbled towards the opened window. The fireman who had guided Claire out the window stood with her on top of a hydraulic platform. It was like some kind of cherry picker used for rescuing people. It seemed to be already full with just the fireman and Claire. The fireman carrying John transferred him to his colleague who, although wasn't able to carry him, kept him somewhat upright.

'Take him,' he shouted. 'He'll be fine until you get down.'

The fireman in the hydraulic platform grabbed the controls and guided it to the ground. Two paramedics were waiting with a stretcher. One of them looked like he was just out of school. The other was grey-haired and looked like he had seen many similar situations in the past. They grabbed John from the fireman and laid him down on the stretcher.

'Are there any more people in there?' the older one asked.

Unsure who the question was aimed at, Claire shook her head. 'No.'

As soon as Claire was out of the platform, the fireman took controls once again, and raised the ladder.

'He was in and out of consciousness up there,' the fireman shouted at the paramedics, pointing at John. The ladder continued its upward journey.

'Thanks,' the grey-haired paramedic shouted back. They quickly placed something over John's mouth and nose. As they wheeled the stretcher towards the ambulance, John suddenly felt the burning sensation in his lungs subside. He could feel a fresh cool stream going down his throat. It felt divine. It gave him strength to open his eyes again. The paramedics lifted the stretcher into the back of the ambulance. He could feel the oxygen mask covering his mouth and nose.

'John! I'm so sorry.'

John moved his head slightly to one side and saw his wife looking down at him. She wore a blanket over her shoulders, and her face was black and tear-stained. John mumbled something, but it was muffled by the oxygen mask. Slowly he moved his hand to the mask so he could remove it for a moment. Gently Claire placed a hand on his to stop him.

'You don't have to say anything right now, John. We have tomorrow. We have the rest of our lives. I don't blame you for Max's death. I don't blame you for anything.'

John could feel his wife's hand grasp tighten.

'We're going to get through this together,' she said into his ear.

He nodded, signalling that he understood her.

'Things will be different, John. I promise.'

He squeezed her hand. A tear trickled down his cheek. The first tear in front of his wife since Max's funeral. There was so much he wanted to tell her, but it would have to wait.

57

Daniel and Grace remained in each other's arms for at least twenty minutes, saying nothing. They were lost in each other's warmth, lost in each other's past. Finally Grace broke the silence.

'Thank you for coming.'

Returning from a million miles away, Daniel said, 'You're welcome.' It was followed by a spontaneous yawn.

She let go of him and made a move to sit up. He let go of her. She turned to him.

'I want to forgive you for what you did,' she said.

'Okay.' He wasn't fully alert. 'What do you mean you *want* to?'

'I want to. But there's one condition.'

'Okay,' he said a little unsure, sitting up straighter.

She picked up the wine glass and knocked back the remains. 'This is probably the most difficult thing I have ever said to someone.' She placed the wine glass back on the coffee table. Slowly, she raised her hand and touched him on the face.

'Please don't ever contact me again.'

The warm atmosphere seemed to disintegrate before Daniel's eyes. He frowned. 'What do you mean?'

'Look, Daniel,' she said as she took her hand away. 'I don't want to go through what I went through more than a decade ago. You were the only person I have ever loved. And here you are, right in front of me. For one day only. I mean, don't get me wrong, I appreciate what you've done for me. I appreciate it more than you could ever imagine, but please, I …' She raised her shoulders, and shook her head. 'I just don't want to see you again.'

Daniel was unsure how to react. 'I thought that…'

She raised a finger to her lips signalling him to stop talking. He got the message.

'Think of it this way,' she said. 'I'm a recovering alcoholic and you're a big chilled bottle of Chardonnay. If I open this Chardonnay there's no way I can shut it again after one glass. It's best that I'm not tempted. It's best that I don't open old wounds that took so long to heal first time round.'

As a song from the laptop faded out, they could hear sounds from outside. Someone was trying to park right below the apartment. They could hear the parking sensors, a short interval of beeps as the car reversed. The beeps turned into one constant beep indicating to the driver it was time to put the car into first gear and move forward. Another song began and the outside world was once again drowned out.

'The truth is,' Grace continued, 'that I might very much still be in love with you. And who knows, maybe deep down you're still in love with me.' She paused for a few moments. 'But we're both in different stages of our lives now. You have a wife and child. We can't ever go back to the way it used to be. And to be honest, I'm not sure if either of us wants to.'

Daniel remained silent, suspecting that she wasn't finished with what she wanted to say. He was right.

'Let's not make a big deal out of it. Chances are that maybe we would never see each other again anyway, unless we made a conscious effort to.'

When it was Daniel's cue to speak, he was lost for words. He took a deep breath. 'Okay.'

Picking up his wine glass that was standing on a stool next to the sofa, he knocked it back and placed it on the coffee table.

'I don't know what I was expecting by coming here. I mean, I knew I wanted to warn you about my prediction, but I wasn't sure if there was going to be anything extra, if you know what I mean.' He was unsure if he was making any sense. 'I understand how you feel. And you're right. What we once had is gone, long gone. And I have nobody else to blame but myself.'

It was time to leave. Rising from the sofa he walked to the hallway. He sensed Grace following him. He took his jacket that was hanging up. He opened the door and turned around. She walked towards him. Without warning, she took his face in her hands and kissed him on the lips. It lasted a few seconds before she pulled away. He could see the tears swelling in Grace's eyes. Her nose twitched slightly. There was so much more he wanted to say to her. So much he didn't understand but wanted her to somehow understand.

'Nobody else in the world would understand what you did today,' she said as a tear rolled down her cheek. 'But I do. And I will be grateful until the day I really do die.'

Daniel swallowed hard. He was unsure whether to smile or not. Grace took the door handle.

'I love you, Daniel. I always will.' She spoke the words softly as he stepped outside. He turned around to meet Grace's eyes one last time, but the door was already closing, obscuring the view. He did nothing to stop it, but just stood there as the door closed on his face.

Standing in the hallway, he could hear her lock the door from the inside. He glanced at his watch. It was two minutes after midnight. His job was complete. Daniel turned around and climbed down the steep stairwell. His journey back to his simple, routine life began here. His dream of becoming a world-famous mathematician was now truly dead. But someone he once loved, maybe even still loved, was still alive.

And that was all that mattered.

58

The A&E of Connolly Hospital was as busy as ever. Nothing new for a Saturday evening. Alcohol was the common factor in many of the accidents. Falls, fights, broken limbs, bloody faces. Domestic disputes that went too far. Car accident victims. Despite the anti-drinking laws and campaigns, some people still took chances. Too many chances.

Like most Irish hospitals, the corridors were used as more than a walkway from one room to another. They were used as *space*, vital space. Incoming patients on stretchers lined up all the way from the A&E department to the ambulance drop off zone.

Lying on one of the stretchers in the corridor was Professor John Redmond. The doctor kept the oxygen mask attached to him and monitored his breathing. Stable. No need for a bed right now. Resources were tight. Time was even more so. Next patient, please.

John drifted in and out of consciousness. The sounds and noise surrounding him were chaotic. Beeps from machines. Rattling as shaky medical equipment rolled by. Underpaid and overworked medical staff doing their best to attend to the needs of every patient, like waiting staff in a busy restaurant. There would be no tips to share after their shift though, only exhaustion to take home with them.

John felt a hand on his. It held him tight and then released the grip. That wasn't the touch of the medical staff. He knew whose touch it was.

At least she's okay.

He was too exhausted to waken fully. His batteries were empty. They needed to be recharged. Or better still, replaced.

A scent of sterility hung in the air. Alcohol hand

dispensers hung on every corner. A first defence in the combat against the resistant super bugs.

He could feel a thin blanket over him. He wondered how many previous patients felt the same blanket. His arm touched against a metal bar. Cold. Although his eyes were shut, he could sense dark shadows passing by, followed by bright ones. Were they the angels and ghosts that waited patiently to take their patients to the next level, wherever that may be?

'Sandra, have you got a spare sphygmomanometer?'

'I saw one in cubicle five.'

Constant background hum.

'No, that's fine. I just wanted to test...'

Radio speaker. Was it an ambulance driver announcing a new arrival?

Constant footsteps. Some harder than others.

A mild draught every time someone passed by. Too exhausted to care.

'We're gonna turn around and come back again. There's no real space around here.'

'What's the story...?'

'Is that sore?'

'Theresa, which one is swollen?'

'Where were you going?'

Sound of cubicle curtain being pulled. Phone ringing. Slap. Latex gloves being put on. Beep, beep. Rattling sound again. Another shaky device being wheeled by.

'Are you okay?'

Another phone ringing.

'...you've got arthritis in the fingers, have you?'

Beep.

Footsteps.

Sneeze. Another one.

Mobile going off. Old fashioned phone ringtone. Or maybe it was just an old fashioned phone somewhere in the A&E department.

Beep.

Phone ringing again.

Whispering.

'That'll be lovely, and she can bring home my walking aid.'

Cough.

Beep. Different tones.

'Remind me to give that to Paula.'

'What time is it?'

'It will dry up tonight.'

Door closing.

'Show this to your doctor.'

Strange sound as if nails are being clipped.

John drifted back into sleep as the sounds around him metamorphosed into a single incomprehensible drone. It was as if his head was submerged into a warm bucket of water.

59

A whirlwind of emotions spiralled within Daniel as he walked down Westlandgracht towards the tram stop. Tempted as he was to look back towards the apartment, he resisted it. He didn't want his last image of Grace to be a sad lonely figure looking through a window. He wondered if she felt the same, if she too resisted from looking out the window so she wouldn't have to watch a sad lonely figure walking down the street.

He felt an ache inside him. Although Grace had forgiven him for what he had done, he wondered if he would ever forgive himself.

A bicycle wobbled by beside him on the street. A giggly girl sat side-saddle on the rear seat, perfectly balanced, as her man pedalled with all his strength, straining to keep up the momentum to prevent the bicycle from toppling. Daniel wondered what rewards would be in store for him once they got home.

When he reached the tram stop, Daniel tried to read the timetable and anticipate the time of the next tram. With everything that was going through his mind, combined with the wine he had enjoyed with Grace, he gave up and decided to just wait patiently. He was in no hurry. Raising his head, he noticed a large spider web between the top of the shelter and the advertisement billboard on the side. A poster of a local beauty magazine showed Beyoncé on the front page, looking beautiful in a red Roberto Cavalli dress. Someone had stuck pieces of chewing gum on the dress she was wearing, roughly where her nipples would be. Next to it, written in black marker were the words: *Koud, he?* He doubted it was funny, even if he knew what it meant.

Looking in the distance, he saw three cranes lit up. They seemed to be all different heights. It reminded Daniel of an award podium for first, second and third places one would see at a sporting event. The middle crane was highest, the one on the left was lower and the one to the right was even lower. He closed his eyes as a gust of wind blew in his face. He had an urge to walk to the cranes and climb up one. Away from the emotions he felt. Was that why he chose to become a crane operator twelve years ago? To get away from everyone? Now it felt like his home. It was where he belonged. He looked from the cranes towards the direction of the apartment. A tram bell rang out and he turned his head to see Tram 2 coming his way. He held out his hand signalling it to stop.

60

As soon as Grace closed the door, she covered her face with her hands. On the verge of crying, she realised that perhaps Daniel would still be standing on the other side of the door. She held back her tears, removed her hands from her face and placed her ear to the cold surface of the door. The door was too solid to really hear any movement coming from the landing on the other side.

She walked to the living room and sat on the edge of the sofa. She looked around. Everything was different now. A deep sorrow flowed through her. Was it the wine that made her feel this way? She took a deep breath. The sorrow seemed to be accumulating in her heart.

How did I end up like this?

It was as if any hope she had in anything, she had unknowingly put it in Daniel. Now she had sent him away, never to come back. Staring at the two empty wine glasses, she wondered if she had done the right thing. Light from the plant-like lamp in the corner fell onto the glasses highlighting fingerprints on one of them. She knew straight away it was Daniel's glass. Although he always held the wine glass by the stem to begin with, after the first sip he usually held it by the bowl. It was the little quirks like that that she loved. A sort of oblivious innocence.

She picked up the wine glass by the stem. Not sure why, she closed her eyes and rubbed the glass against her cheek. Imagining Daniel's hands caressing her. She moved the glass to below her nose and took a gentle whiff. There were only remnants of red wine, and no sign of Daniel's scent. Opening her eyes, she placed the wine glass back on the coffee table.

Her attention turned to her nail on her right index finger. The nail varnish was chipped. She would need to give them a fresh coat of polish before Monday morning.

It was a chore she despised. Her thoughts floated to the time she had started painting her nails regularly. Sure, she had always done it for special occasions, big nights out, weddings, holidays and the like. But when did she start having varnished nails on a daily basis? It didn't take her long to pinpoint when it started. Or, more specifically, who encouraged it.

Otto. When they first met in Edinburgh.

'See how feminine she looks,' Otto would comment on other women when they were out together. 'It's in her finger nails.'

Not long after, Grace did it as a once-off to please him. The once-off became a regular habit, edged on by her husband.

Jesus, didn't I have any backbone?

She reflected on how she allowed Otto to chip away at her self-confidence over the years, like a novice sculptor. He had banged away blindly. His condescending words and unpredictable blows were his hammer and chisel. The result was anything but a work of art.

Grace spread out her fingers in front of her as if she was admiring a recent manicure. Inside however, she despised the appearance of her nails. If a bucket of concentrated acid stood on the coffee table, she would have dipped her fingertips into it and got rid of the nail varnish along with the nails themselves. Possibly even her fingerprints. Her identity had already vanished.

How did it come this far?

She held her hands closer to her and began scraping the nail that already had the chip in it. Taking a deep breath, she vowed that she would regain the confidence and sense of humour that she once had. She would take out the bug that had crawled up her ass all those years ago. She would let her hair down more often. She vowed that she would try to forget every little comment or sly remark Otto had thrown at her over the past nine years. Or if she couldn't forget them, at least manage them differently.

She was no fool. She knew that the memories she wanted to forget would be the hardest ones to lose. But if she could somehow store them somewhere, deep down where they would seldom see the light of day... Then she had a chance.

As Grace contemplated on getting her life back on track, her mind wandered, and she lost track of time. She failed to hear the knock on the door. It was only when a second knock came, a little louder this time, that Grace suddenly became aware of it.

61

Daniel sat next to the window in the tram. A screen hung overhead a few metres away broadcasting muted news and adverts in Dutch. The tram went around Hoofddorpplein and up towards Hoofddorpweg until it came to a standstill.

He reflected on his thesis and how his actions over the past twenty-four hours ensured that it would be worthless now. There was no rescuing it. It suddenly felt like a weight off his shoulders. Something that he once spent so much time on was now really behind him. It felt like an elderly grandparent passing away. On one hand it's extremely sad, especially when you were so fond of them, but on the other hand, if they are so old and often sick, it's for the best.

His simple life had been made that much simpler now. No more skeletons in the closet. No more 'what if' questions. This is what he chose.

Daniel searched in his pockets for his mobile. He pulled it out and glanced at the screen wallpaper. Sean smiled back at him with a sparkle in his eye and a cheeky grin. The photo was taken at Dollymount Strand on a spring day. It dawned on him how happy he really was. Suddenly he missed his son incredibly.

Looking outside the window, he realised the tram still wasn't moving. A small group of cyclists seemed to have congregated. Had there been an accident? What was preventing even cyclists from moving through the streets of Amsterdam? He placed his mobile on his lap, leaned towards the window and cupped his hands around his face. Ahead, it looked like a section of the street was suddenly standing upright at a ninety degree angle. Were his eyes playing tricks on him? Squinting and leaning forward until his forehead touched the cold window, it suddenly became clear. A bridge was open. A trail of boats travelled through the canal to their destinations. He could see the tip of the occasional mast pass behind the upright street. To the side, he could catch a glimpse of the boats continuing their journey into the spider-web of canals.

That's something you don't see every day, he thought to himself. He turned back to his mobile. He was about to put it on sleep mode when something caught his eye. The time on the top of the screen said: 11:22pm. Instinctively Daniel looked at his watch. It read 12:22am.

Of course, he thought. He had never put the clock in his mobile forward when he landed at Schiphol the previous day. There was little point in doing it now, he thought, unless he was going to use it as an alarm clock. He dismissed the idea. He would just set the alarm in the hotel room. He placed his mobile back in his pocket and continued to observe the never-ending stream of boats taking advantage of the open bridge.

Suddenly he felt uncomfortable. Very uncomfortable. It was the second time in the last few hours that he felt that something was not right. He looked at his watch again. It was past midnight indeed. But back in Ireland it wasn't a new day yet. Daniel rubbed his forehead, and fidgeted in his seat.

Was there a time zone factor built into the calculation? He closed his eyes and thought for a moment. He was almost certain there was. It wasn't obvious in the last calculation as it was already taken into account in the generic part of it that automatically included Ireland's time zone.

A cold chill ran through his spine.

'Shit,' he whispered.

What if his prediction for Grace was still valid? He had calculated it based on the Irish time zone. He chewed on his thumbnail. After a few moments, he dismissed the idea. Even it was true, he thought to himself, what were the chances? *She's in the apartment. Probably in bed.*

Daniel scratched his head and tried desperately to accept his latest resolution.

Yes, she's probably already fast asleep.

Staring at the screen hanging overhead, he saw an advertisement for the World Press Photo exhibition in De Oude Kerk. He tried to take his mind of his latest concern.

That would have been nice to attend.

The next ad lost his interested and there it was again, the nagging at his mind.

Grace is still at risk.

'Shit,' he said to himself, louder this time.

He pulled out his phone again and called Grace's number.

Now she's going think that I want to come back for the night.

62

Grace stood up.

Was it Daniel at the door?

Instead of going to the door, she crept to the window and looked down at the front door of the apartment. It was closed. Had Daniel even left the apartment building? She couldn't recall hearing the door of the building open and close. She looked down the street towards the tram stop. It was empty. She jumped slightly, startled by another knock on the door.

Who else could it be?

She walked to the door. It seemed strange that he would have just waited there for the past fifteen or twenty minutes, Grace thought to herself.

'Who is it?' she called out, unsure if the visitor could even hear her through the thick door.

Silence.

'Hello? Grace said, raising her voice. 'Can you hear me?' She repeated it in Dutch, in case the person standing on the other side of the door was an extremely rare species of Dutch person who couldn't understand English.

The knock sounded again.

They obviously can't hear me, she reasoned with herself. 'If it's not Daniel, who in the name of God is knocking on the door after midnight?' she wondered out loud.

Slightly irritated, she unlocked the door and pulled down the handle to open it.

She had opened the door only a fraction when it flew open with an almighty force. The door bashed into Grace's face, breaking her nose instantly and knocking her to the floor. The wallop was so unexpected that she had no time to protect herself as she crashed into the wall on the other side of the hallway. Pain exploded through her head as she reached the floor.

In the sudden chaos, she heard her mobile ringtone somewhere in the apartment.

63

The phone continued to ring.

'Come on.'

Looking out the window, Daniel saw that the bridge had started to go down.

'Pick up your phone ...,' he stopped when he heard an answer.

'Hi, this is Grace. I'm not available right now, but leave a message and I'll get back to you.'

Daniel hesitated for a moment. Before he had time to decide what to do, he heard the beep.

'Sorry... Hi Grace. It's Daniel here,...um. I'm not really sure what to say. If you hear this message within the next half hour can you call me back? Please. Otherwise just forget about it. You don't have to call me back.' He cringed as he hung up.

Looking outside he saw that the bridge was almost horizontal once again. Scooters and cars that had their engines off were starting up again. Cyclists had their feet on their pedals, ready to kick off. It reminded Daniel of a strange version of *Wacky Races*.

He looked at his mobile and prayed for it to burst to life. He longed to see Grace's name appearing on the screen. Nothing. Only Sean's cheeky grin stared back at him.

He took a deep breath and tried to forget about it. *What were the chances?* He looked out the window again.

Would anything really happen to her in the space of an hour?

The bridge was down fully.

'Fuck it.'

He jumped out of his seat and ran to one of the exits. He pressed the red button to open the doors, but they didn't budge. He looked towards the front and saw the barriers before the bridge going up. He turned towards the conductor near the back of the tram and shouted, 'Hey! I need to get off.' He continued to press on the red button. 'Can you open the door!' The conductor shouted something in a grumpy tone. The doors swung open nevertheless. Daniel jumped out to a chorus of bicycle bells of cyclists that were on the move again.

'Kijk uit!

Eikel!'

Daniel ignored them and ran back in the direction the tram had come. He couldn't really believe what he was doing. Was the alcohol causing him to be so paranoid?

Half afraid that he would lose his way, he ran parallel to the tram line. It seemed a bit complicated as he came to a square called Hoofddorpplein, but he just went around it, keeping his eye on the tram track. He was certain that there was a shorter route back to Grace, but he didn't want to take any chances of getting lost.

'I'm going crazy. I know I am.'

As Daniel caught sight of the tram stop with the Beyoncé poster, he took a right at the corner convenient store into Westlandgracht. Knowing that he was on the correct street now, his run turned to a brisk walking pace as he took his mobile out to see if there were any missed calls. Nothing. Dialling Grace's number, he tried one last time to make contact with her. Again it went to her voicemail.

As he caught sight of the apartment in the distance, he saw that the light was still on in the front living room. *A good sign*, Daniel thought. Maybe she was just in the shower and had missed the calls. Maybe she had her phone on silent mode, especially after visiting the various museums during the day. There were dozens of perfectly reasonable explanations to why Grace was not picking up her phone. He decided not to draw any more conclusions, but to just ring the doorbell and confirm that everything was okay.

Out of breath by the time he arrived at the door, he pressed the doorbell. Looking up he hoped to see Grace looking down at him. Whether or not she would open the door didn't really matter as long as she was all right.

Nobody came to the window. He pressed the button again.

'Come on, Grace.'

He became more aggressive with the doorbell. 'Open the fucking door,' he said under his breath. After a few moments he knocked on the door with his bare knuckles, hoping that would convey the importance of his visit. Opening the letterbox, he peeked in. The stairway was dark. He could just make out the silhouette of the bike blocking the hallway. He was about to pull away when a light in the hallway came on.

Thank God.

There was a buzz and the door opened.

Daniel pushed the door open and glanced up the stairway. What he saw, however, did nothing to reassure him that Grace was okay.

64

As John slowly regained consciousness, he could hear an ambulance siren in the distance. He wondered for a moment if he was inside the ambulance that he was hearing. Unable to sense any movement, he accepted that he was not. In any case, he had a vague recollection of lying in a stretcher in the busy hospital hallway earlier. He was already at his final destination. Unless they were moving him to another hospital?

No. The sound of the siren was now fading. It belonged to the outside world. A world to which he was slowly, reluctantly, coming back to.

A fierce pain pulsed in his head. He felt like his head had been placed in a vice and slowly tightened. It seemed like every cubic inch of the internal workings was affected by this unusual pain. Keeping his eyes closed, he remained in the grey world between sleep and wakefulness.

He tried to swallow, but there was nothing to swallow. His mouth was like sandpaper. As he moved his tongue upwards in his mouth, it attached itself to the palate momentarily, almost like Velcro. He suddenly felt thirsty, parched even. It was time to wake up, escape from the limbo where he found himself.

As he woke, he rattled his dazed mind for the reason he felt this way. In the colourless abyss of his mind, nothing came forth. Could it be just a hangover?

He remembered the pints of Guinness, the English tourists, the match. Did he drink so much as to make him feel this way?

John dismissed the idea almost as soon as he thought of it. Deep down he knew it was more serious than a hangover. Gradually he opened his eyes.

One of the first things he saw was a small television set hanging from the ceiling. He blinked slowly. He felt some kind of foreign object coming from his nose and across each side of his face. Uncomfortable. Almost ticklish. A sensation that could eventually lead to an almighty sneeze. For now the sneeze would not come. John reached up and touched it. It was an oxygen tube.

His attention turned to the hand he had raised. Slowly he placed it back to its resting place on the bed. His gaze followed it. An intravenous drip was attached to it. A plaster kept the tube in place.

He noticed that the skin of his hands seemed dry, leathery, almost as if they had aged overnight. Or was this just the first time he noticed? His hands, John thought, had turned into his father's hands. When had that happened?

Scenes of when he was young flooded back. How much he enjoyed observing his father's hands. They were so big and strong compared to his small, smooth ones. His father's hands had more hair and wrinkles than his. He recalled how he would gather the skin of his father's hand in between two fingers, a very loose pinch, and then let it go. The skin would lie back to its original position, like an obedient dog.

He would do the same to his own youthful hands too. The obedient puppy would return to its original position much quicker. He sometimes wondered why and reckoned it was something to do with the hair on his father's hands. Never had John realised that he too would have hands like that one day. The only difference was that his father's hands worked hard to provide and protect his family. Glancing at his own, he realised how useless they were. Not even being able to protect the one true gift his life had given him.

John raised his head and scanned the room. Three other beds lay in the hospital ward. Judging by the mounds beneath the bed covers, two of them were occupied.

The thirst he encountered moments earlier returned to him. Slowly he glanced towards his bedside locker, hoping he would find a glass of water. It was only then that he noticed his wife.

Claire was fast asleep on the visitor's armchair beside him. A copy of *Woman's Way* lay open on her lap. It lay at an awkward angle, about to slide to the floor. Her hair was unkempt. Something extremely rare for Claire.

'Claire,' he whispered, not to wake her up but more out of affection. He studied his sleeping wife. Her head sloped to one side. It seemed so uncomfortable. *Couldn't she have slept in the empty bed across from him?* John thought.

He continued looking at his wife as if he hadn't seen her in months. Perhaps he hadn't. Perhaps subconsciously he really tried to avoid looking at her. Maybe he was afraid of seeing the resemblances. Claire had the same high cheekbones as Max. The same eyes. How heredity was so much fun when a baby was born and as a child grew up. But how those genetic traits could turn against you and break each parent's heart as they looked at one another, constant reminders of their dead child.

John thought she looked so pretty and peaceful. 'My beautiful Claire.'

It started coming back to him. How he ended up there. He remembered drinking a lot. He remembered stumbling home. And that strange smell in the kitchen. It was so intense. But he did nothing about it, especially with the knowledge that Claire was supposed to die. He did nothing about letting Claire know about the importance of the date. He did nothing to protect her from the possibility of dying. He might as well have flung a match into the bin himself.

He closed his eyes trying not to think of it. It was like the morning after a night out, when something embarrassing had happened. Dancing on tables, arguing with bouncers, French kissing a random stranger, all things he had done when he was much younger and stupid. He would wake up with a shock, often not in his own bed. Or sometimes not in a bed at all and wonder what had happened. Waves of embarrassment would rise as the flashbacks made unwelcome appearances.

But this was very different. This was much more than embarrassing. This was devastating. A shock of reality tore through his body as he shuddered at the thought of what might have happened. He recalled the smoke, the heat, the stinging eyes, the crying, the coughing. He could have prevented all that if he stayed at home and protected his wife. If he stayed sober and alert.

John's head turned back towards Claire, but he was unable to look at her. Instead his gaze floated to a picture hanging on the wall above her. It was a desert road with mountains in the distance, probably taken in one of those American States: Utah, Arizona.

It wasn't enough to stop the flashbacks that haunted him. John's vision became blurred as he felt his eyes water.

'Why?' he muttered quietly. He closed his eyes to clear the tears that were accumulating. As he opened them again, one trickled down his cheek. It was thrown off course when it came to the plastic tube on his face, and disappeared behind his ear onto the pillow.

'John?' whispered a voice.

Taken completely off guard, he glanced over to Claire and saw that she had woken.

'Sorry,' he said blinking his eyes, hoping they would quickly dry up. 'I didn't mean to wake...'

'Shh,' she said as she leaned towards the bed and took John's hands in hers. The *Woman's Way* fell to the floor. 'I was just dozing. How are you feeling?'

'I'm sorry, Claire. For everything.'

She stroked her husband's hand. 'There's no more apologising from now on.'

He wiped his eyes with his non-intravenous-tubed hand.

'You don't understand...'

'I understand enough, John.' She squeezed his hand

before realising that she may be hurting him and loosened her grip.

'I want you to understand something,' he said.

'I understand enough.'

He ignored her. 'I knew there was a possibility of you dying today…or yesterday. '

'Shh, John look at me.' He met her eyes. They were bloodshot and puffy. 'You don't know what you're saying.'

'I do,' he said, searching for words. His mind was exhausted. All John could muster up was, 'I'm so sorry.'

'John, if anyone has anything to apologise for, it's me,' she said. She took hold of the armrests of her chair and moved closer to him. She stopped half way, picked up the *Woman's Way* and left it on the locker. She then continued to shuffle closer with the chair.

'Listen to me,' she said as she held John's hand once again and squeezed it. 'We're going to get through this together, do you hear me? Together. No more living our separate lives. No more being afraid to mention him in front of one another. Or to mention his name at all for that matter. Max's name. No more being afraid to cry. If you feel like crying, then cry. If you want to shout, shout. Please. Every tear that falls takes a bit of pain with it. Every minute brings us closer to a day when we can get through it without feeling like we just want to die.'

Claire took a deep breath and smiled at John.

'Max was the most amazing thing that happened to our lives. He gave so much meaning to it. It was the most rewarding experience anyone on earth could wish for. We were privileged to be his parents for ten years. Ten wonderful years. We have to be thankful for that. Because, do you know something?'

John shook his head very slightly.

'There are some parents out there, or even in this hospital right now, who have only enjoyed their child for nine years. Or for five years. Some not even a single week. Or a day.' She raised her hand to John's cheek. 'We had ten years. Ten wonderful years! Think about it. Think about it and then try telling me that we're unlucky.'

John remained silent for a moment, thinking about what his wife was saying. He tried to swallow, but his mouth was still as dry as the desert road picture on the wall.

'But there's something that will always haunt me,' John said.

Claire's head tilted to the side. 'What do you mean?'

John's voice escaped as a whisper. He coughed to clear his throat and spoke again. 'You were a brilliant mother,' he said, this time louder. 'You were the best mother a child could ask for. The thing that is eating me alive is the kind of father I was. I couldn't even find time to buy him bloody football socks. I never had the time to watch a stupid football match. Not one! Not one ninety-minute match.'

'Hang on. If you're trying to tell me that he loved me more than he loved you, then you're wrong,' she said. 'He loved you just as much as me. Sure, you worked hard, so what? We both had our strengths and weaknesses as parents. My weaknesses were made up by your strengths and vice versa. We were a team.'

'Weaknesses? You? What weaknesses did you have?'

Claire dismissed his question. 'It doesn't matter now, John. Trust me. Every parent has them. But together we were great parents. I'm not afraid to say it. You should not be afraid to say it either.' She rubbed her eyes and met her husband's gaze once again. 'Who taught him how to ride his bike?' she asked. 'Who taught him how to tie his laces? To fix a puncture? To do that thing with his finger so it looks like it's broken? What about the swings you both made with rope and tyres? Remember the day he came home saying that he was stung by a nettle and you made it all better with a dock leaf. A goddamn dock leaf? Do you think I would have thought of that? You were his hero, John.'

Somewhere in all of this, the tears started to flow from John's eyes. No sobs, just tears that streamed down.

'Don't feel guilty for not being there one hundred percent of the time. No parent is with their child one hundred percent from the moment they're born. It's not quantity, it's quality.'

She rubbed a tear from John's face.

'He may not have had a long life, but he had a good one. He experienced a lot, and that included unconditional love from his *two* parents. We had good times and bad times. And at the end of the day, he knew that we loved him more than anything else in the world. And he loved us.'

A silence rose. John stared into the distance, unsure what to say. It was the first time they had a conversation about it, a real conversation. Unlikely as it seemed, it helped.

After some time he spoke again in a dry, whispery voice. 'Can I have some water?'

65

Glancing up the steep stairway, Daniel saw the neighbour whom they had ran into earlier standing there. She wore a navy dressing gown, and her dirty blonde hair hung down tangled and untidy. The black lipstick strangely enough was still there.

'Hoe kan ik u helpen meneer? U gaat de hele buurt wakker maken!'

Daniel had no idea what she said but sensed from the tone of her voice that she definitely wasn't impressed.

'Sorry,' he said in between breaths. 'I was here earlier with Grace…' He trailed off as he realised that the woman probably didn't know who Grace was. 'The woman that's staying in the apartment above you,' he clarified as he made his way by the bicycle and began climbing the stairs. 'I just need to check something with her.'

The woman backed into her own apartment as Daniel reached the top of the first flight of stairs.

'You're making a racket,' the woman said. 'When you ring the bell, it's actually outside her door, so everybody in the building can hear it too.'

'My sincere apologies,' he said. He found it funny that the woman didn't sound so angry when she spoke English. Or maybe her tone had changed as result of his proximity to her. He pointed up to the next level, as if asking for approval. 'I won't be long.'

The woman shrugged her shoulders. 'Maybe she's not there, you know.'

He continued up the stairs to the next level. 'Maybe.' *As long as she's safe.*

When he reached the second floor he knocked on the door of the apartment. He put his ear to the door straining for any signs of movement.

'Grace?' he said softly. 'Grace, are you there? You don't

have to open the door but just let me know if you're okay.'

He was unable to hear any signs of life. His knocks became louder as did his voice.

'Please, Grace. If you're there just tell me.'

Silence.

Daniel sensed movement from the corner of his eye and turned his head to see the face of the neighbour peeking from downstairs.

'Did you hear her leave in the last half hour or so?' he asked.

The woman shook her head. 'I'm not sure if she left, but I did hear a bit of a commotion about twenty minutes ago.'

Daniel's blood turned cold. He turned his full attention to the woman. 'Commotion? What do you mean by "commotion"?'

The woman shrugged. 'I don't know. Like some kind of fight. Something heavy falling. Another thing smashing. Heavy footsteps as if someone was running across the floor. Rik has wooden floorboards, meaning you can hear a pin drop sometimes, but this sounded out of the ordinary.'

Daniel turned back to the door and started banging on it. 'Open the door, Grace! This isn't funny.'

As he waited for any signs of life, he studied the door. It was extremely solid. Reinforced with a deadbolt lock both on the top and the bottom. There wasn't a hope in hell in breaking in.

Turning to look at the curious neighbour, he asked, 'You don't have a spare key, by chance?'

'No. Sorry.'

He buried his face in one hand as he tried to think. Was he getting upset over nothing? Or did he really believe that Grace was in trouble? The stories of her violent husband during the day didn't help the situation. And now the story of the commotion that the neighbour just heard.

'There is one thing you could try if you're desperate,'

the woman said, now halfway up the stairway.

Daniel raised his head and looked at the woman. 'I am desperate. What is it?'

'Maybe you could climb from my balcony to the balcony above and get in that way.'

His heart was racing. 'Is it high? I mean the distance from your balcony to hers.'

'You can have a look.'

He followed the woman back downstairs. 'That would be fantastic. Thank you.'

'But don't try anything. I have a Rottweiler.'

The woman led Daniel through to the back of her apartment and opened the door to the balcony. He didn't see any Rottweiler, but could tell from the smell that a dog resided in the apartment.

As he stepped out onto the neighbour's balcony, he looked up to Rik's balcony and then down into the garden below them. It wasn't *too* high, but still high enough to break his neck if he fell the wrong way.

'I'll give it a shot.'

Daniel hopped onto the balcony railing. With a swift movement he stood up straight and caught hold of the bottom edge of Rik's apartment. His legs started shaking suddenly with the nerves. Or was it the alcohol in his bloodstream? Either way, it didn't feel good.

'Are you sure you want to do this?' the woman asked. 'If you're really concerned about something, we could just call the police.'

'I'll be fine,' he said, trying to sound positive. His arms were stretched as far as they could, but he couldn't grab hold of anything that would give him enough grasp to pull his entire weight. Even if he did, he doubted that he *could* pull his entire weight. Doing a chin-up was difficult enough when he had a decent grasp. The gap between the two balconies was just too great. The situation wasn't helped by Daniel's sweaty palms.

Looking to the left, he noticed a wooden divider that

separated the balcony he was on from another neighbour's apartment. He shuffled sideways on the rail, continuing to hold onto the edge of the upper balcony. The divider ran upwards at a diagonal angle. With the best grip he could manage, he threw his foot onto the divider. It gave him enough stability to do the same with his other foot. Although he was in an extremely awkward position, he was higher, and the gap between him and Rik's apartment was now much smaller.

He quickly secured a firmer grip of Rik's railings and pulled himself up and over the balcony. He landed on his back in Rik's balcony and let out a sigh of relief.

That's the hard part done.

He quickly stood up to see how he could get into the actual apartment. The light in the kitchen was still on. Peering through the slits of the Venetian blinds hanging on the door, Daniel observed the kitchen. There didn't seem to be anything out of the ordinary there.

From the kitchen he could see right through to the doorway of the living room. Daniel's world froze when he caught sight of what laid on the floor. He leaned forward until his head touched the glass, and he placed cupped hands around his face. It was unmistakable. He could make out Grace's feet and part of her legs. She was lying face-down on the floor of the living room.

66

Desperately, Daniel tried the handle of the door. Locked. He knocked on the window.

'Grace! Open the door! It's Daniel.'

To hell with waking up the neighbours.

He started banging on the door. 'Grace! This isn't funny!'

Don't let your imagination run away with you, Daniel. She could have tripped. She could be asleep. She could have…

But the words the neighbour said moments earlier came back to him, *I did hear a bit of a commotion…*

He looked through the Venetian blinds again. No movement.

What the hell could have happened?

Another thought struck him. *If she was attacked, could the attacker be still in the apartment?*

'What's happening up there?'

It took Daniel a split-second to realise who had said it. Looking over the balcony, his gaze fell onto the neighbour's face looking up, full of curiosity.

'Something strange has happened,' he replied. 'She's lying down on the floor in the living room and not moving.'

Could it be his worse fear had materialised? He looked back to the door on the balcony and saw that the window above it was open. He poked his head back over the balcony and shouted to the neighbour: 'I'm going to try and get in through the window above the door. If you hear another commotion when I'm inside, don't investigate. Just lock your apartment and call the police.'

Quickly he scanned the balcony for something to stand on. A stack of three Grolsch beer crates stood in the corner. Daniel grabbed hold of the bottom one and pulled them over to the door. Spreading his hand over the bottle tops of the top crate, he pressed down and shook his head.

'It's not going to hold my weight,' he mumbled to himself. He lifted the crate off the stack and quickly pulled the bottles out two or three at a time. He lay them on their sides next to the railing. The gap between the balcony floor and the railing was too narrow for any of the bottles to roll off.

Once the crate was empty, he turned it upside down and placed it back on top of the stack. It still fitted perfectly, despite being upside down. He caught hold of the door handle and climbed onto the stack of beer crates. He managed to pull himself onto the tower of crates in a kneeling position. It swayed slightly with his weight. Still holding onto the door handle for balance, he quickly caught hold of the frame of the opened window. Slowly, one foot at a time, he went from a kneeling position to standing up.

The tower of crates swayed even more. His own legs shook with nerves again, almost like he was getting a mild electric shock. He scanned the window, trying to determine his next move. The window was held open by a metal lever. One end of it was inserted into a bolt on the window frame. Daniel propped it up and grabbed onto it to prevent the window from slamming inwards. Placing his foot on the door handle, he pulled himself up and in through the window. He dangled for a while, half inside, half out. The window rested on Daniel's back. As he shuffled further in, his top got caught on the metal bolt that had been used to prop the window open.

'Shit.'

Unsure of the rest of his plan, Daniel caught sight of a key sticking in the lock of the door he was hanging over. If he could reach that and unlock the door, maybe he could shuffle back out and come in the normal way. As he leaned further into the kitchen and reached down to the key, he could feel his top ripping on the metal bolt.

'Goddammit!'

A little bit more, he told himself as he made contact with the key. No sooner had he touched the key than he realised that he had gone too far. Gravity took control and, in what felt like slow motion, he fell headfirst onto the kitchen floor.

Slightly dazed, the cocktail of alcohol and adrenaline in his body prevented him from feeling any real pain. He looked towards the living room.

'Grace!' he called out again, hoping that she had just dozed off, and the sound of him falling in a heap would have suddenly woken her. He could still see her feet, but still no movement. He composed himself and got up quickly.

'Grace?' he said, softer this time, as he slowly walked towards the living room. He stopped at the main door in the hallway. It was the same door he was banging on moments earlier from the other side. He took the advice of every flight attendant before a flight and checked his nearest exit in case of an emergency. He opened the door and called out to the neighbour in case she was close by. 'I'm in!'

What surprised him was the door was no longer locked from the inside.

Didn't I hear her lock it when I left half an hour ago?

He left the door ajar and continued to the living room. He stopped in his tracks. On the wall opposite the door was blood.

Daniel started breathing heavily. His body was full of adrenaline. His gaze went from the wall to the wooden floor, where he saw more drops of blood leading to the living room. He tried to swallow, but couldn't. He wondered if he should retreat to the kitchen and grab a weapon. Just in case…

As he slowly moved closer to the living room, Grace came into full view; first her feet, then her legs. She still wore the same trousers she had worn the whole day. Daniel's gaze remained glued to Grace as he entered the room.

His worst fear had materialised.

The scene that unfolded in front of him made his blood turn cold. Slowly he lifted a trembling hand to his mouth as he mumbled, 'Oh my God.'

67

Grace lay face down on the living room floor, in a pool of blood.

'Grace!'

Daniel rushed to her side. Kneeling beside her, he pushed her onto her back and was met with a horrific sight. Blood covered her nose, mouth and neck, unseeing eyes stared into space.

'Grace, can you hear me?'

He held her in his arms, wondering where all the blood came from. It was only then that he noticed a deep gash across her throat.

'Oh, Jesus!' Instinctively, he used his hand to press on the wound, but it was no use. The damage was done. He became nauseous with the sight of so much blood.

'Grace,' he said with a quivering voice. 'If you can hear me, I want you to know you're not alone. I'm here. Daniel is here.'

He brushed her hair out of her face, leaving blood streaks on her face, as he continued comforting her on the off-chance that she could still hear something. 'I'm here. Please, Grace. I've come back.'

He fought hard to keep control of his emotions. Deep down, he knew that she was dead. She didn't seem to be actually bleeding anymore, which meant that her heart had stopped beating. Her face was deathly pale. Placing his ear to Grace's chest, he couldn't hear anything. No chest movement. No heartbeat. He placed his fingers to her wrist for any sign of life. Nothing.

Tears started to well up as he recalled the final thing Grace had said to him: *'I love you, Daniel. I always will.'*

'Grace,' he said, as he caressed her face. 'Don't go. Not like this.' Tears trickled down his cheek and landed on her face. In some areas they washed away the blood, ever so slightly, forming tiny skin-coloured islands among a red ocean.

'Grace. Please.' More tear drops fell. He put his hand to his mouth as if he was trying to muffle out his crying. He pulled it away immediately looking at the blood that covered his palms. His tongue touched his upper lip. He could sense a faint salty taste from Grace's blood.

His attention to Grace was broken by the sound of footsteps in the apartment. Daniel's head swung around as his gaze shot to the living room entrance. He forgot about the possibility of the attacker still being in the apartment. The steps came from the hallway and moved closer. He took a deep breath, ready to move in case he too came under attack.

'Hello!' It was the voice of the neighbour. 'The door was open. I just wanted to check if I need to call the pol...' As the woman entered the living room, her jaw dropped and the mobile she was carrying fell from her hand. It landed on the floor with a thud, but remained intact.

'*Mijn God!*'

Daniel, relieved that there was no immediate threat, turned back to Grace and continued to weep.

'Is she... dead?' the neighbour asked.

Daniel nodded.

'Will I call someone?'

They both looked at the mobile she just dropped. He nodded again. The woman picked it up and dialled the Emergency services. She retreated to the hallway. He could hear her speaking Dutch.

He looked at Grace's unseeing eyes staring into nothing. He wondered what kind of monster she had witnessed just before her death. He closed her eyelids with his thumb and index finger. She seemed more peaceful now, more serene. It was as if she were sleeping.

'I'm so sorry,' he said almost in a whisper. 'I'm so sorry I couldn't prevent this.' As he continued to caress her face,

Daniel felt a hand on his shoulder.

'The police are on their way,' the neighbour said. 'I know this is difficult for you, but this is a crime scene. It's probably best that you step away from her.'

He nodded. He kissed Grace on the forehead. He could still smell her hair, which triggered another wave of emotion ready to erupt. He closed his eyes and broke down. Quietly. Shaking with grief.

Despite his emotions, he knew the neighbour was right. This *was* a crime scene, and God only knew what kind of disruption he had already caused. He wiped away his tears and tried to regain composure. As much as he hated doing it, he pushed Grace back into the position he had found her, face down in a pool of her own blood. Slowly, he stood up and stepped away.

His foot hit off what looked like a piece of paper folded in two. As soon as he picked it up he knew what it was. Unfolding it, he looked at the photograph of the two of them. Grace's beautiful smile staring back was too much right now. He closed it again and slipped it into his back pocket.

He suddenly walked towards the window. 'That bastard isn't far.' He half expected to see a dark figure running away in the distance. Or jumping into his BMW and speeding away.

The street was empty, except for someone walking his dog.

The neighbour had no idea who Daniel was referring to. 'What bastard? You know who did this?' she asked surprised.

'Her psycho husband,' he said, as his grief turned to anger. He turned back towards the neighbour. 'Did you see anyone entering…' Daniel trailed off as he caught sight of something on the wall next to Grace. He moved closer, but was careful now not to step in the blood. Not that it mattered. Blood was all over him. The neighbour noticed Daniel's sudden interest in the wall and followed his gaze.

They both spotted it.

On the skirting board they could see what looked like a couple of letters written in blood.

'What is that?' the neighbour asked.

'It looks like an "O" and, beneath that, a "T" maybe. He got down on his hunkers. 'It was as if she was trying to spell something in the last moments of her life.'

'O. T. What was she trying to spell?' she asked.

He thought for a moment and then stood up. It didn't take long for the penny to drop. 'She tried to spell the bastard's name. She was trying to spell "Otto".'

68

Detective Harry Janssen had just pulled over two Moroccan youths when the call came in.

They had been speeding and pulling wheelies with their scooters along the south end of Rembrandtpark.

Janssen was in his late-forties. His skin was like that of a Mediterranean olive farmer, more wrinkled than it should be at his age, as a result of a past chain-smoking habit. The whites of his eyes had a yellow tinge to them, as did his teeth. He had kicked the habit three years previously, but not a day went by that he didn't think of cigarettes. His chesty cough served as a permanent reminder to his past love affair, one that posed a constant threat to reigniting.

Janssen hated dealing with youths, particularly Moroccan youths. All he wanted to do was to give them a break and spend his energy chasing real criminals. But sometimes they only had themselves to blame. It was past midnight. Speeding through a park with a scooter was illegal any time of day. As for in the middle of the night? That was just plain stupid.

He checked their licences and registrations and was in the middle of giving them a small lecture. Depending on how they took it, he would decide whether to issue a fine or not. If they decided to be aggressive or abusive, they would both get one. So far they seemed to be neither.

A warning would probably suffice.

'I mean, come on. It's late. People are sleeping,' Janssen said pointing to a high-rise apartment block close by. 'They can hear you zooming up and down right beneath their bedrooms.'

The youths were seventeen years old. One of them had dark stubble that made him look more like forty. The other had a hatchet face and a gold chain around his neck. They both seemed to be drenched in cheap after-shave.

Sheepish gazes met Janssen's stern look. '*Sorry meneer,*' the one with the stubble said. 'We had no idea people could hear us.'

Although Janssen thought that scooters were a real pain in the ass, pulling a wheelie in the middle of the night wasn't exactly a threat to society. It was kind of innocent in a way. If he was honest, he wouldn't mind having a go himself.

Always trying to appear authoritative, Janssen knew that, deep down, he was soft. It didn't bother him though, and he often relied on people like those to whom he was talking now for information on more serious crimes.

'Well, now you know. Maybe in the future...' Janssen cut himself off as he heard the message come in on the police radio on his waist.

'Just a second,' he held the radio to his ear.

The message was repeated.

'*307 reported at Westlandgracht. House number 29, second floor.*'

Janssen's heart skipped a beat. Westlandgracht was just a stone's throw away. A 307 was *not* something he encountered on a daily basis.

He grabbed his radio and spoke.

'Janssen here. Location: Nachtwachtlaan, south side of Rembrandtpark. Will be there in two minutes.'

The youngsters grinned at each other. They knew immediately that they were off the hook.

Janssen turned his attention back to them and cut his well-rehearsed lecture short. 'A bit more consideration in the future, okay? If I catch you pulling wheelies again, I will fine you and confiscate those scooters.' He already started walking towards his unmarked car. 'Is that clear?' he asked as he glanced behind him.

They both nodded like over-excited school kids.

He hopped into the car and drove out of the park. He took a left on Saskia van Uijlenburgkade and followed it before turning right onto a small bridge that was meant for bicycles and pedestrians. As Janssen drove over it, he hoped he wouldn't encounter any cyclists. Not that he was driving too fast. It was more because the bridge was barely wide enough for his car. The last thing he needed was some drunken cyclist ending up on the bonnet, with his face smashed into the windscreen.

It was a shortcut he used many times in the past, with no incidents up to now. The alternative route would be to drive via Haarlemmermeerstraat, which would have added at least an extra three or four kilometres to the journey.

Literally two minutes later, he arrived on Westlandgracht. As he approached number 29, he glanced up to the second floor and saw that the light was on. Manoeuvring into what seemed to be the only free spot on the street, Janssen switched off the ignition and got out. There was no sign of an ambulance yet.

If the person really is dead, then I suppose there isn't any major hurry.

Janssen pressed the bell. The door opened almost immediately. He figured the occupants of the apartment had seen him park his car and walk towards the building. He rolled his eyes, as he manoeuvred around the bike blocking the entrance, and took the stairwell two steps at a time. On the first floor, the door was ajar.

Nosey neighbour already at the crime scene, Janssen figured. When he reached the second floor, he was met by two figures standing at the doorway. The woman stretched her hand out and introduced herself in Dutch.

'Claudia Schuurman. Ik woon beneden.' *I live downstairs.*

Janssen showed his badge and introduced himself in Dutch.

'It's best if you speak in English,' Claudia said nodding towards Daniel.

Janssen looked towards Daniel and was taken aback by his appearance; his top was ripped and covered with blood. As were his hands. Even his face had a smudge of blood. His eyes were swollen.

'You're English?'

'Irish.'

Janssen narrowed his eyes. 'Forgive me if I don't shake hands,' he said pointing to the bloody hands. 'May I?' Janssen asked as he moved inside. Both Daniel and Claudia moved out of the way.

There was little need for Daniel to point the detective in the right direction. All he had to do was to follow the trail of blood on the floor.

Janssen felt his stomach turn as he entered the living room.

Jezus Christus!

Although he had been a detective for five years, and in the Police Force for a total of eighteen years, he had encountered less than five dead bodies. This was without doubt the bloodiest. His eyes swept the room, taking in a broken wine glass, bottles of wine lying sideways on the floor and a smashed up phone. His first impression was that there had been a drunken domestic dispute that went horribly wrong.

He slipped on a pair of blue latex gloves, crouched down and touched Grace's neck. No surprise there. Zero pulse.

He turned towards Daniel. 'What happened here? Did you kill her?' he asked matter-of-factly.

Unsure if he heard him correctly, Daniel glanced at Claudia and then back at the detective. 'Sorry?'

'Did you kill her?'

'No! Of course not.'

'Don't get all defensive,' he said as he analysed the slit across Grace's throat. 'You should take a look at yourself.'

Daniel glanced down and saw his ripped and bloodstained top. 'I found the body,' he tried to clarify. 'I tried to stop the bleeding.'

'Was she still alive when you found her?'

'No. I don't think so. But I didn't know that until I...'

'Contaminated the entire crime scene,' Janssen

completed his sentence.

Daniel and the neighbour looked at each other. The neighbour turned to the detective and said something in Dutch. Daniel hoped it was something along the lines of *"Don't be so hard on him."*

'You know her name?' Janssen asked, as he rested Grace's head back in its original position and stood up.

'Grace Farrell... ' Daniel stopped abruptly. 'I mean Visser. Grace Visser.'

Janssen raised an eyebrow. 'You don't sound so sure.'

'I'm sure. Farrell was her maiden name.'

'So she's not Dutch?'

Daniel shook her head. 'No. Also Irish.'

Shit. That's all I need. More red tape than normal. It will probably even make front page of the newspapers tomorrow.

'She lived here?' Janssen asked as he removed his latex gloves with a snap and rolled them into a ball.

'In Amsterdam, yes. Not in this apartment.'

'Who lives in this apartment, then? You?' he said pointing at Daniel.

He shook his head. 'A guy called Rik. I don't know his surname.'

'Bergman.' Claudia added.

'They worked together.'

Janssen scanned the living room and picked up one of the empty wine bottles. 'It looked like they did more than work together.'

Daniel shook his head. 'It's not what it looks like. The wine is from me and her.'

'Excuse me?'

'I had dinner with her tonight.'

'In this apartment?'

'Yes.'

'So where's this Rik guy?'

'He's in Belgium at a hockey tournament.'

Silence.

'Why didn't you have dinner in her own house? In Mrs

Visser's house?'

Daniel bit his lip and eventually said, 'She's staying here for a while.'

The detective frowned. 'Why?'

Daniel felt reluctant to give the detective so much information, but figured he had no choice. Sooner or later everything would come out. 'She left her husband.'

'Did she, now?' Janssen took a little box of Tic-Tacs out of his pocket, shook a few into the palm of his hand and threw them in his mouth. 'And what exactly was your relationship?' he asked as he chewed on them straightaway.

'We went to university together.'

The detective rubbed his temples, clearly not getting the full picture. 'Hang on. Just going back a bit. How come you spent the whole evening with her and you are also the person who found her?'

'I left around midnight. When I came back she was...' His words trailed off. 'She was like this.'

'Dead. You can say it. She was dead. Why did you come back?'

Daniel swallowed. His heart was beating faster. Could he be painting a picture of himself as a suspect? Why *did* he come back? He couldn't really tell him the real answer. Could he?

'I forgot something.'

'What did you forget?'

'Look,' he said, 'I realise it's your job to ask questions, and I'm happy to oblige. But I didn't kill her. I left around midnight. I returned a half-hour later and she was dead. This means someone was watching us. Or waiting until I left. It also means that the killer could still be very close by.'

'Maybe. That's up to me to figure out. I just want to know what you forgot.' Janssen walked to the window overlooking Westlandgracht. In the distance he could see flashing blue lights coming from the direction of Slotervaart hospital. The ambulance was on their way. At least he assumed they were heading this way. If it was, he would not be letting them in the apartment for now. The forensics team would need to go in first.

'Did you ever meet her husband?'

Daniel nodded. 'Yes.' He opened his mouth to say something more but changed his mind. He decided not to offer any more information unless Janssen asked for it.

'Nice guy?'

Daniel shrugged. 'I only met him once. But no, I didn't get that impression,' he said trying not to think of the encounter at the front door of Otto's house.

Janssen returned to his previous question as he continued to look out the window. 'What did you forget?'

'A photo.' It wasn't a *complete* lie. He hadn't noticed he had left it behind until he picked it up just moments ago, but still. It was probably more convincing than the truth.

'A photo?'

He nodded.

'And can I see this photo?'

Daniel reached into his back pocket and held it out to the detective.

He unfolded it and analysed it, smiling. 'Sweet. Is that you?'

'Yes.'

'And forgive me for not recognising her, but I assume that smiling girl is Mrs Visser or Farrell.'

'Grace. Yes.'

The detective looked up at Daniel and handed him back the photo. 'Very sweet.'

The blue lights had indeed turned into Westlandgracht and were heading towards the apartment. It wasn't an ambulance, but a police car. Janssen figured it was the forensics team.

'I think it's best if we step outside the apartment, and let the forensics examine the area.' Janssen turned to the neighbour. 'How many other people live in the apartment building?'

'One more on the third floor,' Claudia said, pointing upwards.

'We're going to have to evacuate the building for a few hours for the forensics to get everything they can. Do you have somewhere to stay tonight?'

The neighbour looked at her watch. 1:05am.

'My sister lives in Haarlem, but how am I to get there at this time?'

'After you give a statement, one of my colleagues will drop you there. Perhaps you can call your sister and let her know you'll be there soon.' Janssen turned to Daniel. 'I'd like you to join me...'

'But I've got a dog,' the neighbour said.

Janssen turned back to the neighbour. 'You can take the dog with you.'

'My sister hates dogs.'

'Maybe she can make an exception when you tell her what happened here. Tell her there's a murderer on the loose.' Janssen turned back to Daniel. 'Which I guess is true.' He looked at Daniel for a reaction. Nothing. 'I'd like you to join me down at the station to give a full statement.'

Daniel nodded.

'In the meantime, sit tight, and we'll...' Janssen trailed off as he spotted the letters in blood on the wall.

'What the hell is that?'

69

Daniel was driven in a squad car to a police station on Surinameplein. The conversation he had with Grace about the different modes of transport for the police seemed like a lifetime away.

The police station was a large yellow-bricked building situated next to yet another canal.

Is there any place in this city that isn't in close proximity to water? he wondered as a uniformed policeman escorted him inside. The door beside the reception desk buzzed and Daniel was brought through into the back corridors. After they climbed one flight of stairs the policeman opened the door to a small room. A musky stench hung in the air. It was like the window hadn't been opened in years. The policeman placed his hand out in the direction of a table with four chairs around it.

'Please have a seat there,' the policeman said. 'Someone will be with you shortly. Can I get you something to drink?'

Daniel shook his head. 'No, thanks.'

He held up his bloodstained hands, and turned to the policeman. 'Can I wash my hands?'

The policeman looked at Daniel's hands and then down to his clipboard, as if searching for the answer. Daniel doubted very much it had the answer.

He was right.

'I'm not sure,' the policeman said. 'Did they examine you at the scene?'

He frowned. 'What do you mean examine?'

'Take swabs. Fibre samples. That sort of thing?'

'No.'

'Maybe it's best not to wash your hands just yet. Someone from forensics will be with you shortly. They will be able to advise you.'

Daniel shrugged. He didn't like the answer, but didn't have much of a choice. Once the policeman left, he walked slowly around to the chair that the policeman had pointed to and sat down.

A fluorescent bulb filled the room with artificial light. Every so often it flickered. When it happened the first time, Daniel thought he had just blinked too hard. By the fourth flicker, he could almost sense a headache set in.

Looking around the room, he wondered about all the people who sat there before him. Were they victims or criminals? Witnesses or suspects? He wondered what he was categorised as. As they hadn't handcuffed him, he couldn't be a suspect, could he? Daniel glanced at the door. He hadn't heard the policeman lock it from the outside. He assumed he was just a witness.

He placed his hands on the table. The dried blood made his skin feel tight and uncomfortable. Taking a deep breath, he closed his eyes. Apart from the buzzing of the dodgy light above, he relished the silence. As he opened his eyes again, he muttered: 'Grace.' His throat was dry. He could do with a glass of water or something. He scratched his head. He forgot what he had said to the policeman when he had offered him a drink.

Did I say yes or no?

Unable to remember, a wave of exhaustion suddenly fell over him. He folded his arms on the table and rested his head on them. It felt good. The table wobbled ever so slightly. One leg was just a fraction too short.

Every cell in Daniel's body seemed to sigh a breath of relief. He closed his eyes. Amid the darkness, he saw Grace's face. Her smile. It felt so real. How long ago was Grace wrapped in his arms? It was less than two hours ago. The scent of her hair was still fresh in his mind. Images of her bloody corpse kept interrupting his thoughts, shooting through his mind like uninvited demons. The flashbacks were almost in sync with the faulty light bulb above him.

Daniel's thoughts turned to how exactly Grace could have been murdered. He hadn't noticed anything suspicious whatsoever. Or had he been walking with his head in the clouds? It was an emotional departure. His mind had been completely preoccupied. A van with "Rent a Killer" in neon lights could have pulled up outside the apartment, and he wouldn't have noticed.

What would he say to the detective?

The truth. I have nothing to hide.

The door opened suddenly. Daniel jumped as he raised his head.

'Sorry. I didn't mean to startle you,' said a lady with dark curly hair, in her thirties. Her face was pale, except for the light blue eyeshadow that seemed to match her shoes. 'My name is Officer Van den Berg. A member of the forensics team.'

Daniel stood up. He was about to shake hands but they both saw the blood on his hands and decided unanimously to skip the formal gestures.

Van den Berg carried a pile of neatly folded clothes, on top of which lay a transparent bag.

'I would like you to change into these clothes and place all your bloodstained clothes into the plastic bag provided,' she said as she lay them down on the table. 'Also, do you mind if I take a swab from your hands?'

Daniel looked at the pile of clothes and the transparent bag. He then looked at his hands.

'Is it really necessary? I'm making no secret of the fact that I was in the apartment.'

'It's more routine than anything else,' Van den Berg said. 'The swab will take literally ten seconds.'

Not wanting to give off an impression of guilt, he agreed. Van den Berg undid a sterile piece of tape, placed it over Daniel's bloodstained hand and slowly removed it. Some of the dried blood stuck to the tape. She placed it in a sterile bag and sealed it immediately. She wrote something on it, signed it and passed it to Daniel, together with the pen.

'If you could sign there, I'll fill in the rest.'

Daniel complied. He wondered briefly if he needed a lawyer. 'What will happen to this specimen?'

'It'll be used for comparison, mostly, and a means for ruling out. Right now we assume that the blood on your hands is Grace's blood, but we just need to confirm this.

He liked to hear the words "ruling out", but wondered if she was just saying it to keep him happy. She picked up the transparent bag that lay on the table

'Can you place your clothes in this? These spare clothes should fit you.'

He glanced at the pile and picked up a pair of tracksuit bottoms.

'I know they're not very stylish, but they're clean and hopefully more comfortable than these bloodstained clothes.' She held out a pair of grey brandless runners. 'There are two reasons why we ask you for your clothes. One: As evidence. Two: simply so you don't have to go around like you just escaped from an abattoir.'

'In other words, I shouldn't expect these clothes back, washed and ironed?'

'Correct.'

The lady left the room to allow Daniel some privacy. As he pulled on the tracksuit bottoms and the sweatshirt, he realised they were indeed very comfortable and loose. In fact, if he wanted to make a run for it, he couldn't imagine more appropriate clothes.

He felt like being back at primary school after one of his nose bleeds. It wasn't only the bloody hands, but also the second-hand clothes he had to wear back then too. His parents would wash them, of course, and give them back to the teacher, ready for the next pupil who would have an accident of some kind.

Folding his old trousers, he was about to place them in the plastic bag, when the photo fell from the back pocket. It was also bloodstained. He placed it in a pocket of his new tracksuit bottoms and zipped it closed. Going through the rest of his pockets, he removed a couple of tissues and about five euro in coins. He then placed his trousers and ripped top into the bag, never to be seen again. At least that's what he hoped. The less he had to remind him of the worst night of his life, the better.

Daniel was tying his laces, when there was a knock on the door, and the forensic scientist entered followed by Detective Janssen.

'Everything fit okay?' Van den Berg asked.

He stood with his arms out 'Yes, perfect.'

The woman picked up the plastic bag with his bloodstained clothes. 'Thanks for your cooperation, Mr Geller.'

'No problem,' he said, as Van den Berg left the room.

Janssen pointed to the empty chair that Daniel had been sitting on earlier. 'Please have a seat.' He took a seat opposite and stared at him. 'What a night, eh?'

Daniel nodded in agreement.

Janssen browsed through his notebook and stopped to scribble something. 'So, if my notes are correct, you were Mrs Visser's ex-classmate?'

'Correct.'

'Just friends?'

'Nowadays, yes.'

'Nowadays?'

'It means "at the moment" or "current..."'

'I know what it means, Mr Geller. You're insinuating that it wasn't always that type of relationship?'

'Sorry, yes. We were more than friends when we were at university.'

Janssen scribbled in his notebook. 'And when you say "more than friends", you mean you were lovers?'

'Correct.'

'For how long?'

'Four or five years.'

'When did you break up?'

Officially, half-an-hour before she died, Daniel wanted to say. 'Twelve years ago.'

'That long? But you kept in touch?'

'More or less.' His inside twisted. Was that a lie? Something prevented him from telling the truth.

'Meaning?'

'A couple of times.'

'Who do you think killed her?'

'You really want to know what I think?'

Janssen nodded.

'Her husband.'

Janssen smirked as if he was expecting it. 'And what makes you say that?'

'Nine times out of ten it's the husband, right?'

'Or Ex-boyfriend.'

Daniel couldn't resist smiling this time. It seemed absurd that he was here talking about the murder of a woman he loved and feeling so guilty at the same time.

'You saw the marks on the wall, right?' Daniel asked.

'The O and the T?'

Daniel nodded.

'Yes. I saw them.'

'Do you not think that she was trying to write his name?'

'Maybe,' the detective agreed. 'Or maybe the murderer picked up her hand and wrote the marks himself.'

Daniel contemplated the thought for a moment. 'So why not spell the entire name?'

'To make it look more genuine.'

Daniel had nothing to say to that. Janssen scribbled something else in his notebook and then looked up.

'So, take me through the last time you saw her alive and the circumstances leading to you finding her dead.'

Daniel closed his eyes for a moment. He rubbed them briefly with his thumb and index finger before opening them again. He then looked down at his bloody hands. Slowly he described leaving the apartment and trying to

331

call Grace from the tram. And his decision to return to the apartment.

'Why did you return?'

Daniel frowned. *Didn't I already tell him that?*

'I forgot the photo.'

'Okay. And now pretend I'm not stupid. Why did you return to the apartment?'

Daniel pursed his lips, wondering how much he should give away. He couldn't possibly tell him about his thesis. And his sudden revelation in the tram...

Could he?

'It's a long story.'

Janssen sat back and opened his arms. 'I'm not going anywhere. Neither are you.'

70

Daniel took a deep breath. His heart was beating hard. Never in his life did he feel so nervous in front of someone. It wasn't as if Janssen was really *interrogating* him, but still...

The detective leaned forward and kept eye contact. 'Why did you run back to the apartment?'

Daniel rubbed his day-old stubble, and shook his head. What could he say?

'Before I came in here,' Janssen added, 'I listened to a recording on her mobile.'

Daniel frowned. 'Whose mobile?'

'Who do you think? The victim's, of course. Mrs Visser's.' He glanced down at his notebook and flicked back a few pages. 'You left a message, right?'

Daniel closed his eyes, trying to recall what he had said exactly. He didn't have to. The detective read out a transcript:

'Hi, Grace. It's Daniel here. I'm not really sure what to say. If you hear this message within the next half hour can you call me back? Please. Otherwise just forget about it. You don't have to call me back.'

Janssen looked up. 'Kind of strange, don't you agree? What was so important about the next half hour?'

Daniel twisted in his chair. 'I just wanted to … see she was alright.'

'Why wouldn't she be?'

He could feel the palms of his hands starting to sweat. He wasn't sure how much longer he could go on without telling the detective about his thesis, about the prediction.

'What I find strange,' Janssen continued, 'is that within that time frame of you leaving the apartment, calling her, and running back she was attacked and killed. Exactly that time frame. So the question is: did you know something?

Did you see something that made you worry for her safety? Were you aware that her life was in some kind of danger?'

Daniel's thumb moved to his wedding ring. Grace's blood was still beneath it. He would have to remove it and scrub his hands well. And the ring? He would need a lot of soap just to get it off. He couldn't remember the last time he removed it. Turning his thoughts back to Janssen's question, he mumbled eventually, 'I realised it wasn't midnight in Ireland yet.'

Janssen frowned. He looked towards the wall and then back at Daniel.

'Sorry? What did you say?'

He repeated it, speaking clearer this time.

'What does the time in Ireland have to do with anything?'

Daniel went to run his hand through his hair. Instead he ended up leaning his head on his hand. A short silence followed as the light above flickered again. Eventually he said,

'Twelve years ago I developed a thesis on predicting a person's date of death. I performed the calculation on Grace when I was in university. I predicted yesterday's date. I came over here to warn her, and to spend the day with her to ensure nothing happened to her. When it reached midnight, we said goodbye. Of course, when I was on the tram I realised it was still Saturday in Ireland. Because the calculation was performed in Ireland, I wasn't sure if it meant that my calculation was still valid and ultimately she was still at risk.' He lifted his head and sat up straight. 'That was why I asked her to call me back within the next half hour or not at all. Once I knew she was safe after midnight Irish time, it would be okay.'

Janssen placed his pen and notebook on the table and sat back on his chair. 'I don't understand a single word you just said. I mean, I understand the language, but not what you're telling me.'

'I know it's a difficult concept to grasp. Trust me.'

'Let me see if I can summarise what you said. Are you telling me she died on the exact day that you predicted twelve years ago?'

Daniel nodded and then shook his head.

'Officially, her death will be recorded as today. So I'm one day off.' He paused briefly. 'But if she had been living in Ireland, then yes, it would have been spot on. It would have been the day I predicted.'

Janssen leaned back on the chair so it was balancing on two feet. 'That's the most ridiculous thing I've ever heard.'

Daniel rubbed his eyes again and stifled a yawn. The exhaustion was overwhelming. 'What part exactly?'

'That you can predict someone's date of death. Especially from so far back.'

Daniel didn't say anything for a few moments. Eventually he raised his hands in the air in a surrender gesture.

'Look, that's my story. That's my statement. I'm trying to tell the truth here. If that makes me even more of a suspect, then so be it. *I* know I would never hurt Grace. *I* know I could never hurt *anybody,* come to that. So finish what you're writing in that notebook, and stop asking me questions if you don't want to listen to my answers.'

Janssen sighed as he leaned forward, and the chair was once again on all four feet. 'Look, there's no need to get like that. I need to collect everybody's story. I just can't believe you can predict someone's date of death like that.'

'Neither did a lot of people. Trust me. That's why my thesis was rejected and at some stage I even stopped believing it.'

'Your thesis was rejected?'

'Yes, I mean never mind trying to convince you, try convincing a panel of mathematic professors.'

'I see. So you had a lot of bitterness inside you after they rejected you?'

Daniel took a deep breath. 'Oh, come on. What's that

supposed to mean?'

The detective placed the notebook on the table. 'I mean when you...'

'No, I think I know where this is leading,' he cut him off, 'but one thing is for sure; I did not kill Grace. And I sure as hell wouldn't be telling you about my thesis if I *had* killed her. I'd appreciate it if you could stop going down the path you're going.'

'It's my job to go down every path. It's my job to turn over every stone.'

'Well, don't get too distracted about what you find beneath my stone.'

'I find it intriguing. I find it…'

A knock on the door sounded and the policeman that had led Daniel to the room earlier popped his head in.

'Mag ik je even storen? Het is belangrijk.' 'Can I disturb you? It's important.'

The detective turned to Daniel. 'Excuse me for a moment.' He rose from his chair and left the room.

Two minutes later, the detective returned, along with the policeman. Janssen sat down, as the policeman remained standing.

'The husband has been taken in for questioning,' Janssen said.

Daniel raised an eyebrow. 'I'm sure he's quite upset,' he mumbled, wondering if his sarcasm would be detected.

'Drunk, actually. Very drunk and stoned.'

'Probably nothing new there,' he said as he recalled Grace's story about pulling her from the bath and beating her up.

'He was picked up just one block from the apartment where Grace was killed.'

'Seriously? There you have it.'

The detective took a deep breath. 'It's rarely so simple and straightforward. I am going to interview him now, though, but I want to keep you overnight.'

'Me? Seriously?' Daniel was a little surprised. Although,

when he thought about it, he couldn't blame him.

'We'll put you in a room. It's clean. Get some rest. We'll talk in the morning.'

'I have a flight in the morning.'

'I'm sorry, Mr Geller. You're going to have to cancel or postpone it.'

'How long am I going to be here?'

'Officially, we can keep you up to forty-eight hours without arrest.' The detective stood up. 'Now, if you'll excuse me, Officer Brunenberg here will escort you to the bathroom to get cleaned up and then to your room.'

71

When John woke in the morning, Claire was no longer sitting on the chair next to him. He was actually glad she wasn't. He didn't want her waiting there for him like some kind of trustworthy servant. The guilt was too much for him. Perhaps she had found a bed to lie in. Or even had gone home. *If there was a home to go to*, John thought. Maybe she had simply gone for breakfast.

Although his head still ached, the pain seemed to have subsided somewhat since earlier in the night.

I did wake during the night, didn't I?

For a fearful moment, he thought he might have dreamt his middle-of-the-night conversation with Claire. He glanced next to him and saw the *Woman's Way* lying on the locker.

It was not a dream.

Looking across the room he saw that one of his fellow-patients was awake. He wore his dressing gown and lay on top of an already-made bed, eager to get the day started, by the looks of it. The guy was engrossed in a hardback book. John resisted from wishing him a good morning from his side of the ward, for fear of waking up other patients. The man was at least ten years older than John and wasn't connected to any drip or tubes. John wondered briefly what was wrong with him.

Perhaps nothing anymore. Perhaps it was time to go home today.

Sitting upright and pushing the pillows behind him into a more vertical position, John rested his head on the newly positioned pillows and stared at the ceiling. He wondered how long he would be there. Surely it was just a case of observation and they would release him as soon as possible.

His thoughts then turned to his home, and he wondered how much damage had been done. Would the insurance pay for it? Or would they find some nitty gritty term in the clause that prevented any pay out?

A dizzy spell washed over John. He raised his hand to his forehead and waited for the dizziness to subside. When it did, he kept his hand there as if it was responsible for keeping the dizziness at bay.

John thought of Daniel and how his predicted date of death was wrong. Was this the end of the mathematical formula? His thesis? His "comeback", so to speak? Maybe Daniel *had* lost his mathematical skills after so long. Or maybe he never had them to begin with...

He shook his head suddenly, ridding the doubt accumulating in his mind like flies on a jar of honey. As the scepticism subsided, he recalled the thesis. He had spent days reading through it. The formulae Daniel had developed were nothing short of astounding. How he had taken everything into account. *Everything.* It was so thorough. John recalled thinking that he would be the closest to winning a Fields Medal of anyone he had ever known. Although he may have got this prediction wrong, John felt reluctant to accept that the thesis was now worthless. The thesis, and indeed Daniel, had so much potential. He was certain of that. Maybe it was the pressure he had put on Daniel that led him to stumble. How could he have expected him to deliver a flawless result after so many years?

Suddenly John's stomach rumbled, telling him it was time for breakfast. He glanced at his roommate who was still glued to his book. He didn't see any tray or remnants of breakfast, which meant that he had not missed it. Wondering what time it was, John looked at his wrist. His watch was missing. Of course it was. He noticed that his wedding ring wasn't on his finger either. They had obviously removed all these items for medical reasons when he was still unconscious. He wondered if Claire had them. What about his wallet and mobile phone? Hadn't they been in his trouser pockets when he lay down on

Max's bed the previous night? He hoped Claire had them.

Looking towards the bedside locker, he reached over to open the top drawer. It was reluctant to come out. He gave some extra force, and eventually the drawer opened awkwardly. A wave of relief rushed over him. Everything was there. Neatly arranged. Almost as if they were glued in place like the little props found on an IKEA store display.

John picked up his mobile and examined it. He looked at the display screen to check the time but was distracted by the five missed calls and two new text messages he had. He clicked on one of the text messages and saw that it was from his network provider informing him to check his voice mail. The other message was from Daniel. As John read it, his heart skipped a beat. He paused for a moment and then read it again.

'John, I made an error in my calculation. Please call me.'

'You're kidding me,' John said out loud. The patient on the other side of the ward raised his head. John didn't notice. It was now his turn to be engrossed in something. The patient turned his attention back to his book.

John called his voice mail and listened to the messages. Three of them were silent after the beep, like the caller decided to hang up just as it started recording a message. One of them was from Tommy, a friend of his from UCC, saying he was in Dublin the next week and if he wanted to meet for lunch. The final message was from Daniel. As he listened to the message and the desperation in his voice, his blood ran cold:

'John, this is Daniel. Please call me. There is a mistake in the calculation. I forgot about certain DNA tests specific for women. It's complicated. I'll explain when I see you. I don't think Claire will die today. I'm sorry. I hope you and Claire are okay. Call me, please.'

John lowered his mobile and stared at it. He could hear the faint din of the automated voice giving options of what to do with the message. He hung up.

'How could he have known?' he whispered to himself.

'I don't understand.' He tried to piece together what had happened. Daniel had given him a wrong date of death, a wrong prediction. Claire didn't die. It was somehow back on track. Two pieces of a jigsaw fitted perfectly again. The thesis was still legitimate.

Or was it? His thoughts fell to Daniel's plight in Amsterdam. Had he succeeded in warning Grace?

John glanced at the time display on his mobile. It was 8:05am. Should he call Daniel? Perhaps it was too early. Then he realised it was an hour later in Amsterdam. Still, it was fairly early. He decided to wait an hour or so, and then to return Daniel's call from the previous night and put him at ease.

72

It took Daniel several moments to figure out where he was when he woke up. He looked around. The room was very basic. It was composed of a single bed, a chair, a reading lamp, a toilet and a wash hand basin. He wondered if it was an actual cell for temporary prisoners, or just a room for policemen who were on long shifts and needed to grab some quick shut-eye. Either way, it served its purpose. Daniel had slept soundly.

He had decided to sleep in his clothes. They almost felt like pyjamas anyway. He also slept on top of the bed sheets. It wasn't that the bed was dirty, but it was just in case he had to get out of bed quickly, for whatever reason. The bed was actually immaculate. The mattress was hard though, a sharp contrast to the pillow, which was soft; almost too soft, like those puppies from the toilet paper commercial.

Daniel sat up on the bed and was met with a sharp pain in his neck, an irritating creak, possibly due to the ridiculously soft pillow. Perhaps it was a combination with a neck injury that often resurfaced. It was an injury that he sustained in judo when he was a child. Slowly he moved his head back and forward, and then side to side. The creak remained, like an annoying piece of chewing gum on the sole of a shoe. He rubbed it, but to no avail. It would disappear when it was ready to.

Daniel stood up and tried opening the door to the room. It was locked from the outside. So it *was* a cell. He recalled hearing a latch or something opening during the night. Probably checking that he was still there. Or maybe they were checking if he hadn't done anything strange with his shoe laces.

Am I really such a threat? he wondered as he walked to the toilet. That too was spotless. Afterwards, he sat back on the bed and put on his shoes. He tried to look at the situation from the Dutch authorities' point of view and soon realised they had a fair point in keeping him overnight.

Hopefully, he thought, they wouldn't need the full forty-eight hours before they realised they were barking up the wrong tree.

After he tied his runners, he lay back down on the mattress with his feet hanging over the edge. Rubbing both his eyes, he yawned. His yawn was disturbed by a clank from the door. Seconds later the door swung open, and in walked Detective Janssen carrying a mug of coffee and a plastic cup of coffee. Daniel sat up on the bed once again.

'How did you sleep?' The detective asked.

Daniel looked down at his crumpled clothes and back at the detective. 'Doesn't this say enough?' Although he slept fine, he didn't particularly want to give the impression that he would like to stay there for another night.

'That makes two of us.' Janssen handed him the plastic cup of coffee. He then removed some sachets of powdered milk and sugar and placed them on a small shelf next to the bed. 'I didn't know how you took it.'

'Thanks.' Daniel laid the cup on the shelf. It was very hot. He tore open a couple of sachets, poured the contents into his coffee but left it on the shelf to cool down.

The detective took a noisy slurp from his mug, which had a picture of the Brooklyn Bridge on it. Daniel wondered briefly if he had been to New York or had just received it as a gift. Perhaps it was one of those communal mugs that had ended up in the kitchen.

The detective got straight down to business. 'As you know, we were talking to Mr. Visser.'

Daniel nodded. 'And?'

Janssen grabbed the chair, placed his mug on the floor and opened his notebook. 'He denies it, which is to be expected, of course,' he said as he flicked through the notebook. 'But his fingerprints were found on the doorbell of the front door on street-level.'

'And what about the knife that slit her throat?'

Janssen shook his head. 'No. Not yet. I'm sure you understand that I can't go into too much detail. Basically, he was found in his car, a block away from the apartment. He was wasted. Half asleep, half stoned, half drunk.

Three halves, Daniel thought quickly to himself. *Not good maths.*

'He's sleeping it off in one of the, let's say, non-luxury cells in the other block.'

'So you think he did it?'

'Five minutes ago I received a message from the forensics laboratory. Drops of his wife's blood were found on his shoe. On his laces, to be exact. Together with the fingerprints and those letters on the wall...' Janssen shrugged his shoulders. 'And that's just the evidence accumulated in the first twelve hours after her death. I'm sure there is a lot more to come.'

'So what now?' Daniel asked.

'Well, you're free to go.' Janssen picked up his Brooklyn Bridge mug and stood up. He placed his notebook beneath his arm and held his hand outstretched. 'I'd like to thank you for your cooperation in this incident.'

Daniel stood up too and took the detective's hand. 'Happy to help.' He paused for a moment and eventually asked, 'What will happen to Grace's body?'

Janssen took a quick sip of his coffee before answering, perhaps buying a few seconds.

'It will be held until Monday,' he said, 'at least until the coroner has had a chance to inspect it thoroughly.'

'"It"?' Daniel asked, not impressed. '"Her", you mean.'

'I'm sorry. Her. I think it's pretty clear how she died. The inspection won't take too long, I imagine.'

'And then?'

'She will be released to a family member. Her next of kin was Mr Visser, but obviously we won't be releasing the body to him. It will be an immediate family member. A parent or sibling, I guess.'

'Have they been told? Her family?'

'We've contacted the Irish authorities last night, and they will take care of that.'

Daniel nodded. He pictured her parents and how devastated they would be. They lived in a small close-knit town called Ballyferriter, close to Dingle. Daniel tried to imagine how they would be informed of their daughter's death. Would the local garda approach them as they were coming out of mass? Or perhaps later in the day, when they were preparing a Sunday roast. His heart went out to them. They were such lovely people. Pure. Simple. Well-educated, but almost child-like in their actions, both with rugged skin from the Atlantic wind, and sparkles in their eyes that would draw you into their hearts. And where did the older brother Diarmuid live nowadays? He couldn't recall, but hoped for the sake of the parents it wasn't too far away.

'Is there anything I can do to help?' Daniel asked.

'Can you write down your details, so I can contact you if I have any more questions?' Janssen placed his coffee mug on the chair, opened a new page of his notebook and handed it to Daniel.

He scribbled down his number and email address.

Janssen pulled a card from his wallet and gave it to Daniel. 'Here's my card, just in case you think of something and need to contact me.'

Daniel studied it briefly and was about to place it in his back pocket, when he realised he was wearing the tracksuit bottoms. He placed it in a side pocket instead, next to the photograph.

'Can I get somebody to drive you back to your hotel?' the detective asked.

'That would be great, thank you.'

'You can finish your coffee. Someone will pick you up in five minutes.'

73

When Daniel entered his hotel room, the dog stench hit his senses straight away. He was glad that he would be checking out today. He placed the hotel card in the electrical slot, and plonked himself down on the bed, which was left untouched since the previous day. One of the socks that he hung on the end of the bed fell to the floor. He removed his shoes, each foot taking its turn to push the other shoe off. He gazed at the ceiling. The bed wasn't much more comfortable than that in the police station. Daylight falling through the curtains made random patterns on the ceiling. He closed his eyes.

In the darkness, an image of Grace appeared. Motionless. Dead. Surrounded by blood. Daniel shut his eyes even further, hoping it would make it disappear, a desperate attempt to erase the horrific mental pictures that haunted him. The image of Grace's body stayed there.

Taking a deep breath, he relaxed his eyes. Although they remained closed, the vision in his head metamorphosed to the living Grace from the day before. The transformation took place like a stop-motion film. Her unseeing eyes twinkled once again. It was the same Grace that had kissed him gently on the lips. Unconsciously, Daniel rubbed his tongue along his lower lip, hoping he would be met with one last taste of Grace. Nothing.

Of course nothing.

He saw her laughing. Drinking wine. Walking in Vondel Park. Looking down from the apartment window when he had first rang the doorbell. It felt like it was a lifetime away. He couldn't believe it was just yesterday.

'Why did I come?' he whispered to himself. 'I should have stayed away.' An utterly hopeless feeling inside him made his stomach turn. A shattered heart had dispersed its pieces within. He felt fragments of it inside his body. It was like broken glass on a beach. A beach with no exits, except through the vast ocean of time.

Apart from her killer, Daniel thought, *I was the last person who Grace saw alive. And yet, I had caused her so much grief.* He shook his head as he opened his eyes.

He turned to one side. The clock radio next to his bed stared back at him. The time flicked from 9:52 to 9:53am. He had missed his flight. There would be another one. No doubt the airline would charge exorbitant prices, but there would be another one. At times like this, money didn't matter. Money was so frivolous.

A mild scent of dog seemed to come directly from the top bed sheet, but Daniel ignored it. He listened to his own breathing for a while before he sat up. A sudden rush to his head gave him a brief dizzy spell. The room suddenly felt so big. Too big. He didn't want to be alone. Not now. A hotel room in a strange city, was there anywhere lonelier in the world?

The loneliness was unbearable. It was no wonder rock stars and film actors often ended up overdosing or getting up to no good in their hotel rooms. He couldn't imagine having to stay in one for months on end during touring or filming.

He rose and walked to the window. The carpet beneath his feet was thin and lacked elasticity. It was well passed its replacement date. But who would complain about the carpet? Those who had nothing else to complain about? Not Daniel though.

He heard voices and footsteps as he looked out the window to the outside world. Pedestrians, cyclists, tourists, locals. The world continued as it should. But to Daniel it would never continue as it should. Never in his life was he so devastated, so disappointed in himself. The one thing he set out to do this weekend, he failed. The *one thing*.

If I stayed an extra hour...

As he continued to look out the window, he noticed

347

little Amsterdam pillars on the pavement outside his room, with three X's on each of them. Although he had seen them all over the city, this was the first time he really noticed them. A seagull landed on one.

A seagull?

How close was he to the sea? How ignorant he suddenly felt with his lack of knowledge of Amsterdam's location. Sure, there were water and canals all over the city, but he had no clue where the nearest beach was; the nearest sea. The seagull cried the usual seagull cry and took off as a car rumbled by on the uneven bricked road.

Daniel rubbed his forehead. It felt greasy. It was time for a shower. As he was about to head towards the bathroom, he heard his mobile go off. He took it from his pocket and looked at it.

John Redmond's name showed up on the screen.

Of course. He had forgotten all about his other so-called prediction. Daniel answered the phone.

'Hi, John.'

'Daniel. I just got your message.'

'Great.' His mind went blank. *What message was it again?* 'Sorry, I can't recall exactly what I said.'

'You made a mistake in your calculation. You wanted to make sure everything was okay.'

'Of course. Yes. And? How is Claire?'

'She's fine.' A small silence ensued before John continued. 'We had a fire in the house last night. But we both made it out okay.'

'Are you serious? Jesus.'

'I'll tell you about it when we meet again. What about Grace? Did you find her?'

Daniel rubbed his hand through his unkempt hair. Where would he begin?

'I did find her,' he said, slowly.

John sensed there was more to come. 'And?'

Daniel knew what he had to say, but could not say it.

Say it.

348

He swallowed. He placed his hand over the mouthpiece of his mobile. *Wham!* Before he realised what he had done, he had kicked the first thing that was closest to him. A chair. It tilted back - almost in slow motion. When it reached a certain point, gravity took over and pulled it the rest of the way to the floor. Although it didn't make that much noise, he was sorry he did it. Clearly, anger was building inside him, but there was nowhere to vent the anger in the hotel room. He took a deep breath to try and control himself and his voice. He removed his hand from the mouthpiece.

'She was murdered, John.'

No sound came from the other end. That was to be expected. After a few moments, Daniel wondered if John was still on the line.

'John?'

'I'm here, Daniel. I- I just can't believe what I'm hearing.'

Another silence elapsed. It was John's turn to take a deep breath before he spoke again. 'Who killed her? Did you witness it?'

'No, I didn't see it happening. They think it was her husband. Well, it's pretty obvious it was the husband,' he said as he caressed the small bump on the side of his head. He could feel the anger inside again. Why hadn't he stood up for himself when Otto pushed him from the doorstep on Friday? Why hadn't he found a big rock and flung it through the front window? It might have resulted in a whole different chain of events.

I could go crazy if I keep thinking that way, he thought to himself.

'I'm so sorry to hear that, Daniel. Truly I am.'

Daniel nodded. 'Thanks. To be honest, I don't feel like talking right now. I will contact you when I'm home.' He hung up without the usual niceties. He would see John soon enough. The professor would understand.

Looking down at his mobile, Daniel suddenly got a

shock. He blinked and tried to focus on the screen of his mobile. For a split-moment, he thought he had seen a message appear from Grace. When he looked again, it was gone. His mind was playing tricks with him. He was exhausted. He felt dirty. It was time to shower and check out. It was time to go home.

74

John continued to look at his mobile after Daniel hung up.

Murdered.

He shook his head with disbelief. *How could she be murdered?*

His thoughts turned to Grace herself. Although he didn't have close contact with her during her time at Trinity, he still knew her. The team of PhD students at the time were very close. Often he would have coffee with the group. From what John could recall when he spoke to her, it was mostly maths-related. At least he couldn't recall much about her personal life. Of course that wasn't unusual.

He remembered that he would often see Daniel and Grace together. They weren't the lovey dovey kind of couple that made you want to throw-up. But at the same time they were obviously a couple.

What kind of life had she led in Amsterdam? John wondered to himself. *Obviously, not a happy one, if they believe it was the husband who murdered her.*

He wondered about Daniel's thesis again. Out of all the ways one could die, how could he have predicted a murder from twelve years ago? The question was absurd. The more he thought about it, the more puzzled he felt.

He closed his eyes as he contemplated the question. He tried to picture Grace from twelve years previously. He tried to envisage what this development meant for Daniel's thesis.

As all these questions revolved through his mind, Claire entered the ward. He sensed her presence and opened his eyes. She smiled. It took John a second longer to gather his thoughts and return the smile. It was enough to raise suspicions.

'Are you okay?' she asked as she placed a copy of the

Sunday Independent on his bed.

'Yes, sorry, I was miles away,' he admitted. He decided against telling Claire about the whole Daniel situation. Not now. It would only complicate things. Besides, he wasn't sure what to tell her. He would like to tell her everything, even how he had asked Daniel to predict her own date of death, but not now.

Claire nodded towards a bed tray with a half-eaten boiled egg and toast. 'How's the food?'

John shrugged. 'What can I say? It tastes like hospital food.'

She smiled and looked around to see if anyone was watching them, like a drug dealer on a street corner. She then removed something wrapped in a paper napkin.

'Here. Have this.'

John could smell it before he accepted it. 'A breakfast roll?'

She nodded. 'The works. Sausage, rasher, black pudding, white pudding. I think there might even be an egg in it.'

John smiled. 'Can't remember the last time I had one of these,' he said as he unwrapped it. The contents were already hanging out of the roll. He took a bite.

'Don't worry. You don't have to finish it,' Claire said as her husband tried to smile with a full mouth.

He offered the breakfast roll to Claire. 'You want a bite?'

Reluctant at first, she eventually shrugged her shoulders. 'Sure, why not?'

Her bite was much smaller that John's. The bread holding the contents was already soggy. 'Not bad,' she said, through a full mouth.

John pointed to his chin, indicating to Claire that some ketchup had dripped onto her chin. She wiped it away with the back of her hand.

'I spoke to the nurse,' she said, glancing at what she just wiped away. 'She mentioned the doctor will do his rounds before lunch. There's a good chance you'll be allowed home today.'

The tempo of John's chewing slowed down as he clearly became preoccupied with something. He swallowed before asking the question. 'Is there still a home to go to?'

Claire nodded. 'The fire department called me about half an hour ago. They put out the fire pretty quickly. However, there is substantial damage to the kitchen and the hallway.'

'That's it? It's still standing?'

She nodded.

'Thank God,' he said with a sigh of relief.

'We were lucky,' Claire said matter-of-factly. 'Very lucky, really. Imagine if we lost the whole house?'

'Or our lives,' John mumbled. He looked as if he was in a daze. 'Do they know how it started?'

'They will do a full investigation tomorrow. They think it started from the bin.' She looked away and closed her eyes. Slowly she shook her head.

'What is it?' John asked.

'I threw in a whole load of varnish-soaked cloths into that bin. I was planning to take out the black bag later, but I just fell asleep. It was probably something stupid like that that started it. The heat those cloths would have generated just sitting there. Spontaneous combustion. I read about it online a while ago. It's really more common than you think. People just don't realise how dangerous it can be. How could I have been so careless?'

'It's not your fault, okay?' John said as he touched her on the arm. 'From what I remember, I also smelled it and did nothing about it. I probably even made it worse by stuffing my newspaper on top of everything.'

She smiled, appreciating the way John was accepting responsibility for it. Deep down she knew it was still her fault.

'Thanks.' She took a deep breath. 'To be honest, I think we owe our lives to whoever was trying to call us at

353

that time of the evening.'

John looked towards his mobile remembering the five missed calls. Was it possible that the one person who told him that Claire was going to die was the same person who saved them?

He took another bite of the breakfast roll. A piece fell onto the bed. Claire picked it up and ate it.

'Do you want another bite? I don't want you eating my scraps.'

She shook her head. 'No, thanks.'

Hospital sounds echoed throughout the ward. Beeps from machines. Footsteps from the hallway, less frantic than the ones from the previous night.

John took another bite and then re-wrapped the half-eaten breakfast roll. 'I think I've had enough.'

'You want to keep it for later?'

He shook his head and placed it on the bedside locker. Noticing a glass of water standing there, he picked it up and took a mouthful. When he finished washing down the remains of his breakfast roll, he turned to Claire. 'I just want to go home.'

'We will. Once the doctor has seen you.'

He shook his head slowly. 'I haven't been home for so long.'

Claire frowned and turned her head sideways, clearly confused. Standing up, she took the newspaper that was on John's bed and moved it to the chair she had just been sitting on. She lay down on the bed next to him. John was still in a daze.

'What do you mean you haven't been home for so long?'

'I just feel... mentally I haven't really been home for some time. Physically, yes, but mentally no. My mind has always been somewhere else.' He looked at his wife. Despite the awful night she had, she still smelled good. It was a fragrance she always seemed to emit, like it was *her* scent. It was as if it was part of her. Perhaps it was simply the hand-cream she always used, or a body cream.

Claire took his head and placed it next to her chest. 'We will go home. Together.'

As John relaxed, he noticed a rip in Claire's top. On the sleeve. He wondered if she had noticed it yet. It was a new top. Or, at least, he couldn't recall her wearing it previously. As he focussed on the rip, it broke his heart. Even more than the fact that they had almost lost their home.

Why did such a small detail cause him so much heartbreak? He began to imagine the whole buying process she would have gone through. Where had she bought it? Debenhams? Arnotts? Brown Thomas? Was it love at first sight or did she have to touch it first? Caress it? Like the way she picked out fruit in a supermarket. He imagined her holding it up to her as she looked in a full-length mirror. She would pick out two different sizes. The realistic size and the "wishful thinking" size. Of course the realistic size would fit her best. And even when she had made the decision, still there would have been doubt. Doubt if it would go with anything she already owned. There would be concerns that it would run in the wash.

What would never have crossed her mind, though, was how it would fare should their house go on fire, and whether she would get out of the house safely without damaging it.

John reached out and touched the rip. He didn't say anything, but vowed to buy a similar top for her when his life returned to some kind of normality.

75

Zoe swore under her breath as she arrived at Dublin Airport. It didn't go undetected by Sean, who was sitting in the passenger seat absorbing everything.

'What is it, Mammy?' he asked.

'Nothing, sweetheart,' she lied.

It seemed to Zoe that, every time she drove to Dublin Airport, a completely new parking set-up was introduced: diversions here, a new parking garage there, one section closed-off, that part for set-down only. Now that Terminal 2 had finally opened, yet another parking option led to the never-ending confusion.

Zoe couldn't help recalling the time from years ago, when they used to just park for free at the church within the airport grounds. How simple life was back then. How less busy the airport was. It was a time when going somewhere by plane really was a novelty. Zoe couldn't help thinking that every man and his dog now seemed to be jet setters.

Somehow, the same church remained untouched throughout all the development, like a stubborn treehugger reluctant to budge for development corporations.

Although Zoe's father-in-law had picked her up that very morning (and dropped her there three days previously), it didn't help her now. She was annoyed at herself for not paying more attention when she was the passenger.

'Terminal 2 this way,' she mumbled to herself and followed the signs.

'It's like Terminator 2,' Sean observed. Zoe nodded, not really listening. It suddenly dawned on her that Dublin Airport had been one big building site for the past ten years. Work on Terminal 2 began during the height of the economic boom and was completed just in time for the crisis. One advantage of the crisis was that there didn't seem to be any more development going on in the airport complex. It now seemed to be "finished".

When she came to the entrance of the parking garage, she took a deep breath.

I'm not going to stall. I'm not going to stall.

She hated the barriers. After rolling down the window, she grabbed the parking ticket and revved the engine slightly. The barrier swung upwards and in she drove.

'Woo-hoo.'

Sean gave his mother a strange look.

'Now listen,' Zoe said as she drove up to the second level in search for a free space. 'Daddy might be a bit upset, okay? So go easy on him.'

'Why is he upset?'

She wondered briefly if she should have brought it up. And now that she had, how much detail should she go into.

'A good friend of his just passed away.'

'You mean died?'

'Yes.'

'Oh, that's sad.'

'Yes, it is.' She hoped that it was the final question.

'How did he die?'

Nope, wishful thinking.

'She. It was a "she",' Zoe corrected him, and decided not to go into too much detail. 'I'm not sure, to be honest.'

They didn't have to wait long before Daniel came through Arrivals. Sean ran up to him with his arms outstretched. Daniel bent over and gave him a hug and a kiss. He took his hand in his and walked towards Zoe. They kissed each other on the cheek.

'You look like shit,' she whispered.

'Thanks. Great to see you too.'

'He doesn't look like shit,' Sean offered.

Both his parents tried not to smile.

'Don't be saying those words, Sean,' Zoe said, trying

her best to put on a serious expression. Deep down, she found it so funny when her little boy swore.

'But you said it.'

'I know, but it just slipped out.'

'Well, it just slipped out of me too,' Sean said as he looked towards his father. 'I heard about your friend. It's very sad.'

Daniel looked at Zoe wondering how much she had told the boy. She shook her head trying to convey that she hadn't told him too much. He got down on his hunkers.

'Thank you, Sean. That's a very mature thing to say. You're getting to be such a big boy.'

Daniel hugged him again and kissed him on the head before standing upright.

'Where's the car? Shall we go?'

'Are you okay to drive?' Zoe asked.

'I think so,' he said, despite feeling like he hadn't slept in a week.

'Good. I hate those barrier things.'

Daniel made it through the barrier without stalling, much to Zoe's admiration. As he exited the garage, a bus appeared out of nowhere forcing him to break suddenly. Everyone in the car jolted forward, before their seatbelts locked hard.

'Jesus, where did he come from?' He muttered. 'Sorry.'

Zoe placed her hand on his knee, as everyone sat back again and tried to relax. He twitched slightly. Her hand felt foreign. Like a stranger rubbing off him in a public place. Was he frightened that she would somehow sense the feelings he had over the weekend for Grace? Is this the way cheating husbands behaved when they were back with their partners? A simple touch now feeling like an electric shock?

'You're tense, sweetheart. Are you sure you don't want me to drive?'

'I'm sure,' he said sternly, staring right in front of him, like a horse with blinkers heading for the finishing post.

Only he wasn't moving.

'I mean now that you've done the hard part of getting through the barriers,' she added in an attempt to add humour to the situation. Daniel didn't react.

'Are you okay?' she asked.

The car behind them honked. Daniel gave it some gas and they were on their way again.

Zoe's hand remained on Daniel's knee. She hadn't taken the hint that it made him feel uncomfortable.

'Sorry about Grace,' she said.

Daniel glanced briefly at her and returned his attention to the road. Lowering his voice he said, 'I don't want to talk about it right now.' He nodded towards the back. Little ears would be picking up everything. Zoe removed her hand from his leg and folded her arms.

After several moments of silence, a little voice came from the back: 'Did you bring any presents?'

Daniel smiled at the question and then grimaced when he realised he hadn't. He had planned to buy something at Schiphol but with all the stress of booking a new flight and his head still full of images from the previous night, presents were the last thing on his mind. Mentally, he kicked himself for forgetting.

'I'm sorry, Sean. I didn't get round to it.' He glanced at the rear-view mirror and saw the disappointed look on his son's face. Sean lowered his head in mock disappointment, knowing that his father was looking at him.

'Listen, mate. I'll make it up to you next weekend, okay?'

'Okay. How?' Sean asked.

He glanced back again and saw that his son had already perked up. 'We'll see next weekend, okay. Have a think about what you would like to do.'

'He has been invited to Jack's birthday next weekend,' Zoe said.

Daniel glanced sideways quickly and then turned his attention back to the road. 'I assume Jack's not celebrating the whole weekend?'

She rolled her eyes and raised her voice. 'I'm just saying, that's all.'

Daniel remained silent. Sean could sense the tension in the car. 'Don't be arguing.'

Zoe looked back and smiled at her son. 'We're not arguing, sweetheart, we're just having a discussion.' She reached back and caressed Sean's cheek. 'Did you tell Daddy what you've been up to with Nana and Granddad?'

The remainder of the journey was made up with stories that involved Granddad falling asleep at the cinema. An early morning walk in Phoenix Park with Granddad and Toby (their cocker spaniel) to watch the deer. And a trip to Dublin Zoo where Sean and Nana saw one monkey fling his poo at another monkey. Nobody else believed them.

Part III

The present only is our own,
So live, love, toil with a will,
Place no faith in "Tomorrow,"
For the Clock may then be still."

Robert H Smith

76

John was released from Connolly Hospital on Sunday afternoon with little fuss. There was no shortage of patients in A&E to take his place.

'Make an appointment with your GP for a check-up next week,' the doctor, an attractive Polish lady in her fifties, advised. She wore a pair of half-moon reading glasses. When she finished glancing through John's paperwork she took them off and let them dangle around her neck. 'I'll send the results of the tests we ran to your GP, but judging from the X-ray and your current condition, your lungs escaped any major damage.'

John cleared his throat as if testing the doctor's theory. Any pain he had during the night had faded.

'Thank you.'

They shook hands and the doctor was already making her way towards the next patient. John turned to Claire, who was doing one last check in the bedside locker for any personal belongings.

'How are we going to get home?' he asked.

Claire stood up. 'Taxi?'

Twenty minutes later, they pulled up outside their house, number 9 Beechpark Lawn. John paid the driver and included a generous tip.

The first thing both of them noticed simultaneously as they got out of the taxi was the driveway. It was empty.

'Where's your car?' John mumbled

Claire turned around and saw it on the street, two doors down. 'There.'

The window on the driver's side had been smashed and temporarily taped back up.

'Somebody smashed...' she trailed off as she put one and one together. 'The Fire Brigade probably smashed the window to get into it and roll it away from the fire, as a precaution.'

John nodded. 'You're probably right. The last thing you want is a car exploding in your driveway.'

Turning back to the house, they both walked up the driveway. At first glance, the front door seemed to have escaped any damage. As they got closer, John could see black marks on the top of the doorway and on the sides. It reminded him of dampness, a sort of mildew growing slowly outwards.

'They didn't break the door down?' he wondered out loud.

'Maybe they went in the back or...' Claire trailed off as she noticed some damage around the Yale lock towards the top. 'Or maybe they just got through this lock easily. Aren't these the ones you see on television that burglars open using a credit card?'

'Maybe.' He inserted the key and was about to twist it but stopped. 'I don't suppose the alarm is on?'

Claire gave him a friendly slap on the back.

As he pushed the door open, he could feel some resistance. He gave it more force and the door slid open. The first thing that met John was the smell. It was like burnt toast, only a thousand times stronger. Looking down, he could see the debris that had blocked the door. Smouldered plastic, burnt wood.

'Jesus.'

They both walked into their home and took in the new look. The top part of the walls and the ceiling were black. A burnt piece of wallpaper hung from the wall in the hallway, like a piece of skin that had seen too much sun. John couldn't resist reaching up and pulling it off.

'Never liked that wallpaper, anyway,' he admitted, as he dropped it to the floor.

Claire rubbed her fingers against the wall and looked at the black residue on her fingertips. She glanced at John, who was already rummaging through the debris on the floor. He picked up a photo frame and, with one hand, wiped away the dirt and ash that was covering it. The glass was smashed and the frame warped. The photograph inside was also distorted on the edges, but the image itself was still clear. He pulled the photograph out and dropped the frame back onto the debris with a crash.

It was a photo of all three of them as a family on a beach in Florida.

'Can't believe that survived,' Claire said as she looked from the photo to John.

'Me neither. I guess we need a new frame for it.'

'And the photo reprinted. The edges are all singed.'

John said nothing for a moment and then shook his head softly. 'I think I prefer it this way. We can use it to remind us how lucky we are. To have survived this fire.' He looked at his wife. 'And to have been parents to such a wonderful little boy.'

Claire smiled and turned her head slightly as she analysed the photograph. 'You're right. We were very lucky. In every sense of the word.'

He placed the photograph in his bag and walked to the kitchen. 'Jesus, would you look at this.'

There was little doubt that the fire had started in the kitchen. It was completely destroyed. The walls were black. Some of the cupboards hung awkwardly, barely attached to the wall. Others had fallen off completely, engulfed in the furnace that had paid a visit. Remains of cups, plates and other crockery lay scattered on the counter top and floor. Most of them smashed, others burnt and cracked beyond repair. Cans of food with half-burnt labels lay among the debris. Some of the cans had exploded and still contained dried food remains. The rest of the food had been projected into the inferno.

John walked over to the cooker. The top of it was completely destroyed, as was the extractor fan above it. The oven door was still attached to the oven though, albeit slightly warped.

'Jesus, imagine the heat of the fire to have done this to

an oven door.' he mumbled and then turned his attention to the counter. With his arm, he cleared burnt debris from the counter to the floor. A cloud of ash rose. He waved his hand in front of his face, but knew it had no effect.

'This isn't too damaged,' he said touching the counter. 'Good job we got marble.'

'It's cracked in some places.' Claire said as she examined a section of the counter close to the fridge.

John looked around almost unable to believe that it was their house. The metal wine rack next to the microwave was still intact, but the bottles were all destroyed. Broken, cracked, blackened.

A whiteboard hung on the other side of the kitchen, next to the microwave. It remained on the wall, but was now blackened too. John moved closer and could still see some of the bullet points.

Toilet paper, Eggs, Batteries for smoke alarm.

He reached up and wiped away the last one. 'Just in case the insurance company investigates it and wonders why the smoke alarm wasn't working.' Turning to Claire, he looked for her reaction. Nothing. She was already walking towards the sitting room.

At first glance, the sitting room seemed surprisingly okay.

'I guess the door prevented the fire from getting through,' she said as she examined what was left of the door. It still hung to its hinges, but was badly burnt. The paint that remained was in the form of loose flakes. She felt that if she shook the door hard enough, the paint shavings would fall to the ground, like leaves falling from a tree on a windy autumn's day.

John glanced into the sitting room. Some of the ceiling just inside the door was black. As were the walls next to the door.

'It's in an okay state, considering,' he said.

Claire nodded. She walked back to the hallway and glanced upstairs. John was close behind her.

Most of the stairway was burnt. The banisters were black, but still intact. John placed his foot on the first step. Testing it. Like he was about to step onto a recently frozen lake. It felt solid enough. He placed his full weight on it as he moved his other foot to the next step.

'Sturdy enough?' Claire asked.

'Yeah, I think so. I think it's mainly the carpet that was burnt.'

As he made his way upstairs, the condition of the house improved drastically. By the time he got to the top, the carpet was covering the stairs completely once again. The walls on the landing were coated with a black film, but not as bad as downstairs. The pack of toilet roll that Claire had left there the previous day seemed to be untouched, except for a thin film of soot. The burnt smoky scent remained in the air. John wondered how long it would last.

The door to Max's bedroom was closed. He walked slowly towards it. As he touched the knob, he stopped. He had flashbacks of the previous night.

Entering the bedroom.

Lying next to his wife on their deceased son's bed.

Suddenly he felt a hand on his shoulder.

'It's okay. Don't be afraid,' Claire said. 'It's over.'

He wasn't quite sure what she meant by "it's over". Was she referring to the fire? He turned the knob and pushed the door open.

The room was dark. At first he thought the curtains were drawn. It took him a moment to realise that the window was boarded up. The Fire Brigade had obviously smashed the window. John was unsure if they did it when entering the house or when escaping from it.

The windows throughout the house had locks on them to prevent intruders. Unfortunately, unless you knew where the key was, they weren't the most convenient windows when it came to escaping fires. If the house were a hotel, they would have failed the fire regulations.

John looked towards the bed. It was a complete mess.

The Manchester United duvet had disappeared. Pointing to the bed, he turned towards Claire.

'I think I wrapped the duvet around me when I was being rescued,' she said as if reading his thoughts. 'I can't remember what happened to it after that. Maybe it's out in the garden or maybe I left it in the ambulance.'

'Don't worry about it,' John said. 'One less thing to get rid of, I guess.' He scanned the room further as Claire bent down and retrieved something from beneath the bed.

'I got these yesterday.'

John looked at them. 'Bags?'

'Charity bags.'

He held them. 'Where did you get them?'

'From the charity shop.'

'You went there alone?'

She nodded. 'I was going to talk to you about it yesterday.'

He kissed his wife's forehead. 'No more doing things alone when it comes to Max, okay? From now on we do everything together. No more growing apart.'

Claire didn't need any convincing and wondered briefly if he had somehow overheard her private conversation with Max. She nodded. 'Okay.'

77

Daniel sat at the kitchen table and flicked absent-mindedly through an old issue of the Evening Herald. Although it wasn't a current issue, the news seemed new to him. Dinner had gone smoothly. Sean had helped him take his mind off the recent events. He was a little chatterbox after his weekend at his grandparents.

A scent of spaghetti bolognese and garlic bread hung in the air. The wish-wash sound of the dishwasher indicated that it was in full swing. Daniel visualised the propeller inside spinning around frantically, throwing water onto the dirty plates. The little dishwasher tablet would have been ejected into the storm by now.

Zoe stood at the counter making Sean's sandwiches for school the next day. She wore jeans and a D&G T-shirt. Her hair was held back with a hair band.

'Do you want sandwiches for tomorrow?'

Daniel shook his head. 'No, thanks.'

She turned halfway towards him. '"No" as in you don't need them or "no" as in you're not going to work?'

He looked up at her. 'Both, actually.'

Zoe resumed her evening ritual of making Sean's sandwiches. After balancing the knife on top of the jar of lemon curd, she took out a Ben10 lunch box from the cupboard. Neatly, one by one, she placed the sandwiches in the lunchbox and then placed the lunchbox in the fridge. She sat down at the table in front of Daniel.

'Do you want to talk about it now?'

Daniel looked at her. She wasn't wearing any make-up. He could make out her tiny facial hair, or "fluff" as he would call it. It was always more visible when she didn't wear make-up.

'Honestly?' he said, 'Not really.'

'You look exhausted. Is there anything I can do?'

He closed the newspaper. 'My mind is just full of so many things right now. If only I did this or if only I did that. Every time I close my eyes I see her. Lying there. In a pool of blood.' He rubbed his finger against a coffee stain on the table. The stain started to disappear. 'I never realised how dark blood really is. When you see so much of it. It was horrible. The way it just formed a pool on the wooden floor, like spilled wine.'

Zoe reached over and took his hand. 'Look at me.'

Daniel raised his eyes and met her gaze.

'It's not your fault.'

'I know.'

'No. You don't know. You're still... '

A drilling sound from the next door neighbour distracted both of them. Daniel glanced at his watch. It was 8:22pm.

'Jesus, do they ever stop renovating next door? Not a week goes by that I don't hear drilling.'

Zoe ignored him and steered him back to the subject at hand. It was too easy for Daniel to go off on one of his rants. She raised her voice to be heard above the neighbour's din. 'You have to stop these "What if" games in your mind. Let it go.' She squeezed his hand. 'Let *her* go.'

Daniel wasn't sure what she meant by her last remark. Did she suspect something?

The drilling stopped. Zoe lowered her voice as she continued. 'You tried to prevent it. You did more than anyone could have. Now stop blaming yourself.'

He looked away again. 'Okay. I'll try.'

'No,' Zoe said, 'Don't try. Just do it. There's nothing you could have done, so just leave it at that.'

The dishwasher emitted a beep, announcing that it was moving on to the next cycle. Daniel hated the beep. He often joked with Zoe that it was one big show-off dishwasher. *Look at me. I'm moving on to the next cycle now. What do you think of that?*

Their eyes met once again and, as if thinking of the same past conversation, they smiled.

'Did I ever mention that I hate that dishwasher?' he asked.

'Once or twice.'

78

It was a crisp autumn morning in Dublin. The leaves on the trees were starting to turn yellow. A few of them had already started to fall. It would be another few weeks however before the mass migration downwards would take place.

As Daniel walked down a road called The Pines in Castleknock, he admired the large detached houses, one after the other. The front gardens were beautifully maintained, surrounded by perfectly shaped hedges. It reminded him of a Lego town. He took a left on Beechpark Lawn and continued for a moment until he came to what he assumed was number 9. Although there was no number on it, he based his assumption on the houses on either side of it: 8 and 10. Number 9 was a large red-brick house. On the driveway stood a skip container.

This must be it, he thought to himself.

As he approached it, two workmen were coming out of the house. They were lifting an old kitchen counter that was still intact, but badly cracked.

'Careful does it, Mousey. The fecking thing could give way any second,' said the workman wearing a baseball cap. The one referred to as Mousey was anything but mouse-like. He was tall and muscular. One bulging bicep had a colourful eagle tattooed on it. Both workmen counted to three as they threw the counter into the skip. As soon as it hit the container, it broke into several pieces.

'You see?' the baseball-capped workman said. They both turned back towards the house before Daniel managed to catch Mousey's eye.

'Excuse me?' Daniel asked. 'Is this Professor Redmond's house?'

Mousey frowned for a moment and then called after his colleague who had just stepped through the front door.

'Hey, Anto. What's the name of yer man livin' here?'

Daniel suddenly realised why the workman before him was called Mousey. His voice was high-pitched, a complete mismatch to his physical appearance. Anto appeared at the front door and addressed Daniel.

'Who are you looking for?'

'Professor Redmond?'

Anto frowned, thinking hard. 'I didn't know he was a bleedin' Professor. I thought Professors were old and grey and wore... what d'ya call them things?' he said turning to Mousey and then back to Daniel. 'The long things, like capes, but for very brainy people.'

Daniel glanced in the skip, not really listening to Anto. He caught sight of burnt cupboards, broken dishes and lots of rubble.

'Gowns! I think they're called,' Mousey offered.

'Yeah, gowns.' Anto looked towards Daniel.

'Like Professor Dumbledore,' Mousey added.

Anto burst out laughing. 'Like Dumbledore! D'ya hear your man?' He said nodding towards his colleague.

Daniel offered a false smile. 'Do you know if John Redmond lives here?' The word "professor" was obviously too much of a distraction for them.

The workmen looked at each other before Anto admitted: 'Yeah. I think dat's his name.' He scratched his head. 'Do you want me to get him?'

'That would be great.'

The two workmen disappeared into the house. Anto made off upstairs. Mousey went back to the kitchen. Daniel decided to stay outside, just in case it was the wrong house. He could see Anto stopping halfway up the staircase and calling: 'John! There's someone here to-'

A banging noise from the kitchen drowned out his call. Mousey wasted no time in continuing the demolition job at hand.

A moment later, Anto called out from the doorway. 'He's on his way,' he said pointing behind him. No sooner had he gone back to the kitchen than Daniel saw John coming down.

'Daniel. Good to see you,' he said, hand outstretched as he stepped outside.

Daniel shook his hand.

John wore jeans and a grey sweater. It was the most casual Daniel had ever seen him. It was a sharp contrast to his usual Trinity attire. He noticed a small cut above his eye. That was new. The stubble growing on his face had patches of grey and, despite the recent events, he looked relaxed.

'I wasn't sure if I had the right house,' Daniel said pointing to the doorway. 'I assumed the number would be on the door. But I don't even see a door.'

'True. Yes. We're getting a new one,' John said pointing to a rectangular package wrapped in plastic and bubble wrap, lying beneath the front window. They will put it on when most of the rubble is taken away.'

'Is there a lot of damage?'

'Let's just say it could have been worse.' His last words were drowned out by further banging from the kitchen. He raised his voice. 'Let's take a walk. The place is a mess.'

Daniel nodded towards the house. 'What about Beavis and Butthead?'

'They'll be fine. They're trustworthy enough. They were referred to by a friend.'

As they walked out the driveway, Daniel noticed that John was wearing runners. Bright white ones, looking like he had just bought them. It was another digression from his usual mundane shoes he wore to university.

'Are you going to break into a jog?' Daniel asked pointing to his footwear.

'Those? No. I actually found them on top of the wardrobe, would you believe? I can't remember where they came from. It's amazing the amount of shit you find lying around your house when it comes to tidying up and renovating.'

They walked down Beechpark Lawn alongside a small green.

'I used to play football with Max here,' John said pointing to the open space. At the bottom of the space stood a large wall separating the back gardens from the playing area. 'Sometimes the ball would go over that wall. I would lift Max on my shoulders and ask him if he could see which garden the ball had gone into. Once we knew, more or less, we would go around the front and knock on the door of the specific house. I think he found that more fun than the actual football.'

Daniel said nothing. It dawned on him that it was one of the first times that John spoke about Max with an air of fondness. It was the first time he recounted an event without a big cloud of guilt hovering over him.

'Once our stray ball hit a glasshouse in one of the back gardens. I wanted to teach Max about responsibility and offered to pay for the pane of glass that we had broken. I remember the owner, a lanky guy with yellow teeth came to the door and just smiled at us for a few moments. When we explained what had happened, he went to fetch the ball from his glasshouse. While he was gone I caught a whiff of cannabis floating from his house. I offered to pay for the broken glass, of course, but he waved it away and continued to smile. I then realised why he wasn't bothered about replacing the glass.'

'Which was?'

'Well, he was either too stoned to understand me or just didn't want to draw unnecessary attention to what he was growing in his glasshouse. Try explaining that to a ten-year-old. Or maybe he was about eight at the time.'

Daniel and John came to the end of Beechpark Lawn. They walked across a pavement onto Auburn Avenue. An elderly lady with a chihuahua was in deep conversation with a young mother. Both of them glanced towards whatever bundle of joy lay inside the modern-looking buggy.

'I nearly screwed up, Daniel.'

It was the end of the nostalgia trip. The dark cloud of guilt had caught up.

'In what way?'

'In what way? Wasn't it obvious?'

'You were responsible for the fire?' Daniel asked. 'The burnt-out kitchen?'

John sighed wondering where to start. 'Well, it's not as if I doused the place in petrol and threw a Zippo at it. But I did nothing to prevent it. I avoided Claire the whole day. When I got home, I was so drunk. I smelled something weird but did nothing about it. I was asleep when the fire started, and by the time it was in full force, I was comatose. If Claire didn't wake up on time, we would have both died.'

John scratched his face, still getting accustomed to his facial hair. 'The truth is,' he said as they continued walking. 'If you hadn't realised you made a mistake. If you hadn't tried to call me on the house line, Claire would not have woken up.'

'Really? You believe that?'

'Yes, I do,' he said with utmost sincerity.

The footpath narrowed, forcing Daniel to fall back and walk behind John for a few strides. When the path was wide enough again, he retook his position next to the professor.

'The thing is,' John continued, 'I also hoped that by dying I was leaving you a small gift. To say I'm sorry.'

'A small gift? What kind of gift?'

'I wanted to give your thesis another boost of confidence. I wanted to convince you that your thesis was correct.' He took a deep breath. 'I think subconsciously I wanted Claire to die on the day you predicted for two reason: to end her suffering and give you confidence to return to mathematics.'

They both walked in silence for a while. A filthy vegetable truck passed by with the words "wash me" engraved into the dirt on the back. A couple of other more obscene words were also visible.

'The fact that she didn't die, and you realised that you made a mistake before the end of the day is good news for your thesis, I think. They both kind of cancel each other out.' He pointed to the pavement suddenly. 'Watch out for the dog poo.'

Daniel stepped around the obstacle. Judging from the trail of brown smudge marks that followed, an earlier pedestrian hadn't been so vigilant.

'How can it be good news all of a sudden?' Daniel asked. 'What about all that talk about her not coping with Max's death? And how she was dragging you with her. You practically wanted her to die, didn't you?'

'In a way, yes. But what I really wanted was for her to start living her life again and stop killing herself slowly with the drink.' He trailed off for a moment, searching for the right words. 'I wanted some kind of cure for her. And if dying was the only way, then, yes, in a way I did want her to die. I know it sounds like I'm a monster when I say it, but it's the opposite. I think I wanted her to die because I love her so much and couldn't stand what she was doing to herself. It's like that quote…' He put his hand to his head trying to think. 'Something, something, something… *for death is the cure of all diseases.*'

'*We all labour against our own cure, for death is the cure of all diseases,*' Daniel said, 'by Sir Thomas Browne.'

'Exactly, that's the one,' John said clicking his fingers. 'But something changed that night.' John's foot slipped off the side of the pavement. He quickly hopped back on the footpath. 'Maybe it was the fact that we both came so close to death that we realised how precious life really is.'

The two men made brief eye contact as they continued from Auburn Avenue on to Castleknock Road, towards the Phoenix Park.

'Basically, the woman I woke up next to in the hospital was a new woman. She was… well, sober, for a start. And she just started telling me that she didn't blame me for what happened.'

Daniel seemed a little sceptical. 'You mean the fire? She didn't blame you for the fire?'

'I think everything. The fire, the death of Max.'

'Did you tell her about my prediction? Her possible date of death?'

He shook his head. 'No. Not yet.'

'Are you going to tell her?'

'Maybe. One day. There's enough on our minds for now.'

The two men continued walking down Castleknock Road. Daniel continued to glance around every so often, observing the large houses with beautiful gardens and large driveways. He noticed that some of the houses even had balconies. In his neighbourhood, there were no balconies on houses. He didn't see the point of balconies on a Dublin home, unless it was part an apartment. He saw them as an open invitation for burglars. Turning his attention back to John he said, 'You mentioned this so-called gift was also a way to say you were sorry. What do you mean by that? Sorry for what?'

John stopped walking. Daniel stopped a couple of steps in front of him and looked around. Something definitely changed since the last time they had met. John glanced in the distance briefly before making eye contact with Daniel.

'To say sorry for not recognising your gift sooner. To apologise for practically sending you to work on a building site for twelve years.'

Daniel looked down to his hands. Twelve years of working on a building site had taken its toll. They were rough, rugged, just like what Grace had noticed. Still, they were the same hands from his university years. 'It was my decision to work on a building site,' he said looking up at John. 'It was my decision to become a crane operator.'

'Maybe so. But still. If it weren't for me, you would have been... I don't know, more successful.'

'I know what you're trying to say. And I know you're trying to say it without sounding condescending. But listen, John, you already apologised for the part you played in this. It was you who suffered the greatest loss imaginable. Maybe if the thesis was accepted all those years ago, I could have predicted Max's death. Who knows? But there's nothing left for you to apologise for. Can we agree on that?'

John gave him a pat on the arm and looked him straight in the eyes. 'You're a good friend, Daniel.' They remained caught in each other's gaze for a few short moments before John broke it and continued walking down Castleknock Road. Daniel waited a few moments. It was the first time that John referred to him as a friend. When he reflected on their meetings over the past couple of weeks it made sense. They had shared very personal experiences with each another.

Daniel looked after the man walking ahead of him. He noticed the back of one of the legs of his jeans was tucked into his sock. The bright runners did nothing to improve the image. He smiled as he started walking again. When he caught up, John turned towards him.

'Now, let's hear your story. What happened in Amsterdam?'

79

6 Months Later

Daniel awoke early on the day of his PhD graduation ceremony. Although it was still dark outside, light from a street lamp found its way through a gap in the curtains. He stared at the ceiling as he listened to Zoe sleeping soundly next to him. Her breathing was soothing. Therapeutic some might say. Still, when he thought of the day before him, a cold rush of adrenaline spurted through his body. How could he sleep with so many thoughts in his head? And if that wasn't enough, his stomach started to rumble. The thought of food, though, was the farthest thing from his mind. His appetite seemed to have disappeared to the same place as his ability to sleep.

Daniel's thoughts turned to the last six months.

Attending Grace's funeral down in Ballyferriter, close to Dingle, was heartbreaking. The ceremony was beautiful and the speeches emotional. The burial took place in a small graveyard looking out onto the Blasket Islands, or the 'Sleeping Giant', as it was known to locals. The 'Giant' lay there, oblivious to the dreams and dangers that the surrounding Atlantic Ocean offered. The graveyard seemed a suitable resting place for someone who also lived their life full of dreams and dangers.

As Daniel left Ballyferriter later the following day, he caught sight of a lightning storm brewing in the distance. Stopping the car, he got out and continued to look in the direction of the storm. It started to drizzle. He took out an umbrella from the boot and opened it. Slowly he walked into a nearby field, staring the whole time in the distance. He wasn't sure what he was waiting for. Deep down he knew it wasn't the wisest thing to do, but still...

And there it was: a beautiful lightning bolt stretching across the sky. It came and went in a split second. Just on cue, it was followed by the distant rumbling sound of thunder. It wasn't the bolt of lightning that he found fascinating. It was the unpredictability of it.

But wasn't everything predictable? The question gnawed at him. As it always did. Couldn't mathematics predict everything if applied correctly? Had he really touched on something extraordinary?

The truth is he didn't know. And he would continue to never know, unless he did something about it.

Something dawned on him as he stared into the dark sky before him. Grace would have died in vain if he didn't do something with the so-called gift he had. If he continued life as a crane operator, it would be the biggest insult to her. He reached into the inside pocket of his suit jacket and pulled out the photograph of himself and Grace from all those years earlier. He looked at her as light rain drops landed on the photo.

'I'll do it,' he said as he rubbed the photo gently against his trousers and placed it back into his inside pocket. He stared into the beautiful chaos in the distance. 'I'm going to defend my thesis and publish my work.' The drizzle started to turn into heavier drops. The storm was approaching. 'I owe you that, Grace.'

Then, there was Otto Visser's trial in January. Daniel's return to Amsterdam was not something he had been looking forward to. It became less of an ordeal when John offered to come with him for support. Daniel took him up on his offer.

It was the afternoon of the second day, when Daniel took the stand and gave evidence. Reliving almost every moment of his previous visit to Amsterdam in front of a Dutch court of law was not a pleasant experience, but he knew it had to be done.

His thesis was ridiculed by the panel of three judges, which brought back painful memories of his defence in Trinity College first time round.

John couldn't help thinking the same, only this time he was a spectator. It was like some strange kind of déjà vu for both of them. Daniel kept his cool, stayed with the facts and even went so far as to remind the court that his thesis was not on trial. A few low sniggers could even be heard from the public viewing area. To the viewers, it was a welcome relief to an otherwise long and harrowing day.

More disturbing for Daniel, however, was how the prosecution lawyer revived the sequence of events for the judges. Based on blood stains, Grace's internal injuries and chaotic state of the living room, the forensics team and the coroner were able to piece together a hypothetical series of events. How the intruder kicked open the door that immediately broke Grace's nose and knocked her to the ground. How she made it into the living room and tried to call the emergency services, only to have the phone taken from her and smashed against the wall. How she tried to escape the apartment, only to find it locked from the inside. How she was beaten and kicked about until she could fight no more, until she was lying down helpless. And how the intruder stood over her and finished it by lifting her head and slitting her throat with a knife from the kitchen.

Daniel stayed for the duration of the trial, as did John.

Rik Bergman also took the stand and testified. He spoke mainly about his experiences with Grace during the final week before she died. He recounted how frightened she was of her husband, the panic attack and the text message he had seen.

Daniel met him for coffee on the third day. It was clear that Rik too was devastated by the murder. When the forensic officers had finished collecting all the necessary evidence and had cleaned up the apartment, Rik couldn't bring himself to live there again. He couldn't bear the thought of someone he clearly had feelings for being murdered there. He put it up for sale immediately and accepted the first offer.

The trial continued smoothly, and although Otto continued to protest his innocence, the evidence against him was too strong. There was the history of violence, his fingerprints on the door, Grace's blood on his shoe, and the one that sealed his fate: the "Ot" written on the wall. Otto's law team argued every point. The history of violence was nothing more than some drunken outbursts in the past. His fingerprints were on the door because he had dropped by the apartment earlier that evening to talk to her, but decided to leave. He was too drunk to have any conversation with his wife. Grace's blood on his shoelaces was from a few days earlier when she had a nosebleed, as she packed up and left their house. They didn't say what had caused her nosebleed, or *who* had caused it.

The first two letters of Otto's name on the wall, however, could not be explained. Why would Grace have used her last bit of strength writing her husband's name on the wall? Nobody could think of any logical explanation except for what the prosecution team suggested: 'She had tried desperately to tell us who had done this horrendous crime to her. She had attempted to write her husband's name.'

That piece of evidence was what tipped the scales and sealed Otto's fate. After a trial that lasted five days, he was sentenced to twenty-five years in prison. He broke down in the court, crying and shouting his innocence.

'Ik ben onschuldig!'

As he was led away, he made brief eye contact with Daniel. Although he despised Otto for what he had done, there was something in his eyes that made Daniel feel uneasy. Was this the same feeling that kept Grace and Otto together for so long? It was a mixture of pity and loathing. Daniel felt pity for just how low he must have sank to make him do what he did and hated him for doing it. The look in Otto's eyes was something that would remain etched in his mind forever.

Even now, as he stared at the ceiling, he saw the eyes again, trying desperately to communicate some kind of innocence. Daniel tried to dismiss the doubt. The eyes of a mad man could not communicate anything.

He turned to his side and stared at the back of Zoe's head. He inhaled and took in the familiar "Zoe scent". His hand crept around her waist, and rested on her stomach. Everything felt warm. He was careful not to apply any pressure on the side of her arm. She had received a kick earlier in the week during her kickboxing training. The bruise was still a mixture of purple and yellow. After several moments of holding her in a spoon position, he decided to get up.

Daniel got up and went downstairs to make a cup of tea. As the kettle boiled he sat down at the kitchen table, half of which had become a permanent workplace for his research. He glanced at the folders and notebooks that were neatly stacked to one side. Next to it was a shoe box that contained random stationary and smaller items; pens, a scientific calculator, an adaptor for the laptop, old floppy disks that were in the original box from the attic. He smiled as grabbed one of the diskettes and remembered the evening with Grace all those months ago. How the same design were used as retro coasters.

He was about to throw the diskette back into the shoe box when he noticed something that caused him to freeze. The main label read "Random Notes" in black marker, but beneath that, in faded green ink, it read: "2 More".

'Two more?' His mind raced for an explanation. *Could it be the other calculations I did when I moved in with Zoe all those years ago?* In the past six months, he had not seen anything that referred to those predictions. He had almost begun to doubt he had made them at all. This was the first sign to suggest that they did indeed exist. But what was it that made him not keep the paperwork?

'There was something strange about the dates,' he mumbled. He wanted to have a quick look at what was on the disks, but there was little point in grabbing the laptop from the sitting room as there was no floppy drive in it. In fact, even their previous couple of computers hadn't contained a floppy drive, that's how old the data storage medium was.

Curiosity got the better of him. He knew there were a couple of computers in the library at Trinity College that had floppy drives attached to them via USB. 'It would be interesting to see what's on the disk.' He looked at his watch. If he had time before the ceremony he would pop into the library and have a quick look at the contents. Otherwise, it would have to wait until Monday.

80

After a long shower and a quick shave, Daniel grabbed hold of his suit that had been stored with a plastic cover over it. It was his one and only suit.

Perhaps it's time to buy a new one, he thought as he unzipped the plastic cover and let it fall to the ground. Hanging the suit on the door handle of the bathroom, he pulled the trousers from it. After he put on the trousers, which were coming close to the term "a little too tight", he opened the package of a new shirt and tie that Zoe had bought him in Arnotts. His nails were too short to pull out the pins that held the shirt in shape. After some rummaging in the drawers, he found Zoe's tweezers and used them to pull out the pins. One by one, he placed the pins in the upside-down lid of his shaving gel. He felt like a vet picking out pellets from an animal that had been shot by poachers. As soon as he was satisfied that all the pins were gone, he unfolded the shirt from the cardboard support and held it up. One pin still remained, preventing the shirt from coming free completely.

'There's always one,' he muttered beneath his breath. He picked up the tweezers one more time and removed the final one.

Although there weren't many creases in the shirt, the ones that were visible were pronounced and obvious. Daniel quickly ironed them out. He put the warm shirt on, followed by his tie. Zoe appeared behind him just as he finished tying his tie.

'Oh, I just missed it,' she said in a sleepy voice as she rubbed her eyes. Her hair was a mess. She wore grey silk pyjamas and was still in her bare feet.

'You just missed what?'

'Helping you with your tie. Isn't that what all good

wives do in the mornings?'

'Very funny.' Daniel took his suit jacket from the hanger and handed it to her. 'Here, you can help me with this.' He placed his arms in the jacket as Zoe held it up.

'How do I look?' he asked as he pulled the jacket on. They both glanced in the full-length mirror in the bathroom. Zoe pulled at the front of the jacket to help straighten it and wiped away imaginary fluff.

'Like a true Doctor of Philosophy.'

Placing his hand in the inside chest pocket of the jacket, Daniel pulled out what felt like a piece of cardboard. When he realised what it was, he placed it back quickly.

'What was that?' Zoe asked, her curiosity aroused by the way he had quickly replaced the item.

'Nothing.'

'Come on. Don't give me that. What was it?'

He smiled. 'Seriously. Nothing. Forget about it.'

'If it's nothing, then show it to me.'

'No… just forget about it.'

Zoe made a grab for it, but Daniel blocked her and knocked the shaving gel lid full of pins to the ground.

'Now look what you've done.'

'That was you who knocked that over,' Zoe said, annoyed. 'What are you hiding, Daniel?'

'It's just something that was in my pocket since Grace's funeral last year. It was the last time I wore this jacket.'

Zoe folded her arms.

'Okay. So what's the big deal then?'

He glanced down at the pins and back at his wife. 'I don't want to upset you.'

'Why would it upset me?'

He reached inside his pocket and retrieved the item. It was the photo of him and Grace taken in the Buttery all those years ago. He held it up to Zoe. Her face remained neutral as she took the photo. Finally she looked at Daniel.

'Why would you carry this around?'

'I wasn't *carrying* it around,' he said. 'I just had it going down to the funeral and forgot to take it out of my pocket.'

'But why?'

'I don't know. She was my friend, Zoe.'

'Your *girl*friend, don't forget.'

'Also a friend.'

'Do you still have feelings for her or something?'

'Oh come on, Zoe, don't be ridiculous.' He couldn't believe the conversation he was having. 'She's dead, for Christ's sake. I thought maybe saying goodbye to her was easier if I actually saw her. Why are we even having this conversation? It's not worth it.'

'And if she wasn't dead?'

'What if she wasn't dead?'

'Would you still have feelings for her?'

He raised his hands to his forehead, unable to comprehend where the conversation had led. 'Don't be ridiculous.'

'Get rid of it then,' she said, handing the photo back to Daniel.

'Okay, I will,' he took it and placed it back in his pocket. 'Later.'

'Do it now.'

He looked at his wife like she had gone mad. 'I can't believe this,' he said. 'Are you seriously jealous of someone who is dead?'

'I'm not jealous at all,' she admitted. 'The question is if you are still in love with… someone who is dead?'

Daniel took a deep breath. 'Just leave it, okay?'

'Get rid of it then. Rip it up and throw it away.'

'It's just a bloody photo. Why are you making such a big deal about it?'

'It's not just a bloody photo.' Zoe raised her voice. 'We both know it's more than a bloody photo! It is so much more.'

'Ssh. You'll wake up Sean,' he said trying to calm her

down. 'Why are you doing this, Zoe? On this day out of all days?'

She ran her hand through her hair. 'Because I don't think you ever stopped loving her,' she said as her eyes watered. 'Because I don't think you ever loved me the same way you loved her.'

Daniel was taken aback by Zoe's sudden insecurity.

She continued. 'I feel like a fucking pastime. All these years I felt like you were waiting for something better to come along. Or come back to you.'

A minute passed.

Daniel cleared his throat. 'I'm sorry you felt that way, Zoe. I had no idea.'

She turned away. Daniel stood there, unsure what to say. He stepped towards her and placed his hands on her arms. She pulled away.

'Careful. My arm.'

He moved his hands down to his wife's waist.

'You're not a pastime, Zoe. You're my wife.' He kissed the back of her neck. 'I had no idea you felt this way.' He paused for a moment, unsure how to proceed. 'Let's get through today and then we can discuss this further. Okay? This is an important day for me.'

She nodded. However, she didn't turn back to face him. Instead she walked away, stopping on the landing to remove the plastic wrapping from the new shirt that had stuck to her bare foot. Once it came free, she left it on the landing, went into their bedroom and closed the door behind her.

Daniel did the same with the bathroom door. Taking a deep breath, he grabbed the sink on both sides and looked at himself in the mirror. The person staring back at him looked like a complete stranger. Although he appeared very smart in the suit, was he happy? Did he belong in this suit? Wasn't he happier being a crane operator, leading a simple life?

He reminded himself of Tarzan arriving in the city for

the first time. Would he realise halfway during the graduation that he really didn't belong there? Would he tear off his suit and academic robe as he ran out of the campus and climb the nearest crane?

Now, that would be a sight, he thought to himself.

Once more he reached inside his pocket and retrieved the photo. Staring at it, one question went through his mind:

Do I really deserve today?

81

The atmosphere was still icy as Daniel and Zoe drove Sean to school. It was a rare treat to be driven to school by both his parents. They figured he was too young to really understand or appreciate a graduation ceremony.

'It would bore him to tears,' Zoe had said. 'Old farts calling out hundreds of names one after the other.'

Daniel pulled in on Howth Road close to St. Brigid's National School. It was a narrow street that became overly congested during the school run. Sean poked his head to the front and gave both his parents a kiss. Daniel put on the hazard lights.

'Watch the car,' he said to Zoe. 'I'll walk with him to the yard.' He hopped out of the car, ignoring any response that she might have given. Sean was already getting out of the car on the other side. Daniel took his hand in one hand and his school bag in the other and they walked together towards the school front gate.

It was a fresh spring morning. Although Howth Road was still at least a kilometre from Dublin Bay, Daniel could smell a saltiness in the breeze. If he was a stranger to the area, he would know the sea was not far.

The daffodils in some of the residential gardens seemed to have minds of their own. They were in different stages of their life cycle. Some were in full-bloom, others were withering away for another year.

Daniel turned his attention to Sean's school bag. It was the size and weight of it that caught his eye. 'Do you carry this by yourself every day?'

Sean nodded.

'Janey Mac,' Daniel said. In his mind, all he was thinking was that if the ratio of the bag-size to the person remained constant throughout his son's education, Sean would be carrying a huge backpack to school by the time he would be doing his Leaving Certificate.

When they reached the school gate, Daniel got down on his hunkers and gave him a big hug. Sean pulled away slightly embarrassed and then pointed at Daniel's shoulder.

'What?' he glanced to one side and saw that the breeze had blown his tie over his shoulder.

'You look like Mr O' Malley.'

They both giggled as they imagined the principal of the school with his tie over his shoulder. 'Does he always wear his tie like that?' he asked as he pulled the tie straight and handed the school bag to his son.

Sean nodded. 'Even when it's not windy.' They both shared another giggle.

'You'll be a good boy now, okay?' Daniel said caressing his son's face.

Sean nodded. 'I'm always good.'

'I know you are, pet.' He kissed his forehead. 'Be strong and always be yourself.'

Frowning, Sean asked, 'What do you mean?'

'Never mind. Just enjoy yourself and we'll see you later.'

Another gust of wind blew Daniel's tie over his shoulder.

'Here,' Sean said as he went rummaging in his school bag.

'What is it?'

After a few moments, Sean pulled out a paperclip. Daniel pulled his tie back into place.

'Mr O' Malley sometimes wears these to stop his tie from going all over the place.'

With his nimble hands, Sean attached the paperclip to the tie and clipped it to his shirt.

'That's very clever, Sean, thank you!'

Delighted with himself, he threw his bag over his shoulder and entered the school yard. As Daniel watched his son run over to his little group of pals, another gust of wind blew. This time just the bottom of his tie fluttered a little. Daniel smiled. He knew everything would be okay.

He hopped back into the car and switched off the hazard lights.

'What was that all about?' Zoe asked.

'What?'

'I saw you giving him a hug and talking to him like he was about to...'

'It's not every day I get to bring my boy to school,' he said as he swung a U-turn on Howth Road. An envelope lying on the dashboard flew off onto Zoe's lap. Completing the turn in one manoeuvre was tight. Daniel noticed a street bin that had been knocked over. It was probably by a parent who really should have done a three-point turn.

'In your suit and tie?' Zoe asked.

'What do you mean?'

'It's not every day that you bring him to school while wearing a suit and tie.'

'What is that supposed to mean?' Daniel asked as he straightened up and headed for the city.

'Nothing.'

'No, it's not nothing. Did you think I walked with him so I could show off my suit? My fifteen-year-old suit? With a bloody tie that keeps flying into my face? Is that your idea of showing off?'

In an attempt to change the subject, Zoe began rummaging in the envelope. It was from Trinity College.

'So where will I meet you?' she asked, desperately changing the subject. She browsed through the graduation information that was in the envelope.

Several moments passed. Daniel decided to drop the subject too.

'First I have to pick up the academic gown. I think from the Atrium. After that, all the PhD students have to meet at Number 1, Front Square. You can wait with all the other relatives in the Public Theatre. That's where the ceremony will take place. As far as I know, we will walk in procession to the Public Theatre with all the relevant Professors and Chancellors and what not.'

'Did you already order your gown?'

'Yes, the receipt should be there.'

They drove in silence as they passed Whitehall church and stopped at the traffic lights on the Collins Avenue junction.

'Are you nervous?'

Daniel shrugged. 'Mixed feelings, I suppose.'

She placed her hand on his leg. 'Don't be.'

He forced a smile. All he wanted was the day to be over.

82

Although the salty breeze from Dublin Bay didn't venture so far as the city centre campus, it didn't lessen the swirl of energy within the grounds of Trinity College. Graduands - those who were about to graduate - ran around picking up their gowns, posing for photos, or meeting friends and relatives. Undergraduates attended classes, business as usual, or, in some cases, visited the library. The usual inflow of tourists wandered around the campus, snapping photos and searching for the Book of Kells.

Daniel picked up his gown in the Atrium and put it on over his suit. 'So, how do I look?'

'You look great,' Zoe said smiling. 'I'm very proud of you.'

'Okay, and now say it with a straight face,' he said as he pulled the robe up and manoeuvred his shoulders until the gown sat better on him.

'Sorry. It's the gown. It just looks like something out of a different century.'

'That's because it probably is.'

It was a red and gold gown. The sleeves were wide enough to fit a rugby ball up them. Daniel couldn't help feeling like a clown. An educated clown.

'What time does your procession start?'

'Twenty past ten,' he said as he put his head through the doctoral hood and settled it neatly on his shoulders.

Looking at her watch, Zoe said, 'You have twenty minutes. You should probably get going.' She took hold of the edges of the hood and pulled them up, forming a sort of wide triangle at the front. She signalled to Daniel to turn around. She quickly adjusted it from the back.

'There.'

'Does the thing look okay from behind?'

'Perfect,' she said, as Daniel turned back around and

gave her a kiss.

'Do you have the camera?'

Zoe rummaged in her handbag. She looked up. 'I think I left it in the car.'

Daniel searched in his pockets and took out his keys. He handed them to her. 'Here. You have plenty of time to run back to the car and get it. Only if you want to. I can get a professional photo taken later.'

'You must be joking. An overpriced thing that you have to wait weeks for. I plan to take plenty of photos. It's not every day my darling husband becomes a mathematical genius,' she said. 'Or at least a *recognised* mathematical genius. I'll upload them to Facebook as soon as I get home, so everyone can see.'

Daniel still had time so made a quick visit to library. He made a beeline for the computer section and sat at one of the four models that had a floppy disk drive connected to it. He retrieved the diskette and placed it in the drive. It took a moment to load before he saw the contents appear on the screen. There were a few random Excel and Word documents as well as a separate folder entitled "2 more". He double-clicked and entered a folder containing ten more documents.

'I remember this,' he whispered. He clicked on a document entitled 'Final Result'. It was a half-page document with a conclusion, two names and two dates.

'Jesus. The dates are both the same.' He scratched his head and took a deep breath. 'That's why I didn't think much of the results back then. What were the chances?' The dates reminded him of Grace's prediction and the one he did for Claire. Although Claire's one ended up being incorrect, he did have a brief recollection at the time of these calculations. 'But this can't be right either.'

He froze when he looked at the actual dates and allowed them to sink in.

'You've got to be kidding me.' His heart started beating

faster and his mouth went dry. 'I don't believe it.'

He leaned back on his chair and took a deep breath. What were the consequences if what he saw in front of him was true? He didn't have time to do much about it. He had to attend his graduation ceremony. The chances of both of them coming true must be absurd and yet there was something in the back of his mind. After five minutes of staring into thin air and allowing every possible scenario to go through his mind, Daniel got up, took a sheet of paper from the printers and sat back down. He took a pen from the inside of his jacket and started writing. It took him longer that he thought but when he was finished, he folded the paper in three, took the diskette out of the floppy drive and walked towards the reception. He asked for an internal mail envelope. He placed the paper and diskette inside and closed it. He handed it in to one of the librarians; a short man in his fifties and thick eye-brows. The man appeared a little puzzled at first as Daniel spoke but then nodded his head.

83

Daniel entered Number 1 in the Front Square. A sign saying "Doctoral Degrees Assembly" stood next to the helpdesk, pointing to the ante-room of the Board Room. Fellow graduands were coming and going with their robes in pursuit. Daniel walked inside.

The interior of the room was modern, yet the high ceiling and musky smell were enough to fill any past student with feelings of nostalgia. Daylight filled the room through the large Georgian windows. Tea, coffee and bottles of Ballygowan water were on offer at a small table next to the window. Daniel nodded politely to fellow-researchers who met his gaze. No familiar faces jumped out from the crowd. Most of them looked at least ten years younger. He calculated that those who were getting their undergraduate degrees were probably just starting secondary school, when he left Trinity all those years ago.

They probably didn't even know what calculus was then, he realised.

Small groups of three or four formed throughout the room. The chatting gave rise to a constant hum. Occasionally genuine laughs broke the monotony. Every so often someone from a group would break away and take a photo of the rest of the group with their mobile. Daniel suddenly had that horrible feeling of being at a party where everyone knew each other, except him. He decided to do what he would do if he was at such a party and made his way towards the drinks. The only difference this time was that the drinks were non-alcoholic and had zero chance of giving him the Dutch courage he needed at parties like this.

As he walked towards the table of refreshments, he couldn't help notice that many people, if not all, wore dress suits beneath their gown. Black-tie almost. Bowties instead of ties. Cufflinks instead of buttons. He couldn't help feeling a little underdressed with his fifteen-year-old suit. And a paperclip as a makeshift tiepin.

Did he really care? The paperclip meant more to him than anything else he wore.

He picked up a cool bottle of Ballygowan. His hand became wet from the condensation that had formed on the exterior of the bottle. Unscrewing the top, he poured himself a glass of sparkling water. As he took a mouthful, he felt a hand land on his shoulder.

'You made it!'

Daniel spluttered. Water that went down the wrong way came back up and landed on his chin. He wiped his mouth with his oversized sleeve and turned around. It took him a split moment to realise who it was.

'Hey,' Daniel said eventually, his shocked look transformed into a grin. 'You almost killed me!'

Professor Redmond stood there in the ceremonial attire for professors: a black robe with a blue hood. He held out his hand. Daniel quickly wiped his hand against his robe and shook hands.

'Sorry, my hand was a bit wet from the bottle of water.'

'You look great,' John said.

Daniel gave the professor a once-over. 'You don't look so bad yourself.'

'It's all very formal, you know. Centuries of tradition.'

'Sure. I'm not complaining,' he said looking down both at his own attire and that of the professor's. 'It's just a bit funny. Can't help thinking of Harry Potter.'

A silence hung in the air momentarily. Daniel glanced towards the wall where three framed photos hung. They were black and white, from the 18th Century.

'So,' John said, 'Here we are. After all this time.'

'Yes, here we are.'

'You deserve everything, you know. The PhD. The special recognition.'

'Do I?'

'Of course. Why would you even doubt it?'

Daniel shrugged. 'Sometimes I wish I wasn't so stubborn and chose a simpler thesis. Or at least a less attention-grabbing one.' Looking around the room, he continued. 'If I wasn't so stubborn, I could have enjoyed this day with my own classmates twelve years ago.'

John waited a moment before answering. 'That's perfectly understandable, wanting to share your graduation day with your own classmates. But let's not forget the thesis itself. The mathematics. The ingenuity of it all. Can you imagine if Michelangelo decided to paint a little chapel instead? Or Sir Isaac Newton brought a parasol with him when he sat beneath that apple tree?'

Daniel smiled. 'I had similar thoughts myself a while back.'

John placed both hands on Daniel's shoulders this time and looked him straight in the eye. 'You were meant to do this thesis. This is what you were put on this earth to do.'

Daniel couldn't help but notice several students looking in his direction, as John's hands remained on his shoulder.

'Getting a bit intense there,' he said smirking. 'But sure. I hear you.'

John removed his hands, satisfied that he made his point. 'So, is the whole family with you?'

'By "whole family" you mean Zoe and Sean?'

The professor nodded. 'And your parents, maybe?'

'Just Zoe.' He took a sip of water. 'My parents are on a cruise in the Caribbean. God love them. They booked it a year ago with half their life savings when I was still a plain old crane operator. I insisted that they still go. And we didn't think it was necessary to take Sean out of school to sit through a couple of hours of name calling.'

'I tend to disagree,' John said waving at someone across the room. 'I think this is an important day for you. I always encourage students of mine who have kids to bring them. It's your decision, of course.' He glanced at his watch. 'So, you know the drill?'

Daniel nodded. 'I read the letter. Basically, we walk in a procession to the Public Theatre, and from there we just sit down until our name is call...'

'John, will you join us for a photo?' A young attractive woman with too much lipstick interrupted. She turned to Daniel briefly and back to John. 'Sorry, were you guys...?'

'No. No problem.' Daniel said.

'Will you join us for a photo?' she asked John again. Daniel detected a Cork accent. She wore a skirt that revealed a pair of beautiful legs. The gown, although almost identical to his own, made her look even more attractive. He couldn't help thinking of Grace and what she had worn to her graduation.

'Certainly, Emma' John said. He turned to Daniel. 'If you'll excuse me.'

'Of course. Do you want me to take the photo?' Daniel offered. *Since I'm the outsider here.*

Emma smiled. Daniel noticed a tiny bit of lipstick on one of her teeth. At least he thought it was lipstick. However, he didn't feel it was his duty to mention it and left the task to one of her friends. Subconsciously, he rubbed the front row of his teeth with his tongue.

'That would be great,' Emma said. She gave him her iPhone and showed him where to press. Daniel pointed the mobile at the group of four students with John in the middle.

'Ok. Here we go. Cheese!'

The group repeated on cue, 'Cheese!'

Click.

'I'll take one more just to be sure.' This time he turned the iPhone to its side. Landscape mode.

'Cheese!'

Click.

He handed the phone back to Emma. Quickly she opened the Photo Gallery keeping the phone at an angle towards Daniel, so he could see his own work. He noticed a tattoo on the woman's wrist. The first thing that came to his mind was how painful it must have been. But that was quickly replaced by what the tattoo was.

'Brenda,' Emma said. 'You're supposed to keep your eyes open.' She swiped her finger across the screen, bringing up the next photo. Realising that it was landscape, she turned the phone to the side and admired it.

'Yes. That's a nice one.' She looked up at Daniel. 'Thank you...' She trailed off as she saw him staring at her tattoo.

'Nice tattoo,' Daniel said.

'Oh, this. Thanks. I got it when I was young and stupid. It's the Venus symbol. A symbol of femininity.'

'I know. I once had a friend who used to get mixed up between that and the male symbol. It resulted in some awkward moments in toilets. She could have done with a tattoo like that to remind...' he trailed off as his eyes remained glued to the woman's tattoo.

A flashback shot through his mind.

The blood.

The wrecked apartment.

Grace's body lying on the floor. Lifeless.

The sirens.

Grace's final movements.

Her last ounce of energy spelling the name of her killer on the wall.

An 'O'.

Followed by a 'T' below it. A small 'T'.

Daniel felt goose bumps cover his entire body.

'Jesus.'

He could see it now. The image of Grace's final message. They weren't letters in the alphabet. They weren't the first two letters of Otto's name.

It was the female symbol!

'Jesus.' he mumbled, as he took a step back.

He dropped his glass of water. Glass smashed and water spilled across the wooden floor. An awkward hush fell across the room.

84

Emma put her hand on Daniel's arm, fearing he was about to faint.

'Are you okay?'

He closed his eyes for a moment.

'How could I have been so stupid?'

John, who saw how he was acting, approached. 'Are you okay?'

Daniel was lost in his thoughts, but managed to nod. He opened his eyes. 'I need to make a phone call,' he said, finally coming out of a trance-like moment. He looked from John to Emma. 'Excuse me.'

Ignoring the broken glass on the floor, Daniel rushed towards the entrance. Without thinking, he cut between two professors deep in conversation. When he reached outside, he took a deep breath. Looking up he took another deep breath.

'It was a message to me, wasn't it?' he said to the overcast sky above. 'You weren't spelling your husband's name.'

Two tourists passing by gave him a strange look.

Daniel reached into his pocket and pulled out his mobile. Quickly he scrolled through the contacts until he came to Detective Janssen. He hit call.

Glancing at his watch, he estimated that he had about five minutes before the procession began.

'Come on,' he whispered to his mobile. On the fifth ring a voice answered.

'*Met Janssen.*'

'Detective Janssen?'

'Yes.'

'It's me. Daniel Geller. You know, the Irish guy. The death of...'

'Yes, I remember, of course.'

'I'm calling about those letters Grace wrote on the wall before she died.'

'Can I call you back in an hour or so?'

'No. I'm not available in an hour.'

There was a silence. This was followed by the sound of footsteps and a door closing. 'Okay. Just bear with me.'

Daniel could hear the sound of paper rustling and some clicks of a mouse. Finally the detective said, 'You're referring to the "O" and the "T" that the victim drew on the wall?'

'Yes,' Daniel said nodding. 'What if they weren't letters?'

'Excuse me?'

'What if they weren't letters, but a symbol?'

'A symbol?' Janssen started laughing. 'Come on, Mister... Geller. This isn't *The Da Vinci Code*. This is real life.'

Daniel realised how absurd he must sound, but continued nevertheless.

'I know, I know. But the T was beneath the O, right? They were joined. I remember it was a small "T", almost like a cross.'

'That is correct,' Janssen said. 'And what symbol is that supposed to be?'

'You tell me.'

'I didn't study symbology or whatever the English word is.'

'Neither did I, but it's a symbol that is quite common.'

Silence filled the line. Daniel could almost imagine the detective drawing the symbol on a piece of paper.

'Oh.' It was the sound of recognition. 'You mean *that* symbol.'

'Yes, *that* symbol.'

'For a woman?'

'Yes.'

'You think she was trying to tell us that it was a woman that did that to her?'

'Isn't it a possibility?'

The detective took a moment to answer. 'If you're dying, you don't have time to think about these things. She had very little energy. Blood was spurting out like crazy.' Daniel remained silent. 'Besides,' Janssen continued. 'That initial blow to her face. When the door was first kicked open. That was some power. I remember the autopsy report said that she broke her nose, what was it?' More rustling of paper. 'She broke it in two places from that original blow alone.'

'So you don't think a woman could have done it?'

'Honestly? And no disrespect to women, I don't think so.'

Daniel remained silent.

'Unless,' the detective continued, 'the woman was some kind of a martial arts nut.'

'Martial arts nut?'

'You know, a Kung Fu expert, a black belt in kickboxing or whatever. I don't see how, let's say, an average woman could do something like that.'

It was on hearing the word "kickboxing" that Daniel's world became blurred. His surroundings became nothing as the world spun. All he could think of was his wife. Zoe. Kickboxer fanatic.

Shaking his head he mumbled: 'No. It can't be. She was in London.'

'Excuse me?'

Daniel felt lightheaded. 'Nothing,' he whispered.

'Who was in London?'

'Nobody.' He took a deep breath. *She was in London, wasn't she?* He tried desperately to recall any evidence of her trip to London. Had he seen any photos? Receipts lying around? Plane ticket printout?

He couldn't recall.

'I have to go,' he hung up the phone just as Professor Redmond came out of Number 1.

'I was looking for you. Are you okay?' As he got closer,

he realised Daniel was far from okay.

'You look pale. Are you okay, Daniel?'

Daniel's mind was somewhere else. Miles away. Amsterdam. Eventually he turned to the professor.

'This might seem really strange, but can I borrow your car?'

'What?'

'There's something I need to do.'

'But your graduation! We're leaving in two minutes.'

'It all means nothing if I can't confirm something.'

'What can be so important?'

'I'll explain later, but for now I need to go home. Zoe has the keys to our car. I don't have time to go looking for her.'

John was unable to believe what he was hearing. 'After so long, this is finally your moment.'

'I'm not so sure of that.'

'What do you mean?'

'Listen. Please, John. All I ask is to borrow your car. I'll probably be back within the hour, before the ceremony is over.'

The door to Number 1 opened and out came the Chancellor, the Provost, and the Senior Master Non-Regent, followed by the professors and candidates. The Chancellor waved towards John.

'Professor, when you're ready.'

John looked towards Daniel. 'You're a stubborn bastard,' he said as he rummaged in his pockets. 'What if I see Zoe? She's going to wonder where you are.'

'Just say I forgot something. I will be back in a while.'

John gave him the keys to his car. 'It's a silver Audi Q5 parked in Fleet Street car park. Third story. Just press this button a few times as you walk around and you'll hear the beep when it unlocks.'

'Thank you.' He patted John on the arm. 'You're a good friend.'

'See you later.'

85

As Daniel drove into the driveway of number 48 Springdale Road, he realised he had no key to the house. He got out of the car and walked down the side alley to the back garden. He entered the garden shed and searched in a little box of screws. There he found a spare key to the back door.

He entered the house and stood in the middle of kitchen. Where should he begin? The silence in the air was broken by a long beep coming from the dishwasher. It had finished its cycle. Daniel quickly opened the dishwasher. Steam escaped upwards, like a genie escaping from a magic lamp. Once the steam had dispersed, he bent down and rolled out the bottom tray, allowing the cutlery and dishes to air dry.

'Where should I start?' He whispered. All he wanted was proof that Zoe had been in London that weekend for the hen party. It was six months ago. What possible proof could there be? He couldn't recall seeing any photos on Facebook. This was unusual in itself as she was usually quite active in posting photos. He turned on the laptop in the sitting room. After logging into Facebook he clicked on Zoe's wall. He scrolled through many updates, mainly to do with Sean or kickboxing, but as he went further back he noticed that there simply were no photos of the hen party.

'Whose hen party was it anyway?' Daniel tried to think as he scrolled through Zoe's friends. He stopped at Helen. 'It was yours, wasn't it?' He clicked on Helen's profile only to find the content blocked. It was only available to Friends and Family.

Daniel had another idea. He walked upstairs to their bedroom and looked at the suitcases on top of the wardrobe. The purple one belonging to Zoe lay beneath his. Grabbing a stool from beside the dressing table, he hopped on it. Reaching up, he pulled Zoe's suitcase down. He stepped off the stool and placed the suitcase on top of the bed. Even though Zoe had only been gone for the weekend, she always checked in a bag. It was more to do with the amount of bottles of beauty products she brought with her than anything else.

'Shit.' The airplane tag that usually went around the handle had already been removed. Probably months ago. Probably as soon as Zoe picked it up from the baggage belt. Daniel lay back on the bed and closed his eyes. His mind raced.

There must be something.

He opened his eyes and stared at the ceiling. 'Maybe I'm overreacting,' he said out loud. 'Maybe Grace *was* trying to spell "Otto". I should just get my ass back to the ceremony before I ruin the day completely.' It was when he turned his head towards the suitcase that he saw it. The label. The small back-up label that airport ground staff attach to baggage during check-in. He sat up immediately as his heart started racing again. Slowly he reached for the label and peeled it off. It was a barcode. Nothing more than black lines and random numbers.

'Maybe this will do,' he whispered. Without wasting another moment, he ran downstairs taking two steps at a time, almost tripping over his graduation gown in the process. Sitting down in front of the laptop again, he googled "Aer Lingus" and hit the link for the homepage. Quickly he chose the Contact Us menu followed by Baggage Tracing. He skipped through the information until he came to a telephone number. He grabbed his mobile and dialled the number. A recorded message gave him some options. He chose the options that brought him to a real operator. After several rings, an operator answered.

'Good morning. Thank you for calling the Aer Lingus missing baggage line. You're speaking with Shane. How may I help you?'

'Hi, I'm calling about a suitcase that went missing a few months ago, and I still haven't heard back about it.'

'A few months ago? Do you have the Baggage Reference Number?'

'Um, I'm not sure. Is that the barcode number?'

'Yes, that will do.'

'Okay, it's 56917013'

Daniel could hear the operator type the number in his computer.

'I have no record that this piece of luggage went missing.'

'Really?' Daniel asked, pretending to be surprised. 'Can you confirm that it corresponds to a flight from London Heathrow to Dublin?'

Some more tapping.

'No, sir. Our records say it was on EI 0607 flight from Amsterdam Schiphol to Dublin.'

Daniel's heart stopped. He closed his eyes as the world he knew collapsed around him

'Sir?' the operator asked.

Daniel couldn't believe it. He hung up the phone and stared at the barcode. 'This can't be happening,' he said as he shook his head. Just then he heard the front door open.

'Daniel!'

It was Zoe. He closed the laptop over but remained sitting, unable to accept the reality of what he had just discovered.

Zoe entered the kitchen and stood at the doorway. 'There you are. What is wrong, honey? I saw all the proud students following their professors and you weren't among them.'

It took a few moments before Daniel raised his head slowly and looked his wife in the eye.

86

Daniel remained silent, unable to comprehend the implications of everything if his suspicions were true.

'Daniel,' Zoe said as she moved closer and squatted down before him, so that she was on eye-level. 'What's the matter? I spoke briefly to John, and he told me you forgot something. I could have fetched it for you. This is *your* big day.'

'Really?'

She frowned at Daniel's reaction. 'Yes, really. What's wrong?'

He turned his hand around to reveal the little barcode sticker stuck on his forefinger. Zoe looked down at it and then back at Daniel.

'What's that?'

'A barcode.'

'For what?'

'I found it on your suitcase.' Daniel looked for a reaction. 'The one you used going to London.' Zoe remained expressionless. She looked down at the barcode again and then back at Daniel

'What's that got to do with anything?'

'You know, it's funny. I never saw any photos of that weekend you had in London. The so-called hen party.'

She stood up and leaned her back on the counter. She folded her arms but said nothing.

'There was never a hen party in London, was there? Your suitcase was never on a flight from London to Dublin. I think we both know what flight it *was* on.'

'I see.'

'Is that all you can say?'

'What do you want me to say, Daniel? That I travelled to Amsterdam the same weekend and tracked her down? You made it so easy for me. I went through your stuff and found out her married name. With that it was easy to find out where she worked and I just followed her home to that apartment she was staying in, before you even arrived in Amsterdam. Do you want me to tell you how, on the day in question, I waited for you to leave her apartment and then killed her? I had entered the apartment building hours earlier when someone had left it open while they took out some rubbish, and I just hid on the top floor where they have store rooms belonging to each apartment. When you left at midnight, and Grace closed the door in your face, I was actually looking down at you from the stairwell, two flights above.'

Daniel was devastated by that authentic detail. He knew without doubt that she was telling the truth.

'I just knocked on the door a few moments later, bashed her around and then slit her throat while she pleaded with me. Do you want me to say that I killed Brian four years ago too? Although that was much easier, especially with the amount he drank. It was just a little tampering with his car. The shit country roads did the rest. Do you want me to say that I wanted to prove your thesis so badly, so that the bastards at Trinity would treat you with a bit more respect than just throwing you out?'

Daniel shook his head. Tears formed in his eyes. 'I can't believe what I'm hearing.'

'I was going to tell you at some stage.'

'Tell me what, Zoe? Tell me what?!'

'That I helped prove your thesis.'

He looked around the kitchen. As if searching for anything that would wake him up from this nightmare.

'I remember the day they rejected you,' she continued. 'I remember you walking into the Winding Stair when I was working the lunch shift. The look on your face. In your eyes. You were absolutely ruined. I think you would have thrown yourself into the Liffey if it wasn't for me. I wanted to show those bastards that they can't do that to another human being.'

410

'Stop, Zoe. Please, stop talking.'

'I thought this is what you wanted? The truth? I killed them, Daniel. On their dates of death, predicted by you.'

'No. No, you didn't. Please, Zoe. Please say it's a mistake.'

'Look at me, Daniel. It's okay. It's okay. It's our secret. Nobody suspects a thing. It's our secret.'

'Get away from me! How could you do this?'

'Daniel…'

'How could you… *kill* someone?'

Zoe stepped forward.

'And my thesis? It's fucking worthless!'

'It's not! You did it. You predicted two out of five.'

'But you killed them!'

'That's irrelevant. They might have died anyway.'

'Might? They *might* have died? Well, we'll never know now, will we? The only thing that you proved is that my thesis is the biggest pile of shit that ever existed.'

'No, Daniel, you're wrong. I believed in you.'

'You believed in me? Are you taking the piss?'

Zoe stepped forward with her arms open. 'Daniel -'

'Get away from me!' He turned suddenly. His graduation gown got caught beneath his foot and, before he knew it, he was falling. Only it wasn't the floor he was falling towards, it was the lower rack of the dishwasher that he had pulled out moments earlier. Within the cutlery basket there was a carving knife, its blade sticking upwards.

Before he had time to stop himself, a sharp pain shot through Daniel's abdomen. Letting out a scream of pain, he quickly rolled from the dishwasher onto the floor, sending the rest of the cutlery flying. But it was too late. The knife came with him, embedded in his lower abdomen.

He let out another cry as he lay on the floor. It took Zoe a moment to realise Daniel's injury.

'Jesus, Daniel, are you okay?!'

411

His face twisted with agony. He lifted his head and saw the handle sticking out of the left side of his stomach. Zoe knelt down beside him.

'Jesus, Daniel. What will I do?'

He tried to take a deep breath, but ended up coughing.

'Will I remove it?' she asked.

He shook his head. 'No.' He pointed to a tea towel hanging up beside the oven. Zoe grabbed it and placed it on the wound. Daniel wrapped it the best he could around the wound and the handle of the knife. He was bleeding heavily.

'Okay, we have to get you to the hospital,' Zoe said. 'Can you stand up?'

Daniel nodded. 'I'll try.' With Zoe's help, he stood up. Zoe held the tea towel in place, as he put his arm around her. He placed his other hand on the counter to help take some of his weight. An intense dizziness washed over him. And he started to stumble.

'Daniel!' She helped him steady himself. 'Are you able to walk to the car?'

He nodded. 'Yeah.' His breathing became shallow and his face pale.

'Okay, here we go, Daniel.'

They walked slowly along the hallway to the front door. Carefully they went down the single step outside the entrance. They passed Professor Redmond's car and came to their own Nissan.

'Front or back?'

Daniel's mind was drifting. He was unable to comprehend the question, and went for the last word he heard.

'Back.'

Zoe opened the back door while still supporting her husband. Daniel caught hold of the side of the car and pulled himself in. Unsure of whether he should sit upright or lie down he went for the easy option and lay down on the back seat. His feet dangled out the door he had just climbed in. Zoe pushed his feet in and closed the door quickly. She ran back to the front door of the house and closed it over and then jumped into the driver's seat of their car.

'Are you okay?'

'I'm fine,' Daniel whispered and kept his hand on the wound. Slowly he closed his eyes.

87

'Beaumont! I thought he was bringing me to Beaumont hospital. He's bringing me back to fucking Trinity.'

Although Zoe had searched for the nearest hospital in the GPS device, she forgot to click "Done". It was only when she was on Amiens Street close to the city centre that she realised she was heading back to her previous destination: Trinity College. She quickly pulled over at a bus stop and did a new search. The GPS showed: *Mater Misericordiae University Hospital.*

'I'm bringing you to The Mater.'

She took a right on Talbort Street and drove as far as she could before turning into Marlborough Street. She continued down another side street and suddenly came out onto O' Connell Street.

A street I recognise. Thank God, she thought to herself.

Officially she was not allowed to turn right. She took a chance and crossed it, driving through the pedestrian zone in the middle of the wide street. It was there she almost crashed into a mime dressed as James Joyce. She swung a right and joined the traffic on O' Connell Street.

'Fucking mimes! I nearly ran into him!' she screamed from the driver's seat.

Daniel was sprawled out on the back seat trying to keep pressure on the wound in his stomach. The bump coming off the pavement sent pain through his body. He raised one hand before him and saw blood. Lots of it. It had seeped through the rag that was covering the cut, a futile attempt to reduce the blood loss. The blood was now beneath every fingernail. It had even found its way into the links of his wristwatch. Closing his eyes, he begged the pain to go.

'Stay with me!' Zoe cried from the front, as the GPS navigation system emitted a warning beep that she was driving too fast.

Daniel opened his eyes. He gazed out the window and watched the city speed by. From his angle, all he could see were tops of lamp posts, buildings, trees and road signs. His sense of direction had vanished. He had no clue where in the city he was. Even worse, he couldn't recollect how he ended up in the back seat of a car with such an injury.

What the hell happened?

His hands moved to the pain in his abdomen. He could feel the blood still seeping out. And then the blade and the handle of the knife. It took a moment and then he remembered. He remembered everything.

Stop the car.

The wound stung like hell. The car flew over a speed bump almost knocking him from the backseat. He let out a scream of agony.

'Stop the car,' he moaned.

He could see his wife crying. She was in no state to drive, especially at this speed.

'Zoe, please!'

His wife continued to keep her eyes on the road and her foot on the accelerator.

Daniel's head dropped to the side. He spotted something green sticking out of the pocket of the passenger seat in front of him. All he could think of was Sean. Daniel's bloodstained hand reached towards it and grabbed it. It was a green napkin with two holes cut out, a makeshift mask of a comic book superhero. He had a quick flashback to the time he had worn it. The eye holes had been cut out too close together meaning Sean had looked more like a crossed-eyed villain than a masked crusader. It had made himself and Zoe laugh, but neither of them had the heart to tell him.

He grasped it tight and pulled it close to his chest, to his heart. A tear escaped down the side of his face. Deep down Daniel knew. Could he stop it?

'After 300 metres, turn left,' the GPS device announced

415

with a remarkably calm voice that didn't match the emergency situation it was part of.

Zoe continued for a bit and then slammed on the brake as she took a sharp corner. She placed her foot on the accelerator again and continued to speed through the city.

'Please stop the car,' Daniel mumbled from the back. He took a deep breath and with his last ounce of energy he roared: 'Now!'

She glanced behind. 'You're going to bleed to death if I don't get you to a hosp...'

A cold shiver covered Daniel as he caught a glimpse of a red traffic light fly by. This was followed almost immediately by the screeching brakes. A car coming from the left clipped them from the back, spinning them out of control across the street. Another sound of burning rubber filled the air before an oncoming van hit the Nissan. Pain exploded through Daniel as the car flipped and slid on its roof to the other side of the street. Almost back to where they were first hit.

Daniel let out a roar as gravity flung him onto the roof. The weight of his body pushed the knife further into his abdomen. He lay face down, blood now seeping onto the lining fabric of the interior roof.

The green superhero mask landed an arms-length away.
Sean

He felt faint.
I'm sorry Sean. You'll be okay. I promise.

He heard his wife crying.
'Daniel?'

'I'm here, Zoe. Don't be afraid. I'm here.'

Zoe still sat in the driver's seat but her head was pushed against the roof.

'I'm scared, Daniel.'

Daniel let out a cry. The pain was too much. He tried to be strong. He pushed himself onto his side to ease the pressure from the wound. He was unsure if it would do any good. He picked up the green superhero mask and with the same hand reached out and held his wife's.

'Don't be… scared,' he said almost in a whisper. 'You have nothing to be scared about.'

'I'm sorry for ruining everything. I don't want it to end like this. I don't want you to think that you failed.'

'Listen to me, Zoe. I don't. Look at me.'

Zoe did her best to move her head towards Daniel.

'I don't think I've failed,' he said. 'Not now. You see… I predicted this day… for the two of us.'

A look of confusion fell over her. 'What? What do you mean?'

'I used my thesis years ago on both of us. I never told anyone. I didn't even think the results were valid. I found them this morning... If we die today, then my thesis is still valid.' He tried to catch some breath. 'I think you're right. Perhaps even if you didn't kill them, they would have died anyway on the dates I predicted.'

'Why didn't you tell me? We could have avoided…' Zoe trailed off as another thought came to her. 'What about Sean?'

'He will be fine.' Daniel swallowed hard. He could taste blood. 'He will be fine. I've taken care of it.'

Suddenly he felt dazed. His grasp loosened. Zoe tightened her grip. The green napkin mask remained in place, between the two parents. The pain was subsiding. Was that a good sign? He closed his eyes. It felt good to close them. He could hear his wife in the background, becoming more faint. Was she being rescued from the car? He felt comfortable now. He wanted to stay where he was.

A strong stench attacked Daniel's senses. Memories flooded his mind from his student days, working in a petrol station. He loved the smell, in a strange kind of way.

He could hear a voice. It was a male voice. A voice he recognised.

'Turn around when possible.'

His hopes were dashed. It was the GPS device offering a last piece of navigating advice.

The scent of petrol seemed to get stronger. Then everything went dark.

COUPLE KILLED IN CAR CRASH ON WAY TO
HOSPITAL

*A 34-year-old driver and her 36-year-old male passenger
killed in a crash on Dorset Street have been named.*

*Zoe and Daniel Geller of Raheny died on Thursday from
multiple burns and injuries. Gardai say that Mrs Geller was
rushing her husband to The Mater Hospital after a domestic
accident. Mrs Geller, who was driving a Nissan Almera,
missed a red light and was hit by both a Renault Clio and
Volkswagen Van. Their car caught fire shortly afterwards, and
they were unable to escape on time. The drivers of the other
vehicles suffered minor injuries and were treated in The
Mater. The couple leave behind a six-year-old boy who is
believed to be currently cared for by family.*

There was a knock on the door.

'Come in,' John shouted from behind his desk.

A short man in his fifties, wearing a striped shirt, entered. He had bushy eyebrows and was carrying an internal mail envelope.

'Good afternoon,' he said. 'Are you Professor John Redmond?'

John glanced at the envelope and back at the man, who looked vaguely familiar. 'Yes, I am,' he said standing up.

'Desmond O' Brien from Trinity Library,' the man said as he reached out his hand.

'I thought I recognised you,' John said as he shook his hand. "How can I help you?'

The man cleared his throat with a nervous cough. 'This is about one of your students. Daniel Geller.'

'Oh,' John said with genuine surprise. 'Please take a seat. Would you like anything to drink?'

'No, I'm fine, thank you. I won't take up too much of your time,' O' Brien said as he took a seat. John decided against fetching a drink for himself and slowly sat back down on his chair.

'I just found out that Mr Geller passed away last week.'

'That's right. I attended his funeral. And his wife's.'

'A terrible tragedy.'

'Yes. Especially for his little boy. Losing two parents like that.'

'I'm not sure how to begin as it's all rather strange.'

John frowned and move his head sideways unsure what he meant. 'Well, you have my full attention.'

'On the morning of his graduation. At least I assume it was his graduation as he had one of those robes on.'

John nodded, eager for the man to continue.

'He handed me an envelope,' he said holding it up. 'He

asked me to put it in the internal mail on Monday if I didn't hear from him.'

'If you didn't hear from him? I don't understand.'

'Well... I didn't really understand either. He just said that if he didn't drop by the library on Monday then if I could place it in the internal mail for him. The thing is I was out all week with a stomach flu. It was only this morning when I saw the envelope lying in my locker that I remembered. I was going to put it in the internal mail like he said, but I figured that it was probably better to deliver it to you by hand at this late stage.'

'Do you know what it's about?'

'No idea. He seemed a bit flustered at the time but I assumed that was part of the butterflies you get in your stomach before a graduation ceremony. I thought maybe he was submitting an application to something that was not yet open for submission.'

John looked totally perplexed.

'He *was* a student of yours, right?' the librarian asked again.

John nodded. 'Yes. And a friend.'

'Well here you go,' he said handing the envelope to the professor. 'I apologise for the late delivery.'

John's mind raced for the possibilities of the contents. Could it be to do with a mathematical query? Was he supposed to calculate the date of death of someone else using his thesis?

He took a pen from his desk and tucked it beneath the flap of the envelope.

'You don't have to open it front of me,' the librarian said. 'I'll show myself out.'

'Of course. And thank you.'

As soon as the librarian left the room, John examined the envelope. It was nothing special. Just a plain old yellow internal mail envelope, sealed with tape. He tore it open with the pen and removed the letter. It was a single sheet of A4 paper folded in three, handwriting covering both sides of the paper. He turned the envelope upside down and watched a 3.5 inch diskette slide onto his desk.

Looking towards the door, he contemplated if he should lock it. He decided against it, realising that the letter wouldn't exactly be *top secret*. He unfolded the letter. His curiosity was overwhelming. As he began to read, an invisible force pulled him into the words of his deceased friend. His office and surroundings disappeared.

Halfway through the letter, John looked up and closed his eyes. A tear trickled down his cheek. This was followed quickly by another. They both landed on the letter. John wiped his eyes, rubbing away any fresh tears. He sniffed, as his nose became runny. Through blurred vision, he looked at a photo on his desk. It was the family snapshot taken on a beach in Florida that had been damaged in the fire. He smiled, took a deep breath and turned back to the letter.

When he had finished reading it, he left it on the desk and sat back on his chair. He took another deep breath. Slowly he rose from his seat, went over to his coffee maker and fixed himself a double espresso. Sitting back at the desk, John glanced through the letter again as he sipped his espresso. He had finished his drink by the time he reached the bottom of the page. He shook his head in disbelief.

Looking at his watch, he realised he had about twenty minutes before his next lecture. He would have to postpone it to later in the week if there was a slot. He rang the departmental secretary.

'Fiona, John Redmond here. I need to postpone my eleven o' clock lecture to later this week. Can you take care of it? Something important has come up.'

'That's fine, John,' Fiona said. 'I'll take care of it.'

He folded the letter and placed it back in the envelope. He picked up his jacket and left the office.

Claire was on a call with a client, a biotechnology company based in Switzerland. They were undergoing rebranding and had picked Interactive Blue Ltd. to come up with a new logo.

'I'm uploading them to Dropbox as we speak, and I'll send you the link… yes, there are various formats including jpeg and vector format…. sure we can touch base after lunch and discuss further…. Yes…okay. Talk to you later.'

Claire hung up and checked the progress of the files being uploaded to her client's Dropbox account. She turned to Tim, a fellow graphic designer. 'Is it just me or is the internet slow today? I think I'm…' She trailed off when she saw her husband at the reception. She stood up immediately and walked out of her room.

Rebecca, the receptionist who was talking to John, turned to Claire. 'Well, here she is.'

'Do you have a minute?' John asked, out of breath.

Claire looked at Rebecca and then back at John. 'Of course. Is everything okay?'

'The meeting room is free,' Rebecca offered. 'Do either of you want a drink?'

'A whiskey would be great,' John said.

'No, thanks, Rebecca,' Claire said as she led John to the meeting room, shooting a glance to Rebecca as if to say "please ignore my husband". She had never seen John acting so strange.

As they both entered the room, the feeling of déjà vu was almost tangible.

'What is it, John?' she asked, clearly very worried.

He took a moment to observe his surroundings. A conference phone lay in the middle of the oval-shaped table. On the ceiling almost directly above the phone hung a beamer pointing to a white wall. A strange sound came from it like it had just been used, and the internal fan was still working hard in cooling the internal circuits. A slick-looking black clock with white hands hung at the back of the room.

'This is the room where I told you about Max?'

'That's right.'

He glanced at the floor and wondered where exactly they had collapsed, wrapped in each other's arms, where the living nightmare began.

Claire noticed him looking at the ground.

'John. What is it? I'm here.'

Slowly he raised his head and looked at his wife. He smiled. 'I know you are. We're both here. Now. And that's all that matters.'

Her face twisted with confusion. 'Have you already had a few whiskeys?'

John removed the letter from his jacket and handed it to his wife. 'Daniel wrote me a letter before he died. I want you to read it carefully. We can then decide together.'

Claire swallowed hard as she stepped forward and took the letter. She stared at John looking for possible signs of what it could be.

'What do you mean by "decide"?'

'Just read the letter.' He pulled a chair from the oval-shaped desk. 'You might want to sit down.'

She shook her head as she unfolded the letter. For John to leave work and come running all the way up to Harcourt Street in the middle of the day meant that it was important. Her heart pounded wildly as she began to read.

John,

If you're reading this it means I'm dead. And I probably died today, Friday, the day of my graduation - out of all days! At least that's the date that I calculated for myself twelve years ago, soon after I left university.

What troubles me is that I also performed the calculation on Zoe and predicted the exact same date as myself. I couldn't really bear the thought of us dying on the same day and figured there must have been an error in my calculation. It was around the time when I was turning my back on mathematics and beginning a new life. Just like the rest of the predictions I did my best to push them aside and forget about them. I even threw away all the paperwork related to these calculations. What I didn't realise was that I kept a record of them on the enclosed diskette; a diskette that I just became aware of this morning.

You can imagine my surprise when I opened up the files on a computer here in Trinity Library and was suddenly confronted with today's date.

I don't have time to do anything about it. I need to act normal and go to the graduation ceremony. I need to go to the drinks reception afterwards. I need to go to dinner later. Fingers crossed everything will go smoothly...

And yet, here I am writing you this letter. If my calculations are correct, then I'm not here anymore and neither is Zoe. Now you don't have to be a mathematical genius to know that two parents minus two parents equals zero parents.

It breaks my heart to imagine that our little boy Sean will become an orphan. What a word. Christ, it sounds like something from a Dickens novel. The thought of it breaks my heart. I hope to God I'm wrong. I hope I can avoid what might happen and I can rip this letter up first thing on Monday.

If I'm right however, I need to make arrangements for his welfare.

My parents are Sean's next of kin should anything happen us, but they aren't getting any younger. They would love to take care of him. They would cherish him, I have no doubt. However, their energy levels aren't what they used to be and who knows how long they will be around themselves. (I didn't calculate their predicted dates of death by the way, so I have no idea!) Deep down, I believe if they knew there was another option, they would fully agree to it - as long as they could still see him every so often.

What I'm about to ask you isn't a decision that came lightly. It was just a thought that kept growing and growing. Every time I met you, I knew you were a good guy. And I know you were a brilliant father, even though you might not believe it yourself.

John, I would like to ask you and Claire to look after Sean. I would be honoured if you two became legal guardians to our little boy. To bring him up like you would have brought up Max.

John could see Claire's eyes welling up as she read through the letter. She glanced at John. 'Is this for real?'

John nodded. She continued reading.

When I first met you again after all those years, just a few months ago, at the bottom of that crane, you said something about everybody deserving a second chance. You gave me that second chance, John. Now it's my turn to give you one.

You both have so much love still to give. I know that you are the right choice. Your last "role" as a parent was cut so cruelly short. It's time for your second chance.

And these are not just my thoughts. I mentioned it recently in passing to Zoe and she totally agreed. Although the thought of us both dying before Sean turns eighteen was too upsetting to take it further.

Now, I'm not asking you to see Sean as a replacement for Max. Nobody can ever replace your son; your own flesh and blood. He was part of you and Claire. Nobody can ever change that. However, what I am asking is for you to be parents once again to a loving boy. A boy who needs the same things that Max needed: love, guidance and to be around fun people like you and Claire.

Thank you, John, for reviving my thesis. For giving me hope after all these years. If you are reading this, then I'm dead and my thesis is proof that mathematics can be used to calculate one of the most important dates in anyone's life: the day it ends. It can be a stepping stone for someone else to take further.

You could argue if it really matters what your date of death is? You can live to be a hundred, but unless you live life to the maximum every day, what's the point?

You can live to be ten-years-old, and if you enjoy it, give so much joy and happiness to those around you, and receive so much love in return, then at least you can say you really lived.

If you decide to do it, please take care of him. He also enjoys watching Manchester United matches every now and again. I have confidence that you will watch a match with him from time to time!

You're not obliged to say yes to this letter straight away. It is purely a question. A request. A huge request at that. I know that you are both good people. I trust you both 100% with Sean and if you agree to do this, then you will be rewarded with the heart of a very special boy.

Your friend,
Daniel

The tears were streaming down Claire's face as she reached the end of the letter. She buried her face in John's chest as he wrapped his arms around his wife. They held each other for some time before she looked up to John. Their eyes met. Both pairs of eyes were moist. Tears of a heartbreaking past. Tears of hope. Tears of a new future.

Was there no greater instinct in the world than childless parents taking care of a parentless child?

There was no need to say anything. Claire nodded and smiled. John smiled back and kissed her softly on the forehead.

###

Message from the Author

Thank you for taking the time to read my book. I hope you enjoyed it.

To an unpublished writer, a positive review or rating is like gold dust. It's a tiny step in the journey of getting one's work noticed (and possibly published). If you find the time, I would really appreciate a review or rating on any of the websites like Amazon, Goodreads, LibraryThing, Booklikes etc.

Even if it's just a simple rating or a one word review! Every single rating/review counts.

As a small incentive and token of appreciation, I invite reviewers to check out the latest promotion I have running. Visit: www.darrensugrue.com/promotion/ to find out more.

Many thanks once again for reading my book and feel free to connect with me via the various channels mentioned below.

Best wishes,
Darren Sugrue
Amsterdam, October 2014

Twitter: @predictionnovel
Facebook: www.facebook.com/thepredictionbook
Email: darrensugrue@gmail.com
Web: www.darrensugrue.com

25806445R00260

Printed in Great Britain
by Amazon